BLOOD MAGIC

BLOOD MAGIC

TESSA GRATTON

RANDOM HOUSE  NEW YORK

Text copyright © 2011 by Tessa Gratton
Jacket art: photograph of trees © Stephen Carroll Photography/Flickr/Getty Images; photograph of girl © Sara Haas/Flickr/Getty Images; photograph reference for bird silhouettes by Erik Charlton

All rights reserved. Published in the United States by Random House Children's Books, a division of Random House, Inc., New York.

Random House and the colophon are registered trademarks of Random House, Inc.

Visit us on the Web! www.randomhouse.com/teens

Educators and librarians, for a variety of teaching tools, visit us at www.randomhouse.com/teachers

Library of Congress Cataloging-in-Publication Data
Gratton, Tessa.
Blood magic / Tessa Gratton. — 1st ed.
p. cm.
Summary: In Yaleylah, Missouri, teens Silla and Nick, drawn together by loss and a shared family history of blood magic practitioners, are plunged into a world of dark magic as they try to unravel the mystery of Silla's parents' apparent murder suicide.
ISBN 978-0-375-86733-0 (trade) — ISBN 978-0-375-96733-7 (lib. bdg.) — ISBN 978-0-375-89768-9 (ebook)
[1. Supernatural—Fiction. 2. Magic—Fiction. 3. Death—Fiction. 4. Orphans—Fiction. 5. Brothers and sisters—Fiction. 6. Stepmothers—Fiction. 7. Immortality—Fiction. 8. Family life—Missouri—Fiction. 9. Missouri—Fiction.] I. Title.
PZ7.G77215Blo 2011
[Fic]—dc22   2010024997

Printed in the United States of America

10 9 8 7 6 5 4 3 2 1

First Edition

Thus is the fruit of the earth taken, its flesh torn. Thus is it given over to standing, toward rot. It is the principle of corruption, the death of what is, the birth of what is to be. You are wine.

—Richard Selzer, *Mortal Lessons*

ONE

I am Josephine Darly, and I intend to live forever.

TWO

SILLA

It is impossible to know who you really are until you spend time alone in a cemetery.

The headstone was cold against my back, pressing my thin T-shirt into the sweat trickling down my skin. Dusk washed the cemetery of shadows, lending it a quality of between-ness: neither day nor night, but a gray, teary moment. I sat with my legs crossed and the book in my lap. Beneath me, scraggly grass hid my parents' graves.

I brushed dirt off the front cover of the book. It was the size of a paperback novel, so small and insignificant-seeming between my hands. The mahogany leather cover was soft and scuffed from years of use; the color had worn off the corners. The pages used to be gilded, but that was rubbed off, too. Cracking it open, I read the inscription again, whispering it to myself, making it more real.

Notes on Transformation and Transcendence
Oh, that this too, too solid flesh would melt, thaw,
and resolve itself into a dew. —Shakespeare

It had been one of Dad's favorite quotes. From *Hamlet.* Dad used to recite it whenever Reese or I stormed out of the room to pout. Said we had nothing to complain about compared to the prince of Denmark. I remembered his blue eyes narrowing at me over the rims of his glasses.

The book had arrived in the mail this afternoon, wrapped in brown paper with no return address. DRUSILLA KENNICOT was written in plain block letters, like a summoning. There were six stamps in the corner. It smelled like blood.

That particular raw-penny aroma stuck in the back of my throat, clinging with memory. I closed my eyes and saw a splash of blood streaked across bookshelves.

When I opened my eyes again, I was still alone in the cemetery.

Inside the front cover of the book was a note, folded in thirds and written on thick, unlined paper.

Silla, it began. I shivered every time I saw my name written in the old cursive hand. The bottom of the *s* spiraled into oblivion.

Silla,
 I feel your loss as my own, child. I have known your father for most of his life, and he was a dearest friend. I regret I am unable to present myself for his memorial, though trust that his life is celebrated and his death greatly mourned.
  If there can be any small consolation, I hope that this is it. Here in this book are

the secrets he perfected. Decades of research, a lifetime's worth of knowledge. He was a gloriously talented magician and healer, and he was proud of you, proud of your strength. I know he would like for you to have this record of his work now.

All my brightest hopes be with you and your brother.

It was signed only *The Deacon.* No last name or contact information.

Crows laughed, bursting up through headstones a distance away. The black cloud of them cut through the air in a flapping of wings and raucous cawing. I watched them against the gray sky as they flew west toward my house. Probably to terrorize the blue jays that lived in our front-yard maple.

Wind blew my short hair against my cheeks, and I brushed it back. I wondered who this Deacon was. He claimed friendship with my dad, but I'd never heard of him. And why he would suggest such incredible, ridiculous things: that my dad was a magician and healer, when he'd only been a high school Latin teacher. But despite that, I knew without a doubt that I was holding a book my dad had written: I recognized his fine, delicate handwriting, with its tiny loops in every capital *L* and its perfectly angled *R*s. He'd abhorred typing, and used to lecture Reese and me about learning to write longhand legibly. Reese had compromised by printing block letters, but I'd been too enamored of wild, looping cursive to worry about readability.

No matter where it had come from, this book was Dad's.

As I flipped through it, I saw that every page contained lines and lines of perfect writing and meticulous diagrams sprawling like spiderwebs. The diagrams contained circles within circles, Greek letters or strange pictographs and runes. There were triangles and octagons, pentacles, squares, and seven-pointed stars. Dad had made tiny notes at the edges of the pages, written descriptive paragraphs in Latin, and made lists of ingredients.

Salt dominated the lists, and recognizable items like ginger, wax, fingernails, mirrors, chicken claws, cat teeth, and colored ribbons. But there were words I didn't know, like *carmot* and *agrimony* and *spikenard.*

And blood. Every list included a drop of blood.

They were magic spells. For locating lost items, for blessing new babies and deterring curses. For protecting against evil. For seeing over long distances. For predicting the future. For healing all manner of illness and wound.

I flipped through, heart alight with wonder and fear. I could taste excitement, too, like electricity in the back of my throat. Could it be real? Dad hadn't been one to play elaborate tricks, and was the opposite of fanciful, despite his love for old books and heroic tales.

There had to be a spell I could try. To test it. To see.

As I thought about it, the smell crawled up the back of my throat again, blood clinging to my sinuses and trailing like sticky smoke down my esophagus.

I raised the book to my nose and drew in a long, cleansing breath. And I imagined I could smell him in the book. My dad.

Not the overwhelming blood that had saturated his shirt and the carpet beneath his body, but the slightly oiled cigarettes-and-soap when he came to breakfast every morning, after a shower and quick smoke on the back patio. I dropped the book into my lap and closed my eyes until Dad was right there, sitting in front of me, one hand touching my right knee.

When I was little, he used to come into my bedroom just before lights-out and touch my knee as he sank onto the bed. Gravity would pull me closer and closer until I could lean my head on his shoulder or climb into his lap while he told me condensed versions of literary classics. My favorites had been *Frankenstein* and *Twelfth Night,* and I asked for them again and again.

In the cemetery, another crow cawed, a loner flying slowly after his cousins.

I held the book up in my two hands and let it fall open wherever it willed. When the fanning pages had chosen their sides, I lowered it and glanced at the spell: *Regeneration.*

To bring life. For careful application when flesh is infected or necrotized. To keep flowers strong.

The diagram was a spiral inside a circle that narrowed to the center like a snake. I only needed salt, blood, and breath. Easy.

With a stick, I drew a circle in the cemetery dirt, and from the plastic bag I'd brought of ingredients readily available in my kitchen, I pulled out a box of kosher salt. The crystals glittered between thin blades of grass as I sprinkled them around the circle. *Place the subject in the center of the circle,* Dad had written.

I chewed on the inside of my bottom lip. I had no cuts or dead flesh. And it was too far into autumn for flowers.

But a small cluster of dead leaves had collected against the base of the headstone across from me, and I got up to pick out a good one. Back in my seat, I gently placed the crinkled maple leaf inside my circle. The edges were black and curled, but I could still see lines of scarlet tracing the veins. Trees around here weren't losing many leaves yet, so this was probably left from last winter. It had soaked up a lot of time in the cemetery.

Now came the difficult part. I dug my pocketknife out of my jeans and flipped open the blade. Resting the tip against my left thumb, I paused.

My stomach twisted as I contemplated how much it was going to hurt. What if this spell book was a huge joke? Was I crazy to even try? It was all impossible. Magic couldn't be real.

But it was written in Dad's hand, and he had *never* been that kind of mean. And he wasn't crazy—no matter what anybody said. Dad had believed in this, or he wouldn't have wasted his time with it. And I believed in Dad. I had to.

Either way, it was just a drop of blood.

I pushed the knife against my skin, puckering it but not breaking through. My whole body shivered. I was about to find out if magic was real. The electric thrill of terror was tangy on my tongue.

I cut deep.

A muffled cry escaped my tightly closed lips as blood

welled against my skin, dark as oil. I held out my hand, staring at the thick drop slithering down my thumb. The pain was a dull ache that drew all the way up my arm and settled uncomfortably in my shoulder blade before fading into nothing. My hand trembled, and I wasn't afraid anymore.

Quickly, I let one, two, three drops of blood fall and splatter onto the leaf. They gathered in the center of it in a small pool. I leaned over, staring at the blood as if it could stare right back. I thought of Dad, of how much I missed him. I needed this to be real.

"Ago vita iterum," I whispered slowly, letting my breath brush the leaf and shake the tiny pool of blood.

Nothing happened. Wind fluttered my hair again, and I cupped my hands around the leaf to shield it. I peered down, thinking that the Latin had been bad. Squeezing my wounded thumb, I let more blood gather and drip down. I repeated the phrase.

The leaf shuddered under my breath, and the edges unfurled like growing petals in time-lapse photography. The scarlet center spread out, reaching for the tips and becoming a luscious, bright green. The leaf lay there in the circle, flat and fresh as if new-plucked.

Something rough-sounding against the grass drew my attention up sharply.

A boy was watching me, his eyes wide.

THREE

NICHOLAS

I'd like to say I came to the graveyard in search of my past, or out of sentiment or nostalgia. But I came to get as far away from my psychotic stepmother as possible.

We'd been at dinner: her, my dad, and me, sitting around the long table in the fancy dining room. I plucked at the white linen and wondered whether, if I spilled a few drops of wine onto it, Lilith's eyes would roll back into her head and she'd start spouting Bible verses backward.

"Looking forward to school Monday, Nick?" Dad asked, raising his own wineglass to his mouth. He believed in introducing me to alcohol gradually and in a controlled fashion, as if I hadn't made friends with it in the boys' bathroom at school by the time I was fourteen.

"Like I look forward to sliding down a hill of razor blades."

"It won't be so bad." Lilith slid a chunk of steak off her fork with her teeth: her version of a challenging sneer.

"Right. A new school at the beginning of my senior year in the middle of freaking nowhere. I'm sure it'll be great."

She pursed her Botox-lips. "Come now, Nick, I doubt

you'll have any more trouble alienating yourself and being an outcast here than you did in Chicago."

I deliberately set my glass down too hard, sloshing red wine onto the tablecloth.

"Nick!" Dad frowned at me. He still wore his tie, even though he'd been at home for hours.

"Dad, didn't you hear what she—"

"You're nearly eighteen, son, and you've got to stop—"

"She's thirty-two! I think if anyone needs to act mature, it's her." I shoved to my feet. "But I guess that's what you get for marrying someone thirteen years younger than yourself."

"You are excused," Dad said calmly. He was always calm.

"Great." I grabbed a spear of asparagus and saluted Lilith with it. She won that round, clearly. She always did, since she had Dad wrapped around her finger.

As I strode out into the foyer, I heard Lilith say, "It's nothing to worry about, darling. That's what bleach is for."

Grinding my teeth, I swung by the front closet, snatched a hoodie, and slammed out the front door. If I'd been at home, I could have jogged down the block to Trey's house and we'd have headed for a coffee shop or Mikey's to shoot some aliens on his Xbox. But instead I was alone outside a Missouri farmhouse with nothing nearby but a crumbling old graveyard. I finished chewing the asparagus spear as I marched over the gravel driveway and zipped up the hoodie.

The sun had set below the woods surrounding the house, so everything was pretty dark. But above, the sky was still pale. Only a handful of stars poked through. Shoving my hands into the pockets of the hoodie, I headed for the trees. I could see the cemetery from my bedroom, and now was as good a time as any to see if I could find Grandpa's grave.

Grandpa had died over the summer, leaving the whole of his property to me. Who'd met him once when I was seven and only remembered being sick most of the time and him yelling at my mom about something I didn't understand. But I guess age did strange things to a person, and I was his only living relative besides Mom, who didn't speak to either of us anymore.

Yeah, it was a nice family history.

But then Lilith and Dad descended upon what had probably been a charming farmhouse and tore all the quaint wallpaper off the walls and replaced it with black-and-white art deco soullessness. If only their sex life was so bland.

Lilith had spent several days ooohing and aaahing over the land. "What a perfect atmosphere for a writer!" "Oh, darling, I love it! Look at that view!" and "I'll never spend three thousand bucks on a designer coat again!" Okay, she didn't say the last part, but she should have.

The worst part was that Dad was planning to be gone four days every week, flying to Chicago to keep up with all his needy clients. So not only was I in a hick town where the most popular gathering spot was the Dairy Queen, but I was trapped here alone *with Lilith.*

At least I only had to live here for a few months before graduation. And at least I'd only missed one month of the school year, so I'd actually be *able* to graduate.

I kicked my way through the woods. I don't know an oak from an elm in the best of times, but with the sun down it was pitch-black in the forest and all the trees crowded around me like an arboreal downtown for squirrels. And bugs and frogs, which were making so much buzzing and whining noise I wasn't sure I'd be able to hear myself talk. The ground was covered in layers of old leaves, and when they tossed up under my feet, I smelled delightful things like rot and mold. I nearly tripped a couple of times, but flailed my arms and managed to catch myself on a tree. It was fun smacking through the leaves and low bushes, like it used to be fun to run through piles of raked leaves in our backyard when I was a kid. Mom used to make the leaves dance, and they'd float up around my head and dive-bomb me. She said they were little beetle airplanes and—

See, no. That was why I didn't want to be in Yaleylah. Everything reminded me of Mom, and of all the things I wasn't supposed to think about. In the house, I stopped in front of every door wondering which had been her bedroom. In the kitchen, I wondered if she'd taught herself to make that awesome spaghetti sauce or if her own mom had helped. Had she stared off at the cemetery like I caught myself doing before bed last night? Or had she been totally uninterested in ghosts? These were things I'd never know because she was off in Arizona pretending I didn't exist.

I burst out of the woods really abruptly. I hadn't even noticed the light getting a little better. A road—really just two wheel tracks overgrown with weeds—was between me and the dilapidated cemetery wall. I hiked across to the crumbling stones and climbed over easily. A thin little moon grinned at me beside a scattering of stars. The sky was purplish and clear. And the cemetery spread for at least a quarter mile before ending at a huge hedge keeping it private from our nearest neighbors' house.

It seemed rude to keep kicking through the leaves now that I was in a cemetery, so I slowed down and walked quietly. Most of the headstones were blackened granite or marble, the epitaphs worn down and obscured by darkness. I could read some names and a few dates going back to eighteen-something-something. Touching them was irresistible, so I wandered with my hands out, patting one here and just dragging my fingers against another. The stone was cold and rough, also grimy. A few of the headstones had dying flowers clinging to them. There was no noticeable pattern to the layout of the graves; as soon as I thought I'd found a row, it bent out into a weird oval or courtyard. It wasn't as though I was likely to get lost when I could easily see the black mass of the woods around my house on one end and the neighbors' on the other. I wondered who lived there, and if the fields to the south belonged to them, too, or another farmer.

It was all quiet except for the low hum of bugs from the woods, with the occasional burst from crows yelling at each other. I watched a flock of them fly away, teasing and pecking at each other loudly, and I found myself relaxing. At least I could find some peace with the dead bodies. They were probably all decomposed to dust by now. Except maybe Grandpa. I kept my eyes peeled for a bright, new headstone.

I wondered if I would have liked him, if I'd ever come to visit. I could have. Should have, I guess. But I'd never known him, and Dad never brought up anything having to do with Mom's family, so mostly I just lived my life without thinking about it. There was no point in stressing about it now.

A statue about ten feet ahead of me moved. I froze, then ducked behind a five-foot-tall obelisk like the Washington

Monument. Peering around the corner, I realized the statue was wearing jeans and a T-shirt, and had barrettes in her hair that glittered purple in the moonlight. I was an idiot.

The girl sat on the ground with her back against a fresh headstone. A book rested open beside her, and a blue plastic grocery bag flapped against her knee. She was skinny, with choppy short hair that stuck up in this dramatic way I really liked. Like I could run my hands through it and she wouldn't snap at me for messing it up (like some girls I could mention) because it wouldn't make a difference. I opened my mouth to say hi, but stopped when she lifted a pocketknife and put it against her thumb.

What the hell?

After a hesitation, when her lips pushed together, she cut herself. *No.*

The blood dripped down her skin and I thought of my mom with Band-Aids on all her fingers.

I remembered Mom pricking her finger and smearing blood across a mirror to show me the images that came alive in it, or dripping it onto a small plastic dinosaur toy and whispering a word to make the stegosaurus wag its spiky tail. I didn't want to remember it, didn't want to know that it hadn't been only our shared brand of crazy.

The girl leaned over and whispered to the leaf in front of her. It shuddered, and then unfurled, turning bright green.

HO-lee shit.

She glanced up at me. My mouth was hanging open. There was no effing way I'd seen that. It wasn't possible. Not here. Not again.

As I snapped my mouth shut, she scrambled to her feet, pocketknife thrust behind her back.

I stepped around the headstone, dragging my gaze away from the leaf and up to her face. "Sorry," I managed to gasp out. "I was just wandering past, and I saw . . ." I glanced back at the leaf.

"Saw what?" she whispered, like there was something in her throat.

"Nothing . . . nothing. Just you."

Her face remained guarded. "I don't know you."

"I'm Nicholas Pardee." I didn't usually introduce myself that way, but it was as if in the cemetery I had to tell her my full name. As if it mattered. "I just moved into the old house next to the cemetery." I managed not to wince. Talk about cliché. *Hi, I moved into old man Harleigh's spooky house and like to wander grave-yards. I usually have a big dog named Scooby with me.*

"Oh, yes." She looked off in the direction of my house. "I heard. I'm Silla Kennicot. We live back that way." She waved behind her at the nearby house, then seemed to suddenly remember the knife was in her hand and whipped it behind her back again.

I took a long breath. Okay, so she was my neighbor. And my age. And hot. And possibly messed in the head. Or I was. Because there was no way this was happening. Me, hot girl, and what had looked like . . . no. *No.* I felt prickly, like I'd sprouted porcupine quills all down my back. I wanted to say something obnoxious to make myself feel better, to get my feet back under me, but instead I said something totally lame. "Silla—I've never heard that name. It's pretty."

She looked away, her face going still as glass. When she spoke, her voice was thin enough to shatter into a thousand pieces. "It's short for Drusilla. My dad taught Latin at the high school."

"Oh, Latin, huh." Taught. Past tense.

"It means something like strong." She said it like it was ironic.

We stared at each other. I was torn between grabbing her and yelling that I knew exactly what she'd been doing and that she had to stop before somebody got hurt . . . and pretending we were both normal and didn't care about blood. Maybe she was just a dumb cutter, or it was an accident. I didn't know enough about her. Maybe it didn't have anything to do with my mom. Maybe I hadn't really seen anything. I refused to let myself glance back down at the leaf.

"Have you graduated?" she asked.

Startled, I answered a bit too loudly. "Oh, no. I'm starting school tomorrow." I offered my best wry smile. "Can't wait."

"You must be a senior?"

"Yeah."

"We might not have any classes together, then. I'm a junior."

"I suck at history," I offered.

"I'm in AP." She smiled again, and real humor made her eyes narrow. They didn't seem so ghostly and huge.

I laughed. "Damn."

Silla nodded, and looked down. While we'd been talking, she'd drawn her foot through the spiral etched into the dirt. It was just a mess of lines now, and bits of dry grass and leaves. No sign of anything weird. Relief made me bolder. "Is your hand okay?"

"Oh, um." She brought her hands out, slipping the folded knife into her jeans pocket. A ring hugged each of her fingers. Splaying them wide, she studied her thumb. Blood was smeared across it.

"Peroxide," I said abruptly. That's what Mom had used. I hated the smell.

"What?"

"You should use that to, uh, clean it."

"It isn't so bad. Just a little prick," she murmured.

Silence surrounded us, except for the distant calling of those crows.

Silla opened her mouth, paused, then sighed softly. "I should go home and take care of it."

I wished I had something else to say. But I was trapped between wanting to forget what I might have seen and wanting to demand explanations. All I did know was that I didn't want her to leave. "Can I walk you?"

"No, that's okay. It's just a little ways."

"Sure." I bent and picked up the little book for her. It was plain and ancient-looking, with no title. "Old family heirloom?" I joked.

Silla froze, lips parted for an instant like she was afraid, but then laughed. "Yeah, exactly." She shrugged like we were sharing a grand joke and took the book. "Thanks. See you, Nicholas."

I held up a hand, waving. She darted off, making almost no noise. But I continued to hear my name, long and kind of exotic-sounding in her quiet voice, after she'd disappeared into the shadows.

 # FOUR

SILLA

As the screen door smacked closed behind me, I heard the answering machine pick up Gram Judy's call. "Hey, kiddos, bunko's dragging, probably thanks to the vodka I dropped into Margie's punch. I'll miss supper, but if you need me to pick anything up, give a call. Ciao."

Good. I was shaking with excitement, and I wanted to talk to Reese before she got home. Making my way down the hall to the kitchen, I thought about Nicholas Pardee, who'd nearly seen the magic. It hadn't occurred to me that I needed to be so careful in the cemetery—nobody went there but me. Nicholas's grandpa, Mr. Harleigh, had been buried across town in the newer cemetery with everyone else. It was only by a special request in Dad's will that he and Mom were so close to home.

But Nicholas had been gentle about my hand, and watched me with the oddest, most intriguing expression. Like he knew my secret. Even though he couldn't. Because if he'd seen the leaf, he would surely have decided he'd imagined it. Nobody believed in magic.

Nodding to myself, as if I accepted my own reasoning, I

flipped on the kitchen light and placed the spell book on the table. At the sink, I turned on the water and rinsed my thumb. The ruffled curtains over the sink fluttered in the breeze pushing through the open window, and I imagined singing my favorite show tune of the week while Mom hummed along next to me, peeling potatoes in her favorite apron, with the cartoon rabbits all over it. That apron was folded in the bottom of a drawer next to the oven now.

I patted my hand dry and looked at the wound. It was small and smooth from the sharp knife, and it stung. Part of me still couldn't believe the magic had worked, and that I'd actually cut myself for it. That I'd had the guts to do it. Turning to lean against the counter, I stared at the spell book. My stomach pinched and I felt my lungs contract. Magic was real. I'd changed that leaf with just some lines in the dirt, my blood, and a few little words.

Magic was real, and my dad wasn't crazy.

The relief was heavy enough that I needed to sit down at the table. All I could hear was the soft ticking of the grandfather clock in the hall and my own breath. I pressed my elbows into the wood and folded my hands together. My feet tapped on the hardwood floor, frantically, like they were trying to run far, far away. But I couldn't stop them. I wanted to run, to scream, to fly up into the sky and laugh as I looked down at the changed world.

Two hours ago I'd been lost, just a girl with two dead parents and an angry, distant brother. Now I knew my dad lived on through the spell book. Through the magic.

A smile quirked across my face. I imagined a mask settled against my skin: brilliant yellow and blue, with gold glitter sprinkled everywhere and cheerful pink flowers at the corners of the wide smile.

It was eight p.m. Reese would be home anytime. I couldn't focus on homework while I waited, but I wasn't hungry and the house was perfectly clean. I'd spent a lot of time the past few months cleaning and cooking to keep myself busy and distracted, but there was only so much bleach a toilet could take. I hopped to my feet anyway. The brown paper the spell book had arrived in rested on the floor near the entryway. I wrinkled it up and dumped it in the recycling bin under the sink. I unloaded the dishwasher and rearranged the daisies in the vase in the dining room. I swept the hardwood hallway floor and around all the rugs in the den and Gram Judy's bedroom. Even after going over the kitchen, I didn't have enough detritus to fill the dustpan. I dusted everywhere except Dad's office, but it didn't take more than a single Swiffer sheet, since I'd dusted only two days ago. Then I grabbed one of Reese's paperbacks, a historical murder mystery. It started with blood, and I couldn't read it. So I tried one of Gram Judy's left-wing magazines, and the words swam around on the page, making me think of runes and magical ingredients.

A car door slammed outside. My heart thudded hard and I closed my eyes, sucking in a long, calming breath. Reese's familiar footsteps clomped up the porch, and the front screen door creaked open.

I held the spell book to my chest as I went to meet him.

Reese propped himself half in, half out of the house, with the screen against his butt, as he scraped mud off his boots.

He was two years older than me, and should have been up

at Kansas State getting his bachelor's. But he'd deferred his admission after Mom and Dad had died, and I couldn't bring myself to argue.

When he turned to step inside, Reese startled, flinging a hand out. It smacked into the door frame. "Christ, Sil, what the hell are you doing?"

I held out the spell book in both hands, like an offering.

"What's this?" He tromped in, snatching the book carelessly. I swallowed a whimper of distress and bit my lip.

Reese pushed around me into the kitchen. He tossed his wallet onto the table, and the book beside it. Going to the cabinet, he pulled out a glass to fill with water. "Where'd it come from?"

Appalled by his lack of concern, I said, "It's Dad's."

He stopped, glass halfway to his lips. Then he carefully set the glass on the counter and turned. His jaw was locked.

"Here." I opened the book and pulled out the Deacon's note, keeping my eyes away from Dad's handwriting. I fluttered it at Reese.

Slowly, as if pushing his hand through water, he took it. I stared at his face while he unfolded it and read. He needed to shave, but he usually did. His skin was darker than it had ever been, from all the time he spent working in the sun with the harvest crew these days. It had gilded his hair and sunk into all his pores. Made him look older. Or maybe Mom and Dad had more to do with that.

His mouth fell into a hard frown, and two blotches of muddy color flushed his cheeks. Suddenly, he crumpled the note into his fist.

I leapt forward. "Reese!"

"It's crap," he said.

"No it isn't!"

"You want this to be real?" He stepped forward, brandishing his fist.

"It *is* real." I took his fist in my hands and pried up his fingers until I could get to the note. My fingers were shaking again.

"It's crazy. If this was Dad's, it proves what everyone says. He was crazy and he did it on purpose."

My tongue dried up and shriveled into the back of my throat. I couldn't say anything, as usual, against Reese's horrible certainty.

"Yeah, Sil. On purpose. Planning to shoot her." His voice wavered. His fingers curled as if he might punch the wall again.

"No." I scuttled back to the table and grabbed the spell book. "I tried it. The magic works. I—"

"Bull."

The sharp tone cracked through my joyful mask, and it slid off my face.

Reese crossed his arms over his chest. "Don't bullshit me, Silla. I'm tired and not in the mood."

"I'm not." My voice was reasonable, smooth. "It worked. I transformed a dead leaf, Reese, and if the magic is real, then Dad wasn't crazy. He didn't do what they say he did."

"Say it, Silla. Killed Mom. That's what they say because that's what happened."

I shook my head and set the book deliberately on the table. "Look at it. Really look at it. Then I'll show you." I had to get outside.

Threading through the hallway, I went out the back of the house and ran down the patio stairs onto the grass. Crickets and cicadas screamed through the darkness. I closed my eyes and saw Mom and Dad, limbs twined together in a great splatter of blood. The rivulets reached for my shoes, but I couldn't move, could only stare and stare and suck in air sticky with blood and death. Would it have helped to tear at my eyes until the memory of them sprawled in the study was scratched away forever?

"Silla." Reese came out of the house. He had the book.

"Why don't you believe in him?" I begged.

"I saw"—Reese grabbed for me, caught my arm—"I saw them, just like you did. Why don't you see it now?"

I jerked away. "I do."

"You see what you want to see, Silla. Have you ever heard of this Deacon person? No. We don't know anything about him, or if he's real or what. At best this is a sick joke, and at worst it's something Dad really believed in and that doesn't prove he's innocent, it proves he was psycho."

The magic is real, Reese. The world is different tonight. I let out a long, slow sigh. He couldn't know without seeing. Couldn't have faith. "He was our dad. I know he didn't do it."

Throwing the book to the grass, Reese said, "He did—the police proved it, for chrissake. There was no doubt in anyone's mind. It doesn't matter if some crazy spells work. He pulled that damned trigger. Sheriff Todd was Dad's friend. Don't you think he'd do everything he could to . . ." He trailed off, shaking his head with frustration. We'd had this conversation before.

"He didn't do it. The magic—"

He cut me off with a slash of his hand through the air. But then his anger crumpled. "Bumblebee," he said, and when he stepped forward again, I didn't move away. "It's been three months. You have to accept it."

"Like you have?"

He put his arms around me, and I leaned into his chest. Hay dust tickled my nose, and behind it sweat and tractor oil. Familiar and solid, like Reese had always been. What was it like to be so sure the way he was? To be confident and strong, to pound your anger out against a wall, to work it out in the fields?

"Yeah," he answered. The word was tinged with bitterness, and I was relieved that Reese didn't like it, even if he believed Dad had killed her. It didn't make sense to him, either.

After a moment, he said, "I need a beer. Want one?"

"No." I was numb enough.

"Where's Gram?"

"Bilking Mrs. Margaret and Patty Grander for all they have."

"Oh, yeah. Bunko night." For a moment, he tilted his face and I thought he'd apologize for yelling. But then I'd have to apologize, too. Instead Reese sighed. "I'll make sandwiches, okay?"

"Okay. I'll—I'll stay out here for a while."

Nodding, Reese went back inside. My sneakers gradually sank into the grass. I waited for the earth to grow up over my ankles and shins and knees, trapping me until I turned into stone.

FIVE

March 18, 1904

Philip insists that I write what I remember. It is ridiculous and a waste of my time, because I do not wish to remember where I came from. But the Awful Beast will not teach me more unless I do!

And so, against my Will, this is the tale of how I came to meet Dr. Philip Osborn (the Beast).

It was last year, when I was fourteen years old, and I remember the smell of the mill and how I hated it so very much that when the dizziness came to me, I was thrilled. Influenza would send me to St. James! I was the oldest, and dreadful Mrs. Wheelock was furious to lose me because of how fast I could thread the warp. I laughed at her even as the fever shook my bones. I was piled with the others in a narrow infirmary room at the back of St. James, quartered off from the rest of the world. I expected them to burn the hall when we died, and never bother to give us a proper burial.

The little girl shaking in the bed next to me was certain we were Doomed, the gutless creature. She clutched at me and her prayers rattled in my ears, as useless as rats. I was not going to die.

When I saw Philip's face for the first time, I knew that the girl at my side had prayed to the wrong person. Philip's eyes had a thickness to them, and his copper hair and long-fingered surgeon's hands Awoke something in me that has never Slept again. He had come to help us, to make the sick children comfortable if he couldn't make us well. I stared at the corner of his mouth as he concentrated, at the way it twitched when he tried to hide the Truth as he listened to the little girl beside me breathe. I stared and stared, and when he turned to me, he said, "You aren't going to die, are you?" and I said, "No, sir."

A week later, I was the only one left. Philip took me out of St. James and to his tall house in Town. He let them think I was dead, and it was no trouble for me! I had always hated it with Mrs. Wheelock, and escape was worth the risk of going with a stranger like him. Philip cleaned me up, gave me my own bedroom and a cast-iron bathtub with a bar of soap he cooked himself. It smelled of flowers! But even with the soap and scalding water, I could not get the tangles out of my hair. I remember being terrified for one brief moment that he would throw me back to the mill. But when he found me crying on the floor, he cut it all off with a skinny little dagger and said, "All problems have a solution, Josephine Darly. Learn that and you will do well here. I will teach you to read and write, and if you apply yourself, perhaps other things." I thought he meant man and woman things, which I already knew but did not tell him because I wished him to think me Innocent. Besides, I liked the idea of learning to read and write. With an Education, I'd never have to go back to the mill, and I would impress him so very much with my wits and spirit and prettiness that he would love me above all other things!

How could I have known that what he would teach me is ever so much greater than Love?

SIX

NICHOLAS

Yaleylah High School was two buildings: a three-story academic hall and a gym. Between those yellow brick disappointments was a parking lot, and to the south a field of grass that I guessed was a field for football, soccer, track, and baseball rolled into one, depending on the season. You'd think with all the open spaces and farms they could find a place for each sport. Even in Chicago, the baseball team had only had to share with the softball team.

My natural inclination to irritability was totally made worse by the fact that I hadn't slept well thanks to nightlong dreams about being trapped in a dog's body. (Don't get me started on that favorite recurring nightmare. I don't know the Freudian explanation, and I don't want to.) Plus, I was the new kid and from the Big City and had a totally different fashion sense (I'd say the only fashion sense) and taste in music, food, and culture. I talked differently, for chrissake, and at lunch a cheerleader asked me to repeat what I'd just said. I flipped her off.

The girl in the cemetery distracted me, too. I hadn't seen

her again, though I'd wandered out to the graves last night. Hoping because I couldn't stop thinking about her, and fearing because I really didn't want her to be doing what I thought I'd seen her doing.

As I walked between classrooms, I kept my eyes out for her. I was used to dashing, and occasionally sprinting, between classes, but most senior rooms here were on the first floor, all clustered together. I estimated that there were only about four hundred kids total at the school, and they all clearly knew each other's names and family histories and et cetera. The herd of cowboy boots made me want to puke.

On Wednesday, in my calculus class, Mrs. Trenchess told us to pair up and go over homework. I didn't have any homework, but this guy in the desk next to me snaked his hand across the aisle. "Hey, I'm Eric."

I looked up from the dirty haiku I was writing between notes on logarithmic functions. *And?* I asked with my eyebrows.

He smacked his hand on the desktop, grinning. "You really are an asshole. That's what they're saying."

I still didn't answer.

Eric dug a silver Zippo out of his jeans and flicked it open, then shut, slouching down in his desk to conceal it from Mrs. Trenchess. "It's okay, I already know your name, Nick." He fisted his hand around the lighter, leaned way across the aisle— so precariously I expected him to fall—and read the poem in the margin of my textbook. " 'Cramped without recourse / Mrs. Trenchess is against / student survival.' " He paused. "Haiku?"

I couldn't be totally rude to somebody who knew his poetry. "I thought about etching it into the desk next to ONLY MOFOS PLAY CHESS but wasn't sure it was clever enough."

His laugh was a high-pitched bark. "Do you have any others?"

I debated for a second, then thought, what the hell. Flipping my notebook over, I found the last poems.

Formulas, algorithms and graphs
Make for boredom not laughs
I won't need this stuff
Whiskey's enough
To set me on the right paths.

And:

Skanky girl with eyes
Too heavy under powder
Thinks I give a shit

"That sounds like Sarah Turner," Eric mused.

"It was Western Civ this morning. She was pissed I wouldn't talk to her. I didn't even try to catch her name."

"So you want to be a poet?"

"No."

Leaning back into his desk, he waited for me to continue. When I didn't, Eric shook his head. "I hear poets get themselves a lot of tail."

We shared a grin. "Hey," I said. "You know Silla Kennicot?"

His face stilled, then the skin around his mouth tightened like he was trying not to frown. "Yeah. Why?"

"She's just my neighbor." I shrugged, as if it didn't matter. *What the hell?*

"Oh, that's right. I forgot. You meet her?"

"Yeah. She seemed a bit odd."

He paused, flicking his lighter open again. "No kidding. Ever since her parents died, she's been messed up." Eric stopped. "Can't blame her."

I was clearly supposed to ask for details. Instead I asked if he needed help with his homework. He replied that if he'd done it, he would.

After class, Eric walked with me to my free period. As we passed a bulletin board, he paused and pointed at a neon or-ange flyer. MACBETH, it read, and WE NEED CREW! ALL THE GLORY, NONE OF THE MEMORIZATION! "You should come join up," Eric said. "You don't have to be liked to be on stage crew."

The river of students pressed me closer to the orange paper. At the very bottom, it said in tiny letters, SPONSORED BY THE RAZORBACK DRAMA CLUB. ERIC LEILENTHAL, ACTING PRESIDENT. "Acting president? You're just pretending?" Frankly, Eric didn't look the part. I'd put him in the home-fried baseball category.

He pulled a pen out of his jeans pocket and scratched out the word *acting*. "That bitch." Replacing the pen, he continued, "Wendy Cole keeps insisting we have a vote, but I was vice prez, and when the president gives up on you, the vice just steps in."

"Wow. Drama in drama club."

"Yeah, well, your girlfriend Silla is in the show. That make you want to come?" He sneered.

I liked that Eric was kind of an asshole, too. And I needed something to do after school to avoid Lilith. "Sure. Where?"

"After school, in the auditorium. Later, okay? I gotta find Wendy."

As he marched down the hallway, I thought, *Where the hell are they hiding an auditorium?*

SILLA

School rushed by in its usual blur. Since Saturday night, I'd spent every moment I could up in my bedroom, hunched over the spell book and reading it out loud the way I used to read scripts to memorize my lines. I read cover to cover, and then over again, brushing my fingers against the indentations my dad's pen had made in the thick paper. The patterns swam in my imagination, and I could hear his voice: *Sympathetic magic works with our own associations. Quicken the tincture with a drop of blood. Draw poison out with fire, bind with red ribbons. Fresh beeswax is best for transformations. Drop of blood. Hint of blood. Cut. Sacrifice. Give.*

So many questions I had for him. What does sympathetic magic mean? Why is ginger for burning curses away, and salt best for protection and neutral spells? What do you mean by *neutral?*

It all intruded on my school day, memories pressing at me. Not just of reading, of Dad, but of the moment the magic had unfurled that dead leaf, and of Nicholas Pardee rising out of the shadows where he'd crouched like a goblin. They eclipsed the video Mr. Edwards showed in AP History, and Physics lecture, and even Mrs. Sackville's discussion on *The Return of the Native*. I tried to push all of it out of my mind and listen to Sackville's questions about the nature of misfits and sexual identity, but everyone in my classes seemed pale and stony. They were mere gravestones, and only the magic was real.

And tonight, I'd show it to Reese. I'd prepared all I could, read through everything. Now I needed Reese. Needed to prove to him it was real so that he could stop hating Dad, so that he could help me unlock all the secrets. I'd resurrect something more impressive than a leaf, and he'd have to believe me.

Finally it was three-thirty, and I escaped to the auditorium. There, I could pull on the masks of the theater and lose myself in the words that weren't my own. It was a relief to sit on the edge of the stage, to dangle my feet as Wendy and Melissa argued about whether all the songs from *Wicked* were overdone on the audition circuit. Their conversation echoed up the rows and rows of red seats, and the smells of old paint and musty curtains grounded me back into my body. I'd always loved the theater. Here, I could be anyone, not just the girl who'd found her parents murdered on the floor, not just the skinny, fading kid with dropping grades and choppy hair, but Ophelia or Laura Wingfield or Christine Daaé. Pretending I was someone else, that their words were my words, their heartaches and loves my own; it made me feel like I knew who I was.

Or it had. When I'd been Silla Kennicot: most likely to star in movies, president of the drama club, and forensics champion.

Eric walked in with Nicholas Pardee and raised his middle

finger in my direction. I frowned, but Wendy giggled. "He probably found my flyers," she said.

Melissa laughed, too. "I saw that."

I pulled my feet up onto the stage and sat cross-legged, watching Nicholas. I'd been thinking of him that way, the way he'd introduced himself to me in the cemetery, of him being something that belonged there, with a long, old-fashioned name to go with it. But here in the real world, everyone was calling him just Nick. And away from all the death and blood and magic, it was hard to see him as anything more mysterious. It suited the way he walked between the rows of seats and the sharp way he sat down next to Stokes, the teacher, while Eric stomped up the stairs and glared at the three of us. "Cute flyers," he said.

"Like your butt, sweetie." Wendy kissed the air in his direction.

Flipping her off again, Eric joined Trent upstage, and they kicked off their shoes to start some warm-up stretches.

"I want my witches front and center!" Stokes called before turning to Nick, who stood beside him.

It was good I knew the layout of the stage well, because I didn't stop watching Nick even to head out with Wendy and Melissa to wait for our cue. He was tall, even all cramped up in the small theater seat where he'd sat after talking to Stokes. His hair was longish and sort of slicked back in a way none of the boys here wore it. It opened up his face so that I could see it better than I had Saturday night.

"Jeez, Silla, you might want to close your mouth," Melissa said.

I glanced down at the scuffed stage, then up at Melissa with my lips pursed into a frown.

Wendy nudged her. "Leave her alone. It's great she's showing interest at all."

My gratitude for her intercession dried up, and I glared at them both.

"He is cute," Melissa offered.

"He lives in that old farmhouse up the road from me," I said. "Just moved in."

They both watched me like I'd sprouted a conjoined twin on the side of my face. Wendy winced as Melissa laughed. "No kidding, Sil, we know. Everybody's been talking about him all day. Jerry said he's Mr. Harleigh's grandson."

"Oh." He didn't look like Mr. Harleigh, who'd been stooped over like he was holding a secret against his stomach.

"*And* his stepmother is like some huge, famous writer. She must use a pen name, though. Weren't you listening at lunch when Eric and Doug were starting up the betting pool on what she writes?"

Stokes waved his pudgy hands toward the stage, and the three of us shifted to where he wanted us. "Why would a famous author move here?" I asked, but didn't hear any reply because Nick lifted his gaze right then, and caught mine. He smiled crookedly. His knees jutted out, as did his elbows. He was like a giant scarecrow folded up into the seat, smiling at me. I glanced away.

"Let's see the start of act four!" called Stokes.

NICHOLAS

I'd never been a theater guy. But even I saw it as Silla stepped into her role.

It was like—I don't know. Silla was there, but she was more than herself. It was a witch up on the stage, talking about eyeballs and lizard parts, and even though I'd seen her out in the cemetery, this was different. But it was also real.

So, acting. Apparently it wasn't just something kids did when they couldn't get into college.

Mr. Stokes paused the scene, and Silla fell out of character. Like flipping a switch. She flicked her stare past the director, to me. I smiled a little. Silla glanced away.

Even when Stokes moved on to a scene Silla wasn't in, I watched her. She stood at the edge of the stage, leaning against the arch. Her hands were covered in rings. She fidgeted, causing the rings to glitter under the multihued lights, making colors dart crazily across the black stage floor.

 # SEVEN

SILLA

In the parking lot after rehearsal, Nick was waiting. He rested his butt against the passenger door of a sleek black convertible.

Wendy bumped her shoulder into mine. "He's staring at you again. He could be crazy. You know, I heard that his mom spent time in an institution."

"An institution?"

"A mental one."

"Hey!" Melissa cackled. "You two might have been made for each other."

I should have done it myself, but Wendy smacked Melissa's arm for me. "God, Melissa. Insensitive much?"

We were close enough then that Nick said, "Hey, Silla."

I cautiously approached, knowing Wendy was going with Melissa and her boyfriend in Melissa's old Camry to Evanstown for burgers. I didn't want to go, and maybe Nick was my excuse. "Hi, Nick."

"Can I give you a lift home? It's right on my way."

Low gray light filtering through the afternoon clouds softened all the shadows. I could see all the angles of his face. His eyes were brown, a dark, greenish sort of brown like a freshly turned field. His lashes curled like birthday ribbons. "Silla?" he said.

"Oh, sorry." I lowered my chin and looked at the asphalt for a moment, at his black combat boots. Wendy's fingers brushed against mine. *Go, dummy,* she meant. I smiled up at Nick. "Yeah. Yes, I'd love a ride."

"Great." He opened the door for me.

I waved to Wendy, who bounced after Melissa. As I slid into the passenger seat, I said, "Nice car," because I was supposed to.

"It's my dad's, but thanks."

As he jogged around the front and got behind the wheel, I studied his profile. He'd broken his nose at some point. Before I could ask, Nick revved the engine and pulled out of the lot. Wind grabbed my short hair and ruffled it, and for a moment, I missed the feel of its length whipping against my cheeks and neck. I closed my eyes and leaned my head back against the soft leather.

"I don't know if this is an appropriate question or not," Nick said.

My guts rolled. He was going to ask about my parents. I kept my eyes shut.

"How come you aren't playing Lady Macbeth? I mean, you're the best one up there. Way better than that blond girl they have in the role."

Startled, I glanced at him. His hands were on the wheel

and his eyes on the road. But he did flick a quick look my way, once and then again. I felt my lips soften and let myself smile. "Thanks. I don't mind the role, though. The witches are fun."

"Yeah, but . . . I mean, I don't know much about theater, and I can tell you're better." He winced, shrugging as though apologizing for the compliment.

Inexplicably, I wanted to touch him. To put my fingers on his shoulder or knee. I folded my hands in my lap and watched the winking glass in my rings. Each one reminded me of a different word, or a different expression on Dad's face. I took a breath and said, "Casting me as a witch was the kindest thing that's ever been done for me."

Nick frowned into the silence, but it wasn't until we'd passed through the third block of Main Street and were turning up Ellison toward our part of the township that he asked, "Why?"

I couldn't look at him while I said it, so I turned to watch the broken brown stalks of old corn flashing past. The gray sky above made the stalks seem almost golden. "Because of my parents." I paused, and when he remained silent, I assumed he understood. "I read for Lady Macbeth, but there's a scene where she's kind of lost it, and she keeps seeing blood all over her hands." My shudder melted into the vibration of the racing car. "Stokes didn't want me to have to go through that every performance. Not to mention at rehearsals. And if it was me onstage, nobody in the audience would be thinking about Macbeth or the play—they'd be thinking about my parents." I licked my lips and looked back at my lap.

Nick didn't say anything. It wasn't like there was anything that needed to be said.

After another moment, the car slowed and pulled onto the crunching gravel of my driveway. I remembered ruining the white dust under my bloody fingers. If I won the lottery, the first thing I'd do would be to pave the road. Then I'd move to New Mexico.

NICHOLAS

I stopped the convertible behind a Volkswagen Rabbit with a mess of stickers on the bumper and rear window. My Sebring's engine ticked quietly, and I pulled out the keys while I read all the Rabbit's stickers. Did people really still have SAVE THE WHALES bumper stickers? Answer: yep. And every Democratic presidential campaign sticker since Dukakis.

Turning, I leaned my back on the door and hooked my knee up a little onto the seat. Still as stone except for the wind in her dark pixie hair, Silla stared at her hands where they clenched together in her lap. Where'd all the rings come from? They didn't look like cheap crap from Claire's or Hot Topic. The antique settings twisted in knot patterns and graceful swirls. I'd have bet that at least some of the jewels were real. I drew my gaze up her arms to her face. "Hey, so, Silla."

She slowly raised her head.

"That your car?"

Her lips parted as though it was the very last thing she'd expected. "Um. No, that would be Gram Judy. She's rabid." Silla smiled fondly.

I wanted to ask her about Saturday night. If I'd imagined it on a dark, lonely night in a cemetery. She looked tired, though. And sad. And what if she said I was crazy? I touched her wrist. "How's your finger?"

"My finger?" She lifted it up, and then her eyelashes fluttered really fast. "Oh, um. That. It's fine. I used peroxide, like you said." She showed me the Band-Aid wrapped around the cut.

"You should be more careful." It wasn't supposed to sound as condescending as it did. But the Band-Aid on her thumb reminded me so sharply of Mom.

She moved suddenly, like she'd realized she was on fire, grabbing her backpack off the floor at her feet and opening the door. "Thanks for the ride."

I winced while her back was turned, realizing I'd probably scared her off by being a prick. "Sure, anytime. I'll be at rehearsal most nights, I think."

"Oh, really?" She paused after shutting the door gently, and leaned in, maybe a little eagerly. Or I was imagining it. "I meant to ask what you were talking about with Stokes."

"I'm going to be on the stage crew."

Her smile widened, and was undeniably real. "Good." Then the smile folded back under the quiet mask she was carrying around. "See you, Nick."

"Good night, Silla." I forced myself not to wait until she'd gotten up the porch and into the house. Instead I fired the engine and zipped out onto the road.

SILLA

From the porch, I listened to Nick drive away. It was cool in the shade, and I had my usual moment to wonder what I'd find when I entered the house *this* time. If I'd invited Nick in to meet Gram Judy, I wouldn't have to go in alone. It was a weird thought to have: wanting someone to share the horror with.

I pressed my forehead against the cool front door. Inside I heard folksy strains of Joni Mitchell, one of Gram's favorites. *"You're in my blood like holy wine,"* she sang.

A cheerful mask would be good: blue like a mountain lake, with silver spirals around the eyeholes. Imagining it covering my face, I pushed open the door.

"That you, Drusilla?"

My backpack hit the entryway floor with a thud. "Yes, Gram."

"Judy," she corrected, without looking up from her magazine, when I entered the kitchen.

Pulling out one of the chairs, I remembered vividly the spell book all wrapped up and safe behind layers of brown paper before I'd opened it and let out all the demons inside. But now the book was tucked under my mattress upstairs. I dropped my chin into my hand and looked at Gram Judy's magazine. *Mother Jones.* "Good reading?"

"Oh, you know, enough to keep me informed and angry." She slapped the magazine down onto the table and smiled. It looked like the smile of a hungry little terrier, but I'd learned over the past weeks that it was as friendly-looking as Gram Judy got. When she'd shown up at the funeral, we'd all thought she was some city jackal come down to report more on the horrific small-town murder. Reese had barred her from the house until she smacked him on the shoulder and said, "I was your dad's favorite stepmother—get out of my way and let me cook some supper." Neither my brother nor I had had it in us to argue. And eventually she'd shown us pictures from when we were little, with her and Mom and Dad on a trip up to St. Louis that neither Reese nor I remembered. It turned into a blessing, because she knew a lot about managing bills and helped us put Mom and Dad's life insurance money in the right places.

Her hair was pure white and long enough to braid in a crown around her head—which she had, ever since I'd cut all mine off. It was as close to mourning solidarity as she could get. I didn't tell her the reason I'd gotten rid of mine was that the ends had been soaked in my mom's blood. Every time one of the strands touched my neck, it reminded me of talking to Sheriff Todd that night over stale coffee, all my hair stiff and hard with dried brown blood.

"Silla, honey, what in God's name are you thinking about?"

I blinked.

Gram Judy continued, sighing and reaching for her tumbler of ice and bourbon. "As if I don't know." With one snap of her wrist, she finished off the drink and gestured toward the kitchen window. "Who was that boy you drove in with?"

"A new boy at school. Nick Pardee." I stood up and went to get a glass of water. I brought Judy more ice so that she could refill her drink. "He's Mr. Harleigh's grandson."

When I returned to the table, Gram Judy's frown was thoughtful as she tilted back in her chair. "Oh, from the house back in those woods, is it? Your dad dated a girl from there in high school."

"Really?"

"Yes, Daisy or Delilah or something. I can't quite recall. They broke up a few months before he met your mom. It was sudden, I do believe. But then, your dad was getting ready to go off to college and whatnot, and that's never a good time to really tie yourself down to a relationship." Gram Judy seemed to think no time was a good time to tie yourself down.

My rings clinked like wineglasses as I rubbed my cold hands together. "He's joined the crew for the play, and offered to drive me home since it's on his way."

"How polite!"

I glanced up. Judy twisted open the bottle of bourbon and splashed some over her fresh ice. Her fingers were long and knobby, as tan as the rest of her and as wrinkled. But they ended in a French manicure. She took a drink, watching me over the rim of the tumbler. She wouldn't ask anything, just let me tell her what I wanted to—or what I had to. That was how she learned everything about everyone without seeming like a busybody. Patience, and the easy application of alcohol. I stuck to my water. "He's cute."

"You should ask him out."

"Gram!"

"Why not?"

"I just . . . I don't know." *The way he looks at me makes me feel like I could burst out of my skin.*

"You have to have a reason. Bad breath? Not handsome?"

I shrugged again.

"Silla, really. If you don't like him, I wouldn't expect you to date him."

"No, I—he seems nice." I wiggled on my chair. This conversation would never have happened with my mother, who would have immediately started reminding me not to even kiss on a first date. Gram Judy probably assumed I'd already gone all the way with a guy.

"Then what's the problem?"

"I don't feel like it."

"Ah!" She rolled her eyes dramatically. "That's a piss-poor reason. You need to get out into the world again, get your mind off its morbid cycle."

"I don't."

Gram Judy lowered her chin and glared at me.

"Judy, I just . . ." I shuffled for an excuse, settled on the graveyard. "I think I didn't make a good first impression." Though, strangely, it hadn't seemed to bother him.

"Oh, posh." She stretched both her arms across the table and reached for my hands. "Sweetie, it'll be good for you to go out with someone who hasn't known you your whole life, who didn't know you before."

I bit down on the side of my tongue and looked at our hands: mine so pale and covered in the rings that looked too heavy against the bones; Gram Judy's wise and old and elegant. "Because I'm so much less than I was?" I whispered it, knowing it was true.

She squeezed, and my skin pinched between the rings. "Not less, just a little faded. You need a good romance to remind you about love and put some heat back in that body of yours."

That was my limit. Fighting a fierce blush, I tugged my hands away. "I have homework."

The best thing about Gram Judy was that she knew when to let go. Leaning back into her chair, she said, "Supper at eight."

NICHOLAS

All the radio stations out here were country or Jesus rock, so I kept a cluster of CDs on the floor of the passenger side and tended to shove them in at random. That afternoon's lucky selection was an Ella Fitzgerald album. It was scratchy and old, having belonged to my mom, and most of "Over the Rainbow" just skipped.

Which was fine, since it was only a minute and a half to my house from Silla's.

But I punched the radio dial to turn off the music almost as soon as it started. It just frustrated me. Why hadn't I stopped the car with Silla still in it, on the side of the road, and asked her about the leaf? I didn't usually mind being rude or even mean. So what if she was pretty? So what if her parents just died? If she was doing magic, I had to know. I'd spent five years ignoring it, pushing the memories away, but I couldn't get that image of Silla crouched in the graveyard out of my head. When I thought about Mom's Band-Aid fingers, they were covered in Silla's rings.

My knuckles whitened as I gripped the steering wheel. I didn't want this back in my life, screwing everything up. I wanted to just forget it, to push through my last few months of high school and drive away from Dad and Lilith, and from this shithole where crazy was in the water.

Except . . . except I couldn't stop thinking about Silla.

Grunting at myself, I parked in the drive behind the open two-car garage. Dad's *other* convertible was beside Lilith's posh Grand Cherokee. How exciting that they were both home. I didn't want to think too deeply about what they'd been doing all day. Climbing out of the car, I reached in back for my messenger bag, slung it over my shoulder, and headed through the garage door and into the kitchen. Maybe I could get to my bedroom and pretend I'd been there doing homework for the past two hours.

But no, Lilith was in the kitchen with a flowered apron tied around her waist like a goddamn Susie Homemaker. Her maroon nails were curled into claws and dripped gore as she turned away from the half-demolished chicken corpse. My lips twitched. It was so fitting. "Hey," I said before she could accuse me of being morose.

"Nick!" She smiled and took a towel from the granite counter to wipe her hands. "You're so late. You didn't get a detention, did you?"

I blinked. It would be easy to lie, and neither of them would check. But I'd have to spill eventually. "No."

She paused. "Where've you been?"

"Around." I hooked a foot onto one of the tall bar stools under the center island and sat. There was a bowl of jalapeno-stuffed olives next to a ceramic chicken holding an egg that read: THE COOK CAME FIRST. I popped an olive into my mouth. "What's for dinner?"

"Chicken caprese."

"Where's Dad?"

"Up in his office."

I ate another olive. Had I been social enough to earn an easy evening alone in my room? It all depended on Lilith's mood. She continued to clean the chicken. She was taller than me when she wore even short heels, and taller than Dad barefoot. Skinny, long, and sharp, with black hair styled even when she slept, and with this way of arching her eyebrows in constant disapproval. "Well," I said, standing up from the stool. "Later." Lilith nodded, and I stared out over the checkerboard tiles.

"Oh, Nick."

"Yeah?" I paused with my back to her. That light tone always meant she was about to slam me with something.

"We have flashlights in the front hall closet, and also just inside the basement door."

Not what I'd been expecting. "Okay, whatever." I let myself make a face of annoyance since she couldn't see.

"For sneaking around the wilderness in the dark."

I held my breath.

The faucet turned on, and I heard the oven door creak open. But it felt like she was directly behind me, flicking her dragon tongue on the back of my neck in order to smell my fear. She'd played this game all the months I'd known her. *I know what you're doing, Nicky, and I can tell your father anytime I want to.*

I took a deep, quiet breath and pushed it away. Dad heard me go outside every evening, too. It wasn't like Lilith could possibly know about Silla and the cemetery. I turned, flashed her a smile, and said, "I'll do that. Thanks."

I tromped up the curved stairs, one hand loosely dragging along the twisted steel banister, bypassed the second floor completely, and ran up to my attic bedroom. The chaos of my room was always a relief after the starkness downstairs. I'd plastered my walls with movie posters and flyers I'd taken from bulletin boards back home. They were confetti-colored reminders of what I'd loved and what I wouldn't get here in Yaleylah, punk rock bands and slam poetry in particular. Not to mention coffee shops and being able to walk to Lincoln Square. The only nightlife around here was the bar on the corner next to that Dairy Queen.

Dumping my bag on the desk, I grabbed my angriest CD and shoved it into the player. NARKOTIKA hissed to life in a rattle of drums and pounding keyboard. I turned the sound up, then dragged a small box out from under the bed.

The trunk was scratched and old, decorated in lacquer with black birds flying against a purple sky. The key had broken off in the locked position when I threw the trunk across the room once after Mom left. A couple of years later, I had pried it back open. Now the bronze lock hung ruined, and I flicked it aside before opening the box.

Inside were three rows of six small wooden compartments, and slim glass jars slid perfectly into fifteen of them. Each jar contained powder or chunks of metal, dried flower petals, seeds, or, in one, gold shavings. In another, tiny, rough rubies.

The jars were labeled in small, perfect handwriting: *carmot, iron, bone dust, nettle, blessed thistle, snake scales,* and more. In the three empty compartments were black squares of vellum, thin lengths of wax, and spools of colored thread. The tools of Mom's trade. Her bloodletting needle was a sharp quill. I ran my fingers along the speckled brown feather. Turkey, I guessed. I'd never thought to ask her when she was around.

I ripped down five brightly colored handbills from my walls and knelt on the floor again, tearing them into rough shapes. Triangles, squares, and jagged lightning bolts in yellow, red, and orange. I put them flat on the floor, then pulled the jar labeled *holy water* out and uncorked it. Dipping the quill into the water, I drew a circle in the palm of my left hand. I didn't push hard enough to cut. Not yet.

Mom and I had played this game a hundred times when I was small. She drew a circle on my hand with the water, then cut her finger and used blood to etch a seven-pointed star inside the circle. It tickled, and I always laughed but never tugged my hand away. Mom would kiss each of my fingers and tell me I was strong. Then she'd prick my palm quickly. A drop of my blood welled to mingle with hers, and my whole body was warm and tingling. She pressed her finger into the blood and anointed each of the paper shapes with a bloody fingerprint. Together, we whispered, "Paper shapes fly free, dance high, watch over me," in a continuous round.

I did it all, there on my attic floor. The water circle, then a seven-point star of blood. Water dripped down to dilute the blood, giving my star weak pink edges. It still tickled, but I didn't laugh now. The laughter was trapped in my throat and sharp like a chunk of rock. I pressed fingerprints onto all my torn-up, ragged shapes and said, "Paper shapes fly free, dance high, watch over me."

For a second, it was all bullshit. The memories of Mom were these broken bones poking up through my skin. She'd deluded me, tricked me, made me believe in magic that didn't exist.

But then I thought of her delighted smile, and the paper shapes trembled against my carpet as if a light draft teased at them. They shook harder, several of them jumping up to dance a foot in the air.

I scrambled back. My palm smeared across the floor, breaking the spell, and the paper fluttered back down.

I jammed the holy water back into the box and slammed it shut, shoving the whole thing back under the bed. Gathering the shreds of paper, I tried not to think of being a little boy and going to sleep with dozens of rainbow-colored paper stars shaking over my head as they clung near the ceiling. They'd been better than any night-light, better than a blankie or stuffed bear or Power Ranger toy. Because nothing had kept them up there but the power of my mom's love, she said. As long as they hung up there, her blood and mine were connected. Nothing could hurt me.

Now I crumpled my aborted paper spell in my fist and threw the pieces into the plastic bag I'd been using for trash.

Because I'd only been eight when the first bright-yellow star, shrouded with dust, had slowly fallen to the carpet.

 # EIGHT

March 27, 1904

This is how I found out about the Magic:

I had been with him for nine months, and all he had me do was read and read and read, and write and write and write. I copied pages from Mrs. Radcliffe's Romances and Mr. Twain's silly book, and at night Philip would read Whitman or Poe, and I would write down what I heard as he read, until I could write as quickly as he spoke. I preferred the rhyming, because it was easier to predict the direction in which the words would flow. Philip's Library is small and cramped, but the books pile on top of each other until I feel their Weight will bring down the very house around our heads. One entire wall is these creaking old books with pictures in them of Dead bodies and body parts! There is a shelf of Shakespeare, which he told me I was not sophisticated enough for, so I grabbed up a play named The Tempest, *and I read a speech by a creature named Ariel again and again, until it was trapped in my mind. After dinner I stood and recited it for Philip. He slowly clapped his hands and called me his little air sprite. His face became sad, and he asked if I understood what Ariel said. "He has made a storm and destroyed men, for love of Prospero!" I said.*

"For love of Prospero," he said, and he laughed quietly. "Little sprite, tomorrow will you come with me, to assist with my Work?"

Of course I did agree.

I began to help him gather the Blood the very next day.

It comes from his patients. He bleeds them as physicians did Long Ago, but not to drain the Illness away. That is old superstition with no Truth in it. Philip says this with disgust. But his patients do not know better than to let him do it, and if they did, no one would listen to such people as he helps. I do not know WHY he helps them, people who will not or cannot go to hospital, who are poor and dark and dirty.

I did not want to go back into those places, but I am clean and fine now, and they would never Know me. The smells did not disgust me before, but now everything is horrible. Philip does not care! He kneels at their beds and does not notice when a woman is black with dirt or a child has vomit crusted in the corners of his mouth! I stare and stand beside him holding the ceramic cup as the blood flows in, trying to pretend I was never on a bed like that, all Lumpy and Infested, that I was never ugly and that my hands have always been so soft from Philip's oils. I close my eyes and pretend that I do not recall the repetition of the shuttle and the heat when I had to touch the thread to untangle it before Mrs. Wheelock noticed. I do not think about the smell of boiled onions coming from the patients' fire and that once such things were all I had to eat.

I hate this! I hate him for making me remember what I was. What I swear on my immortal soul I shall never, ever be again.

I close myself off to the memories, and we are suddenly players on a dark stage, my Prospero and I, gathering the Blood for our midnight secrets. Although it is only a small amount that we take from each patient, I imagine the cup growing heavy in my hands until my arms tremble with the effort. I measure it into flasks from his leather bag and label them with different-colored inks and different letters. The colors for stages of health and the letters for which ailment affects them. When I arrive home, I take the flasks into the laboratory and lay them out in groups and rows where they belong.

One afternoon, I stood in the shadowy corner of the laboratory, holding a flask up to stare at the way the Blood separated. It was so strange, and I remember I was curious why it did not do that inside my skin.

Philip came in with sweat on his forehead, and did not notice me there. He yawned until his jaw cracked, and collapsed behind his desk. The windows were drawn tightly shut, and only two gas lamps were lit, because I prefer the dimness. He leaned back into his chair and whispered, "I will never find it."

I was unable to resist walking behind him. I rubbed his shoulders as Mrs. Wheelock rubbed Mr. Wheelock's when he came to the mill on Fridays.

"Josephine," Philip said, reaching up to touch my hands. "I did not see you, child."

I bent and kissed his fingers. I am not a child. I am his airy sprite.

With my hand in his, he drew me around and turned his chair so we faced one another. "It truly does not bother you to be here, with the lights so low and surrounded by blood?"

I laughed.

"No, not you." He shook his head. "Come here." He stood with my hand in his. His fingers were cold. I followed him to one of the long tables, the one bare of phials and flasks. A circle was etched into it, and dark stains smeared through the line, soaking the grain of the wood. Philip took a piece of chalk and drew a circle inside the circle.

He connected the two with more lines and then drew a strange letter in the center. "Give me your kerchief."

I drew the square of linen from my skirt's pocket. He gave it to me my first week here. It is embroidered with a tiny butterfly, blue and yellow, in the corner.

"Thank you." Philip took it and folded it over his strange chalk letter, with the butterfly facing up. He whispered something in another language, two words repeated again and again. Then he held out his hand for mine. I gave it.

With his other, he lifted the same tiny knife with which he'd cut my hair. I sucked in a sharp breath, but he said, "Do not fear me, Josephine. I am about to show you your power."

I clenched my jaw and ignored the burning in my stomach. I spread my fingers wide to stop them from shaking. Philip put the knife against my longest finger, and I whimpered. Stopping, he looked to me with a patient expression. I shook my head and whispered, "Please. Please, I want you to show me."

When he pricked my finger, I bit the tip of my tongue as the sharp pain dragged at my spirit. A drop of blood welled up like a tear. It slowly stretched until it dripped off of my skin and fell onto the kerchief, staining the butterfly red.

Into my ear, Philip whispered, "Lean over and say to it: 'I give you life.'"

I tilted my face to him. We were as close as we had ever been. His dark eyes drew in all the light. My breath shook and I needed to be here, needed this closeness more than anything in the world. And so I stared down at the blood soaking into the embroidery thread and said, "I give you life, little butterfly."

It leapt off the linen, alive and frisky. I fell back, only keeping my feet because Philip had his arm around me. My heart beat as fast as the butterfly's wings, and I flew, too, trapped in my Prospero's arms, as landscapes of possibility unfurled below me.

"All blood is life and energy, Josephine," he said as I stared at the fluttering creature. "But some, like mine and yours, holds the power of God and his angels."

The butterfly's wings flashed blue and gold and scarlet in the gaslight.

 # NINE

SILLA

After dinner, I retired up to my room to wait for Gram Judy to go to bed. Reese had gone for a run, and once he was back and Judy was asleep, I'd be able to tiptoe down the hall and drag him outside to prove the magic was real.

I waited, rereading the regeneration spell and reciting the instructions to myself while pacing in a circle under the watchful eyes of the theater masks hanging on my walls. My own secret audience.

Reese came home, slamming the front door. He clomped up to shower, and at 8:37 p.m. Judy called up the stairs, "Night, kids!"

"Night!" I yelled back, and heard Reese's muffled goodnight through the coursing water. He finished, and I listened to him move down to his bedroom.

At my window, I pushed my forehead against the cool glass, blinking out at the dark front yard. Yellow light from the porch revealed our bare maple tree. Most of its leaves had fallen into scarlet piles. I imagined breathing life into them all, making them dance up like butterflies to reattach to the branches. A fiery maple lasting until the springtime. It would be a bloody glow against the whites and grays of winter.

Waiting fifteen more minutes was like watching the moon rise.

Finally I pulled on my boots and sweater and gathered up salt, a half-dozen candles, and the spell book, and put them in a plastic sack. Safe in the back pocket of my jeans was the pocketknife.

Down the hall, I knocked quietly on Reese's door before pushing it open. The knock was worthless, though, given that he was stretched out on his bed with headphones totally covering his ears.

Before Mom and Dad died, I'd probably have found him hunched over a puzzle that sprawled in five thousand pieces across his desk. Something impossible, like the night sky or a beach with nothing on it. He'd have been playing games online with his friends in St. Louis, or reading a huge old science fiction paperback and grumbling at the bad physics.

Instead his face was drawn and still, eyes closed, and only his index finger moved, tapping out a frenetic drumbeat.

He'd torn all his posters down after the funeral, and every time I came in here I felt as empty as the walls. The only thing breaking up their vastness was the crater a foot from the door-jamb, where Reese had punched through. I'd tried to help bandage his knuckles, and Gram Judy had nearly fainted at the huge noise. He was lucky he hadn't broken his hand, that he hadn't hit a post.

Tonight, I had to make him believe in the magic. It would give him something new to sink his teeth into. A problem to solve. He'd chew on it and dissect it until we understood it from every angle, inside and out.

"Hey," I said, touching his forehead.

Reese's eyes snapped open. For a moment, we just looked at each other. My practiced confidence fell away under his dark scrutiny until I flicked my gaze down to the iPod resting on his chest.

He swung his legs off the bed and sat. "What's wrong, bumblebee?"

"Nothing. I just want a favor." I met his eyes again. His eyebrows rose, and I rushed on. "Come out to the cemetery and let me show you the magic."

"I thought you'd given that crap up, Silla." His frown reminded me of Dad.

I shook my head. "I've been studying it. I want to show you."

"It's bullshit. Didn't we go through this?"

"It isn't!"

"This Deacon guy is just messing with you. With us. Probably a joker from school, or that asshole Fenley at the sheriff's station. He always hated me."

"Then how'd he get Dad's handwriting so good?"

"He stole something, I don't know."

"It works, though, the magic."

Reese pressed his lips into a line.

I raised my chin a little, daring him to call me crazy.

"Silla."

"Let me show you."

"Bumblebee—"

"No, Reese. Please." I touched his hands, and he wrapped them around my freezing fingers. He didn't want to look at the rings. "Let me show you. If you think I'm losing it an hour from now, I'll do whatever you want. See Ms. Tripp at school every day, or even a real therapist in Cape Girardeau. Anything."

His jaw remained clenched. I saw the fear in his eyes and wondered what he was thinking. Was he terrified that I was insane? Or that I wasn't? Slowly, he nodded. "Okay. One hour." His voice was strained, and his hands tightened on mine.

Relieved, I immediately stood up. "Bring that." I pointed at the sparrow skeleton he'd painstakingly put together his freshman year of high school, during his zoology phase.

"What? Really?" His eyes scrunched up.

"Yes." Before he could protest again, I turned away and slipped out the door. On my way downstairs, I imagined a perfect mask. It needed to be fierce and dramatic: a black shimmer with red lips and a thick red slash across the eyes. It fit over my face like a second skin.

"This is ridiculous," Reese grumbled as we crouched together in front of Mom's and Dad's graves. I'd fought for them to be buried together the way Dad had requested in his will, though everyone else thought Dad didn't deserve it.

"Just wait." Settling on the cold ground with my legs crossed, I presented the spell book. "Here, open it to the regeneration spell at the end."

Reese took it and cracked it open. "It's messed up, Sil. Dad was messed up."

"Or scared."

"Like psychotics are scared people are out to get them."

I shook my head and began setting out candles while Reese skimmed through the book again. The flares of the matches were tiny explosions against the darkness. When we were protected by the circle of flames, I opened the ziplock bag of salt and sprinkled a line of it in a circle all the way around Mom's and Dad's graves. The grains sparkled like diamonds against the dark earth.

A thin breeze kicked up suddenly, and I shivered as it snaked down my neck and under my jacket. "Did you read the stuff about sympathetic magic?"

"Yeah, and the elemental properties of the spell components. And the symbolism. Ribbons for binding, wax for transformation, a river-bored stone for easing pain—I'm telling you, it's just folk magic. There's no reason for it to work. Dad was probably writing a paper or something."

"What about the blood? As a catalyst?"

"Ancient. Blood has always been seen as magical by less scientifically advanced people. Even in Christianity, for chrissake."

"That doesn't mean it isn't magical."

"It does, Silla. Blood is just proteins and oxygen and hormones and *water*. If blood really had unique properties, we'd know. Somebody would have discovered it."

"Like Dad. He discovered it."

Reese shook his head, his face as much a mask as mine in the flickering candlelight. "It's all symbolism. Unconscious stuff, psychology. Focusing the will to get what you want—or to think you're getting what you want."

"How can you tell that just from flipping through the book a couple of times? You're only seeing what you want to see in it."

"And you aren't?"

I clenched my hands together until my rings pinched, and raised my chin. "I just didn't know you knew so much about old folk magic."

He didn't answer, just clenched his jaw. Even in the poor light I could see the muscles working.

"Reese?"

He glared at me. "Dad had some books on it."

I was quiet.

Wind rushed through the dying leaves in the nearby forest. The one surrounding Nick's house. The breeze knocked leaves into the headstones around us, and the salt circle shivered but didn't break.

"Reese," I said, reaching to touch his hand. The knuckles stood out where he clenched the spell book. "It's amazing, Reese. Not horrible. It feels like a warm tingle in your blood. Welcoming and . . . powerful."

His frown deepened. "Sounds addictive."

"Maybe." I tugged his hand off the book and wove our fingers together. "Just come with me on this. For a few moments, let go of your anger at Dad. I know he deserves it, but this . . . let this be for us. For me. Please. Imagine the possibilities."

Reese's eyes lifted to mine and I held his gaze even as it bored into me. I tightened my grip on his hand, which was as cold as mine. "God, you look just like him. That look, right now," he whispered. I didn't glance away, but felt nostalgia and sadness taint my expression. "Okay, bumblebee."

Relieved that the moment was over, I leaned back and briskly said, "Just—just put the bird in the center of the salt circle."

The skeleton was so delicate, positioned with its wings spread. I'd been wary of the large eye sockets when he'd first constructed it, until Reese had said, "A skull is just like one of your masks. Only, this one lives under the face."

I set the small blue and gray feathers Reese had also grabbed around the skeleton. They'd belonged to the bird when Reese found it dead on the front steps. Maybe it would remember the feeling of wind ruffling them. *Sympathetic magic,* I hoped.

Moving to sit across the circle from Reese so that we faced each other over the skeleton, I flipped out the blade of my pocketknife and put it to my palm. Since this was no mere leaf, I probably needed more blood than a prick to the thumb could manage. I couldn't risk its not working for Reese. I bit the inside of my lip, readying myself for the queasy pain to come. This was the worst part. But I understood that you had to sacrifice for the magic to work. And I didn't want to hesitate in front of my brother.

I slashed.

Reese hissed through his teeth and stared at the blood pooling in my cupped palm.

It was so beautiful, dark and shimmering like the night sky itself oozing out of my hand. I pressed the blade against my skin to make the blood flow faster. Pain cracked up my wrist and curled around my forearm like hot barbed wire.

"Silla, hurry. We have to get that bandaged."

"It's okay, Reese." I took a deep breath, pushing at the pain. Tears stung my eyes. The late October night smelled like burning leaves. I leaned over the bird and let a stream of my blood patter down over the yellowing bones. It splashed like thin paint, dark in the candlelight. I imagined the skeleton growing muscles and tendons and flesh and feathers. Imagined it bursting into life and singing for us. Then I whispered, *"Ago vita iterum."*

Make it live again.

Bending so that my lips were inches from the bones, I breathed the imprecise Latin words over the skeleton again and again. *"Ago vita iterum. Ago vita iterum. Ago vita iterum."*

With each phrase, another bulbous drop of my blood fell off my hand.

I felt the moment the magic began, buzzing through my palm and up my arm like a swarm of tiny bees. Hissing, I pulled my hand away from the skeleton.

"Silla." Reese took my unwounded hand and squeezed. His voice was reedy and shaking.

The skeleton trembled. Its wings shuddered and extended outward, stretching like it would take off. Feathers suddenly sprouted out of the bones, rangy and thin, and a single eyeball bubbled up in the skull. I couldn't look away, even as strips of muscle wove onto the bones and the feathers spread, becoming fuller. Reese's fingers crushed mine. My heart expanded and I wanted to sing—to laugh and shriek in amazement.

"*Ago vita iterum!*" I cried at it. The candles sputtered and went out, and the tiny bird leapt into the air, flapping its wings frenetically. It wailed a song before vanishing up into the dark sky.

We were alone in the cemetery, covered in shadows.

"Whoa," Reese said, letting go of me. He leaned forward and skimmed his hand over the dirt where the bones had been. The scattered feathers were gone, too.

I shivered, suddenly dizzy, and clutched my hands together. The moon spilled down. My skin was cold in the absence of fire. But I laughed. Quietly, triumphantly.

"Oh my God." Reese relit one of the candles, then dug into the plastic bag for rags. "Here."

I only shook my head. Reese grabbed hold of my hand and pressed the cloth against it. "Jesus. You might need stitches," he said.

My palm tingled with warmth; pain teetered at the edge of magic.

But a dozen feet away, the bird fell from the sky. Its bones shattered, and feathers scattered out, dry as dead leaves.

 # TEN

May 3, 1904

Oh, the magic! This I do want to remember.

It is like nothing I can say. No words Capture what it feels like when my dark blood smears against a red ribbon, or leaks into the lines of a rune carved into wood. The Thrill of the Blood as the magic burned through me, the way it tickles and teases when I am doing other things, begging me to slice my skin open and let it out!

It hurts, of course, cutting my living flesh to free the blood. I have not conquered the sickening pause before every prick of my needle, every slick cut of Philip's knife. I hold my breath for the moment, and I feel the world holding its breath with me, awaiting the wash of pain that releases the power. Sacrifice, Philip says, is the key. We give in order to create.

Oh, but this is Heaven. Philip is my announcing angel—or I am Morgan and he is the wizard teaching me how to rule the world. By candlelight we mix potions, boiling them in an iron cauldron like witches of old. The smoke turns my cheeks pink and I smile at him often, hoping he might notice.

Philip heals, is obsessed with it, and believes that the gift of our blood is meant to help mankind. Or at least Boston. Most of his charms are for healing, for headaches and fevers, for easy births and gentle deaths. He wants bigger spells, better spells, to heal great swaths of folk at a time, and so he needs all the blood he steals. But in his book are spells for turning stone into gold and discovering lost items. He's used them to accumulate his power, but now that he is comfortable, he leaves such things alone. But I do not. I practice transforming air into fire with a snap of my bloody fingers, and I turn water into ice, or boil it with a word.

Who could imagine such magic in the twist of ribbon or a dried-up duck's beak? Who could imagine blessed water could cure a cough, if only there were a drop of my blood mingled with it? And the stones! Rough and small, oftentimes sharp. Philip showed me how to hold them in my hand and breathe magic into them with intricate patterns of almost-words. They focus my spells and hold my power. With one tucked into my pocket or down my corset, I feel the tingle all the day, feel it pulsing there with my heart.

I never want to lose this.

We can do anything.

 # ELEVEN

SILLA

I didn't make it to school on Thursday.

Reese and I had stayed in the cemetery until after midnight, digging into the spell book together. For Reese's first attempt at his own magic, he used the regeneration spell to heal the wound on my palm. It was pink and aching still, but closed. No bandages necessary.

After the healing, we regenerated a hundred dead leaves, experimenting with the words and amount of blood and how many leaves we could do at once. It was intoxicating—only a single drop was needed, and if we bled onto the salt circle, we could make them all snap back to life together in a great, blossoming pattern.

We'd both felt more alive than we'd been in months, excited and laughing with each other, tossing the leaves up into the air with a smear of blood on them so that they unfurled into emerald life as they slowly fluttered back to the ground.

I imagined Mom and Dad, brought back to life with a whispered word.

But then I remembered the bird falling out of the sky in a

heap of bone and feathers. The spell wasn't permanent. Reese thought the energy of our blood was only enough to give a kick start, not to create real life. I thought it was because the little bird's soul was long gone.

Like Mom's and Dad's. Their spirits had fled.

Unreachable.

When I'd finally crawled into bed, I'd fallen into such a deep sleep there'd been no dreaming, and I didn't hear my alarm. Judy came in to shut it off, and shook me awake. My tongue had been heavy and thick and my forehead sticky with sweat. It felt like my flesh was melting off my bones, and so Judy'd called the school and I had a day off to sleep and recover. Reese stayed home from work, too, though he felt less drained than me. We spent the afternoon between bowls of Judy's tomato soup whispering to each other about the ingredients we should get online and what spells to try over the weekend. Clearly we needed rest between spells, and the magic itself used more energy than we could readily spare. Neither of us had lost enough blood to account for the lethargy.

But I never wanted the day to end. Watching Reese talk about the magic was like seeing him reborn into the brother he'd been before the summer. For his whole life, Reese had learned as if his brain was a sponge: he'd choose a subject, like grafting or genetics, and for three weeks or so read every book he could get his hands on. It had been common to find him in his bedroom surrounded by a pile of twenty library books and Internet printouts. And then they'd be gone. For a week or so, he wouldn't mention the subject, like everything was being processed into all the parts of his brain. Finally, *blam,* the information reappeared, woven into the rest of his life as if it had always been there. It would be the same with the spell book.

Friday, Reese had to be back out in the fields and I was energized enough for school. I'd have rather stayed home and worked on more magic, but there was no getting out of school when both Reese and Gram Judy noticed I was doing better.

In third period Physics, I was lost in daydreams about feeling that tingle of power in my blood when Wendy passed me a note asking if I'd been sick.

Day bug, I wrote back.

Glad better. What hpnd w/Nick?

Oh, yeah. Nick had driven me home on Wednesday night. I scrawled my reply. *Drove home.*

Wendy: ?

Me: *Nothing.*

Wendy lifted both her eyebrows, and underlined her question mark twice. I just shrugged a little and looked back at the diagram Mr. Faulks was drawing on the blackboard. After a moment, Wendy got out her pink lip gloss and pretended to concentrate on reapplying, when what she was really doing was letting me ignore her.

Guilt pushed at my ribs. If I drove Wendy away, there'd be none of my old friends left. I wrote, *I like him,* and slid it to the side of my desk so that she could see.

Her eyes widened, and she smiled. She bobbed her head and the pink barrettes holding back her blond hair glittered in the fluorescent lights. Then she wrote, *Good! I'm glad. B/c u won't mind if I ask Eric out.*

WHAT?

Don't want to step on yr toes.

You HATE him.

He's so cute!

I boggled at her. I'd gone out with Eric for a few months two years ago because we'd been the only two freshmen cast in *Oklahoma!*, but since then he and Wendy had had this wicked rivalry going on. Now that he was president of the drama club in my place, she'd done nothing but jerk him around.

Wendy shrugged, then smiled a sinful little smile.

After class, she grasped my elbow and leaned in to whisper, "You have to come to the party tonight, to be my backup."

"Party?"

She rolled her eyes dramatically. "Sil! The Anti-Football Party! At Eric's place. Duh."

Oh, that. It was a big thing for all the nonsports clubs at the school, held every fall by the drama club president. Always the night the football team played our chief rivals, the Glouster Panthers. I winced. Reese and I had agreed to try more magic tonight . . . but Wendy was smiling at me in that way that meant she was being more lighthearted than she wanted to be. She was pretending it was less of a deal than it was. I softened my expression. "You think Eric will really go for it?"

"Only one way to find out," she said lightly. "And you need a party. You haven't been out since."

I chewed the side of my tongue.

"It's important, Silla. And I need you."

How could I say no to that? Reese could entertain himself. "Okay. I'll be there."

"Yay!" she squeed, her curls bouncing like Slinkys.

NICHOLAS

I stared at her in the cafeteria as she stood in line, putting a single cup of Jell-O on her tray. Her hair stuck in a half-dozen directions today, with only a thin blue headband holding any of it back from her face. She'd finally been in the cemetery again Wednesday night, but there'd been a guy with her—a guy with seriously broad shoulders who could probably have crushed my head between his hands if he felt like it. Her brother, I hoped. I'd started to watch them, but that was pretty stalker-boy even for my tastes.

Speaking of stalker-boy behavior, it hadn't taken more than two minutes on Google to find out the bare bones of Silla's issues. Over the summer, her dad had shot her mom, then killed himself. She'd been the one to find them inside the house. It had been a couple of hours before her brother arrived home and called the police.

No wonder she was hanging out in the graveyard. I mean, she had to be seriously messed in the head. I knew what it was like to see more of your mom's blood than was healthy, and you didn't get over it.

Silla hadn't been in school yesterday, and it's possible I spent the entire day grumpier than usual because of it. Sitting at rehearsal while Stokes read her lines was annoying enough that I'd promised myself if she wasn't there again, I was cutting play practice. Of course, I wondered if she was sick from the magic. Mom used to spend hours in bed sometimes. *Migraines, Nicky, that's all,* she'd said. But I knew better.

Fortunately for my theater career, Silla was there on Friday. She seemed tired, but I was starting to think she always did. And I didn't really care when I watched how her jeans hugged her thighs and pressed right into her hips. Her friend Wendy grabbed an extra serving of green-bean casserole and plunked it onto Silla's tray. Silla's lips curled back in disgust, but she didn't remove the casserole. And she let Wendy pick out a blue carton of 2 percent chocolate milk.

"You just can't take your eyes off," Eric laughed as he plopped down next to me. "She's bad news, bro."

"Because of her parents?"

"Because she's nuts."

"Really?" I chewed my own helping of bean casserole. It tasted a lot better than the same in Chicago.

"Really."

"Isn't everybody?"

"Oh, man, you have it bad."

I skewered a hunk of meat loaf and pointed at him with it on my fork. "Look, just because you didn't get there first . . ."

"Yeah, I did, actually." Eric's eyes drifted to Silla and Wendy as they sat with a handful of other girls near the windows. "Freshman year, when she was still hot."

"Still? She's gorgeous."

"Not compared to before."

"Before what?"

"Before the summer . . . her parents . . ." He shoved meat

loaf into his mouth but turned to shoot a look at me that plainly said, *Duh.*

I nodded like I knew. But I still hadn't asked anyone the details beyond what I'd read on the Internet. It almost came up several times, but I didn't—quite—make it. I wanted to ask her, not someone else.

"She was hot. And eager, man. A few of us were looking forward to her brother going away to college. But then, with her parents . . . she dropped like twenty pounds from all the wrong places, ya know, and hacked off all her hair. And stopped flirting. I can't really blame her. But she's just bony like a skeleton now."

"I guess I'm lucky not to have the comparison," I said, but knew I'd prefer her current incarnation.

SILLA

Ms. Tripp had a desk pushed back against the windows, but she never used it when I was in her office. She preferred to invite me to join her on the plush yellow sofa, as if we were just sitting down to tea.

"So, Drusilla, tell me one interesting thing you've done this week." Ms. Tripp folded her hands over her crossed knees and smiled.

"I met my new neighbor," I mumbled, perching on the couch. I dragged one of the bright purple throw pillows onto my lap and skimmed my fingers over the embroidery. Talking to Ms. Tripp was awful, no matter how nice she was. I fixed my calm mask back into place. The ocean-green one, with seashells glued to the edges and some bright coral emblazoned over the cheeks like a false smile.

"Ah, yes, the new boy. Nicholas, isn't it? I'm sure he appreciates you being welcoming. I was thrilled with the kindness everyone showed me when I arrived." Her tone was gentle, asking me without asking if I would look at her.

There was no reason to be surly, so I did. Ms. Tripp had one of those sweet faces they write romance novels about, with piles of curling hair always escaping the ponytail on the back of her head. She wore cardigans like they were going out of style. Her smile probably would have soothed less damaged girls. When I'd first shown up, she'd asked, "What would you like to talk about today?" but had quickly realized the depths of my desire not to talk to her at all. Now she always had something prepared. When I hesitantly returned her smile (the better to escape on time), she said, "What is the best gift your father ever gave you?"

The spell book, even though he hadn't exactly given it to me. But I wasn't about to tell Ms. Tripp about it. My eyes lowered to my hands, flat against the purple pillow. The rings glittered dully. I flicked my fingers, wanting to be peeling away the skin for fresh blood. For new magic. "He gave these rings to me." He'd given Reese a matching bracelet with a bright tiger's-eye jewel. Reese hadn't worn it since July. He wouldn't even look at it.

"They're lovely."

"One every birthday since I turned nine. My eighteenth should have been the last." My right ring finger stood out naked. What would it have looked like? They kept getting more complex and more expensive as I aged. Last spring had been a white gold band tightly clutching what Dad had called an emerald-cut emerald. I wore it on my left middle finger. "He said, when I was nine, that he'd build a rainbow around me like armor."

"To keep you safe?"

"Yeah."

"From what?"

She was staring at my hands. I wove my fingers together and pulled them closer to my stomach. I could feel the scar from Wednesday night tingling. "Whatever, I guess."

"From the regular monsters that stalk little children? Strangers? Death?" Her voice was light, but when she raised her eyes, they were thick with emotion. I wondered how such a sympathetic person could handle being a counselor. Then she continued: "Or from himself?"

It was like being hit in the diaphragm, and all my breath froze painfully.

"Maybe you wish he'd better protected your mom instead?"

"He didn't kill her," I said tightly. My rings cut into my skin as my hands convulsed.

"Drusilla, honey, I want you to imagine, just for a moment, that he could have. It doesn't make you disloyal or a bad daughter. Do you think he'd have wanted you to hide from the truth?"

"Why is everyone always trying to make me hate my dad?"

"That's not what we're doing, Drusilla."

"That's what it feels like."

She nodded, like I'd said something good. Blood warmed my cheeks. She'd gotten me talking about my feelings again. I pressed my lips together and grasped at the mask I'd invoked before coming in; the mask of calm, of order, of the bottomless, cold ocean. The flush drained away. Ms. Tripp sighed. "Drusilla"—she said my name as though wanting to remind me what it was—"I want to help you. There's nothing wrong with anything you're feeling, all right? I'm here to listen, to help you figure out what those feeling are, why you have them, to untangle any confusions and get you on track. But I'm not here to condemn you, or your needs, or your dad."

"Can I go?" It was early; we usually had a half hour.

"Of course. You aren't a prisoner." She stood and held out her hand. When I let her have mine and joined her on my feet, she squeezed it warmly. Everyone's hands were warmer than mine. "I'll see you next week, unless you want to come sooner. The door's always open."

"Sure." I slid my hand away and grabbed my backpack. The pink line of tender skin on my palm tingled, reminding me of what I'd done. Of what I could do again.

TWELVE

April 17, 1905

It is not all beautiful.

I hardly know how to put this down, but Philip said, "You need to remember." And I do not want to, this more than anything that has happened.

But a small part of me understands what I did not understand before. About memory.

The beginning first. That is how these things are done.

In December, Philip brought home a basket of kittens. He gave them to me, showed me how to soak cloth in milk for them to suck at, and as they grew, I cared for them. The darling, little, mewling things. So soft, with their sharp little teeth and playful paws. I carried their basket into my bed and slept with them curled all around me. For three weeks they were my friends.

And this morning, Philip called me to his laboratory and said I should bring one of my kittens.

I should have known. Somehow, I should have known.

When I arrived, already he had laid out a working circle. A thin black braid of human hair coiled at its edge, along with his blood knife, ribbons, a bundle of sticks, and honeycomb. He explained that his services had been sought for a great protection charm, that a woman was being beaten by her husband, and her grandmother had come begging. I held my cat, which I'd named Serenity, and petted her tawny fur while Philip constructed a doll with the wax and sticks. He pushed in eyes and cut a gash for a leering grin. He tied a ribbon around the doll's neck and pressed the hair into its head.

"How did this grandmother know to come here?" I asked.

Philip was frowning, rather fiercely, I recall. He did not like this kind of work. "The Deacon knew her, and he performed these sorts of charms for the whole of the lower side and much of the towns and villages beyond. She thought perhaps I followed his magic. And she was correct, of course."

I still do not know what happened to this Deacon, the one who taught Philip these bloody ways. Some days I want to meet him, other days I fear it. "Why don't you make charms like this more often?"

"It is filthy work, little sprite, and people will ask things I am not willing to give. Charms for healing and life, but also curses and death—like this one. And the more who know what we do, the less able I will be to experiment." He set the doll into the circle and contemplated it quietly.

"But you're helping some poor woman."

"At a cost, darling."

"To her husband? He deserves it, if he's beating her." I said it rather harshly, I am certain, and Philip snapped his head up to frown at me.

"To all of us." He held out his hands for Serenity.

And then I knew. "What? No!" I held her against my chest, and she squeaked and pressed at me with her paws.

"They were brought here for this very reason, Josephine. Give it to me."

"But a cat! You said our blood is special, that it holds the power. If other human blood cannot quicken the charms, why a cat's?"

Philip came around the table to me, slowly and steadily. I could not move. "Some animals," he said quietly, "share our powerful blood. The ones you would expect. Cats. Crows. Some dogs. Rats. They make strong familiars, though they must give their lifeblood to the magic, not a mere drop."

I was still shaking my head. "Just prick your finger, Philip."

"I won't put my blood into a charm like this, nor yours. Not when it could be used against us."

"Against us?"

"Others know the cunning ways. And even if their blood is not special, with ours they could curse us, turn the doll against us, or any number of other things."

Serenity shoved her head into my chin. I felt tears in my eyes. I feel them again now.

He cornered me and said, "This is not a game. You take it all too lightly. You must understand the sacrifices. The balance that must be kept."

And I understood that he'd given me the kittens to care for with this very thing in mind. My fingers clutched at Serenity, but Philip took her, and killed her on his laboratory table. I remember how her blood shone on the doll's face.

It was the first night since coming to live with him that I did not read with him or even speak to him before retiring to my room in order to write this.

Now I hear them, the rest of the kittens, crying for me to feed them. I want to press their heads under the bathtub water.

 # THIRTEEN

NICHOLAS

For better or worse, tonight I was going to make my mark on the Yaleylah High School drama club and all its various hangers-on.

Too bad I had to get a ride to the party with my evil stepmother.

The left rear tire on the Sebring was flat. Punctured by some random piece of gravel or road crap that liked cosmic jokes. It left me either stuck in the house with Dad and Lilith or hitching a ride. I was desperate enough that if I'd had Silla's phone number, I might have called her. But I was the genius who hadn't gotten it, or even Eric's. Nobody else could come get me. I'd asked Dad for the ride, but Lilith had leapt to it like a rabid wolf on roadkill.

Enter one tin flask filled with whiskey and Coke.

Slinking down the stairs, I hoped that I could get to the kitchen where her keys were hanging and borrow her Jeep or Dad's. But there she was, waiting by the front door in an I-want-to-suck-your-blood red coat, swinging her key ring around her finger. "You're wearing that?" she said.

I sneered involuntarily. "Sorry my fashion sense doesn't run toward cougar-approved."

Lilith lifted her eyebrows at my nasty tone. "You'll certainly stand out."

"Great. Let's get this over with." I pushed past her and out the door. As Lilith called bye to Dad and followed me, I pulled the directions out of my jacket pocket. I'd triple-checked them against the possibility of being lost on backcountry roads with her. Talk about the setup for some slasher movie. And I didn't know which of us would end up dead on the side of the road.

Instead of turning around in the massive driveway, Lilith backed all the way down our gravel lane, her body twisted to stare out through the rear window and her fingers clenching the back of my seat for leverage. Her sharp fingernails were way too close to my shoulder for comfort.

Skinny black tree branches reached out and slid along the passenger side of the car as she swerved slightly off the road. Clearly Lilith wasn't a girl worried about her paint job. I considered complaining. But since I'd seen her turn around plenty of times before, I knew she was doing this just to piss me off after my cougar comment, and I refused to give her the satisfaction of seeing me tense. So I leaned forward and flicked on the radio. Scratchy National Public Radio growled to life, reporting on some massive explosion in the Philippines. It was impressive we picked the station up way out here. And also that Lilith listened to it.

As she managed to get us onto the road leading past Silla's house and finally pointed forward, I hit SCAN to try and deter conversation.

But scanning picked up three static channels for every single decent one, and by decent I mean so filled with twang and heartache it made your eardrums bleed.

"So, Nick."

"Turn left up here." I angled the directions toward the window so that I could read them by the surprisingly bright moonlight.

She did, leaving the single-lane road for what counted as a county highway out here. At least it was two lanes. "Tell me, Nick, about this new morbid fascination with the cemetery? It's rare for you to have an *interesting* interest."

"In about three quarters of a mile we turn left again, and then it's not far. Jesus. I could have walked."

"In the dark, darling? You don't know what's out there waiting to snatch you up."

"Whatever it is, I'm sure it'd be more pleasant than this."

From the corner of my eye, I noticed Lilith grin. "That wasn't nearly as sharp a retort as I was expecting. You must be losing your touch."

"It was a lousy setup. I can only do so much when you throw me a foul ball."

She shrugged and tapped her fingernails on the steering wheel.

I turned off the damn radio, which had totally failed to find anything remotely appealing. If this foray into my own personal horror movie didn't get any better real soon, I'd be praying for an ax.

SILLA

The truck bounced along the uneven road toward the Leilenthal farm. I flipped down the visor and stared at my eyes in the mirror.

"You doing okay?" Reese glanced at me.

"I don't really want to go to a party. I want to practice more."

"It will do you good to relax."

"I know. It just doesn't come close to comparing to the . . . the excitement of the magic. I want to be out there making leaves fly! Or trying the possession spell. Can you imagine what it would be like to inhabit the mind of an animal? Like a crow, the way he says in the book? Soaring over the fields and dipping and darting through the clouds . . ." I closed my eyes, picturing the cemetery from above, the gravestones and rolling autumn fields spreading into forever.

"Yeah," Reese said. "But not tonight. Tomorrow afternoon. Tonight we're going to pretend we're normal."

"Ugh. Normal." I'd lost normal a long time ago. Holding my palm open in my lap, I traced the healing pink line. Against the oh-so-normal background of my jeans and Reese's car, the gash seemed like such an odd thing. Wrong and unsuitable. Why should I look forward so strongly to taking a knife and watching the blade slice open my skin? What was wrong with me? Queasiness suffused my stomach and throat. I closed my hand.

"I thought you liked this party. You used to."

"It's mostly people I don't spend time with anymore."

"Isn't Doug's little brother in your play?"

"Yes. Eric."

"Hang with him."

"I wish you were staying."

"Really? You want to hang with your brother at a party?" He grimaced, but his eyes, when he glanced at me again, were filled with sympathy.

"I'd rather be at home."

He turned down the lane toward the barn. It had only been a three-minute drive. Wendy had promised to run her little sister over to spend the night with a friend, and I could have walked—should have—but Reese was on his way to the football game since his evening was suddenly free.

Ahead, bonfire glow lit the trees into black reaching silhouettes. Pulling his truck up alongside a row of parked cars, Reese turned off the engine and faced me. "Call me if you need anything. I can be here in fifteen minutes. And afterward, we're going to head down to Barley's. Also, call me if you get a ride home. Otherwise, I'll be here around midnight, okay?"

"Yeah." I started to slide out but paused, balancing on the edge of the seat. "Reese?"

"Yeah?"

I opened my mouth. *Don't drink.* "I'm glad you have friends you still want to spend time with."

He reached out and touched my elbow, started to say something, then both his eyes and his hand dropped. He shrugged. "Ya know, if I was in college, I wouldn't be seeing these guys at all, so that's one benefit, huh?" Reese forced a smile. It wasn't a bad lie, as they go.

"Good point. See you later, Reese."

"Night, bumblebee."

Rust flaked off the old door when I banged it shut. I stood there, leaning against Sherry Oliss's blue Chevy as Reese backed away, turned, and drove off.

Behind me, peppy country music blared out of the Leilenthal brothers' huge speakers, which they'd set up on either side of the barn doors. I'd have preferred Johnny Cash. Something deadly, upbeat, and appropriate for a girl who was obsessed with cutting herself. I closed my eyes and hugged myself, wishing the desire to socialize would rush up from the ground and consume me.

It didn't.

I turned around anyway, and picked my way through the weedy grass toward the party.

It was about nine, and maybe thirty people mingled around the fire. More were inside the barn. At the edge of the light, I peered through the orange shadows for a familiar face. Or rather, a welcome face. Everyone was familiar. A handful of drama club members chatted near the barn, including Nick, who was dressed in a pinstripe three-piece suit like he'd walked out of a production of *Guys and Dolls*. He was surrounded by not only Eric and a couple of the other guys but a bunch of girls. Kelsey Abrigale kept touching his lapel in this ingratiating way, and Molly Morris laughed way too loudly when Nick said something.

For a moment, I considered crossing straight over to him to find out if he'd driven me home because he liked me or because he just liked to flirt and fit in. Maybe last year I'd have been right there, in his face and teasing him about his sexy hat. But now . . . since others were preening and displaying their interest, why would he think about a weird girl who liked to hang out in the cemetery?

I didn't need it, either. I had the magic. Real magic. So instead I perched on a toppled tree trunk, watching the fire, the dark outlines of students, and the twinkling stars above. The full moon hung to my left, and I started to think about one of the healing potions that was supposed to sit out overnight, and that Dad's notes indicated would work better when the moon was large. Reese thought that was B.S. until I reminded him that we'd turned a skeleton into a living bird with salt and blood, so who was to say what the moonlight could do?

The afternoon had been so mild, perfect for October, but now it was chilly and I missed having a jacket. Here I was, sitting alone feeling sorry for myself instead of going to talk to my friends and getting to know a cute guy. Pathetic. "Get up and go to the fire," I ordered myself, and rubbed my hands together. In the chill, my rings rolled loosely on my fingers. Last semester, I'd had no trouble at all inviting people to chat, or dance. Talking to my classmates and rambling about teachers, boys, plays, and music were things I enjoyed. Now . . . it felt fake. Like it could fall apart at any moment. Only the blood was real.

I licked my lips. They were dry and cold.

A crack of laughter caught my attention. Erin Pills. She'd been in *Into the Woods* with me last year, and was a year younger. Surely I could think of something to say to her and the cluster of girls with her. I moved around the edge of the circle. Even from ten feet away I could feel the warmth of the bonfire caress my arm.

Oh, and thank God, there was Wendy. "Hey," I said.

"Silla." Wendy grinned, and her pink lip gloss sparkled. I could never wear that glittery stuff—it felt like grit trapped against my skin.

When I nodded, she grabbed my hands and pulled me away from the crowd. Glancing all around, she asked, "What do you think my plan of attack should be? Throw him off guard? Like, just kiss him? Or be all nice?"

"Wouldn't you being all nice throw him off as much as suddenly shoving your tongue in his mouth?"

"Hmm. Good point."

I looked back at Eric where he stood near Nick. "I'd kiss him." I was watching Nick's lips, though, as he flirted with Molly.

"Yeah. You're right. I will." She grinned. "He is so hot with that sword—I can't wait to see him in a kilt."

"I think Stokes said we aren't doing traditional garb."

Her face fell. "Damn. Well, anyway. I like him." Wendy paused and gave me a sidelong glance. She used to rely on me to make all her decisions. "You don't think I should?"

"I don't know him anymore," I said, but I took her hand and tried to give her what she needed. "But I think if you like him, you should go for it. He was always fun. You remember."

"He's over there with Nick. We could"—Wendy rubbed her lips together—"double-date."

I followed her gaze back toward the barn. The group was laughing at something Nick had said, and Nick was staring straight at me. *Oh, God.* My protective mask melted away and he could see my gray eyes, my cold skin. I snapped my eyes back to Wendy. "I'm not sure I'm ready. You know."

"To date?" Wendy caught herself before rolling her eyes. "But, Sil, you have to."

"You sound like my gram."

"I just mean, it will only get better when you let it get better."

I bit the inside of my bottom lip. I didn't want my parents' deaths to get *better.*

"Come over with me," she said, and began dragging me. I had no choice but to go with her or pull violently away.

Nick smiled when he saw us, and I felt a tingle all the way down to my toes. "Hey, Silla," he said when we were close enough. He stood with his elbow propped on Eric's shoulder. A plastic cup sloshed as he lifted it in greeting. "Hi, Nick." I glanced at Eric and Molly and Kelsey and smiled.

"Hey." Eric jerked his chin in greeting.

"Hi, Silla." Molly nudged Kelsey with her elbow and they giggled.

"Want a drink?" Wendy said, looking only at Eric.

Shrugging out from under Nick's elbow, Eric held out a hand to Wendy. "Sure."

She looked back at me with a fast, bright smile. They went off, leaving me with Nick and the girls. I pursed my lips a little. "Your first Anti-Football Party, Nick. How's it going?"

"Better now." Nick stepped closer to me, effectively cutting Molly and Kels out of the conversation. "Want to dance?" He held out his hand.

A simple smile lifted my lips, and I met Nick's gaze. I imagined pink sequins glittering in a swirl down my cheek. "Sure." The music had switched to a sweet, twanging love song. I slid my hand into his, and he pulled me away from the group, closer to the bonfire.

Molly and Kels scowled my way. Delighted, I said almost merrily, "Eric sure can't get away from me fast enough."

"It isn't you," Nick said, resting his hand lightly against the small of my back. His touch was hot through my layers of T-shirt. "He thinks he's doing me a favor."

"Is he?" My smile widened.

Nick paused; then he raised a finger to tip the brim of his fedora lower in a bow. "You bet." He wrapped his fingers around mine. "Christ, you're freezing. Here," he said as he reached into his inner jacket pocket and pulled out a flask. "This will warm you."

"No, thanks."

"It's just Jameson. Whiskey."

I winced.

"Good for the soul?"

His hopeful expression made me laugh.

"Okay, okay!" Nick tucked the flask away. "Just dancing, then, to warm you up." He pulled my hand, drawing me through the crowd to the bonfire. No one else was dancing. Nick spun so that his back was to the fire, and grinned. I could barely make out his features with all the orange light behind him. He leaned in, took my other hand, and brought me closer. Under the brim of his hat, his eyes were shrouded in darkness. My heart beat faster, and I had to blink away the halo surrounding him. He was Mephistopheles, smiling and tempting me, his Dr. Faustus, to dance.

I closed my eyes and stepped in. My hands found his shoulders, and my finger bones sucked up heat from the fire. Nick was warm, too. I followed his movements, letting my feet go freely where he took me, and his hands pressed just over the belt of my low-riding jeans, guiding me, pulling me, pushing me, willing me to twirl and step and glide. His fingers dug into my hips, not painful but making me want to grip his shoulders and climb up into his arms. To forget myself in the dancing, in the flickering orange fire and black night.

The song shifted and he murmured in my ear, "It's practically a swing beat. Can you swing?" He let go of me except for one hand on mine, and spun me under his arm. I snapped out and back in, hitting his body, but he moved with it, catching me against his chest so we sank into a shallow dip. I gasped. He swung me up and around and I couldn't pay attention, could only close my eyes and feel the pressure of his hands pushing and pulling, his hip tapping mine, telling my body where to go, what to do. I felt my blood racing through me, powerful and strong, singing the way it did right before magic happened. But we were only dancing.

As he twisted my arms overhead and spun me again, I let my head fall back. The stars swirled and there was the moon, so full and close to us. I laughed, releasing some of the weight that had rested heavy on my shoulders for so long.

Nick tugged me sharply. My body snapped against his. His hands flattened on my back and he dipped me again, deeper this time, and held me there. I clung to his shoulders.

"I've got you," he said. "No worries, Silla."

I remembered how he'd risen from behind the grave marker last Saturday night, so at ease and belonging there with me, and I wondered if anybody's blood would work. Could he do magic? Nicholas, my boy from the cemetery? Could I invoke that part of him that had met me the first night I bled for magic? The laughter drained out of me. I glanced away.

Slowly, he drew me upright. "Silla, what did I say?"

His chest was so warm under my palms, for a moment, I almost leaned in and rested my cheek against it, buried my face in his neck. I wanted what his hands promised. Stepping away instead, I put on a bright smile. "Nothing."

"Silla." His frown pulled at the shadows hiding his eyes.

"Haven't you heard? I'm crazy." I turned away and added, "It's in the genes."

NICHOLAS

She left a great black hole of cold air behind. As she moved away, she wrapped her arms around herself again. The sparkle of her rings winked back at me. "Shit," I hissed, and jogged after her.

"Silla." I swung around in front of her. "Wait."

She stopped, eyes down. The light punching out of the barn hit her face. There was glitter in her eye shadow, and her lips were painted a soft maroon to match her clingy shirts. Finally she looked up. Even standing this close, I'd barely have to bend to kiss her. But she looked so tired; it was scratched into the edges of her eyelids, pressing down the corners of her mouth. For a moment, I could see through her ivory skin to the webbing of capillaries and muscles and tendons beneath.

It hurt, I wanted to kiss her so badly.

"What?" Her fingers tightened on her elbows.

"Let me get you a drink."

She nodded once. "There's a water jug in the barn. Eric's mother insists on it, because it would be tough to spike."

"Brilliant." I considered offering my hand but didn't. Instead I gestured for her to go first.

A long fluorescent light glared over the wooden floor and hay bales for benches. Three mostly depleted trays of food waited on a card table, and beside it was a bench spread with two-liter soda bottles and piles of plastic cups. I grabbed two cups and followed Silla to the corner with the water cooler.

Armed with water, we found a hay bale. I straddled it and Silla sat with her knees together. The cowboy boots peeking out from under her jeans were red. And adorable. I took back every nasty thought I'd ever had about cowboy boots.

Only three other people congregated in the barn, over near the snacks. I tasted my water and watched Silla's delicate profile. "I haven't heard," I said. It was a lie, of course. I'd heard plenty from Eric.

Startled out of some reverie, she said, "Heard what?"

"That you're crazy."

"Oh." She dropped her eyes again. Swirled the water in her cup. "Well, you've only been here a week or something."

"You should tell me."

She laughed.

"No, really. If you tell me, your version will be the first I hear." I grinned and pushed my hat slightly higher on my forehead.

"You're really something, Nick." Silla turned and hooked her leg up on the hay bale.

"I'm not used to all this small-town, everybody-knows-everything-about-everybody business. Where I come from, gossip is just gossip, and everybody's crazy."

"Sounds like a castle on a cloud." Her smile faded as she studied my face. I crossed my eyes.

"Okay, Nick." She smiled at my expression, then gulped the rest of her water. "Here's what happened. I came home from spending the afternoon with Wendy and Beth and Melissa. We'd been shopping, and I had a really nice new pair of jeans. I got home and Mom's and Dad's cars were both there, which wasn't that weird. It was summer, so Dad didn't have regular classes. But the front door was open, even though it was like a hundred degrees outside. I went in, dropped my bag, and smelled this awful, reeking smell." She licked her lips and raised her chin.

Staring into my eyes, she continued, "It was blood. I found them in the study, Dad's office. They were collapsed on top of each other. Huge holes were blown in Mom's chest and Dad's head. It was like someone had spilled gallons of bright red paint everywhere. The floor was sticky with it. I stopped in the doorway and just couldn't move. It smelled, and . . . their arms were around each other. There was blood on the desk and bookshelves. I wish I'd thought to look for a pattern, but who'd—" She shook her head, blinking and pressing her fists into her lap. She looked away. Took a deep breath. For a moment, I thought she was finished. Then she said softly, "Reese found me, like an hour later. I was just kneeling on the floor, staring. Blood had soaked into my jeans. He dragged me outside and left me in the sun while he called the police. I hadn't even called the police. I found my parents dead in their own blood and I didn't do anything."

I didn't say the obvious things. *What could you have done? Who could blame you?* "So that's why people think you're nuts?"

"No." She smiled: a weird, twisted smile. "They think I'm crazy because the official report, or whatever, claims my dad went crazy, killed Mom, and then killed himself. And I flipped out when they told me. It got around."

"That . . . seems like a pretty normal reaction to me. I'd be pretty pissed in your shoes."

"It was the most violent crime in the history of our town, and until it happened, everybody loved my dad. He was quiet and kind and a really good teacher. But lurking inside, apparently, was a psychopathic killer." Silla's jaw clenched.

"And it scared people. Especially because he worked at the school, right?"

She darted a glance of surprise at me. "Yeah, exactly. They were a bunch of cowards and didn't really believe in Dad. I mean, they should have tried to catch somebody else harder, if they really had faith in him." Color soaked into her cheeks, blotchy and mad. With one thumb, she was rubbing the palm of her other hand in jagged little strokes.

I took her hand and started to rub the palm with both my thumbs. Her skin was warmer than I'd ever felt it. Almost hot. I looked down. In the center of her palm was a thin pink line.

Like an old wound. The edges pulled at her skin, distorting her life line a little. It could have been an accident, could have happened when she tripped and caught herself on some rock, or when she grabbed a broken plate. Anything.

But I knew it wasn't. As sure as I knew this cowboy town wasn't where I wanted to spend the rest of my life, I knew Silla had made this cut herself.

Silla hissed sharply, and tugged at her hand.

"Silla." I watched her face. *Tell me about the magic.*

She didn't meet my eyes. "I have to get out of here."

"Let's go." I stood up, pulling her by the hand.

"Nick, you don't have to—I mean, you should stay."

"Nah. Not my thing. Honestly, and speaking of flipping out, I'm about to take an ax to those speakers."

"Can you drive me home?"

I grimaced. "Actually, no. I don't have my car here. It got a massive flat this morning."

Silla hesitated, her lower lip sucked in just slightly, then she said, "Walk me, then?"

"You bet."

We left the barn, hand in hand. I managed to catch Eric's eye and waved. "Which way?" Several people glanced at us, noted our hands and that we were leaving together. Good.

Silla pulled us to the right. "It's only about two miles that way." She pointed.

"Not a problem, unless you get cold."

"I'll survive."

"Whiskey will keep you from hypothermia."

She stopped, threw me a sideways glance. "And you?"

A smile spread across my mouth. "God, I hope so."

We walked silently for a few minutes. There was no path, and we tromped through knee-high grass and weeds. My pants were going to need dry cleaning, and I wished I'd worn something more practical, like jeans. Oh, well. Silla, on the other hand, dove straight into the grass with total disregard for her clothes. I tried to imagine my ex tromping over anything but concrete or manicured lawns. Made myself chuckle.

"What?" Silla asked.

"I was just thinking about girls from Chicago dragging me off through fields like this."

"Do you miss it?"

"Prissy girls? No way. I like this better." I squeezed her hand.

"I mean Chicago."

"Oh." I dragged the sound out, like I was only just realizing what she'd meant. She rolled her eyes and smiled. "In that case, yes. Almost constantly. There was always something to do. Movies, clubs, libraries. I could hop on the El and get anywhere in the city." I shrugged. "Didn't need a car."

"Sounds crowded."

"Yeah. It was great."

"Why'd you move here?"

"Ha—well, that's because my dad is a lawyer and he thought it was in my stepmom's best interest to get out of Chicago. Some stalker or something, they tell me. Real hush-hush. I wouldn't be surprised if it was more illegal than that. Or she made it up in an impressive play for Dad's sympathy. They've only been married for a few months, so maybe she used it to get her hooks in more securely. And to drag us out here."

"Wow."

"It was extremely convenient that Grandpa Harleigh croaked when he did."

"Did you know him?"

"Nope. Just met him the once. I don't know why he left me the house. No other family, I guess."

"Will you go back to Chicago after graduation?"

"Sure, eventually. Periodically."

"But not to live?"

"No."

"What are you going to do? College?"

We hopped together over a tiny irrigation stream. "Find my mom."

"You don't know where she is?"

"Last I heard, somewhere in New Mexico pretending to be Native American."

"What?"

"We're, like, a sixty-fourth Cherokee or something totally minuscule like that, and she said she felt called to the 'old ways.' There wasn't a forwarding address so that I could tell her the Cherokee were never a desert people."

"How old were you when she left?"

"The first time? Eight. I don't really remember, except being at the hospital. She'd bled all over the bathroom after a really stereotypical suicide attempt. And drugs, Dad says. She got clean, cracked up again when I was nine, tried to kill herself again, got clean, in this constant cycle. Then she screwed her dealer and Dad used that as an excuse to divorce her. He got full custody, and basically a restraining order. I haven't seen her since I was thirteen. Just random postcards. She claims she went through rehab and is on the right track. I'll find out after school, maybe. Dad can't keep me from her when I'm eighteen." I fell silent. It had been a long time since I'd laid it all out like that. I guess it was the night for stories.

Silla didn't respond for a while. I watched my shiny black shoes kick through dead grass and thought of Mom sitting down in a hostel or bus station, scrawling a few words to me and putting on the stamp, then forgetting I existed for another few months. Or taking a razor to her wrists again. It was too much to ask that Mom had really given that up. It was an addiction. She hated her own blood for some reason she never shared. And when she couldn't drain herself dry, she'd turned to drugs to dilute the magic's power.

"That sucks, Nicholas," Silla finally said, sounding very formal. Like she was closing off some ritual. Acknowledging what I'd gone through in a way nobody ever had before.

"I like it when you call me that," I admitted. "It's real."

"Nicholas," she said again, but more slowly.

I shivered and had to roll my shoulders back to regain some firm ground. "So what about you, Silla? What are you going to do after high school?"

She winced and I wanted to know what had crossed her mind. But she said, "I don't know. Go to college, I guess. I was going to apply to Southwestern State, in Springfield. They have a great theater program."

"You want to act, then."

"I've always loved it. Performance. The audience, the language, the action, and just the energy that's all around it. But you know, I have to feel it again."

"I guess you aren't feeling much these days."

"Easier that way."

It was too perfect an opportunity to pass up. I stopped. When she realized, she did, too, and turned to me with eyebrows raised. I took one step, let go of her hand, and put both of mine under her jaw. I kissed her.

Just a gentle press of lips, to gauge her reaction. I could smell her makeup, powdery and light. Her lipstick tasted vaguely of sweet, sharp fruit.

Silla curled her fingers into the hem of my vest, and she leaned in. I was abruptly aware of the rush of blood in my ears, drowning out the night bugs and the rattle of wind through dry leaves. Silla shuddered and broke her lips from mine, then pushed her forehead against my neck. Her nose was freezing. I wrapped both arms around her and hugged her, tucking my chin over her head. She hunched into me, like she was taking shelter. I kissed her hair, and she lifted her face. "Nicholas."

"Yeah?" I whispered.

Her hands crawled up my chest, and she raised them to bury in my hair. The fedora was knocked off and fell to the ground. She kissed me, hard. Like she was going to break my teeth. I gasped, grabbed her shoulders. Then I bit her lip and kissed back. We kissed like it was a competition, desperately clutching at each other.

Suddenly, Silla flung herself away. She turned her back. Her panting mirrored mine.

I was a little dizzy. And severely turned on. "Silla? Are you okay?"

She nodded and spun to me. Her eyes were bright as the moon. She held up her left hand, the one with the tiny pink scar. The tip of her middle finger was slick and dark. "I'm bleeding."

"Oh, shit. I'm sorry." I cringed, reached for her hand.

"No, no, that's okay. It's just, you know—blood." She shook her head like she was rattling nasty thoughts free, then smiled rigidly. I saw the drop of blood on her lip.

I got it. The harsh smell, especially from inside her own mouth, had to hit her hard after finding her parents like that. How did she manage the magic? I swallowed a shaky breath. "We can keep walking."

"Yeah."

Neither of us moved. And then we were kissing again, pushing against each other. I tasted the tang of her blood and it made me dizzy, but elated—I was flying high, and my heart pumped hot, boiling blood through my veins.

Silla stumbled and fell, tearing out of my arms. I grabbed at her, but she landed with a girlish grunt in a tuft of thick grass. "Silla, sorry, I . . ."

She pressed her hands down, and the grass began to transform.

It shivered, green and gold turning bright, eye-popping yellow. Magenta flowers blossomed up the stalks, and violet, electric-blue, neon-orange buds exploded. Silla was surrounded by a Technicolor land of Oz.

From the center of it all, her mouth parted and she brushed her fingers over the tips of grass and petals.

My brain whirred like a toy helicopter, spinning and spinning until all I heard was the roar of rotator blades. I'd never seen anything like it.

Silla pressed both hands to her mouth. She scrambled up and backed away. "I didn't even say anything!" she said, as though explaining would change them back. She bumped into my chest. The wind began plucking petals up and tossing them around. For one ridiculous moment, I thought of Skittles commercials. *Taste the rainbow.*

She turned around to face me. "Oh God, Nick. You, um . . ." She continued babbling. This was the perfect opportunity for me to tell her everything. I should have. I should have taken her shoulders and calmly explained that she didn't have to worry or freak out. I knew. About everything.

"Nick," Silla whispered. Her cold fingers groped at mine.

"It's okay," I said slowly, for some reason unable to confess. Maybe because all I could really think about was whether she'd kiss me again. "I didn't imagine that, did I."

"No. It's . . . magic. I—I know you can't believe me, that it's too impossible," she said, and drew her hands away.

"No, no, I saw that thing with the leaf on Saturday night. I saw what you did then. I wasn't sure, but I thought I saw it. This is like . . . proof." All true. I hadn't been sure. Hadn't wanted to be.

Air hissed out through her teeth. "I wouldn't believe it if I wasn't the one *doing* it."

I didn't answer. Just licked my lips. They still tingled from her kisses. All of me tingled with the need to grab her up again and kiss her, to drive her into more magic. The helicopter roared in my head.

"It's magic, Nicholas. Blood magic. You shouldn't believe in it."

Taking her hands, I drew her closer and kissed her. "But I do," I said. *You, in the middle of all those flowers, are the most beautiful thing I've ever seen.*

SILLA

As we trudged across Mr. Meroon's cow pasture, eyes out for patties, I continued to throw glances at Nick. I wanted to grab his hair again, dig my fingers in until the hat tumbled off, and kiss him. The expression on his face was difficult to read in the moonlight, but he was obviously thinking hard about something. Me, probably. And blood magic. I hoped he wasn't planning his escape.

The cool wind raised goose pimples on my arms, and I picked up my pace. I should have been more upset that I'd done magic accidentally, but I just couldn't be. It was a beautiful night; I was with a really great guy who made me smile and didn't think I was psycho. The magic had just been a spontaneous explosion of my general mood and excitement, catalyzed by the blood from my lip. From our kisses. It had been *our* mood.

"Is that the cemetery?" Nick asked. I popped back into the moment. My fingers tingled.

Milky tombstones were just becoming visible beyond the

low stone wall. "Yeah. Your house is that way." I pointed off to our right. "That bunch of darkness is the woods around it."

"Okay." He nodded thoughtfully. "Why were you there the other night? With the leaf? Does it have to be a cemetery?"

"No, I guess not. But I like it there, near my father."

We climbed over the cemetery wall. "Does this place get used by many?"

"No. My parents were the first in years. Your grandpa is over in the nicer, more modern one on the north side of Yaleylah. I don't know why anyone would want to be buried there, though. It's so sterile. Fake." My voice lowered. "Death isn't either of those things."

"People might want it to be. Take those military cemeteries. All rows of little white headstones, exactly the same. Ordered, simple. Not like war."

I wanted to be holding his hand again. He got slightly ahead of me, picking his way around a long, low tomb, and I watched him walk. He was so gangly and tall. Like half-grown animals, when their paws are still too big, and their legs way too long, and you know they're going to grow into it all eventually and be the handsomest thing you ever saw. With messed-up hat-hair.

Wiping the smile off my lips as I realized I was crushing on Nick in the graveyard where my parents were buried, I hurried to catch up. He glanced over. "You okay?" His eyebrows rose, opening his face.

"Yeah." I tucked in my chin and paced on, almost jogging around the bend in the overgrown path. "If we cut back this way, we can just follow the wall around to my house."

His eyebrows arched up higher.

I paused and laughed nervously. "If you, um, want to come back to my house. You're welcome."

Stalking toward me, Nick kissed me again, arms going around me. He dipped me back like he had when we were dancing. "I'd love to," he said against my mouth before leaning us back up.

My breath stuck in my throat, so I only nodded and turned away to lead him quickly down the treacherous path.

 # FOURTEEN

SILLA

I stared at the kettle, focusing on the tinny hiss of bubbles bursting inside, and tried not to be so aware of Nick's arm nearly brushing mine as he reached past me and flicked the white ruffle of the kitchen curtain.

"My stepmom would drop dead if she walked in here. Can I invite her over?"

"Why don't you like her?" I lifted myself onto the counter to sit beside the two matching mugs. The paper flags from the tea bags dangled over the rims.

"She showed up at Dad's offices, to hire him to help out with that stalker thing, and I'm pretty sure they were in bed by suppertime." He shrugged, still looking out the window.

I crossed my ankles and swung my legs slightly. My heels knocked into the cabinets.

Nick turned his gaze and caught me staring. I licked my lips and glanced down at my rings.

"Anyway," he continued, backing up to the kitchen table and pulling out a chair, "Lilith talks, Dad obeys. When we heard about Grandpa dying, she was all, 'What a perfect place for a novelist,' and besides her literary career, she didn't want to raise any kids in the city. Kids. Can you believe it? I mean, he's almost fifty."

"What about her?"

"Oh, younger. Thirty-two."

The teakettle whined, and I slid off the counter just as it began to shriek. I poured the steaming water into the mugs, and placed saucers over the tops. "To help it steep," I explained to Nick's questioning eyebrows, walking the mugs over to the kitchen table very carefully. I sat a third of the way around the table from him and leaned on my elbows for support. "You don't—have to stay, you know."

He didn't move at all, keeping still as a statue. "Do you want me to leave?" he asked quietly, eyes on mine, then sinking to my lips.

Before I knew what I was doing, I pushed back my chair. I was standing, walking to Nick. He tilted his head back to hold my gaze. Under the bright kitchen lights, he looked older, and calm. Strong. His hands rested on his knees, and they were wide and large, like they could hold anything I offered. The brown of his eyes washed out in the full-spectrum light shining from the brass chandelier. He blinked, and I touched his cheek, brushing my fingers down from the corner of his eye, where someday wrinkles would press.

My eyelids fluttered closed just as I kissed him.

We were still for a long moment, lips touching, barely breathing. Then Nick put his hands on my hips and I sank onto his lap. I opened my eyes, and he was so close. I kissed the corner of his mouth, his cheek, his mouth again, and parted my lips to offer him a taste. It was slow and I was comfortable there, kissing and breathing in the smell of his skin and the gel he used to slick back his hair. My skin tingled, but kissing didn't hurt like the magic did.

His hands found my neck and cupped my jaw, fingers teasing at the hair behind my ears. Shivers rushed down my spine, and we kissed and kissed. I never wanted to let go.

A car door slammed, and the muffled noise managed to penetrate my bliss. I leaned away, breathless, and caught Nick's eyes. They were dazed and clouded, and he said, "Why?" very softly, like a child who's just been put in the corner for arcane adult reasons.

I kissed him again lightly. "Someone's home."

He frowned, slowly catching up with what I was saying. Then he blinked slowly, several times. The soft skin beneath his eyes begged to be touched. "Oh. Your brother?"

"Maybe. Maybe Gram Judy." Reluctantly, I stood up from his lap.

Nick ran his hands back through his hair, paused, and rolled his eyes up as if trying to see the damage.

His hair stuck up in every possible direction. I giggled.

"Christ, do you have a bathroom?"

"Down the hall, first door on the left."

He went in a hurry, and I uncovered our tea. Steam billowed out. We hadn't been kissing for that long, then. Not quite as forever as it'd seemed. I closed my eyes and shivered, leaning my hands on the table. My cheeks felt flushed and my lips raw. The thin gash inside my lip that had bled earlier throbbed with my heartbeat. I'd never felt this way before. So electrified.

The front door unlocked and opened, and I heard Gram's footsteps and the smack of her leather purse on the hard tiles of the entryway. I was glad it wasn't Reese—though I suddenly remembered I needed to call him before long and tell him I wasn't at the party.

I grabbed my cell out of my pocket and texted him: HOME SAFE! just as Judy came into the kitchen. "Hey," I said to her, and putting down my cell, I took my untouched mug and offered it to her.

"Why, Silla, you're home. Thank you, dear." She took the tea and collapsed into a chair. One hand unbuttoned her jacket and the other pinched free the clip-on pearls dangling from her ears. "What an evening. These girls out here watch ridiculous movies."

"It was at Mrs. Pensimonry's house?"

"Yes! Did you know it would be awful?"

"Her grandson was in Reese's class—told Reese she can't get enough Animal Planet since she got satellite TV."

"Did you know, Silla, that there are entire shows about rescuing animals from cruel owners? They're almost like documentaries. I nearly laughed, before I saw that all the others had these looks of absolute horror on their faces. I'd have been a pariah for requesting something more thought-provoking."

"Are you going next month?" I poured a third mug and dug a tea bag out of the drawer.

"Well, Penny promised me some Cary Grant, so yes, probably." She sipped her tea. "How was your party?"

I shrugged as I sat. "Okay."

"How'd you get home?"

With perfect timing, Nick walked in. He'd managed to pull his hair into a semblance of neatness.

"This is Nicholas Pardee, Gram Judy." I wrapped both hands around my mug, reveling in the long form of his name.

Judy stood. "Oh, I see," she said, offering her hand.

They shook. Nick said, "Pleasure to meet you. You're Silla's grandmother?"

"Judy, please. And no, I was married to her grandpa for a few years, but after her dad was born."

"Not from here, are you?"

"No, and I hear by those vowels that neither are you."

Nick grinned and Judy mirrored it. I watched their moment of camaraderie with slight envy.

Judy, who had of course lived in Chicago, grilled Nick about the waterfront and exhibits at the Atlas Galleries, which had been her favorite. He'd never heard of the galleries but told her what was happening at the Shedd Aquarium. Soon Judy was talking about her third husband (just after Grandpa), who'd had a flat in the city in the early 1980s. Nick seemed interested, or he was a better actor than most boys I knew. He nodded and asked questions, and the corner of his lips curved up just a little. I rested my chin in my hand and studied the bend of his cheekbone, his ear, the stiff chunks of hair rather desperately in need of a comb or gel. But the mess suited him.

I'd never wanted so suddenly to be with someone. I'd dated a little, mostly flirting and putting boys off from anything serious because I knew I was going away to college and not interested in long-term relationships. I'd been friends with a bunch of boys in theater, and had always been around Reese's friends, two of whom I'd majorly crushed on. There'd been Eric, of course, and Petey sophomore year. But with Nick, I wasn't yearning for him to notice me or to smile, or ask me out. After tonight, it was clear the yearning was mutual. And the way he looked at me, not just like he wanted to kiss me forever but like he saw through the masks. I shivered with anticipation.

Just like the spell book, he'd dropped into my life when I was only trying to forget everything and survive. The book tempted me with answers. With the possibility of a real explanation for my parents' deaths. With *magic*. What was Nick tempting me with? Everything I'd given up while kneeling in their blood? Everything that had melted out of me to make room for the smell and the fear. Fun, laughter, dating, driving fast, imagining next year and the next with hope—

Or maybe just kisses. Maybe just a few hours away from home. Some trust, if I was lucky. Love, even?

"Silla?"

"Hmm?"

Nick and Gram Judy were both looking at me.

"You're falling asleep in your hand." Judy shook her head, unable to wipe the smile away. "You should get to bed, after the week you've had."

"I can walk home." Nick stood. "It's close."

"No, I'll drive you—I can borrow your car, can't I, Gram?" I pressed to my feet, and my head swam. It must have been the flowers. I'd made them so quickly, so suddenly. All my energy had been used up by flowers and kissing.

"Pish-posh, that's ridiculous. Nick is a big boy; he can walk. You're much too tired, and he's a gentleman." She waved dismissively, then gathered all three tea mugs and dumped them into the sink.

"It's fine, Sil." Nick took my hand. "Walk me halfway?" He wove his fingers in with mine.

The healed pink scar on my palm prickled. "Yeah."

Out back, I took him to the edge of our yard, where the forsythia bushes created a tall, lanky hedge. There was a thin spot, and we pushed through. It was only a dozen steps to the crumbling old graveyard wall.

We walked in silence, fingers woven together. The moon was bright enough that only the strongest stars shone, and some wispy clouds had blown in from the west. Like dark gray brushstrokes on the horizon. I sighed, and squeezed Nick's fingers. And then came the intruding thought: *Mom would have liked him.*

My throat closed, and I turned my face away from Nick so that he wouldn't see the surge of pain slash over my face. It didn't matter, now or ever, how much I liked a boy. I'd never again go through that mildly uncomfortable moment when I introduced him to my mom. Or feel the shaky nerves as Dad looked him up and down before saying, "No worse than Ophelia did." And if the boy laughed, he passed the test.

"Silla?"

Nick gently tugged at my hand so I'd face him. We were halfway between our houses, beside a grimy statue of a cherub. I kept my eyes lowered, not sure I was in control of myself yet. My sea-green mask waited just beneath the surface.

"What are you thinking about?" he asked.

"Ophelia."

"Hamlet's girlfriend?"

"Yeah."

"The one who drowned herself."

"Yeah."

He stepped closer so that I had to look up or let him crush my nose with his chin. Our lips met, and when Nick pulled away, he murmured, "How about a happier one? Like . . . no. Um . . . no. Jesus, all the Shakespeare girls I know are from tragedies. What's a good one who gets to live happily ever after?"

"Miranda. From *The Tempest*. She grew up with magic." *Her dad was a great magician.* I laughed without humor.

"Okay, Miranda, babe. Thanks for the tea."

Moonlight shone on the angles of his face. "I had . . . a good time," I said, and was immediately struck by what a stupid thing it was to say. To salvage the moment, I kissed him. He returned it, keeping the rest of his body back. Only our lips touched. I wanted to open his mouth and dive inside it. But Nick pulled away. "So, Magic Girl, will you show me more?"

A thrill raced up my spine. "Yes. Come to the cemetery tomorrow afternoon around two." I kissed him again. Pressed against him. I didn't want him to go.

Nick groaned and pushed back. "Babe, you keep doing that and I won't be able to leave."

I hugged myself, stepped away. "Sorry." I already missed his warmth.

"Don't be—just . . ." He reached out a hand, but let it fall. "I'll see you tomorrow."

"Yeah."

He didn't move. We stared at each other until Nick very slowly grinned. "Want to go out to dinner?"

I giggled, surprised at the genuine delight the idea of a date with Nick gave me. "Yes."

"Rock on." With a jaunty little salute, he dashed off through the rows of graves.

"Bye," I whispered, and stayed out under the moonlight until my teeth began to chatter.

NICHOLAS

Girl surrounded by flowers
Technicolor kiss
For all the night's lengthy hours
I'll miss . . .

I was in an awesome mood. That's probably why the rhymes were spilling through my head and I didn't even bother trying to sneak in. I went straight in through the garage, kicked aside Lilith's muddy gardening boots, and pushed through to the kitchen. I might have been humming.

My shoes clacked on the tile floor as I headed for the fridge. I dragged out orange juice and a half-eaten summer sausage.

"Nick, is that you?"

"Yep!" I called, not even caring that Lilith was probably going to come try and be social.

She swept into the room, trailing the silk hem of her robe on the floor. "Darling, I can cook you something if you're hungry."

"Give it a rest, okay?" I smiled.

Her body stilled. "What, exactly?"

"You know, the mom thing. The homemaker thing." I didn't really expect anything but a tantrum, or maybe a cold scoff and exit. Thinking of Silla, I hopped onto the counter. My flask pinched my ass, but I didn't want to remove it in front of Lilith.

"Off the counter, Nick."

I remained, and chewed directly into the sausage log.

"I'm only making it worse, I see." She pulled a stool away from the center island and sat delicately, folding her long fingers together like she was about to pray to God for my soul. "What, then, would you like for me to do? Ignore you? Treat you like garbage that I can't wait to throw out when you graduate?"

"That might be a nice change."

"It wouldn't make your father happy."

"He ignores me pretty well, so you never know."

For a moment, I thought she might argue in Dad's defense. But she sighed instead. "Did you have a nice party? You weren't out late."

"I hooked up, no worries."

Her lips pinched into a frown. "Hooked up? I hope that doesn't mean you had sex, Nicholas."

I decided right then that only Silla ever got to call me that again. "Nick. It's Nick, okay? And God, this conversation is just a bad idea." I slid off the counter, thumping down onto my feet. "I'm going to bed." Wrapping the sausage back into its plastic, I replaced it in the fridge and turned to glance at Lilith. "The tow truck's coming at nine. See ya."

"Good night, Nick." She oozed to her feet.

I left, aware of her stare prickling between my shoulder blades. Ugh.

SILLA

The full moon lit my path almost as well as the sun. I allowed myself to wander, unconcerned with getting home too quickly.

My fingers skimmed over the familiar gravestones. DAVID KLAUSER-KEATING, MAY HIS SOUL FIND PEACE, DIED 1953. The Klausers still lived in town, and owned one of the gas stations. Beside him: MISS MARGARET BARRYWOOD, 1912–1929, BELOVED DAUGHTER. My age when she died. I paused there, fingers playing over the rough granite grave marker, wondering if she'd ever been kissed.

I hoped so.

I smiled. The kind of secret smile that changes your whole face, from lips to hairline. A laugh spilled out and I clapped my hands over my mouth, embarrassed I'd let it escape. My head fell back and I grinned up at the moon, directly overhead, shining down like a spotlight: *Here's Silla Kennicot.* For the first time in a long time, I couldn't wait to be back onstage, the curtains drawn, my arms out as I used gesture and tone to plead with the audience to bear me up on their applause. The headstones were my audience here, and I wanted them to remember this moment as much as they remembered the night I'd spilled blood and brought life back into the cemetery.

The moment I'd felt alive again.

Filled with inspiration, I ran for my parents. I didn't know if they were listening, too, or if their spirits would even recognize a burning, living girl, but I had to tell them about Nick.

My stone audience flashed by as I hurried on, cold air burning down my throat and into my lungs. I slid to a stop, leaves crunching under my boots. Something was wrong. A tangy scent in the otherwise clear air.

Slowly, I walked around their wide double headstone, holding my breath.

It all rushed out of me in a sob of horror.

A splash of red tore across their names. I pressed my fists into my stomach. The earth over their graves was disturbed in a pattern. My breath fluttered in and out like I had a bird trapped on my tongue, beating its wings against my teeth. Slowly, I crouched down and touched my palms to the ground. They tingled, especially my left palm where the scar was. It pulsed, as though the blood just under my skin wanted out.

I traced the pattern as best I could. Angles and lines, all of them sharp. Definitely purposeful. A symbol. But I didn't recognize it at all from Dad's book. Which meant Reese couldn't have done this, even if I could think of a single reason he might have.

Someone else knew the magic. And they were here. Nearby.

Someone who could have used the magic against Dad. To kill him and Mom.

I stumbled back, slamming a shoulder into the corner of a headstone. Standing, I looked in every direction for anything out of place. Any movement. But in all this silvery moonlight, everything was still. Not even the wind blew. In the silence, the dead who had cheered me a moment ago pressed close. The weight of eyes raked down my neck, sending shivers all the way to the tips of my fingers.

But I was alone.

I ran.

FIFTEEN

SILLA

Reese's cell phone rang and rang and rang.

I pushed my back against my bedroom door and drew my knees up to my chest. "Answer," I hissed at the phone.

But it only kept ringing, and eventually his voice mail picked up. "This is Reese." Beep.

"Reese, you have to come home. I'm home, and I was in the cemetery and someone else knows the magic. I told you, I *told you* that this could explain so many things about what happened to Dad and Mom, and I was right. Somebody else knows. Come home, please. Be all right." The last words were merely a whisper, and I snapped my cell shut, clenching it in my fist.

What was I going to do?

I pressed the phone against my forehead and closed my eyes. Downstairs, Gram Judy was in her room with the TV on, and canned laughter was the only sound other than the wind in the trees outside.

Pushing to my knees, I crawled across the carpet to my bed and pulled the spell book from under my mattress. I flipped through, searching for anything similar to the symbol dug into my parents' graves. The black drawings stood out against the old paper as I turned pages, hunting.

Nothing. None of them were right. The closest was a seven-pointed star for breaking curses.

I called Reese again. Nothing. Again.

Maybe he was just having a blast at a bar, where he couldn't hear his phone. Nothing was wrong. He'd probably gotten my earlier message that I was safe, so he'd stopped worrying about me. I shouldn't worry, either, until it was after midnight and he should have been home. That wasn't for another half hour.

There wasn't anything for me to do until he got home. I didn't even know what we'd do when he *did* get home.

I climbed onto my bed and lay there, staring up at the ceiling. Beneath me, the bed seemed to swing gently, as though it was a hammock and a breeze rocked me. If I closed my eyes, the sensation went away, but all I saw was the slash of blood across the headstone, the huge puddle of it soaking into the office carpet.

It was better to stare at the ceiling and feel the dizzy motion beneath me.

The magic had drained me. Even though I'd barely lost any blood when I made the flowers. My power had rushed out, leaving me exhausted. And I was sure the excitement of kissing Nick followed by the surge of fear and adrenaline hadn't helped.

There had to be a way to regulate the effects of the magic. Maybe just practice would work. Like honing muscles. This was just another muscle that gets sore when you start using it.

Or maybe . . . maybe it didn't have to be my blood. Maybe I could get the power from something else. An animal. Witch stories were rife with animal sacrifice and familiars, weren't they?

I leapt out of bed. It made sense.

Grabbing a sweatshirt and my cell phone in case Reese called, I carefully opened my door and crept downstairs. In the dark kitchen, I drank a glass of water and leaned against the counter with my eyes closed, just listening to the patterns of night. My house creaked gently, and the wind outside tapped thin branches against the upstairs windows. The same wind hissed through the fields. I'd always loved that noise—it was like being surrounded by water.

Quiet conversation from Gram Judy's TV interrupted my silence, and I momentarily wished I could ask her advice.

Instead I imagined sitting at the kitchen table with Dad, asking him all my questions. Why could we do it? Why did my blood turn dead grass into flowers? Why did I burn with the power? Then he'd use a pen and scrap of paper to sketch out the answer, the way he'd diagramed Latin sentences for me after dinner almost every night when I was in junior high. Mom would have cleared the table around us, taking a moment to run her fingers through Dad's hair. Absently, like she wasn't even thinking about it.

Then Dad would tell me it was because I was special. My blood was strong.

Turning to the counter, I put my glass down and leaned both hands against the cold, flat tile. The kitchen knives glittered against the magnetic strips glued to the wall. I grabbed the butcher knife. The wooden handle was cool and smooth. I'd need something to carry the blood in, too.

My throat dried out, and I swallowed repeatedly.

Mr. Meroon had rabbit traps set up throughout the trees at the far end of his fields. Reese and I, when we were little, had hunted for them to set the bunnies free. We reset the traps so that Mr. Meroon never knew they'd been triggered, and he never moved them around much. Even ten years later, I knew exactly where to find them.

By the time I got there, it was nearly one. This time of night, everything slept. The cicadas and frogs had given up their moaning, and the only sound accompanying me was the wind. My boots crackled sharply through the underbrush as I carefully pushed aside blackberry bushes and low ferns to find the traps.

The third long box I came to had a guest. Kneeling, I put down the knife and Tupperware I'd brought. When I touched the wood, my hands were shaking. "Stop," I whispered. It was just a rabbit. A rodent. And Mr. Meroon was going to kill it anyway, and skin it. I might as well use the blood. I set the Tupperware in my lap and opened the lid. The thick plastic was stained from years of use, and should probably have been thrown out. I thought of Mom carefully measuring leftover casserole into it. She never wanted to overfill the containers so that the lid squished the food down or stuck to the top layer. Even her leftovers were supposed to look good.

But memories of Mom had no place in the little midnight grove.

It was easier than ever to open the trap. Quickly, I reached in and grabbed one of the paws to drag it out. The scruffy brown thing was huffing and scraping its claws along the trap's walls. I bit my lip and pinned it to the ground with both hands. The rear legs kicked and jerked. Scrambling for the butcher knife with my right hand, I leaned up on my knees. My heart thumped in my ears; my stomach was filled with heavy, tumbling rocks. *You can do this, Silla. One, two, three.* I was in a daze, and couldn't move.

The rabbit scooted, and as I grappled for a better grip on its fur, it *shrieked.* Over and over like a siren, like a baby, screaming and screaming. My throat closed and I couldn't breathe—I pushed down, but it struggled, the cries not ceasing. My fingers caught the hilt of the knife. I blinked back panicky tears. Did I really need this? Could I really do it? My stomach rolled over and over, crawling up my chest, and in one more minute I was going to puke.

I thought of Mom and Dad, dead. Thought of Reese, who was still alive, and I had to learn everything I could to protect him. I had to figure this out. There was nobody to ask.

I had to.

Shoving the blade against the rabbit's neck, I pressed down, all my weight behind the knife.

The screaming stopped as the blade popped through the fur and skin and muscles and bone and dug into the earth beneath. Blood immediately gushed over my hand and the blade, melting into the ground. I released the body and the knife, yanking backward onto my heels and wiping my hands frantically on my jeans. I sucked air in a huge, painful gulp. My ribs pulsed in and out, barely keeping my lungs and heart and terror from spilling up my throat. I stared at the decapitated rabbit, at the blood trickling out.

And remembered the Tupperware.

I whirled and grabbed it, my head swimming, then ordered my hand to curl around the rabbit's rear legs and lift it up to dangle over the container. My body obeyed that determined voice, though I felt as though I had no part of it.

The blood flowed quickly, at first pattering into the container, then gathering in a crimson pool that spread to fill the bottom. I could barely breathe. What little air I managed came in short, gasping bursts. The arm holding the rabbit up grew tired, and I transferred the corpse to the other. I stared at the blood, like a thick string connecting my mother's old Tupperware to the torn neck.

It didn't take long for the rabbit to bleed out, and there was hardly any blood in my Tupperware. I'd wasted a lot, flailing around. And the rabbit couldn't have weighed more than three pounds. The poor thing.

I stood up with it, swelling the ball of nausea that clung to the back of my tongue. I'd done it. I couldn't believe I'd done it. And . . . suddenly all my enthusiasm fell away. I tossed the body aside. It would feed a local coyote.

The head had rolled beside the knife, and I picked it up by one ear. With all my strength, I heaved it as far as possible. I heard it crash through the dry bushes.

In the dark, I put the lid on the container and picked up

my knife. My hands were sticky with blood, and the container was already cooling. In the center of the tiny clearing, I listened to the quiet forest. My breath was loud in my ears.

Then the smell hit me. The overwhelming stench of blood. I gagged and fell to my knees.

By the time I'd crawled far enough away from the smell to get to my feet, it was so late that the sky in the east was tinged with the first trace of light. As I stumbled across the front lawn, Reese's truck pulled into the drive, wheels crunching over gravel. It was still the worst sound in the world. Blood on my hands, in my nose, on the gravel—if I shut my eyes, I'd see it all again with perfect clarity.

Reese climbed slowly out of his truck. He shut the door carefully and turned around, obviously trying not to wake Judy or me. When he saw me, he jumped back so that his elbow slammed into the truck. "Silla?" Shaking his head, he walked toward me. As he peered through the shadows, his steps slowed and then picked up until he ran the final feet. "Are you okay? What happened?"

He tried to grab me, but the knife was clutched in one of my hands and the Tupperware in the other. "Silla? What are you doing with that knife?" His tone shifted into wariness, as if I was a wild animal.

"I killed a rabbit." I offered him the Tupperware.

Automatically, he took it, then nearly dropped it. "Jesus!"

"It's just blood."

"You . . ." He stared at me, eyes wide, then at the container, and back at me. "You sacrificed an animal?"

"Mr. Meroon would have killed it anyway."

"And eaten it! Jesus."

"I fed it to the forest."

I could see him steeling himself. His fingers twitched and he clenched his jaw. "Okay, bumblebee, you're freaking me out a bit. You sound totally psycho."

"Like father like daughter." Dizziness swamped my head and I almost floated away.

Reese ignored my raving and put the Tupperware on the ground like it was poison, then daintily removed the knife from my hand. "You're covered with blood." He bent to stab the knife into the ground.

"More on me than in the Tupperware. Mom would disapprove."

His eyes darted to mine, sharply. "No shit."

We faced each other over two feet of nothing. We were the same height, though he was broader, thanks to that Y chromosome and years of football. Mom used to say we had Dad's eyes. Pale and curious. I thought, suddenly, that the rabbit blood would never work now. It was old and dead. Wasted. I said, "You should check your phone messages."

He frowned. "I did. You got home fine . . . didn't you?" As he spoke, he reached into his jeans pocket for his cell.

"Yeah," I whispered, "but . . ."

He flicked it open with his thumb and pushed a button before putting it to his ear.

I walked, feet heavy as concrete, and sat on the porch steps.

Reese's eyes flashed wide. He stared at me, mouth pressing together. I shrugged and leaned my head against the railing.

"Jesus Christ, Silla!"

He was right in front of me, hands on my shoulders, dragging me up. "You're okay? What else happened? Who did it?"

"I don't know." My head shook involuntarily.

"Take me out there."

"I'm too tired. Wait . . . wait a few hours. Until the sun is up high enough to burn away all the moon shadows."

"Jesus."

I leaned forward against him, my head on his shoulder with my arms crossed, hands fisted against my ribs. "I don't think it will work."

"What?"

"The rabbit blood."

"Sil, you—"

"It's dead now. Old. Not used quickly enough. And God. A rabbit. What was I thinking?"

Reese wrapped his arms around me and pulled me with him back to the porch, where we sat beside each other. I put my head down on his shoulder.

"Tell me what happened."

I did. Everything from kissing Nick to the flowers to finding the desecrated graves. To hoping—needing—for there to be some truth about the magic that didn't lead straight back to my blood.

When I finished, Reese was so quiet I had to open my eyes and look at his face. He was glaring off toward Nick's house. "Oh, Reese."

"He made you bleed, goddammit."

"That isn't the point of this story." I took his chin in one hand and forced it toward me. "Stop being overprotective."

Reese jerked out of my grip. "Never."

I held his gaze, trying to make my expression as stern as possible.

Finally he nodded.

"Good, because he's coming over this afternoon to work with us. To try."

"Silla!"

"It will be good to know if he can do it. If it's just our blood or anybody's."

Reese actually growled in frustration. But after a moment, his curiosity made him admit through his teeth, "You're right! It'll be good experimentation."

I put my head back on his shoulder and, as casually as possible, said, "I've been thinking how the magic could have been used to kill Mom and Dad. Since we know now that somebody besides us can do it."

His jaw clenched. I felt the muscles move against the top of my head.

"The possession spell. Dad's notes mention birds, but why couldn't you do it to a person, too?"

"Holy shit, Silla." Reese drew away from me. He blinked slowly, his brain's version of the egg timer that shows up when the computer needs you to wait while it processes something. Then he said, "That makes sense. There are a lot of stories about witches possessing other animals, and people, too. Witches, and the demons, of course." His voice was soft, and he looked away. "You mean that someone possessed Dad and made him kill Mom, then shoot himself."

"Yeah." I settled back against his shoulder.

"But who, Silla? Who would do that? Who could?"

"I don't know. Another wizard, maybe."

"Sil, this isn't *Harry Potter.*"

"It's weird to call Dad a witch."

"The Deacon calls him a magician."

"Like Houdini."

"Maybe." Reese bonked his head lightly on mine. "Houdini was into the occult."

I grumbled and tightened my arms around myself. Reese put an arm around my shoulders.

"We have to try the possession spell. To see if it works," I said.

"That's too advanced, Sil, we should keep working up to it."

"There might not be time."

"Maybe there's a way to protect against it."

"Like one of the protection-against-evil charms?"

Reese sighed. "But Dad had to have known all of them. And he was vulnerable."

The thought made me grab his hand and squeeze. "We have to do something."

"We should focus on finding out who it is."

"I wonder if we could alter the spell for finding lost things. Whoever it is is sort of lost. From us."

"Maybe." He yawned widely enough to crack his jaw.

It passed to me, and as I yawned, I pressed closer to my brother.

Our house faced northwest, so all the stars were visible, and would be for at least an hour. I picked out the constellations I knew. The Big Dipper. Perseus. The cool dawn air smelled of dank leaves and dry smoke. And perfume. "You smell like perfume."

"I was with Danielle."

"Gross."

"Oh, yeah, after your escapades, with Nick Pardee, you don't get to throw stones."

"I guess."

"You really trust him?"

"Gram likes him," I said in a small voice.

Reese sighed. "We'll figure it out, Silla. We have to."

I just kept watching the stars. I wanted to see them move. I always had.

SIXTEEN

June 14, 1905

I have seen our destiny!

Philip took me out into the forest today and taught me the art of Possession. He cautioned me first, as he tends to do, that while possession is a valuable tool for learning, it is a dangerous and tempting weapon. I adore temptation.

I expected it to be so difficult, because Philip struggles, despite his vast practice, to claim his spirit's ownership over even a small jaybird. But I—I leap into it as though I had always known how to fly! When I tumbled out of the sky and back into my body that first time, I was laughing and exhilarated. Philip lay beside me, watching as I stood and twirled. "You are not exhausted?" he asked, leaning up on his elbows. I stopped and smiled at him, at the blond hair falling over his forehead, at his unbuttoned vest and the long stretch of his legs. I shook my head. "I am alive," I said, collapsing beside him and flinging my arms around his neck. I kissed his lips through my smiles.

"Josie," he protested, pushing me back. I showed him my greatest pout, and had him chuckling as he shook his head and touched my hot cheek. "Josie, you are drunk on the magic."

"Yes!"

Philip laughed. "I have never been good at possessions. They leave me laid out and ruined for hours. I suspect you could take a person, if you liked, for as long as you liked."

"A person?" The thought flared through me, faster than lightning. A million ideas for pleasure and mischief battered inside my mind.

But Philip shook his head. "Josephine, it is not a game. In the Deacon's time, men and women were killed for this—for everything we do."

"Killed? Why should we be murdered for the magic? For healing and finding charms?"

"We're witches, little sprite."

My hands flew to my mouth, and I glanced all around at the shadows in the forest. I had thought it but never spoken the word aloud. "Witches." I said it again, more calmly. "But our magic is not from the Devil."

"You don't think I'm your Devilish familiar? Teaching you dark secrets?"

"I know you're not—you won't even kiss me."

He laughed, and his eyes lowered to my lips. I know he will kiss me soon.

I thought about what he said about our kind being killed, but I am not concerned. I have real power—no one could keep me chained, because my blood can transform iron into water. I could walk through walls if I needed, and now—now I know I can throw my mind into another's, and how easy, then, would it be to unlock any cage? We are invincible, Philip and I. Like unto God. Or the Devil.

I have forgiven Philip everything, for all that he has shown me. When he closes us into his workroom or takes us out of the city to collect herbs and stones and rich earth, I think perhaps that he will love me as well as I adore him. Our fingers brush and our blood blends together.

SEVENTEEN

NICHOLAS

I slept with my window open, and by the morning I was wrapped up in my sheets like a burrito. That stupid dog dream had woken me up (again), so it was a pain in the ass to drag myself out of bed when my cell phone blared its techno-beat alarm.

By the time I was dressed and downstairs, I only had time to grab a Pop-Tart before running outside to meet the tow truck. I was in such a hurry, I tripped on Lilith's gardening boots again.

I wished she'd keep the damn things somewhere else, as I picked them up and put them several feet away from the door. It wasn't like she needed to be gardening right now, anyway. It was practically November, and the ground was freaking cold.

After dealing with the joy of sitting in the tow truck cab with a dude in a flannel shirt, trying to avoid telling him that actually, no, I didn't give a crap about the St. Louis Rams having a game on Sunday and could he please just ignore me so that I could stare out the window and think about Silla, I met up with Eric at Mercer's Grocer. It was right next to the mechanic slash gas station. And the Dairy Queen. And the bar with the neon Budweiser frogs in the window. And a hardware store. And a trio of antique stores already throwing open their doors for customers. Okay, pretty convenient to only have to walk a block for anything in town. If you needed old furniture or beer or hammers.

Just inside the sliding glass doors of the grocery was a little coffee cart run by a Mrs. April McGee, and there was a line at 9:45 a.m. on a Saturday.

"Color me shocked," I said. "The Dairy Queen *isn't* the only hangout for the youth of Yaleylah."

"For that, you're buying, asshole. I like two packs of sugar in mine."

Laughing, I did, and joined him across the street in the hardware store a few minutes later. Handing him the cardboard cup, I stood next to him and stared at the wall of tools. "What are you looking for?"

"Hammers."

I grinned.

"What's so funny? You don't have hammers in Chicago? Or you don't know what one looks like?"

"Nothing, it's nothing. Did you say ham*mers*, plural?"

"Yeah. For drama club. We—actually, you, oh member of the stage crew—need to make some platforms for the show this week after school."

"Joy." I sipped the surprisingly good coffee and stepped forward to inspect the hammers hanging from their little metal hooks. They varied in size from as short as my hand to as long as my forearm. What did you do with a tiny hammer? There were wooden handles and heavy plastic handles. Some painted, some not. It occurred to me that I really didn't need to know there were so many varieties of hammer. So I spun around and faced Eric while he shopped, as if one hammer wouldn't do as well as another. "Can I ask you something that's going to sound weird?"

He shrugged. "Sure."

"Did you ever hear strange things about my grandpa?"

"Mr. Harleigh?" Eric flicked his eyes at me, then shrugged again. "Sure. He lived alone next to a cemetery, man. What weird crap *didn't* we talk about?"

"So it was all made up."

The look he gave me said, *Seriously?*

"Look, I didn't know him."

"And you just want some colorful stuff to fill in the blanks."

"Got it in one."

"Okay, here was the best one. Ready?" He went all still, so that the only motion was the steam still rising from his coffee. Then he said in a low, half-whispered voice, "They say Mr. Harleigh was two hundred years old when he died. That for a half dozen generations he used the bones out in the cemetery to make a potion of immortality, but gave it up when—" He paused, glancing away guiltily, as if realizing he was about to say something bad about my family.

I stopped holding my breath and shook myself. "When what?"

All the dramatic affectation fell off him. "When your mom lost it."

"Oh." Goose bumps screamed down my arms. But I tried

to play it off with a wry smile. "Well, she did pretty much go nutso."

Eric clapped me on the shoulder, looking relieved. "Yeah. We all know. Glad you do, too."

"It was pretty hard to miss."

"You should watch out, too."

"What, like it runs in the family? Don't worry. My dad is the most boringly sane person on the planet."

"No, dude." Eric grinned. "Not genes. The cemetery."

"The cemetery?"

"It's like a vortex of evil." His face lit up. "There've been stories about that cemetery forever. My grandma used to talk about the animals avoiding the place—like cows and horses and dogs and stuff—and about seeing strange lights. And think about it. Who lives near the cemetery, and in the last thirty years, who are the only people to have gone crazy and/or been viciously murdered within a hundred miles?"

Coffee turned sour in my stomach. "When you put it that way."

Eric laughed. "Gives you something else to think about when you're gazing longingly at Silla."

I didn't want him to be, but Eric was right. And he didn't even know about the magic.

SILLA

Crows flapped lazily a dozen feet from my parents' graves. Reese and I had tossed an old loaf of bread for them, in several chunks, to keep them around. They seemed content to hop and chatter at each other as they argued over crumbs. Overhead, a solid sheet of blue stretched. All around us, the world rolled away in golden colors, and here we were in the cemetery, surrounded by crumbling headstones and patches of dying grass.

I lay on the ground in the center of a circle of salt and candles.

My blood rushed and throbbed in my fingers and toes, and the grass prickled at my skin. Squeezing my eyes closed, I breathed in and out, concentrating on the motion of my diaphragm. I dug my fingernails into the earth. It smelled cool and fresh. The spell burned through my veins, and my head ached like I'd been hung upside down and shaken.

But the magic wasn't working.

I let out a sigh and tried to relax, to melt into the ground and let go of myself.

"No luck?" Reese asked.

"Clearly!"

"It isn't like you're learning to draw a triangle. This is a whole new language, Sil."

I opened my eyes. The bright blue sky framed Reese's head so that I couldn't see his actual expression to know how serious he was. I guessed not very, and stuck out my tongue.

He laughed.

"I want to do it!" I pushed up to sit. "Everything else has come to me, why not this? I feel—I feel it rushing through me, from the top of my head"—I touched the flaky blood drawn onto my forehead—"to my hands." I showed him the blood runes he'd drawn on my palms. "It's pounding with my heartbeat and I want it. God, Reese, I . . ."

"Maybe you want it too much."

"That doesn't make any sense. Dad says *willpower* and *belief.* Wanting it more should make it easier."

"So part of you doesn't believe this should be possible."

I chewed on the inside of my lip. "It's . . . different from everything else. The other spells were about affecting other things, not myself. This is like throwing myself away."

Reese snorted. "You just like who you are, Silla. You've always been like that. Known who you are."

"I don't feel that way anymore."

Reese's face fell into thoughtfulness. "Are you afraid?"

Was I afraid? The idea made me shift uncomfortably on the cool ground. "Are you?"

"I don't think so. Think what I could learn by spending time in an animal's body. Flying, or hunting with a fox . . ." He turned his face toward the forest.

I gripped his hand. "You could lose yourself. How can a crow hold a whole person? My soul?"

He shook his head and turned back to me. "No, there isn't a physical manifestation of the soul—not like it has mass. It should be able to rest on the head of a pin, like all the angels."

Despite the sun, I shivered. The crows jerked and bobbed, oblivious of us.

"I'll try," he said. "I'm not worried about losing myself."

I heaved in a deep breath and nodded. "Okay. Trade." I very slowly got to my feet and stepped out of the circle. My knees wavered, and the cemetery ground tilted.

Reese caught my hand. "Whoa, Sil."

"I'm totally dizzy."

"That bad?"

"Yeah. I was trying really hard, and could feel the magic trying to work. Draining me." Reese steadied me as I knelt and leaned my back against Mom and Dad's headstone. "God, I'm nauseated, too."

"Dad has this note about that, did you see it?"

"Yeah."

Reese read it aloud anyway. " 'Recommend ginger or chamomile tea to settle stomach after possession. Can have deleterious effect upon body. Water and sugar for head.' There's raisins and cookies in the bag."

He handed me the backpack and I dug out our water bottle and a plastic bag of raisins. "Ugh." I wasn't hungry.

"Drink."

"I guess my body doesn't like the idea of being an empty shell."

"Smart of it."

"Bleh." I opened the bag and pulled out a couple of raisins.

"My turn. You have the knife?" Reese leaned back onto his haunches inside the circle. I handed him the pocketknife and watched as he slashed his palm. Wrinkling his lips, he said, "It's too bad about the rabbit blood."

The blood had coagulated into a disgusting, lumpy Jell-O. Instead of scraping it out of the Tupperware, I'd tossed the whole thing. Poor, wasted bunny. "Maybe we should stick with our own. To make it a real sacrifice, you know? Like Dad says. But I wish we could ask him."

Reese cupped his palm. "Yeah, and at least we know where it's been."

I reached out and tentatively put my finger in the scarlet pool. It was warm and sticky and gross. I winced, but painted a shaky rune on Reese's forehead. With his free hand, he pulled down the collar of his sweater. I painted the same rune over his heart and palms. Then Reese moved his bleeding hand out and let his blood drip in a circle around him, reinforcing the ring of salt already in place. It was supposed to let the soul more easily find its way back to the body, according to one of Dad's arrow points. And those were all the ingredients for this one. Blood, fire for transformation, imagination, and a few little Latin words. I'd noticed that most of the instantaneous spells required less ritual. It was the things meant to last, like warding charms and potions for health and fortune, that took time and planning.

Folding a piece of washcloth, I pressed it against Reese's palm. "So relax, and say the chant. Just focus on the syllables and then imagine yourself in the bird."

"I read the spell, too, Sil." Reese closed his eyes. "And you tried quite a bit, so I got to hear the chant several times."

I smacked his arm. "It was hard, okay?"

"Uh-huh." Reese took a deep, slow breath and folded his hands together in his lap with the bloody towel between them. As he relaxed, his jaw loosened and his eyelashes fluttered. A breeze flicked at his bangs, and my skin lifted into goose pimples. I glanced over to where the crows flapped about, and wished the sun was less bright. The bread was nearly gone. The flock played here all the time, veering toward our house frequently enough that when I'd been little, I'd named them all. Different birds, of course, and I probably couldn't really tell them apart, but I was six, so no one said otherwise.

Reese's breath changed suddenly, becoming shallower and faster, like he was trying to match his breathing to the bird's. Then, without any warning, his whole body relaxed. His head lolled and his fingers loosened. He slumped backward.

The candles went out.

I scrambled closer. He'd done it!

The crows flapped their wings and I swung my head to them. Dizziness swept up from my stomach. Pushing my fists into my belly, I swallowed it back, and looked carefully through narrow eyes. One crow had frozen. As I watched, it shook itself, hopped up onto a headstone, and then slowly blinked its inner eyelids. A cloud passed over the sun, casting us in shade, and the crow suddenly flapped its wings and shuddered. It leapt from the marble and flew out over the cemetery.

The rest of the crows cawed and cackled and chased after it. I stood, using Mom and Dad's stone for support. Too quickly I lost track of which of the spinning and diving birds was my brother. I walked as close to the salt circle as I could get without disturbing it. Reese's chest rose and fell slowly, like he was in a deep sleep. I thought again of souls. *I'm not worried about losing myself,* he'd said. I wondered if that was because he wanted to.

It was nice to see his face calm and peaceful. Some days I thought I wanted to feel more than I did, to break out of my numbness as if it was a shell. But Reese felt everything. My share, too. It made him throw things and drink too much and sleep with ex-girlfriends who he didn't really like in the first place.

The earth dropped out from under me, and I clutched at the nearest gravestone. I had to eat one of those damn cookies, and get to the water. Why couldn't I do this one? I'd made a hundred flowers bloom without trying, like the power in my blood had awakened completely and was starved for magic. But now . . . now I was failing.

Suddenly Reese's body lurched up. His hips lifted off the ground, and his eyes flew open. Then he collapsed and laughed. He flung out his arms, destroying the circle. "Silla! Oh my God."

My heart sank back down into my chest where it belonged. He was okay.

Flipping onto his stomach, Reese grinned. "Silla, it was amazing. I was flying. The wind was as thick as water under my wings. I couldn't fall—there wasn't enough weight in the world to push me down!"

"Wow," I whispered, trying and failing not to be completely jealous.

He nodded, and pushed to his knees. His head turned until he found the crow he'd abandoned, hopping jerkily in a circle. "I can hardly think of how to tell you—I just knew what things meant. And"—he closed his eyes—"the colors were . . . the trees were a million different greens, the sky—God, the sky. Not blue but blue-white-silver-green-blue-blue-blue—there isn't a name for it. Wind in my feathers, dipping, spinning, swirling, always knowing what was up, where the clouds were, what was too high, and my wings—my wings!—my muscles and bones remembered how to move, my feet tucked up." Reese swayed in place, opened his eyes. "Whoa. Dizzy." He reached out for me and I caught his hand. He looked like a little boy.

"That sounds amazing."

"It was. You'll get it. I'll help you." He squeezed my hand. I pulled him out of the circle and shoved the bag of cookies into his lap.

NICHOLAS

When I arrived at the graveyard, Silla and her brother were sitting together snacking on cookies. They both wore jeans and sweaters and had blood on their foreheads. Like a gruesome splotch jerking you out of an otherwise pastoral scene. That happened to be a cemetery. Okay, it was all pretty gruesome.

I lifted my hand and said, "Hi."

Silla slowly got to her feet. Her eyes were pinched as if her head hurt. "Hey, Nick. This is my brother, Reese."

Also standing, Reese held out his hand. "Hey."

I shook it, and was glad he didn't do any of those macho competitive hand-squeezing things. "Nice to meet you." He was bigger than me in every way except height. But he stood casually, like a guy who gets his size from actually working, not from spending hours in epic battles with weight machines.

"You too." Reese leaned his butt against the headstone, arms folded across his chest.

Normally, I'd have made some comment about his attitude being big enough to hold the headstone up without the help of his ass, but I didn't want to piss him off right away. Or piss Silla off.

"Hungry?" Silla asked. She was still standing, her hands clutched together in front of her. A blue strip of cloth was tied around her left hand.

I wanted to kiss her. It had been somewhere around fifteen hours since the last time. I wanted to take her face in my hands and kiss until I couldn't breathe. But instead I just shook my head. "Thanks, but I'm good."

"We were resting, eating. This spell is pretty tiring. Want to sit?" She gestured at the ground, her gaze following her hand.

I glanced down at the edge of the salt circle. The chunky crystals glittered like diamonds in the sun. There wasn't anything I wanted to say that I could say to Reese, too. "So. Magic. What have you done today?"

"Reese flew."

"Flew?" I darted a look at him, but he only offered a smug smile.

Silla said, "It's a spell called possession, and he willed his mind into the body of one of those crows over there. And flew."

Over to my left, the crows were hopping around, some on headstones, others tearing at the grass, arguing over bits of red leaves. "That's incredible," I said to Silla. The drying blood on her forehead had dripped one streak down to the bridge of her nose, and she looked like she'd been beamed with a two-by-four. So did Reese. "The blood on your face—that's part of the spell?"

Warm liquid falling into my eye. I rub at it, and Mom's voice: "Nicky, honey, don't do that."

I frowned and pushed away the flash of memory as Silla

said, "To open up our ability to separate mind from body. Or something."

"Right over your third eye chakra." That's right, I covered up my discomfort with major geekitude.

Reese glowered. "Our what?"

"Oh, um, you know—the points of energy in your body that . . ." Neither of them nodded. I tried again. "From Hindu traditions . . . and also very New Agey . . . never mind."

Silla took my hand and drew me to sit down beside her. "I'm glad you came."

I wove my fingers with her freezing ones. "Me too." This close, I could tell the smeared symbol on her forehead was familiar. *Think about the doggie, Nick, pretend you're running with him across that grass. What's it feel like under your paws? What do your floppy ears feel like?* I shuddered. Possession.

"Nick?" She squeezed my hand and kissed the knuckle of my forefinger.

"I . . ." I smiled tightly, glancing at Reese. "I'm just kind of nervous, I guess. Blood isn't my thing." It was almost the truth.

Reese shot a look at Silla, clearly letting her know he was not impressed with me. "You'll have to get used to it if you want to participate," he said wryly, and flicked open the blade of a pocketknife.

SILLA

We sat in a triangle, just inside the salt circle. Reese and I had talked about what spell to try with Nick before leaving the house. The problem with most of the spells was that you couldn't tell immediately that they were working. A protection spell was only apparent if it *didn't* work. A charm for luck was long-term. We could have tried the far-sight spell to look for whoever'd killed Mom and Dad, but neither of us wanted to talk with Nick about that quite yet. And it called for yarrow, which we didn't have. Several other spells called for harder-to-get ingredients, or things I'd never even heard of.

So we were going to try transformation. A famous one.

When we were situated, knees almost touching at the corners of our triangle, Reese grabbed a pale ceramic bowl from beside the headstone. The edges were scalloped like a pie crust and the bottom etched with the figure of an orange koi. Gram Judy had bought it from a catalog in August, and when it arrived she tucked it into the china cabinet and never touched it again.

I unpacked a bottle of wine from the backpack and set it between Reese and me.

"You're sure you're up for this, Sil?" Reese asked. "Not too tired?"

"I'm good. I have to do at least one thing today." I took the pocketknife from the grass. For the possession, Reese and I had slashed the meaty parts of our palms, since we'd needed enough blood to paint the runes on ourselves. It had *hurt,* and my left hand continued to throb quietly. But for this spell, just a drop would do.

Reese poured water from a sport bottle into Gram Judy's ceramic bowl. The clear water splashed up the sides as it glugged out.

Crows laughed as if they knew something we didn't, and the three of us waited for the water to settle. Glints of the sun

145

flashed in the uneven ripples, moments of silver brilliance that made me blink and look away. I caught Nick watching me, and smiled. He returned it.

Reese shifted in place as he brought the bottle of wine close and untwisted the screw top.

"Wine?" Nick raised his eyebrows.

"Oldest trick in the book." Reese grinned.

A frown wrinkled Nick's forehead for a moment, then he glanced at the water and at me. "Water into wine."

I nodded, feeling my pulse quicken. "Can you imagine?" I whispered.

"Won't have to." He reached over our knees and took my hand.

Reese cleared his throat. "Ready?"

Nick and I took deep breaths and let them out through pursed lips, simultaneously. As though we'd planned it. If he hadn't been holding my fingers tight, they'd have been shaking: we were meant to do this together.

"Ready, Nick?" I asked quietly. "After Reese drips in wine, we say, '*Fio novus.*' It means 'Become a new thing.' "

"Why Latin?" He didn't look curious so much as puzzled.

"Because that's . . . what's in the book," I said sheepishly, tapping the spell book's cover. It blended into the dry grass.

"We teach it what we want to become with the drops of wine," Reese said. "Our blood provides the energy, and our words the will."

Nick nodded. "Okay. Got it."

"Wine," Reese said as he tilted the open bottle and allowed a thin stream of dark maroon liquid to spill. It fell in, dispersing almost immediately. The water in the center of the bowl turned a shade darker. The sun spots flickering in my eyes were less bright.

I leaned over the bowl, and Nick and Reese each put a hand on one of my knees. Pricking my forefinger, I held it out and watched a drop of blood slowly, slowly gather at the tip.

My hand burned, and I felt the surge of energy push out from my guts and down my arm to gather in my hand. The power pulsed in that tiny drop of blood, trembling at the tip of my finger as I held my breath, and then finally—finally—falling to the water.

The blood landed with a tiny *plunk,* staying gathered in a sphere. A crimson bubble of blood floating in the water.

"*Fio novus,*" I murmured. *Become a new thing.*

"*Fio novus,*" the boys repeated. We all said it a third time, bending close so that our breath whispered against the water.

The surface trembled, shifting up and down in tiny eddies like an earthquake had disturbed it. In the middle, where my blood had landed, a strange vortex of purple grew, reaching out with tentacles for the edges of the bowl, for the surface, for the little orange koi at the bottom. Like oil, the vines didn't mingle with the water at first. It was a living organism, a water plant, growing to fill the space. My stomach was tight, and I bit the tip of my tongue, hardly daring to breathe.

"*Fio novus!*" I hissed.

The organism exploded, instantly turning all the water into dark, glittering liquid that lapped gently at the scalloped edges of the bowl.

We three just stared. I thought of Macbeth's witches

huddled around their cauldron. *How now, you secret, black, and midnight hags. What is't you do?*

A deed without a name.

We were as quiet as the gravestones around us.

NICHOLAS

I reached forward and dipped my finger into the bowl. Bringing it to my mouth, I hesitated only a second before popping it in. Sweet-sour taste flooded my tongue.

Silla watched me, wide-eyed, and Reese said, "Well?"

"Wine." I shrugged and laughed in amazement. "Bad wine, but wine."

With a shout of triumph, Silla dunked her finger, too. When she tasted it, she winced. "Gah. I guess I need practice."

"You don't like wine anyway." Reese grinned. "Maybe we should try water into chocolate milk next."

She laughed, and they shared a moment of understanding. It practically glowed in this sparkling freaking line between them. I told myself I wouldn't have gotten along with any siblings anyway.

In unison, they turned to me. Reese said, "Your turn, man."

My mouth opened, but for once I didn't have anything obnoxious to say.

"Don't you want to?" Silla rested her hand on my knee, and it was impossible to think.

"We want to know if it's just us. Our family. Or if it's you, too." Reese stood up in a single motion, bowl of bad wine in his hands. He walked a few feet away and tossed it in a long arch over some dude's grave.

"Nicholas."

The invocation of my full name gave me my words back. "Yeah," I muttered, reaching down to take her hand off my leg. I kept it in mine, and raised her finger up to kiss the tiny cut. "Yeah, I want to try."

Of course, I knew I could do it.

Reese sat back down and plunked the bowl into the center again. He poured the rest of the water in. Silla squeezed my hand before letting go, and searched around in the grass for her dropped pocketknife. Finding it, she offered it to me.

"Wait," Reese said. "You don't have any diseases, do you?"

Silla pursed her lips in annoyance. "You're the one sleeping with Danielle Fenton."

But Reese kept his eyes on me. I held them, making my expression casual and uninterested, like I didn't care about this additional display of dominance. It was mildly irritating that I had to do it again, but thanks to Lilith, I was good at responding to this kind of game. And Reese didn't dislike me, I thought. He just didn't want me touching his sister, which I could totally respect. He'd have to get over it, but I could respect it.

Finally he nodded, and Silla handed me the knife with a little exasperated sigh.

Reese poured in another stream of wine, and then they both put their hands on my knees to complete the circle, just as we'd done for Silla.

I put the knife to my finger and pressed. The pain was immediate—I'd cut too deep, but the pocketknife wasn't as precise as Mom's quill blood-letter. Trying not to blanch and look like a loser, I held my finger over the bowl and focused on what I wanted. More than one drop fell, splashing heavily. My body itched all over as the magic hissed out. I didn't remember it itching.

"Water be wine," I said, not thinking and distracted by the surge of the magic. "Tears of the heavens, become fruit of the vine."

I felt more than saw Silla and Reese hesitate.

But I kept going. "Water be wine. Water be wine. Blood from my body, the power is mine. Water be wine."

With a silent clap of energy, the entire bowl of water transformed into dark wine.

"Nick!" Silla said, muffled because she was pressing her hands to her mouth.

Reese dipped his finger into the bowl and tasted it. His lips turned down thoughtfully. "Better," he said.

I shrugged. "I, uh, think of spells in rhyme. You know, like in movies." *And my mom taught me to make spells like poems.*

"And Shakespeare!" Silla laughed, shaking her head at me.

"That answers two questions, though." Reese took another taste of the wine I'd created. "You can do it, and we don't need Latin."

"Just meaning," Silla said.

I sucked on my finger. It still bled sluggishly. The taste reminded me of kissing Silla.

Reese clapped his hands together, then hissed and glanced down at his wounded palm. "We should go. Clean up, and make dinner. Get some sleep. Nick, this could knock you on your ass. You should take it easy tonight."

"Sure." I flexed my finger. The blood was slowing.

"Maybe"—Reese glanced up at the sky and around the wide-open cemetery—"we should do any more spells at our house, in the backyard. Make sure Judy isn't around, and then we'll have privacy."

Silla said, "No. We have to do it here, with Dad and Mom."

"They aren't here, Silla."

"I can't forget them here, though. I mean . . ." She avoided Reese's eyes by concentrating on erasing the salt circle, picking the spell book off the ground, and dumping it into her bag. I helped her pack the box of kosher salt, the pocketknife, and a pile of used candles.

When the backpack was zipped, she said to her silent brother, "I mean, this is a connection to them, the magic is, and being here reminds me why I'm doing it in the first place." She poured the wine out at the foot of her parents' headstone like an offering.

"I guess." Reese took the bowl and backpack. "I'm gonna run back and shower first."

"Okay." Silla tossed him a quick smile. He did not return it.

"Hey," I said, something suddenly occurring to me. "Can you leave the spell book? I'd like to read it, if that's okay."

Reese held out the bag so that Silla could fish out the book. "Later," Reese said. He took off. I wondered what exactly had soured his mood.

Silla and I stood facing one another. She held the little spell book to her chest, hands splayed over it protectively.

Stepping close, I touched the spine with my finger. "I'll take care of it, babe."

"I know."

"I promise."

"I know."

I curled my hand around the book, but she didn't let go. She just stared at me, her eyes moving all over my face. "You okay, Silla?" I used the spell book to pull her nearer. Inch by inch.

"Yeah." Her bottom lip moved like she was chewing on the inside. I wanted to be the one chewing on her lip. As if she'd heard me, she let go of the book abruptly and put her arms around me instead.

Hugging her back, I asked, "When can I take you to dinner? Monday? Tuesday?"

"I don't have rehearsal call on Wednesday."

"Sounds perfect."

I did what I'd wanted to do since arriving. I tilted her chin up and kissed her. It was different in daylight, with my own magic still ringing in my ears. More real, like this was proof that I hadn't dreamed everything after the party last night.

She smiled into the kiss. I pushed closer, loving the feel of her whole body pressed up to mine, with only the spell book between us. I wanted more.

"Nick." Silla stepped back and took a deep breath, leaving the book in my hands. "Gram's expecting us for dinner in a bit. I have to go. I'm sorry."

"Me too." *Very sorry.*

I only watched her walk away for a few seconds. But they were a *good* few seconds.

SILLA

The afternoon shone cheerily all around me. As I climbed over the crumbling cemetery wall, I could hear songbirds chattering and singing as if they approved of our magic. I was light-headed, but whether from the magic or kissing, I didn't know. I didn't really want to know—it didn't matter, because I planned to be doing a lot more of both in the very near future.

When Reese spoke, I nearly tripped over myself.

"Hey, bumblebee, come and look at this."

It took a moment to find him, ducked down by the base of the forsythia line marking the boundary into our backyard. I made my way to him and crouched. "What?"

"Here." His finger pointed at the yellow grass. It was spotty, with whole chunks of earth visible in places. "If you imagine the dirt in a pattern, like this"—he traced his finger in the air over it—"does that look like part of a rune to you?"

"Oh my God. Do you think Dad did it?"

"Yeah. It kind of looks like the triple star thing in the pro-tection spell. And check this out." He stood, pulling me with him, and backed me up. "See how the dead grass is right there along the bushes? I think it goes all the way around the house. A circle of dead grass."

My mouth dropped open, and I looked in either direction. It was hard to make out, because all the grass was dying as the season changed. "How did you even notice this?"

"When I was"—Reese flashed a look up at the sky—"flying, I thought I noticed it around the whole house. Discoloration. I told you I saw things differently up there."

"Go around that way." I pointed to the south. "I'll go this way. See if there are more."

It was like a yellow brick road now that I knew what to look for. A golden path all around our property. Just beside the driveway gate, I found another patchy area. I traced the rune with my eyes.

We met up a few minutes later. My fingers were shaking a little, so I hid them in my pockets. I said, "I found another one a quarter of the way."

"Me too." Reese's solemnity told me he wasn't any more thrilled than I was about this. "It probably died because he did."

My knees locked before I fell. He was right. The grass hadn't been this dead in the spring or early summer. Mom would have noticed and thrown a fit.

"It was to protect us," I whispered, thinking about the mechanics of the magic so that I didn't have to think about the dead grass. "It makes sense if it's the same rune as from the protection spell. Dad was protecting the house."

Reese was silent, but I know he was thinking, *Not well enough.*

 # EIGHTEEN

August 10, 1905

I saw how he looked at her last week, when we tended to her father's servants.

We were there for an outbreak of influenza, that same sickness that had nearly claimed me, had shown me to Philip. He thought to heal them, as always, but I refused to let him discover a new girl as he had discovered me.

She was the daughter of the house, the only child. Miss Maria Foster. She brought us cool tea and cloths for washing. His eyes lingered on her lips and the long, dark lashes that fluttered on her cheek. When he thanked her, it was with gentler words than he'd ever used with me, and a much too long touch of hands.

And then he did not forget her. I sat beside him, tickling his ear, combing my fingers through his hair, teasing his attention to me. But he would only continue writing in that blasted diary of his. In it, I saw her name. I tore the diary from him and threw it across the room. He lifted me up and said I was improper and unpleasant. I screamed at him, that he'd prefer the soft graces of a stupid rich girl to someone like me, devoted to him and to his secrets.

He said I was right. He did prefer her graces.

I left. I left his house that night and returned to hers. I waited until she was at her window, and when I saw her face, I threw myself into her. My own body fell against the alley wall, and I didn't care. I was Miss Maria Foster. I stood in her corset and crinoline, in her little boots, and I breathed through her lips with her very own lungs.

When you're treated differently, you change. I had a maid to come see to my dinner gown and another to serve my plate. I was bowed to and my chair pulled back. Mr. Foster patted my hand, and Mrs. Foster chided me for taking too much, but kindly. And my new brothers — they teased me, and when we retired to a sitting room it was I they asked to play. I cannot play any piano, of course, but I agreed to read them poems from a collection of Tennyson. One of the dinner guests, a Mr. Dunbar, was attentive, holding my elbow and chatting with me about all manner of things. I fear I left them all with the sense that Miss Maria was weary, for I was forced to put off many of the topics. It is no wonder Philip likes her — she is not only graceful but sweet and educated. I can tell by the way she is treated. Everyone admires her.

As I retired upstairs, I was dizzy and overcome with the sensation that I might float out of her body. Quickly, I took her to her window so that I might return to my own body. There in the alley, on all fours, I vomited repeatedly and had to remain for some time.

But I have gone back every day this week, and borrowed Miss Maria Foster. She has told no one of her blackouts, but that will not last long. I must use her while I can.

In her, I am admired by all.

 # NINETEEN

NICHOLAS

Dad and Lilith sat on the back patio drinking margaritas. After stashing the spell book behind some dried-out flower bushes, I headed for them.

The margarita pitcher glinted neon green in the sun, and they had a small plate of salt and limes. Lilith was, as far as I could tell, staring off into space while Dad skimmed through a pile of paper with a red pen and highlighter. I hoped he was reading testimonies and not editing a manuscript for her or anything so cute and couple-like. "Hey," I said, rubbing the back of my neck with one hand. It didn't alleviate any of the tension tightening around my skull.

"Nick. How was your afternoon?" Dad set the pen down.

"And your car?" Lilith added, skimming a finger around the rim of her margarita glass.

"Fine, and yeah, it's all fixed." My voice was tight because my head hurt. It wasn't the magic, either. It was memory pushing behind my eyes. *Mom pushes her fingers against my forehead and says, "I banish thee from this body." A snap-pull in my stomach and I'm sitting*

on the floor looking at Mom with her hand covering a dog's face. Our dog Ape.
From my goddamn dream.

"Oh, good," Lilith was saying. "But if we ever need to, we can tow it up to Cape Girardeau and avoid the local color."

I scowled. "Isn't that why we're here? Local color?"

She eyed me over the rim as she sipped.

"Dad, I need to talk to you for a minute."

"Sure, Nick, what's up?"

I paused meaningfully. "Um. Alone?"

Lilith slid out of the patio chair. "I'll get some bruschetta. I was just thinking how lovely tomatoes sounded."

After she vanished through the glass doors, Dad and I just looked at each other.

Dad, even in his Saturday, relax-around-the-house state, could have walked into a courtroom and not been out of place. Ironed jeans, button-up shirt, hair combed. And he waited for me to speak. God forbid he waste words prodding me.

Spit it out, Nick, Christ. Where to start? My throat was dry. I didn't want to talk to him about this. But I couldn't talk to Mom or Grandpa, and surely—surely—he knew something about what had happened to me here. Either that or he sucked even more than I expected. I rolled onto the balls of my feet and then back onto my heels. "Why didn't I know Grandpa?"

His brow lowered. Was he scowling? "Your mother didn't speak to him."

The sun warmed my shoulders and neck as I stood there, trying to boil my thoughts down into a question Dad could possibly understand. "I know, but why? What happened that time she brought me down here? When I was seven?"

"What do you remember?"

"Dad."

"You were sick the whole time, Nick. Your mother told me that her father acted as though you'd been cursed or something. Went crazy, she said. Cut your cheek with his knife, and she brought you home."

But it had been Mom who cut me. I remembered that clearly enough. Her comforting smile, her promises, as the blade sliced my cheek. What had she been doing? The cut on my finger itched.

"Nick, what's wrong, son?"

My distress must have been scrawled over my face like I was in a made-for-TV movie. "Don't you know how she got all those injuries?" Was he lying to me? Or had she kept it a secret? Why the hell didn't he know? Hadn't he cared?

"She was very clumsy, which you fortunately didn't inherit. She always cut herself in the kitchen and on whatever little sharp surface was poking out. Paper, nails, splinters—you name it, she managed to get her fingers sliced up with it. Why?"

He didn't know. Hadn't wanted to know. So he would never have to try to help her. "I just remember all the Band-Aids."

Dad's lips bent down. "She stopped with all that when you were very little. Before—"

"Before the first time in the bathtub," I supplied. *Right after we visited Grandpa.*

He nodded once. "This is a strange conversation for such a nice day, Nick."

The urge to cuss at him pressed behind my teeth. Instead I

gave him a suitable excuse, one that his stupid Vulcan brain might pretend to understand. "Well, I'm here where she lived, you know? Going to school where she went to school."

"That's true."

"I think about her here sometimes, and just wonder if she'd have been so nuts if she hadn't left."

Without moving anything but his left eyebrow, Dad managed to look sad. But he wasn't getting pity points from me. "It was this place that she was always looking to escape, Nick. Her history and her family. She never stopped trying to leave her family here, even when she made a new one."

What had been so horrible that she'd needed to try so freaking hard? Abuse? Had it been Grandpa? Or the magic? Something in the cemetery, like Eric suggested? Me? "She never said anything to you about what she hated?" *You never asked?*

Dad's growing irritability was plain in the tight sigh that huffed through his nose. "Nick, what she said only became less and less lucid. I didn't want to remember. I'm sorry."

Yeah, you are.

The sliding glass door opened, and Lilith emerged with a platter of toast and chopped tomatoes. "You boys finished with your tête-à-tête? Hungry?"

"Yeah," I said.

"That looks delicious." Dad stood to pull Lilith's chair out for her. God.

"Why, thank you, darling."

I asked, "Which room was Mom's? Do you know?"

We raised our eyes to the back of the farmhouse. My attic window was open, but all the others hid their interiors with curtains. It was Lilith who said, "That last room there on the right. When you go all the way down the hall on the second floor."

"How do you know that?" It came out more sharply than it should've.

But Lilith's face remained light. "Her name was painted in the closet. I found it during the initial sweep with my contractor in July."

I should have apologized. It was a totally rational reason. Dad clearly thought I should. But I ignored it and went around front to grab the spell book before going inside.

All the way at the end of the second-story hall was my mom's old room. I paused in front of the door, one hand against the wood. Closing my eyes, I leaned my head against it. *"You used him, Donna! How dare you!" "Daddy, I had to, I didn't have a choice." "You did—he isn't your familiar, he's a child. Your child. My grandchild." "There was no other way."*

My hands shook and my face hurt from the contorted expression holding back all this sudden anger. I remembered crawling out of bed, covered in sweat and shaking, just like I was now, but from a fever. And I'd heard them arguing. Heard Mom crying. Sobbing.

Get out. Take that boy home, and you stop this. You're evil, girl, what you're doing is evil.

But they were gone. This was only a memory.

A few deep breaths later, I pushed inside.

The room was empty. Maybe twelve by twelve, with plain cotton-white walls and some old furniture shoved into the corner.

Hoping to find Mom's name, I threw open the closet door. But the whole interior had been painted to match the eggshell color of the room. What did Lilith have against color, anyway? I flung open the curtains and glared down into the backyard. It was a bad angle for directing my hatred at Lilith, so I looked out toward Silla's house. But the forest was too high. I couldn't even see the cemetery from here. Only trees with brownish-green leaves.

I sat in the center of the room with the spell book. It was heavy in my hands. Carefully, I flipped through. Some of the symbols looked vaguely familiar, like versions of spells I knew. Like a slightly different style, based on the same system. The ingredients were mostly the same as the ones in Mom's lacquered box. Not that I'd really doubted, but this was definitely the same kind of magic.

Robert Kennicot.

The name was signed at the bottom of one of the pages.

I dropped the book, and it hit the hardwood with a crack that echoed in the empty room.

"Robbie Kennicot," Mom whispers. I lean against her knee, pressing my hands onto the floor next to her mirror. The glass distorts, and I open my mouth as Mom's reflection disappears into gray clouds. A new face is there, a man's. I don't know him. He's dorky-looking, with little round glasses. I think they're weird because the lenses are pink. "Oh, Robbie," Mom says. A splash of water hits the glass, and in a snap like lightning Mom's face is back. She turns

the mirror over and touches my cheek. "My baby. We're going to save him, aren't we, Nicky?"

I flung myself to my feet and dashed upstairs for the lacquered box. I grabbed a handheld mirror from the bathroom, and matches. Salt from the kitchen and Lilith's bag of tea candles from the pantry. I knew exactly what spell I was going to do, and I didn't need the damn spell book for it. I remembered this one.

I remembered all of them.

Like something had blown open, or been torn down, I remembered the lessons from my childhood that I'd tried so freaking hard to forget. Where to buy herbs, how to dry your own, how to draw what I wanted when I couldn't spell it. That rhyming helped focus the intention. That a drop of blood on the earth anchored you so that you wouldn't be so slammed after the spell. Mom's words rushed through me in a huge roar, and I couldn't hear them all but understood them anyway.

My veins burned. The temperature of the room was a hundred degrees.

I set my spell up quickly. Salt circle, candles at the four corners. I sprinkled dried yarrow flowers into my hand from their jar and crushed them over the mirror.

With Mom's quill, I pricked my forefinger and smeared the blood onto the face of the mirror in the appropriate rune. Underneath the hand mirror went the last postcard from Mom, which I'd tucked into the lid of the magic box when it had arrived eight months ago. Her loopy writing said, *The desert suits me, Nicky, and it's so easy to get lost—which is nice if you're used to being lost. I love you. Mama.* I put the mirror flat on the floor and stared through the thin smudge of my blood. My hands pressed on either side, just as they had when I was a boy, as I crouched over it and whispered her name onto the drying rune. Like I was trying to see through one of those 3-D images, I unfocused my eyes and my own features blurred.

"Donna Harleigh," I said. "Mom."

A breeze brushed the hairs on my forearms. I heard wind through leaves and young laughter. In the mirror, my eyes faded out and were replaced by even darker ones, in a face older and narrower than mine. Her hair snaked over her fore-head, and she reached up a hand to sweep it away. The motion pulled back her sleeve, and tiny silver scars shone against her wrist. She was smiling.

The image snapped away.

Only my own angry eyes stared back at me from the mirror.

TWENTY

August 23, 1905

 I brought her here, to Philip. He'd gone to see her twice, pretending to bring the house more physick. Both times leaving me at home alone. He was falling in love with her, and I would make it me.

 I rang the bell to my own home and he answered, surprise written plain on his handsome face. I made her smile. "Come in, Miss Foster," he said, stumbling a little.

 I did, offering my hand.

 "What can I do for you?" he asked.

 The awe in his eyes was so overwhelming and ridiculous I laughed. He started back, and I caught his face between my hands. "Oh, Dr. Osborn, I adore you." And I kissed him.

 For a moment, he let me, his hands soft on my waist, welcoming my lips and the sweet smell of Miss Foster's perfume. Then he pushed back, still gently—he never is so gentle with me!—and said, "Miss Foster, I should speak with your father."

 But before I could get a word out, he froze. "Josephine!" he hissed.

 "How did you know?" I was amazed, and danced back, laughing.

 "Your eyes." He crossed his arms over his chest. "Your eyes, Josie. How could you?"

I twisted Miss Foster's face into a snarl. "You would marry her! You would give over everything we have for her. Because she is gentle and sweet and STUPID."

His fingers tightened on his elbows, the knuckles whitening. "Come with me now, Josephine."

We returned to the Foster house, and I left Miss Foster there, choking on her own fears for her health. When I opened my own eyes, Philip slapped me. "Never use her again. Never anyone else, Josephine. I did not teach you these gifts so that you might hurt others."

"You hurt me." I flung my arms out. "You promise me everything and then drop it the moment you see a lovely girl. Who is everything that I am NOT!"

"You cannot be her; you can only be your conniving, jealous self."

Before furious tears betrayed me, I left him in the alley.

I gave him several hours to cool off, and myself, as well. Then I brought him a bottle of his favorite brandy. He took it wordlessly and poured us each a glass. We sat down and were quiet for some time. My brandy was nearly gone when I finally asked, "What was in my eyes?"

"I couldn't see my reflection in them. Sure sign of enchantment."

I sighed. "Why do you love her?"

"I don't." Philip swallowed the last of his brandy, too. "I don't love her."

"Yes, you do."

"No, but she is lovely and is so many other things that I am not."

"You're a gentleman, Philip. You could marry her if you liked."

"And what? Teach her to measure blood as you do? Besides, I am no gentleman. I was born lower than you, Josie."

"You've risen above it, then, and no one would know."

"The Deacon found me in a cemetery," he said, his head falling back onto the sofa. "I was running with a gang of resurrectionists, stealing corpses to sell to medical colleges. He recognized my strong blood, as I did yours, and took me away to teach me all these things. God Almighty, that was a long time ago."

I joined him on the sofa, placing my hand on his knee. "It only seems so, Philip. You aren't so much older than I."

His lips turned up. "I am a hundred years old, Josephine."

I had not thought I could still be startled by him. "How?" I whispered.

"A charm, of course. Or a potion, truthfully. And it will not work on those without our magical blood. The Deacon has tried it on others, and always it fails."

"What spell?" I sat up straight.

"Carmot. He called it carmot."

I grabbed his hands. "Show me, Philip. Show me."

Weaving his fingers with mine, he still hesitated.

"I swear I shall not touch her again, or anyone. I will be good, Philip. You can help me, and together we will Please."

"We do deserve each other, do we not?" he said.

I smiled. "I promise we do." I took his face in my hands. "You do not need her, or anyone, Philip." I kissed him, and he kissed me back. I want always to remember the desperate way his fingers clung to my hips.

TWENTY-ONE

NICHOLAS

I slept like ass, exhausted and sweating, as if I could squeeze all my frustration out through my pores. Every time I actually fell asleep, I jerked awake again like there was this fail-safe refusing to let me dream.

What I wanted was to see Silla. To confess everything to her. I wanted to tell her that I'd known about the magic, I'd known it was possible, but that all I'd remembered before yesterday was that it hurt, that it broke my mom into a billion bloody pieces.

But I decided I needed to wait until at least lunch. Didn't want to come on too strong and then tell her I knew about the magic and I was sorry for lying. She'd think I was psycho. If I was lucky.

So I snuck downstairs to grab a box of cereal. Back in my room, I flicked on my computer. In order to try and make sense of the jumble of memories swimming around in my skull, I laid out all the ingredients from Mom's lacquered box and began making a list of the spells in Mr. Kennicot's book, and a list of ingredients. I cross-referenced them with the ingredients

Mom had. The spells seemed to fit into three categories: healing, transformation, protection. Except the possession spell. I ended up putting it into the transformation category, but really, it was more offensive, wasn't it? Closing my eyes, I tried to remember what other things Mom had done. But it had been so long ago, and the specific memories were almost impossible to access consciously. It had felt like she was mostly entertaining me, and teaching me the rules . . . not how to do particular things. When I'd been so young, I hadn't thought seriously about learning it all, and by the time I was old enough, Mom had gone off the deep end and I hated the stuff.

Most of the ingredients I didn't recognize I found in quick Internet searches. They were mostly obscure names for common plants, a couple of which were poisonous. Or had a history of being used in medieval magic for potions called things like "flying ointment" or "all-remedy." Except for carmot. The jar in the box was nearly empty. Just a quarter inch of rusty red powder was left. The word itself didn't explain what it was. Carmot, according to the Net, was the secret ingredient in the philosopher's stone, that great alchemical grail that would let the alchemist live forever.

But nobody knew what it was.

Except, apparently, my mom. And she definitely hadn't wanted to live forever.

I glanced at the computer clock. Only ten. Probably it was too early to head to Silla's. So I reluctantly checked my email for the first time in a week. Not much there besides a few alerts from the Chicago music scene, letting me know about the bands headlining the Anthem Dog downtown and discount tickets to Red Velvet for Dinner. There were three from Mikey, though, and one from Kate, both wanting to know what the hell I was up to and why I hadn't called or emailed.

I fell in with some blood witches, I thought. *Then I didn't even think about you for a week.*

I couldn't possibly explain Silla to them, or what it was like here in Yaleylah. But I wasted some time skimming through a handful of social networking sites I used to hang out on. I didn't update my status or respond to notifications. It felt so distant from where I was, but when I logged in to Facebook, I had a swarm of friend requests from Yaleylah High, and I didn't respond to those, either.

By the time my stomach let me know I'd dicked around long enough, it was almost noon.

Dropping the spell book into my messenger bag, I headed downstairs. Lilith was working on her laptop in the dining room, with a bunch of papers strewn around and marked up with purple. She glanced up, but seemed so in the zone she didn't even recognize me. I decided to take small miracles, and built myself a sandwich in the kitchen. I had no idea where Dad was.

After stuffing the sandwich down my throat, I called, "Going out, back later!" and took off.

Reese's truck wasn't in the driveway, but the little VW Rabbit was, along with a shiny silver Toyota Avalon crusted with fresh gravel dust. I frowned, but continued up the creaky porch steps to knock on the door. In the shade, it was about ten degrees cooler and I didn't have to squint through the sunlight. There wasn't a cloud in the sky.

"Coming!" Judy's voice rang through the open windows. Maybe the guest was just one of her friends. As Judy opened the door, I straightened and put on a smile. "Hi, Nick!" She grinned. Gold bangles swayed from her ears, and her white hair was tucked up under a blue and purple scarf. "Come on in. Silla's upstairs napping. She and Reese were awake pretty late last night. I can run up to see if she's still asleep." Judy trotted back down the hall, her heels clicking on the wood floor like the patter of raindrops. I followed more slowly back toward the stairs and noticed two mugs sitting on the kitchen table as I passed.

One of the hallway doors opened, and a woman popped out. Behind her head I saw packed bookshelves. A library or study, I guessed. "Hello," she said, smiling smoothly.

I jerked my chin in greeting.

"You must be Nick Pardee."

God, I hated small towns. The woman looked like she'd come from church: knee-length skirt, pearl-edged sweater, thick hair up in one of those twists that's supposed to make you look elegant or something. She was probably only thirty or so. Maybe younger. Hard to tell. Would probably get along with Lilith.

"It's nice to meet you, Nick. I'm Ms. Tripp. I work at the school."

"Friend of Judy's?" I glanced toward the stairs Judy'd scuttled up.

"Of Silla's, really. I was stopping by to see how she's doing."

"She's fine." It was a struggle not to cross my arms over my chest.

Ms. Tripp smiled again. "I'm sure she is, Nick."

"I didn't know teachers made house calls."

"I'm a counselor, and I've been helping Silla these past few months. She needs it." Ms. Tripp's eyes went back toward the library.

I gripped the strap of my bag. "She's doing fine."

"Nick, you must know what a horrible shock she's had, and I'm sure you can imagine she needs all the support she can get." Her lips curved into a pout. It wasn't the kind of expression I was used to from a teacher, but I guess she was trying to appear empathetic.

"What were you doing in there?" I nodded at the study. I didn't want to talk about Silla anymore. Was this another messed-up small-town thing? School counselors making house calls?

"Oh, getting a feel for what happened. That's where she found them." Ms. Tripp twisted around to glance through the study door. "So, in a way, that's the center of all her pain."

Despite myself, I stepped forward to get a better look. But I didn't go in. The wide desk sat almost in the center, on a braided rug. All the walls were lined with books, antiques and paperbacks piled together as if the owner didn't differentiate much. A family portrait hung opposite the desk. Silla must've been about eight when it was taken, and she looked pink and healthy in a fluffy white dress—like she'd been plucked out of some camera commercial. Reese seemed to smile against his will, like he resented having to stand still for so long. I guessed I would have, too, at that age. You know, if we'd had a family to take pictures of. Their dad had his hands on his wife's and daughter's shoulders. Nothing about him suggested he regularly delved into anything remotely esoteric. He looked exactly like a Latin teacher. And just as dorky as he had when I was a kid.

"Have you known Silla long enough to see any changes in her lately?" Ms. Tripp was right behind me.

I grabbed the doorknob and pulled the study door shut. Then I put my back to it, facing the counselor. "She's fine."

"She doesn't have to be sick or in trouble to need help, to need someone to talk to. There are a lot of things she might need."

"Are you even supposed to talk to me about this?" I couldn't help it: I crossed my arms.

Her thin brows drew down. "In some circumstances, Nick, it's necessary to reach out. Especially if I'm worried about one of my kids hurting herself."

I was saved from a defensive answer by Judy coming down the stairs. "So sorry, both of you. She's just zonked out completely."

"Thank you, Mrs. Fosgate," Ms. Tripp said. "I'm sure I'll have a chance to talk to her at school tomorrow."

"Yeah, me too," I cut in. "I'll just head out. Have her call me, will you, Judy, if she wakes up soon?"

"Are you sure you don't want some tea?"

"Totally." I smiled at her, hiding my unease as best I could.

"It was good to meet you, Nick," said Ms. Tripp. "If you

need anything, feel free to stop by my office. Or if you ever get worried. About anything."

"Sure . . ." I dragged the word out to let her know how unlikely it was that that would ever happen. "Later, Judy."

I showed myself out.

TWENTY-TWO

November 2, 1906

We use the bodies of the dead to live forever. This, as Philip says, is irony.

It is filthy business, and although we could pay someone money to dig up or steal a body for us, Philip believes, as with all things, that it is best to do our own dirty work. Like my cats—one must learn to sacrifice for the magic. So I went out with him to a cemetery and learned to exhume a coffin. We take bones and strip the flesh, then grind them up. We make a powder with cemetery mushrooms and ginger, of all things, and add pieces of our own hair and fingernails. Then three drops of blood for each potion.

I drank, my hands tight around the cup so that they did not shake and reveal to Philip how excited I was. It did not thrill him. As he drank, he scowled. I touched his face and said I was glad we could be together forever. That none of the dead missed their bones.

"It is wrong," he whispered. "Unnatural. But I have lived so long I am afraid to die now."

"I will not let you die, my Prospero."

He kissed me then, and told me in my ear that I make him feel everything is worth it. That I have brought the magic to life in him again.

In the morning, with my head against his shoulder, I asked how often we needed the bones.

"It will sustain us for three years, if we're lucky," he said. And he told me that once the Deacon used the bones of a fellow witch. That potion lasted three decades, and after taking it the Deacon had been able to will his flesh to split to reveal blood, and then will it whole again. His very touch became holy.

"When you die," I said to Philip, kissing his skin, "I will grind your bones and live forever."

TWENTY-THREE

SILLA

Monday morning brought the first real hint of cold autumn along with the sun. I waited at the front doors of school for Nick as long as I could. The first bell rang, echoing dully across the parking lot. I was feeling grumpy because Judy had told me that Ms. Tripp had come to the house while I was asleep, and Judy hadn't wanted to wake me up because she didn't think I should be forced to talk to the woman outside of school if I didn't want to. But Nick had stopped by at the same time, so I hadn't gotten to see him, either. *Plus* Reese had driven without me down to an antique and curio shop about two hours away to grab as many herbs and bunches of beeswax and ribbons and other odds and ends to use in the magic as he could find. I couldn't help being a little glad he hadn't found some stuff, since he hadn't taken me with him. We'd have to order it on the Internet.

Students streamed past me from the parking lot. I hadn't seen Wendy or Melissa, but they were both chronically late, especially when they drove in together. Eric, though, waved a little at me for the first time in months. I was too surprised to respond, so he probably wouldn't ever try it again. Had Wendy gotten around to asking him out? Or possibly they'd just hooked up at his party. God, how had I not thought to call and find out?

The sun climbed high enough to glare over the tops of the oaks surrounding the school. The second bell was going to ring at any second when finally Nick's convertible screamed into the lot. Even from fifty yards, I could see him slamming the gears into place and grabbing his bag with jerky motions. I nearly fled into the school, not sure I wanted to deal with him pissy. What was wrong? My own grumpiness melted away.

His elbows were like hammers as he jogged toward the building. He scraped a hand through his hair, fixing it back into place after what had obviously been a windy drive. He was grinding his jaw. "Nick?" I said tentatively.

"What?" he snapped, and then his whole face was flooded with regret. "Silla, I'm sorry."

"What's wrong?" I touched his hand.

He turned it over, weaving his fingers with mine. "My freaking stepmom is going to be here all damn day."

"Why?"

"She's talking to, like, all the English classes or something about what it's like to be a real live author."

"Sounds interesting."

"It'll be like—" He sighed. "You probably will like it. God *damn* it."

I giggled and wrapped my arms around his waist. "Nobody will think she's cooler than you."

"That's not—it's just—I know what she's really like. Cold and bitchy. I don't need people talking to me about her after she puts on her sophisticated, successful, NYC badass self. You know, the one who snagged my dad and all."

"Here, let me help." I tilted my face up and Nick pushed his lips against mine.

"That does help," he said against my mouth. He kissed harder and bent me back, arms around behind me for support. "Sorry I missed you yesterday," he said as we straightened again.

Tugging my sweater down over my hips where it had ridden up, I nodded. "Yeah, I wanted to chew Judy out for not waking me up."

"You were up late, she said?"

"Yeah, Reese and I tried to heal each other's hands. With moderate success." I held out my left palm. Next to the thin pink scar was Saturday's cut, scabbed over and looking more like it was a week old. "We were just too tired."

Nick skimmed his thumb over the cut. "I have some ideas about that."

Before I could ask about them, he patted his messenger bag. "I have the book. And some things to tell you."

The final bell rang.

"After school?" I backed toward the doors. "At rehearsal?"

"Lunch?"

"I promised Wendy I'd help her with her audition pieces."

"Okay, three-thirty it is, then. I might find you between classes for some more pick-me-ups." He swept in for a quick kiss.

"I hope so," I murmured just before we hurried down the hall in opposite directions.

NICHOLAS

It was worse than I expected.

Lilith swept in wearing a knee-length silk jacket with some sort of bright embroidery on the bell sleeves. Dramatic makeup, bloodred fingernails, and her eat-your-soul smile grabbed the attention of every single student in my class, and Mr. Alford was probably going to take the memory home with him for some alone time. I slumped down in my desk and stared up at the ceiling tiles.

SILLA

In second period, Nick's stepmother dropped a box onto Mrs. Sackville's desk and began pulling out novels. She looked like a movie star, with her wide sunglasses tucked into her hair and the long necklace hanging down to her waist. Her heels were at least four inches, and matched her fingernails. Sackville clasped her hands together and introduced Mary Pardee to the class, totally throwing me. Mary?

"Mrs. Pardee writes fiction under the name Tonia Eastlake, and three of her books have been optioned for movies. Just last year, *Murder in Silver* went into production. She's been writing since she was in high school, just like you! So let's give her our best attention, all right?"

Hands shot up immediately. Mrs. Pardee laughed, showing us perfect white teeth, and when she said, "Everyone will have a chance. I'm here all day," her voice was so rich and smooth I knew immediately why Nick hated her.

Wendy hissed for my attention and showed me the note scrawled in the margins of her textbook. *Nick's stepmom? Srsly?*

I nodded and shrugged. Wendy's eyes got wider, and she pursed her lips as if whistling silently. Pulling out a piece of scrap paper, I wrote, *He doesn't like her.*

Why?

Bitchy, he says.

Mom loves her books.

My dad called them tripe. Read one a couple years ago, the sex was totally ridiculous. It was nice to talk about something normal. *They did it on the floor.*

Oooo.

Yeah, the kitchen floor.

LOL. Wendy's hand paused, and she glanced at me with a little frown. *Ms. T asked me to stop by her office tdy.*

I pressed my lips together.

I don't know what she wants, Wendy wrote when I didn't respond.

She was at my house ystrdy.

Y?

Thinks I might kill myself.

Srsly?!?

Judy said Tripp wanted intervention yesterday.

When I shrugged, Wendy rolled her eyes. *What hpnd 2 hand?*

Rusty nail.

TETANUS!

S'okay. If we weren't going to have the energy to heal our hands, we'd have to stick to the spells that only needed a prick, or start cutting in less obvious places. I went for distraction. And I was dying to know. *Ask Eric out?*

Oh, GOD, yes. Dude is a fine kisser. You were holding out on me.

You weren't drunk, were you?

She tapped her pen on the desk and glared at me.

Sorry. Just thinking of kissing Eric makes me gag.

Good! Wendy smiled. *Mine.*

I was starting to write, *Did you see Stepmom's shoes?* when Mrs. Pardee mentioned the cemetery.

"It's an ideal setting for someone like me. So many old spirits, and the atmosphere—atmosphere is quite important to a writer. I can just barely see the whole thing from my bedroom window, and you know"—her voice lowered conspiratorially—"some nights I've seen lights out there, flickering like candles or lost, lonely ghosts." There were chuckles from my classmates, since we'd all grown up with that story. Mrs. Pardee's eyes scanned the classroom, and when she found me, she paused, letting her smile widen slightly.

Goose bumps rose on my forearms, and I clutched the pen tightly in my fingers.

NICHOLAS

Silla dumped a thick black textbook into her locker.

I brushed a hand down her back. "Hey, babe, how's it going?"

"Your stepmom is seriously creepy." Silla turned, closing the locker with her shoulder. I put my hands on either side of her, caging her in.

"Tell me about it."

"Do you think she knows what we're doing in the cemetery?"

"Maybe. What'd she say to you?"

"She was just talking about seeing lights and ghosts moving around at night. She looked at me. I didn't think she knew what I look like, Nick."

The bell rang. "We'll figure it out. If she does, she won't do anything here at school."

"You're right."

I caught her hand as she pushed off the locker wall to go. "Hey, what else is it?" Her fingers were cold, and her rings almost burned.

Her eyelids fluttered closed for a moment, and she sighed. "My counselor is really getting on my back. She's coming through my friends now. Wendy I trust, but what if she gets to Melissa or Beth? They'd totally tell her all the gossip and mean things they can think of."

"You mean Ms. Tripp?"

Silla's lip puckered out. She tugged away from me, crossing her arms around her stomach. "Yeah. Did she go after you, too? My freaking boyfriend?"

I smiled and took one slow step closer. Silla backed up, glancing down. "Your what?" I murmured.

"Don't be obnoxious," she said, slapping her palms against my chest. She avoided my eyes, but her lips were twitching as she held back a smile.

"I can't help it."

"I know." Silla rose up on her tiptoes and kissed me.

I breathed her in, thought of her surrounded by all those magical colored flowers, and said, "Silla, I have to talk to you about something important."

Her eyebrows rose. "Sure."

"It—"

"Aren't you late for class?"

Lilith's voice froze me in my tracks. It was joined by another: "Mr. Pardee, Miss Kennicot, it's two minutes past the bell."

Silla lowered down to her heels, eyes wide. We turned. There was Lilith standing beside the vice-principal, whose frown dripped off his face. He was carrying Lilith's box of novels. "Sorry," Silla said, and she bent down to grab her backpack off the tiles. I managed not to sneer at Lilith as Silla hurried away.

"You too, Mr. Pardee," the vice said.

"Enjoy class," Lilith added.

"Whatever," I called over my shoulder, ignoring the tingle of their eyes on my back.

SILLA

Wendy had to cancel on lunch to go see Ms. Tripp. I tried not to resent it, but it sure made me want to ignore the counselor all week. And Nick was forced into a lunch with his stepmother, so I couldn't spend it with him. What I really wanted to do was curl up in a bed and take another nap. So I slipped backstage in the auditorium, found the sofa from the set of *A Doll's House,* and fell asleep in an instant. I was late for Physics.

When school let out, I hurried to the parking lot to catch

Nick and let him know I needed to give Wendy a few minutes for her audition. He said he'd help the stage crew spray paint some background flats out in the football field. "I'll come find you when I'm done," I promised.

I found Wendy waiting in Mr. Stokes's classroom with all her sheet music spread across a couple of desks. "Hey," I said, sliding in near her. I relaxed into the familiar smell of chalk dust and turpentine. "Have you narrowed it down yet?"

She glanced up, and I only barely caught myself before frowning. It might have been the afternoon light pouring in through the wall of windows behind her, but Wendy looked odd. She smiled and shrugged. "That's what you're here for?"

"Yeah. Are you okay?"

"I'm fine!" Wendy laughed at me.

Nodding, I reached for the nearest pile of music. On top was "A New Life" from *Jekyll and Hyde*. One of Wendy's favorites to sing in the car. It suited her mezzo voice really well. "I hope this is on top because it's one of your first choices," I said.

"It sure is." Wendy watched me, one hand up to fiddle with the silver and red stars dangling from her ear. She didn't continue.

"Well . . ." I thought for a second. "They want one song and two monologues, right? So what monologues did Stokes suggest?"

She looked startled, but then leaned over to dig into her backpack. "Um, this one and this one," she declared as she pulled a folder out and opened it. Two photocopied monologues were tucked inside, already marked up with pink directions. "Queen Katharine from *Henry VIII* and this one from

CSI: Neverland." She smirked. "It's actually pretty funny. 'Nine-one-one, what's the emergency? You are being kidnapped by pirates?' "

I smiled. She was being ditzier than usual. "Why Katharine?"

"It's serious?"

"Duh. But it isn't that popular, is it?"

"Maybe that's a good reason to do it."

"I'd pick one of the younger queens, though. I mean—she's kind of mature."

"I can do it." Wendy pressed her lips together and stood. That was what was wrong: she wasn't wearing her lip gloss. Weird. But figuring it out made me feel a lot better. Stepping up onto the raised, carpeted stage at the front of Stokes's classroom, she held the sheet of paper out and began, "Alas, sir, in what have I offended you? What cause hath my behavior given to your displeasure, that thus you should proceed to put me off, and take your good grace from me?" Wendy's face fell into sorrow, and for a second I was impressed. It was a drastic shift. "Heaven witness," she continued in almost a whisper, "I have been to you a true and humble wife, at all times to your will conformable; ever in fear to kindle your dislike, yea, subject to your countenance, glad or sorry as I saw it inclined." Wendy sighed. "When was the hour I ever contradicted your desire . . . or made it not mine, too?" She stopped, staring at the words.

My laugh startled a frown out of her. "Okay, I'm convinced. That was really good."

Her eyebrows rose and she lifted her chin haughtily. "Of course it was."

It reminded me of Nick's stepmom, which made me think of Nick, of his hair-gel smell and the warmth of his fingers. *Focus!* I ordered myself. *On Wendy.* I tapped the sheet music on the desk. "So, with those, I think Lucy's song will work just fine. The only thing you might consider is something more dramatic, I guess? Though this one is really nice for your voice." I flipped "A New Life" over and saw "Your Daddy's Son" from *Ragtime* under it. "Ooooh—this is a good one, too." There was no response, so I glanced up. Wendy was staring at me, her eyes slightly narrower than usual and her hands hanging loose at her sides. The monologue had fallen to the carpet. "Wen?"

She stepped off the little stage. "Silla."

"What's wrong?" Had Ms. Tripp said something to her? Freaked her out enough that she was upset or nervous around me?

"Nothing."

"You seem . . . different."

"Do I?" She put on an exaggerated innocent face. Like we would in a pantomime.

She never tried to hide things from me. "What did Ms. Tripp say?"

"The counselor?" Wendy giggled. "She thinks you're utterly crazed."

Utterly crazed? It was like Wendy was barreling through generations of theater: Shakespeare, commedia dell'arte, Tennessee Williams psychodrama. "Maybe—maybe you should lie down."

Her body shifted: one shoulder drooping, head tilted, small pout on her lips. "I was thinking about your dad."

The wooden desk chair was suddenly hard and sharp. "My dad?"

Drifting to me, Wendy nodded. "Do you ever wonder what he was thinking in those last moments? About you? About your mother? About his past, maybe?"

"I don't think about it." My back was glued to the desk.

"Why not?"

"I just don't. Come on, Wendy, I don't want to talk about this. If you're done with me, I'll just go."

"I don't want you to go." Grabbing a chair, she swung it around and straddled it, despite her skirt. She leaned her elbows on the backrest and smiled. "I like you, Silla."

Without glittery pink lip gloss, and wearing that bemused expression, I barely recognized her. The windows flooded the room with light, but none of it was reflected in Wendy's eyes. Like she wasn't there. *No, oh, no.* I just knew, suddenly: Wendy's body, Wendy's lips and hands, but not Wendy. Not my friend. A shiver tickled at the small of my back, forcing me to sit straighter. I whispered, "You aren't Wendy."

Her lips parted, and we stared at each other for a moment while the world continued to move without us. Slowly, she smiled. Her shoulders pulled back and she slouched, sliding down in the desk until she lounged there like a lion. "Quick as light, just like your dad," she drawled.

My heart beat erratically, punching at my lungs as if they were pillows, so I could barely breathe.

She ran her hands through Wendy's hair, fluffing it out.

"Who are you?" I hated that my voice trembled.

"Just an old friend of your daddy's." The way she said it, teeth bared, made my stomach twist tighter.

I bit the inside of my lip, gathering my courage. "The Deacon."

"Ah!" Wendy's head fell back and she laughed. "No, never, not dear Arthur. You should be so lucky."

"Let her go—Wendy doesn't know anything."

Leaning forward onto the top of the desk she was sitting at, she folded Wendy's hands together as if in prayer. "I thought maybe I'd see if you'd told her anything, find out what the students are saying. But my guess now is you've told more to your boyfriend than your girlfriend."

"Anything about what?"

Wendy's lips twisted up on one side. "You know."

I shook my head. I was cold all over. "What do you want?"

"I want your dad's grave."

"You dug it up. You did that."

"I tried." The annoyance didn't sit well on Wendy's face. This thing, person, whatever it was inside her twisted Wendy's sweet, young features into a scowl. "But you did something to it."

"I don't know what you're talking about."

"Some warding, a protection spell so that I can't get to them without making them turn to ashes or some such thing. Whatever he told you to do, you're going to undo it." She waved a hand breezily. As if we were discussing place settings.

Slowly, unbelievingly, I shook my head. "Nothing. I didn't do anything."

The thing made Wendy sneer. "Yes, Drusilla, you did. I can feel your blood soaked into the ground like a poison."

"Good!" I spat it at her, wanting to strike with my hands, too, but I could only grip the sides of the desk as if letting go would send me spinning off into oblivion.

The thing in Wendy bent down and reached into her backpack. When her hand reappeared, a silver letter opener was clasped in her fist. "I picked this up off Mr. Edmer's desk. He left it right out in the open like that, in this day and age. Can you believe it?"

"Stop."

"Silla." Wendy's possessor raised the sharp point and placed it delicately against the soft flesh under Wendy's jaw. "If I want to, I'll jab this up into your friend's brain."

"You'll die." But I knew it couldn't be true. I thought about the possession charm, how easily Reese had possessed the crow. How easily it seemed this person was possessing Wendy. What happened to Wendy? Where was Wendy? Trapped?

"My body is close, darling. I'll just jump right on home."

"Like . . ." The realization hit as slowly as poured molasses. "Like you did when you killed my parents."

"Yes." She—it—snapped on a grin like the bite of a shark. "Tell me what you did."

"I didn't do anything, I swear. Just some spells there." The tip of the letter opener cut up into Wendy's neck. "Dad didn't teach me *anything*. He never . . ." I sucked a desperate breath in through my teeth, trying to stay calm. "He didn't teach me the magic. I only have the book."

Wendy's body stilled. She stared at me, unblinking. I could see nothing in her eyes. No spark, no personality. They were flat like a dead thing's eyes. "What book?" She enunciated like a vocal coach. Sharp *t*, sharper *k*.

I didn't answer right away. Part of me wanted to leap at her, disregarding the danger to Wendy. I drew myself up. I had power, too, since I had what she wanted. "Trade. Answer for answer." I found a mask for courage: a red dragon face, long and snarling.

"I have your friend's life in my hands, girl. And if I kill her, you'll be blamed." The smile snaking across Wendy's face made my stomach roll over.

"Just tell me your name, and I'll tell you the book's name."

Wendy's fingernails drummed once on the back of her chair. "You do have guts. I like that. Josephine. My name is Josephine Darly."

Imagining the words hissing through razor teeth, I said, *"Notes on Transformation and Transcendence."*

"Oh, that sounds just like him!" Wendy laughed. "What is it?"

"Why do you want it?"

"No, I know what it is. His spell book. That old thing he was always putting his finished spells into. I thought it died in the fire."

I didn't let myself ask about the fire. I couldn't waste a question. "It's filled with spells. Powerful spells. Why do you want it? Clearly you can—you can use the spells already." I needed a weapon. Stokes's desk had some heavy books on it, but they were too far away. All I had in front of me were slips of loose-leaf paper. My pocketknife was barred from school grounds.

"Silla." She pressed the point in again, puckering Wendy's skin. "Don't be coy."

I opened my mouth, closed it, and stared at the thin trickle of blood slipping down Wendy's neck. "I don't have it."

"Who does?"

"I'm not telling you."

"Where did you hide it? I searched your house before I killed them, and it was not there."

An image of my dad's body, possessed, lurching around our house, digging through our things, with this monster's soul looking out through his eyes, broke something in me. "I will *not* tell you!" I yelled, and jerked forward, grabbing at the letter opener and knocking both of us to the floor. The desks crashed down around us, and Wendy's head smacked back. She yelped. I seized her wrist with both hands, forcing the blade back with all my weight. "Leave her alone!"

"Tell me where—the spell book—is," Wendy ground out, teeth clenched as she fought me for the letter opener.

"No."

She relaxed suddenly, and I tumbled forward with a little shriek. The letter opener hit the floor with a clang, and Wendy crawled away from me, scuttling back on her hands and feet. I sat on the floor cradling the blade and panting.

Silence reigned in Stokes's classroom. My head ached again, like the pain had only been waiting for a moment of weakness to come roaring back.

"Silla," Wendy finally said, "help me, and I'll teach you to live forever."

Here was what I'd wanted most the past week: someone to teach me. Someone to answer my questions and show me the depths and heights of the magic. I imagined sitting across the kitchen table from her, poring over the spell book, excitement and wonder electric between us. But she was the one person in all the world I could never, ever accept. "Why did you kill my dad?"

"More quid pro quo?" She brushed hair back from Wendy's face and met my eyes. "He made me his enemy, Silla. Don't think for a moment he was a good person. He killed and he lied. He lied a lot."

"No."

Wendy's hand reached out. "Come with me. I'll teach you to be everything you have the potential to be, Silla. Think of the power, the magic."

I swallowed. My fist tightened around the letter opener.

She smiled, and still there was nothing behind Wendy's eyes. "I can teach you to live forever. With your father's bones—"

"His *bones*!" That was why she wanted the grave. I got to my feet, brandishing the letter opener like a sword.

"Essential ingredients, my darling."

"You can't have them."

"Why protect him? It is because of him that your mother is dead," she sneered.

"You killed my mother. Not Dad." My voice lowered. The urge to fling myself at her, to attack, made my bones shake.

"You did. Get away, go away. Leave. Us. Alone." I stood over Wendy, the letter opener shining in the afternoon light.

"Give me the spell book, and I'll consider it."

"No." The letter opener shook in my hand as Wendy climbed to her feet and offered me a wide grin.

"I can take more away from you, Silla, dearest."

I didn't—couldn't—say anything. I'd find a way to protect Reese and Judy. And everyone.

Her grin slowly fell away. "I bet . . . I bet your boyfriend knows."

Before I could react, she leapt up and bowled into me. Her shoulder hit me, and I went down, crashing back into a desk. I slammed into the floor, cracking my tailbone and the back of my ribs against the edge of the desk. For a moment, I sat there, barely breathing as my vision blackened and then returned and my brain wailed at all the jarring.

Josephine was gone, along with Wendy's body. Where did she go?

I threw myself to my feet. Whirled around the empty room.

Nick. She'd gone after Nick.

TWENTY-FOUR

June 13, 1937

    So many years since I left Boston, where this old book slept in the library amongst tomes of forgotten lore and poetry of the last century.

    Does it matter what I have done, and where I have lived between then and now?

    Philip would say that it does. That I should remember, though I say to myself, How could I ever forget?

    It was the Great War that drew us away from Boston.

    The aftermath, the devastation in Europe called to my Prospero like a haunting ghost, keeping him from sleep until I agreed to cross the ocean with him.

    Once there, I found solace in society, while Philip preferred the low streets, the towns and villages devastated. In the cities, where many had nothing, a few had enough to drown their sorrows in dancing and drink. We moved through London and Edinburgh, and on into France, where I found my home in Paris.

    Oh, how I remember the nights I have made Philip forget—with dancing and theater and the company of the finest in Europe. I excel at gathering a crowd to me, and Philip is so quiet, so handsome and gentle, that it is impossible not to adore him. He found joy in running off to meetings on science and philosophy, while I held delightful séances to entertain those more interested in the esoteric realms of nature. We came back to each other in whatever flat or house I'd bought with transmuted gold, and he regaled me with all the ideas battering his head—I listened, and loved him all the more for the passionate glow in his cheeks, for the way knowledge lights up in him. All night we might spend talking of theories and imagining the great potential of our blood. Philip sees it still as a privilege, a responsibility, while I view it as a gift. It makes us stronger, better, capable of anything. Most often our arguing transmutes into laughter or love as readily as granite into gold.

How happy I am! When he calls my name, it thrills me, and our charms are never as keen as when we create them together, blood with blood. The only shadow falling over my joy is that he refuses to wed me, after all these years. It is the one thing he is more than willing to lie about, and when I ask again why, with all his morality and strict ethical views, he does not care that we live as husband and wife but are not so.

"Josephine," he invariably says, "one day you will tire of me, and if I marry you, you will be trapped."

"That is the thing for which divorces were made, darling," I reply, though only because he does not believe any protestations of mine that I shall never tire of him in a thousand years.

"You know the power of rituals. They are not so easy to undo with pen and paper and a legion of lawyers."

"But I love you."

He kisses me. "And I love you."

I believe him, and that is why tomorrow we leave Boston again in our new Tin Lizzie and travel west into the state of Kansas, where the

Deacon has carved himself land among the flint hills. He sent word to Philip that he wishes, finally, to meet me and to share with Philip some new method of cooking medicine. Kansas! I do not have high hopes for the society there, and wonder why the Deacon chose it.

My time in Europe seems but a dream now, perhaps because I did not take my book, and did not write things as they happened. I will tuck this into my bag, for all those years ago my Philip was correct: to write memory is the only sure way to preserve it.

TWENTY-FIVE

NICHOLAS

I caught myself whistling as I slathered paint onto a circular-cut piece of plywood. The paint was purple, and I had no clue what it was eventually going to be. But I didn't care. The late afternoon was warm, and starting to get that weird golden glow we totally lacked in Chicago. I didn't know if it was about different pollution or the lack of reflective steel skyscrapers, but I kind of liked it. It made the leaves thicker and puffier as they changed for the autumn, instead of just brown and dead. Leaning back on my heels, I contemplated the ridge of trees and the way the sky behind them was so pale a blue it was almost silver. Had I ever noticed that kind of thing before?

A few yards off, the other crew guys hammered away at what I think was going to be a platform, and I was glad to be on my own. Wind blew over the trees, and the leaves moved in a long wave like dorks at a football game. And that's when I realized I was whistling.

It wasn't any tune in particular, and probably pretty off pitch. But that didn't change the fact that my lips were pursed and noise was coming out of them. I stopped. In the silence around me, I heard the laughter of the rest of the crew swell, and the roar of a car engine. Over on the soccer field, the football team was grunting in a weird staccato pattern. Probably beating each other up.

And I was whistling.

Because of Silla.

As soon as she got here, I'd tell her about my mom, about the lacquered box, the magic I used to do—I'd show her something beautiful, and watch her face light up. I'd kiss her, and we'd go home to make the amulets with her brother, and then for a long walk. Something really romantic, like girls wanted. Out to the meadow behind my house, the one next to the cemetery wall. I'd spread out a blanket. Steal a bottle of wine from Lilith, if I could convince Silla to drink it. Grab some dark chocolate and we'd have a real picnic, alone out here. All night, if I could help it.

> *Kisses offered up*
> *Like leaves turning red as blood*
> *Red as tongues and hearts*

I needed to write that one down, despite the lack of rhyming. Turning around, I saw my messenger bag lying wide open in the grass. I stood and walked toward it. A crow cawed behind me, landing in one of the trees so hard it startled a flock of little birds up into the sky, where they flew around like crazy confetti. My neck tingled with that you're-being-watched sensation. Glancing back at the school, I realized Lilith's Jeep was still lording it over the parking lot. What the hell was she still doing around? I sighed in disgust just as the rear doors of the building flew open and Wendy, Silla's friend, came running out toward me. "Nick!"

Straightening, I frowned. She pelted toward me as if her life depended on it.

Silla. There had to be something wrong with—

I ran. "Where's Silla?"

"Do you have the book?"

"The book? The . . ." I slowed my pace as I approached her. "Where's Silla?"

"She's inside." Wendy panted, but managed a fast smile. Her hair was all over the place. "She's fine. Just wants me to bring her the spell book."

"Why?"

The rear doors slammed open again, and Silla came running, too. Desperation in every step. I looked back at Wendy. Her expression hardly moved. But her lips tightened.

I stepped back.

"Nick," Silla yelled, halfway to us. "It isn't Wendy. It isn't—"

Wendy leaned away, then out of nowhere punched me in the mouth. The pain detonated across my skull and I tasted blood. Stumbling back, I touched my lips. Wendy whirled and ran past me toward my bag.

"No!" Silla grabbed at Wendy's hair, but it slipped through her fingers. I ran with them, catching up in three long strides and snatching Wendy's arm. She tried to tear her hand from me, but I jerked her around. She bared her teeth like a wolf and snarled, "Let go!"

"It isn't Wendy," Silla gasped again.

Wendy's body kicked out at me, but I held her away. I smeared my free hand across my bloody mouth and then slapped it onto her forehead. "I banish thee from this body," I said, willing it to be true. The power rushed through my hand, burning my palm. *A stranger's face, angry before mine: "I banish thee," he snarls.*

She collapsed like a pile of sticks.

"Wendy!" Silla knelt beside her friend's body, but Wendy's eyes didn't open. She was breathing, though, calmly, like she'd fainted.

It was totally silent. Even the hammering had stopped. I glanced over to see the handful of crew guys standing and staring, tools lowered to their sides and mouths hanging open.

God, I hoped they hadn't heard what we'd said.

A crow shrieked from the edge of the forest. Followed by another.

"Nicholas."

I looked at Silla. She sat with Wendy's head in her lap. "How did you do that?" Her wide eyes reflected the expansive sky. "That wasn't in the book."

Improvisation, I could have said. Or *inspiration.* But looking at her eyes, I couldn't lie again. "My mother taught me." It wasn't as romantic a moment as I'd been hoping for. My voice was low and flat. This was going to go very badly.

It was amazing how her face changed. One moment raw with emotion, and the next turned hard and still.

The crows cackled again. They lifted out of the trees and flew toward us. Silla's gaze darted at them, but I couldn't stop staring at her. She climbed to her feet and slowly bent to pick up my messenger bag. Lifting it high, she yelled at the crows, "I have it! Here. Come and get me!" And without wasting another look on me, she ran back toward the parking lot.

I ran after her. "Silla, wait! My car."

She completely ignored me. I caught up, reached out, and grasped at her elbow. "Silla, stop."

Whirling, she tore loose. "Let me go!" Her eyes narrowed, and they flicked behind me. "They're coming. I have to get them away from Wendy."

"Come to my car, we'll get out of . . ." I touched her elbow again.

"How do I know you aren't possessed?" Silla jerked back from me. Her eyes looked behind me again, and stayed there.

I turned my head, saw the crows were staring. Just watching us with their heads cocked. Some of them wobbled dizzily, like they didn't know what was happening. "Ask me anything," I said, turned back to Silla.

"Maybe you've always been someone else."

The quiet accusation slammed into my chest. "Silla," I whispered, unable to dredge up more voice than that.

She pushed her lips together and spun on her heels. But her steps didn't pick up. "She could possess anyone in the school," she said. Her fingers tightened around the strap of my messenger bag. "I have to keep her away from Wendy. From everybody. From the spell book."

"Let—let me drive you home," I said.

Slowly, she nodded. Then she glanced back through the cloud of crows spread across the grass to Wendy, who was slowly sitting up, surrounded by a couple of guys from the theater crew. Silla's lips pressed together again, and she made fists. "Let's go."

The crows didn't fly after us. They didn't have to. Whoever was possessing them, or had possessed Wendy, knew we had the spell book and exactly where we were going.

So I didn't head for Silla's house.

She scanned the trees, the fields, the road, the sky. Because the bad guy could be anywhere. In any of the birds, in those cows we were passing, or that dog—in anything. I gripped the wheel and drove. Wind tore at us as I pushed the convertible faster and faster. At least I knew I was me.

It was only a few minutes before Silla said, "This isn't the way to my house." She shrank away from me, pressing herself as far into the side door as she could. "Stop the car!"

I shook my head, but didn't look at her. "He knows where you're going. He could be waiting there. We can't walk right into his hands."

"Or she's hurting my brother, or Judy. Take. Me. Home."

"No."

"You're kidnapping me?" A gust of wind jerked her words away.

"No!"

"That's what this feels like. Stop the car."

"Silla—"

Before I could finish, she unfastened her seat belt and reached for the door.

I hit the brakes. The car swerved and Silla slammed forward, catching herself with her hands against the dashboard.

The world spun, and I was being torn in twelve directions at once. Then—we stopped.

I was shaking. The car was shaking. But the road and the fields were firmly fixed in place.

Slowly, I took my foot off the brake. It weighed a ton. The back wheels dipped off the asphalt and onto the gravelly shoulder. I breathed again. "Silla?" I said, just as she opened the door and fell out.

I heard her scrambling up as I turned off the car and climbed out, too. "Wait!" I dashed around after her as she stumbled down into the ditch and up the other side into a field of harvested corn. My bag still slung over her back.

My combat boots dug into the damp grass, but once I was on level ground with her, it was easy to catch up. "Silla," I called again, from just a couple of feet behind her.

Silla spun, swinging my bag at me, and smashed it into my gut.

All the air slammed out of me and I bent over. "Christ," I hissed when I could gulp in some breath. Thank God it hadn't been a little lower.

"You lied to me."

Straightening, I met her glare. "I was going to tell you."

"Right! That's so lame, Nick." Her lips pulled into a frown, tipping from anger into hurt.

"I was—I told you I had something important to talk about."

"Conveniently."

"Look, it was just bad timing, okay?"

"I can't trust you." She stepped back, her face sliding back into stillness.

I ignored the grinding in my chest and held out my hands. "What was I supposed to say? It's magic. A secret. You don't just go around talking about it."

"But you saw me doing it. You knew. And you did it with us. Come on, you had so, so, so many chances." She crossed her fists over her stomach. "Like Friday night. After we . . . Or Saturday in the cemetery."

"I—"

"We've just been screwing around, guessing, trying our best with the slightest information, and you've known the whole time! How could you just go along like you were new to it?"

"Silla—"

She shook her head. "Why should I trust you? How can I?"

I stepped forward and grabbed her. *"Listen."*

Silence. She was stiff in my hands, but watched me. Her hair spiked up crazily from all the wind, and her cheeks were flushed.

Licking my lips, I released her slowly. "I hated the magic. I didn't want to think about it, much less talk about it."

Nothing.

"And I didn't remember everything. Not clearly. My mom—you know she didn't stick around. And when we did it together . . . I was young. Before my eighth birthday, okay?"

"But you recognized it." Her voice was quiet. Her eyes lowered from mine. Settled on my lips. Then she closed them. As if expecting my answer to be too painful.

I didn't want her bracing herself from me. Withdrawing. "Don't do that."

Her eyes flew open. "Do what?" She tugged away from me.

"Hide. That thing you do, like when you're onstage. The masquerade."

"I'm not hiding. I'm—I'm coping. I'm surviving. Getting through the worst thing that's ever happened to me. I'm sorry if you don't like my methods, Nick." My name spat off her tongue.

"Don't be a bitch, either."

Silla turned and stomped away.

"That's hiding, too!" My mouth curled into a snarl.

She paused, turned back, and came at me. "What do you want from me? You lied to me, and now you're attacking me? Fine. Go ahead. I can take it. I can take a whole lot." Her fists pushed hard into her stomach.

"Maybe it isn't about you, Silla. Maybe it's about me."

"Really? My parents being murdered by some psycho body stealer has anything to do with you? How so?"

"What?"

"*What* what?"

"Murder? You think your parents were murdered by someone doing the magic? I didn't know you thought that. Nice thing to leave out, speaking of lies. 'By the way, *dear Nick,* this person chasing us might *be a murderer?* How long have you known? How long have you been keeping that a secret?"

Silla's mouth snapped shut. Her knees bent, and she just plopped down on her ass, dragged her legs up, and wrapped her hands around her shins. I stared down at her, panting like I'd run a marathon.

"You're right," she said in a monotone. Toward my toes. "It was dangerous for you not to know. For me to involve you without telling you the possible stakes."

I crouched.

"If you thought it was just a game, or just fun, and then you got hurt, or . . ." She squeezed her eyes closed. "I'm sorry."

"Remember I told you my mom tried to kill herself?"

"Yes."

"She slit her wrists. To get rid of her blood."

Silla's head rose just enough to meet my eyes. "Oh." I could see the realization in her face, that she knew what Mom's suicide attempt meant.

"My grandfather told her she was evil. That the magic was evil."

"Why?"

"I don't know." I sank down to sit in front of her. "I don't remember, but I think I should."

We stared at each other for a moment.

I said, "I wasn't lying about not remembering it all. What I did remember was . . . tainted. Because even though it had been fun at first, it all led to my mom trying to kill herself and get high to dilute the power. I even wonder if she put a spell on me to make me forget. Because it just all came crashing back on Saturday, after I saw you and Reese doing the possession. My mom could do that. And she taught me to do it."

"You didn't know if you could trust *me*," Silla whispered. "If I was—was evil, too. Or using it for evil purposes."

"Yeah."

She nodded clumsily. "I get that."

"I also think . . ." I hesitated.

Her eyebrows rose a little.

I cleared my throat. "My mom might have done something wrong, but I went through your dad's book and there isn't even the slightest curse or negative magic. It's all healing, protection, transformation. I think your dad was good."

And just like that she was crying.

I felt a little like That Guy who holds a baby at arm's length because he's afraid it's going to pee on him.

Her hands pressed to her face and she made actual sounds. Like, sobs. And sniffing. It was all muffled, though, as she hunched down, bending over herself and becoming this tiny ball. Her shoulders shook. I touched the top of her head. Just gently, not sure she wanted real comfort or my arm around her.

It didn't last long. Only a few moments, while the corn moved all around us in dry ocean waves.

Sniffing hugely, Silla sat up. She wiped at her cheeks and eyes, and muttered "Sorry" several times. I just waited. Offered my sleeve. She smiled a tremulous smile and shook her head. "I'm okay. God, I'm sorry."

"Don't worry about it. Feel better?" I'd heard that crying really helped some people.

"Ugh." Sniff. "No. Not at all. I feel like my brain turned to snot and cotton balls."

"That's how you look, too," I said. Very seriously.

It got a laugh from her. "God, don't make me laugh. It hurts." She pushed the butts of her hands into her eyes.

So I waited another moment while she gathered herself up.

"I've been afraid, you know?" she said to her hands, now

folded in her lap. "That he deserved it. That he brought this upon us. And the woman who killed them told me that he was a liar and a horrible person. That Dad betrayed her. And it's what everyone says."

"They're wrong."

She took a huge breath and held it, then let it hiss out slowly. Blotches of pink stained her face, and her eyes were puffy. Good thing I wasn't a mirror. Her eyes widened. "Oh my God, I need to call Reese," she said. "Warn him, get him home. But I . . . I left my backpack at school."

"My cell's in my bag." I touched her knuckle. "I'll take you wherever you need to go."

TWENTY-SIX

SILLA

My breath rattled up my throat, sounding like the wind through the brown cornstalks behind me. Shaky, dry, and empty.

I closed my eyes, felt the weak sunlight against the back of my neck, the hard twigs of grass under my butt. A distant crow called, and my stomach tightened.

I dialed Reese's number on Nick's cell, and watched the display until it began ringing.

Please be Reese. Please be my brother.

On the fifth ring he picked up. "Yeah?"

"Hey, it's Silla."

"You've been crying, bumblebee."

Relief like cool rain poured over me. It was him. "I'm okay. I need you to go home. The person who killed Dad and Mom is definitely still around. Her name is Josephine Darly, and she possessed Wendy today and tried to steal the spell book. I'm afraid of what she'll try next. We need to talk, and to find a way to protect ourselves."

Reese didn't say anything for a moment. I could hear the

roar of a tractor and yelled conversation faintly in the background. Then he said, "We can try the protection charms in the spell book. Is Nick with you? Do you have the book?"

"Yes."

"We'll have to go through it and look for—" He stopped, then whispered, "Look, I can't talk about this here. I'll head home."

"I hate that the important ones are the complicated ones. Why can't we just bleed on each other and voila?" I tried to make my tone light, to insert some levity, but it fell flat.

"Yeah."

"I'll see you at home."

"Be careful, Silla."

"You too."

Reese hung up.

Nick, on the other side of the ditch, climbed into the convertible and pulled it all the way off the road. As I watched him, the twist in my stomach slowly relaxed. He moved like an awkward marionette as he climbed out of the car, and it was easy to imagine someone else manipulating the strings. But I didn't believe it. The sun caught some surprisingly bright auburn highlights in his hair, and I wondered if he even knew they were there. I wished I could forget Josephine and my parents, forget the magic, possession, blood, all of it, and just draw Nick back up here so that I could run my fingers through his hair and find more colors.

Instead I dialed Wendy's number. Went straight to voice mail. Her voice, peppy and bright, declared, "Hiya, you've almost reached Wendy—leave a message!"

"Hey, it's—it's Silla. I wanted to make sure you're okay. I flaked, I know. It was just . . ." I licked my lips and then lied, "Um, the blood. I lost it, you know. The blood." My voice fell to a whisper. "Anyway. I know you're okay, but I don't have my cell. You can call the house or something. Or this—it's Nick's phone. Sorry."

Before I babbled for another twenty minutes, I snapped the phone shut. Wendy would believe me. I'd been so stupidly delicate about blood and everything lately, it wouldn't be a stretch.

I shoved to my feet, head pounding with gentle but constant waves in time with my heartbeat. God, I hated crying like that. I didn't feel right again for days. And doing it in front of anyone who wasn't my mom . . . who, of course, would never care if I cried or not again . . . I stopped, closed my eyes, and took a long breath. I had to calm down. So much had happened in just an hour. Less than an hour. I could be steady. I could be fine.

The calm, sea-green mask settled into its place. As Nick got out and moved around to the trunk, popping it with his key, I thought about what he'd said. That I was hiding behind masks. Maybe he was right about the silver and white one. It was cold and meant to be empty. But this one, or the sky and sun mask for joy, so many of the others, they were just part of who I was.

After a final steadying breath, I walked to the car. Nick pulled a box out of the trunk. He tucked it under one arm and slammed the trunk shut, then placed the box on top of it.

"What's that?" I leaned my hip into the taillight, touching

one finger to the lovely glossed finish of the box. Black crows were inlaid in the lid, against a purple sky.

"My mom's magic box," he said, pushing aside the broken lock and opening it.

I gasped, despite myself, at the contents. Tiny glass jars filled with differently colored powders and flakes of dry plants, seeds, metal filings, a feather quill, little slips of paper, ribbon. Wax. "Nick," I breathed.

He pulled out a jar. The glass was thin and cloudy, with a cork stopper. The jar was labeled *blessed thistle*. In Dad's handwriting.

"Nick!" I took it, caressed the curling paper glued to the bottle. "My dad wrote this."

Tugging at his bag, which hung off my shoulder, he dug in for the spell book. Flipping it open, he held up a page and compared. It was perfectly, obviously Dad's writing. "They must have shared it," he said. He glanced up at my face.

"Judy said they dated in high school." If my cheeks hadn't already been blotchy from crying, I'd probably have blushed.

Nick set the book on the car and rubbed his face. "Jesus, this is complicated."

I leaned into him, putting my cheek against his. "Yeah," I whispered. "Let's get home."

TWENTY-SEVEN

September 1937

The Deacon! What a man — what a creature.

He is simple, and as young and beautiful as an angel — a demon. When he says our power comes from Devil's blood, it only makes sense to believe him. The Deacon could charm his way into a priest's pants if he wanted. But he doesn't — that is what makes him so strange to me. So strange and wonderful. He doesn't use his charm to lie to or trick others. He just . . . is. Just as a storm seems like rage and desperation and need but is only wind and rain, not caring how you respond to it. The Deacon is a living part of nature.

Philip immerses himself in this new experimenting of theirs. Drugs and aromas to cure ailments. Boring things. I watch the Deacon and wonder how he became what he is. He looked up at me this morning and smiled. In his eyes was something I had never seen in Philip's.

Challenge.

While Philip dripped tinctures from one test tube into another, the Deacon asked me to venture into the wilderness with him, into the tall prairie grasses, with the promise of new magics for me.

And oh, I am ever so glad that I accepted. He has opened my mind!

I never imagined I could possess a flock of geese as they alit upon a lake, or possess a tree—a tree! Oh my soul. I can hardly put into words what it was like coursing through roots and up into the highest reaches of leaves, waving like hair in the wind. Endless power, endless peace, I think. The Deacon says it is the feeling of God.

But peace does not entertain me for long. I prefer running with the coyotes or cutting through the sky with the eagles. With the Deacon at my side, I hunted. I killed, and felt the charge of filling my stomach with flesh ruined by my own claws.

So long ago, Philip taught me that to possess was to dance with dangerous temptation. There is no temptation here, for I do not resist the wildness, the danger. I am the whole world.

TWENTY-EIGHT

NICHOLAS

As I drove, I told Silla what I remembered about my mom, and about the slippery memory where Mom had said we were going to save Robbie Kennicot. Silla told me about the grave desecration and the letter from some guy named Deacon, who'd sent her the spell book.

"Hang on," I stopped her, just as I turned up our mutual street. "Friday night, the night of the party—that's when Josephine tried to get at your dad's bones?"

"Had to have been."

"Holy shit." Gardening boots. Muddy gardening boots when the ground was too cold for gardening.

"What, Nick?" Silla touched my arm.

I shook my head. So many pieces fell into place. I had to focus on not scratching the Sebring's paint on the gate when I turned onto the gravel driveway. When I'd parked, I swung to face her. "Lilith."

Silla waited.

"I tripped over her muddy boots when I got home Friday night. And your folks died in July, right? She was here doing remodeling. And she was at school today." It was like the whole world was folding in around me. I hated Lilith, but I hadn't really thought she was a *murderer.*

Silla put her hands on my face. "Nick. Nick." She kissed me, just smooshing her mouth against mine.

Everything fell back into place. I mirrored her gesture, holding her face in my hands. Our kiss broke apart, and we leaned our foreheads together.

"Let's go inside, Nick, and we'll talk it through. We'll figure it out."

Half my mouth turned up in a smile. In just a short time, I'd gone from comforter to comfortee. "Okay, babe."

Just as I climbed out, Reese's truck pulled into the driveway. I shut my door and was turning to say hi to Reese when Silla screamed.

Wings flashed in my face and pain shot across my forehead as a little bird raked at my eyes. I ducked down, batting at the bird, and started to run around the car. "Silla! The house!" I could just make her out, flailing against a half dozen blue jays. They made awful croaking noises, and screeched. Little claws jabbed at my neck. I spun. They tore at my hands, pecking and trying to land on my head. They were everywhere. A cloud of them.

I ran. I blacked out suddenly, like a giant blink, and then was still running, tripped and caught myself with my hands, and—

SILLA

The birds reared back as one, and I had a moment to breathe. "Nick!" I looked all around. One of his hands fished into his messenger bag and pulled out the book. A twisted smile spread across his face. *No, oh, no.*

I darted for Nick, and just as I was there, reaching out, his face contorted and he slumped to his knees. The blue jays screamed, and a huge weight of them crashed into my back, tearing through my T-shirt. I wheeled my arms for balance, spinning to bat the birds away as painful heat blossomed through my body.

A roar from Reese's throat sounded like a war cry. He held a shovel and a plastic trash can lid. With the shovel, he slapped the birds out of the sky, and he used the lid like a shield. I fell next to Nick, who was struggling to stand. The spell book lay open, facedown on the gravel, pages bent. I grabbed it, and Nick grabbed my arm. "I'm okay," he said quickly. We got up and lurched to Reese.

"Behind me!" Reese bellowed, swinging his shovel in a huge arc. The *thwack* as he connected made my stomach churn, again and again. We backed up toward the house. Judy flung the door open for us. Nick and I nearly tripped up the porch steps, but Reese was firm and calm. The moment we were inside, Reese dropped the shovel and slammed the door.

NICHOLAS

Judy took Silla upstairs so that she could get some bandages on her back and change shirts. I leaned against the counter beside Reese, waiting for my turn with the nurse. Reese didn't say anything, and I wasn't inclined to, either. I kept my eyes closed and my jaw clenched against the sting from the cuts on my neck and hands, remembering what it had felt like for that long moment I'd been possessed. Disorientation. Numbness. Like being paralyzed, or in a weird waking coma. But I'd felt the second her grip had loosened—triumph at holding the spell book had disrupted her hold on me, and I'd pushed free.

But I didn't know if I could do it again. I shuddered.

Reese stood abruptly. "I'll be right back." He strode to the front door and grabbed the shovel.

"Hang on, what are you doing?"

"You dropped the spell book. We've gotta have it."

Standing, I dug my car keys out of my jeans. "I'll go. You cover me. There's something in my trunk we need, too."

On the count of three, we flung open the door and ran out. I skidded in the gravel, catching myself painfully on one hand, and picked up the spell book. I realized Reese wasn't swinging, and all the birds were gone. The sky was empty. Not a leaf fluttered, and there wasn't a sound disturbing the afternoon. "I hate this," I muttered, jamming the key into the trunk.

Reese grunted. He continued moving around, half crouched in a batter's stance, with the shovel gripped tight. When I had the box under one arm, and the book in the other hand, I nodded, slammed the trunk closed, and then we were back in the house, having only been gone about two minutes.

We collapsed at the kitchen table, box and spell book between us. My messenger bag swung from the back of my chair.

After a moment, Reese abruptly stood again and went to the counter. I just closed my eyes and didn't open them until I heard the *thunk* of a mug hitting the table. I smelled coffee. "Oh, God." Wrapping my sore hands around the hot drink, I inhaled.

Reese pulled out the chair next to mine and held his coffee in his lap.

"Reese," I began. He flicked his eyes at me. Unconcerned. "I've always known about the magic."

He just freaking blinked. Then some tiny change in expression darkened his whole face. Kind of like one of my dad's nonreactions.

"My mom did it, and taught some of it to me when I was a kid."

His jaw muscles tightened and then released. I think he relaxed them deliberately. Setting his coffee down, he splayed his hands on the table and slid them toward me. Glaring. "Your mom did it."

"Yeah."

"Seriously."

"Yeah."

"And you just . . . pretended not to know."

"It was the safest thing to do."

He leaned forward, the chair creaking under him like an echoed threat. Before he opened his mouth again, I said, "Look, it was my decision not to say anything, and I'm not going to feel guilty about it, so get over it."

"Does Silla know?" His voice was so low.

"Yes. She just found out. And she told me about your parents and—and everything." I wanted to add something about getting what it felt like, but was pretty damn sure Reese wasn't feeling the bonding.

"Okay." He sat back, letting breath hiss out through his teeth. "Apparently, we all have a lot to talk about."

"I'll, uh, go get Silla." I forced myself not to move too quickly, but yeah, I was totally fleeing. I couldn't tell if he was relaxing for real or just biding his time until he could punch me. Whichever, I wanted Silla there as a witness.

SILLA

"Whew! Wasn't that exciting?" Judy buzzed into the bathroom and jerked open the mirrored cabinet. Her hands flapped around like if she was still she'd pass out. "Crazy birds! Must be a storm coming, or maybe there was a slight earthquake or something that we couldn't even feel. Birds are sensitive to those kinds of harmonies, you know."

I plunked down on the toilet seat, holding my hands out. The tiny scrapes glistened. Judy crouched in front of me with a cardboard box of Band-Aids, a washcloth, cotton balls, and the bottle of hydrogen peroxide. She wet the washcloth in the sink, and wiped at my neck. I winced, though it didn't really hurt. "Yeah. Crazy birds," I whispered.

"You okay, honey?" Gram Judy paused.

"No." I stared down at her face. What did I know about her? Only what she'd told me. Like I'd said to Nick, she could have always been another person. She showed up right after Mom and Dad died, and we only vaguely remembered her. Not enough to know if her personality had changed.

My stomach flipped, and I slid off the toilet in case I needed to use it.

"There, there, honey." Judy rubbed her hand in circles on my back. "There, there. Did something else happen? What's wrong?"

Pressing my forehead into the cold porcelain of the toilet lid, I just shook my head. But I couldn't let this beat me. I wouldn't be able to function if everybody was the bad guy. It couldn't be Gram. Why would she have bided her time like this? She could have murdered us in our sleep anytime she'd wanted to.

The thought was oddly comforting. I sighed and twisted so that I was curled on the tile floor between the toilet and the sink. I offered Judy my hands, and she began washing them with her cloth, eyes lowered. The pinch of her lips let me know she wasn't going to give up.

I bit my lip against the sting of peroxide when she began dabbing it on the cuts with a cotton ball. Like cold water, it woke me up enough that I asked, "Judy, do you remember anything else about Nick's mom? Anything . . . weird?"

Sitting back on her heels, Judy kept my hands folded in hers and cocked her head thoughtfully. Her silver hair was bound up in a single braid, and it swung heavily, the tip just brushing the tiles. "It was, God"—Judy frowned and glanced up at the ceiling—"a year, maybe, since I'd married Douglas. His mama, what was her name? Daisy?"

"Donna," I whispered.

"Yes, that's right. She and Robbie had been going out for a while before I arrived, but they broke it off rather suddenly at the beginning of their senior year. Doug and I were a little worried, because Robbie had gotten much quieter and some of his tastes had changed, you know, like he quit the football team and spent more time studying. It wasn't as though he didn't study at all before that, but it was strange how suddenly it happened. But then, he was growing up, and getting prepared to go up to St. Louis for college." Judy reached up and tugged at a piece of hair that had escaped its braid. Her French manicure looked dull in the bathroom light.

"What happened, Judy?" I wrapped my wounded hands together and pressed them gently against my swirling stomach.

"I woke up one night. I'd had a headache all day, and went downstairs to get some milk. I heard voices outside, and it was so late. Two in the morning or so. I peered outside. Donna was there, crouched by the front porch. She was doing something to the ground at the bottom of the stairs. I opened the front door to invite her in. I thought maybe she couldn't sleep, either, and came here for—for, I don't know. To be closer to Robbie. They'd only been apart a week or so, and I remembered what it was like when you were first in love." Judy smiled tightly, and her fingers twitched away from her hair. She folded her hands together. "Be that as it may, I went out and she ran. I looked at what she'd been doing, and there was something half buried. I lifted it out of the dirt. It was a little pouch made of thin leather, like an Indian medicine bag." Judy held her fingers up to indicate the size. "Robbie came out. He asked, 'What's wrong, Judy?' I showed him the bag and told him what I'd seen. I remember how he frowned and stared out into the darkness after Donna. 'I'll take care of it,' he said. I gave him the bag and told him it would be okay. That she'd forgive him. He didn't seem to believe me. The next afternoon I asked him what it had been. He shrugged it off, said it was a folk charm. Nothing to worry over."

A tiny movement in the corner of my eye made me look at the bathroom door. Nick stood there, one hand against the doorjamb, fingers clutching it tightly as if he needed it to stand up.

"Nick," I whispered, using the toilet to push myself up. I went to him, touched his chest.

"I, uh, came up to see how you're doing." He didn't look at me, though. He was staring at Judy.

She stood, too, and with all three of us in the bathroom it was pretty crowded. "Let me patch up your hands, Nick," she said, bringing her handfuls of home nursing supplies with her. She dumped them into the sink.

I got out of the way, and Nick just stood there, watching Judy's fingers move. His shoulders were stiff, and I wanted to press up against him, to kiss his neck and rub my hands over the tight muscles. Help him calm down.

Casually, Gram Judy said, "Donna left before graduation, I recall. Mr. and Mrs. Harleigh said she was going up north to stay with an aunt."

Nick's head jerked up, and he met Judy's eyes in the mirror. "She was institutionalized. It happened on and off for my whole life. She was nuts. Is nuts."

Judy nodded sympathetically, then patted his hand.

I stepped forward and put my hands on Nick's waist. But

since Judy was there, I left a lot of air between us. "Did you really think she was doing magic?" I asked Judy.

"Oh, I don't know." She scooted Nick back and began putting away the Band-Aids and other things. Nick took one of my hands, and we stood side by side while we listened. I wished I could still see his face without it being obvious.

Judy closed the cabinet with a snap. "I suppose that's what she thought. At the time, I wasn't very interested in that sort of thing. But I spent several years in Hungary, you know, after Doug and I divorced, and I learned quite a bit about folk beliefs. There were these two ladies I stayed with who never left the house without money tucked in their left shoe to prevent being cursed. And I swear one of them cured a little baby of a fever just by bathing her in a bowl of milk and singing a little song." She smiled. "I prefer Tylenol, of course, but it's not my place to judge. And I'd never dismiss the power of prayer."

"We think someone is trying to use magic to hurt us, Gram," I said, diving straight into the deep end, so that the truth would drown us all. "The same person who killed Mom and Dad."

"What? Oh, no, dear, that's not possible. You can't really hurt people with folk magic. Especially not somebody like your dad, with his head screwed on so tight."

I squeezed Nick's hand. "Do you really believe Dad, the Robbie you knew, would kill Mom? He didn't just go crazy like everybody said."

Judy slowly shook her head. "Oh, Silla, now, I don't know. I'm not sure we can know."

"We can." Taking a deep breath, I nodded once. Determined. "Come back downstairs and I'll show you."

NICHOLAS

Silla led me downstairs and sat me at the kitchen table, like I was brain damaged. Maybe I was. I kept thinking about my mom, about her being my age and desperate for something, and then I shied away because I didn't want to think about her at all. *The sick-sweet smell of puke, and Mom bent over the toilet, yacking on herself. Me, slamming the bathroom door and hiding in my room, thinking of the needle rolling across the bathroom tiles.*

I watched as Silla grabbed a dried-out flower from the vase in the hallway and put it on the table before Judy. Silla pricked her finger and whispered in Latin to make the shriveled yellow petals brighten and stretch out. Judy gasped, but I didn't feel the wonder this time. My brain felt like cheese.

"Oh." Judy blinked and reached out to poke at the flower with her bony old finger.

"Don't even need salt anymore," Silla whispered, leaning back into her chair.

As Judy lifted the flower and inspected it, clearly needing a moment for the reality of the magic to sink in, Reese took turns glaring at me and Silla, presumably because she'd spilled the beans to Judy without asking him. I tried to take some comfort in his irritation, but only kept thinking about Mom. Trying to plant magic at Silla's house. Being in love with Silla's dad.

"We need a plan," Reese said. "Silla, tell us what happened."

Silla gripped her coffee mug and told them about Josephine and Wendy at school. She didn't mention my suspicions about Lilith. When she finished, she ducked her head for a gulp of coffee, and Judy shook her head. "Doesn't that just beat all? I am particularly keen to meet that old bag and give her a slap or ten."

Reese opened the spell book flat on the table, holding the corners down with his spread hands. "Here's what sounds like the best protection charm. We need something silver to hold it in, like actual silver charms, unless somebody wants to skin a cat and tan the hide for leather."

Silla pressed her lips together. I winced. Judy said, "Oh my God!"

"I didn't think so." Reese cracked a humorless smile. "In that case, it's more complicated, because we have to make a potion and soak the silver in it. And the potion requires some things we don't have. Rue, agrimony, and motherwort, the first of which I ordered online but won't be here until Wednesday. Large feather from wild bird, a black candle—I got a bunch of those yesterday—salt, of course, blood, of course, fresh running water we can get from Meroon's stream, and focus stones, whatever the hell that means. Thanks for that ambiguity, Dad."

"I have agrimony and motherwort," I said, unlatching the lacquered box slowly. My hands still felt like lead. I needed to get over this already. I flipped the lid open, and Reese and Judy leaned around to peer inside.

"Damn," Reese said. "This was your mom's?"

"Yeah."

"There's . . . tons. This is excellent. A turkey feather?" He ran his finger along the blood-letter quill.

"That's a blood-letter. Not an ingredient."

"There are crow feathers all over the cemetery," Silla said.

"Okay," Reese muttered, totally distracted as he lifted out bottles, read the labels, and slid them back in. He held out a triangular vial filled with tiny silver beads, and smoothed a thumb over the lettering. His dad's writing. The vial slammed back into its slot a little too hard.

"So that's everything, right?" Silla chewed on her bottom lip. "Except silver and focus stones."

I nodded.

"Nick and I should run out to the mall in Cape Girardeau for charms. It's open until nine. We'll look for stones, too. Or something."

"I'll get the feather and spring water, and start cooking up the potion. It's supposed to soak in the moonlight overnight. Moon's just past full, but hopefully there will be enough . . . oh, shit . . . it isn't—" Reese looked at the window.

"Bright and sunny," Gram Judy said breathlessly. "And we're due for a starry night."

Reese blew out a sigh. "Great. So."

The four of us stared at each other. It was intensely surreal. Four people in a country kitchen, plotting bloody magic. With a psycho, body-snatching murderer stalking us through flocks of birds.

Silla broke the silence. "Before we go, we need a password, so that we can know we're all really—really ourselves."

Reese looked grim. "Good idea, bumblebee."

We were all silent again. But instead of it being weird, I suddenly felt like we'd been waiting for this exact moment.

Everything since I moved here had built up to this. Everything since before I was born, maybe. Who knew how far back this went?

One of the lightbulbs in the brass chandelier flickered, breaking the moment.

Silla whispered, "I am in blood stepp'd in so far that, should I wade no more, returning were as tedious as go o'er."

Reese rolled his eyes. "Something we can all remember?"

"You can't remember *Macbeth,* you heathen?" A ghostly smile caught the corner of her lips.

"Out, out, damn spot?"

"How about this one: 'Stars, hide your fires; let not light see my black and deep desires.' "

Automatically, I replied, "I'd like to see your deep—" but thank God I stopped before I said something unforgivable in front of her grandma.

And her brother.

Reese scowled. "Let's go with something simple, okay?"

Gram Judy held up a finger. "I've got it. Supercalifragilistic-expialidocious!"

SILLA

The phone shrieked, and I almost fell out of my chair.

I leapt up, hoping it was Wendy, and grabbed it off the cradle. "Hello?"

"Silla?"

My mouth fell open and I turned to face my family and boyfriend in abject horror. "Ms. Tripp."

"I'm very glad that you sound all right, Silla. I wanted to

check up, and also to make very certain that you're coming to school tomorrow. It is imperative that we move your appointment up from Friday to discuss this incident with Ms. Cole this afternoon."

"Incident?" I clunked my head back against the wall. Reese was practically ignoring me, his nose still tucked into Nick's box, but Nick and Gram Judy watched me supportively.

"Ms. Cole is very disoriented, and there is a witness claiming you and Nick Pardee attacked her. I've spoken with Nick's father just now, and we're all very concerned."

"Is that—is that what Wendy said?" I whispered, eyes finding Nick's.

"I'm afraid so. She's quite upset, and at home now."

I closed my eyes tightly, my throat closing. Oh, God, Wendy. I didn't know what to say.

"Silla?"

"Yes," I whispered again. My voice wouldn't work properly.

"You'll be in tomorrow?"

"I . . ."

"I insist. I don't want to get the police involved. It's better if we can just sit down and talk about this. Is Judy Fosgate your legal guardian?"

"What? Legal guardian?" As I said it, Reese lifted his head. "I don't have one, I mean, I don't think. I'm almost eighteen and it didn't . . . didn't come up."

Reese swung out of his chair and came toward me with his hand out while Ms. Tripp said, "Well, Silla, someone is responsible for you. I—"

I didn't fight as Reese slipped the phone from my limp hand. "This is Reese Kennicot. What can I do for you?" I backed away, right into Nick. He put his hands on my shoulders.

"Yes," Reese said, looking at me. "She'll be there. But there wasn't anything illegal happening—if you thought so, you'd have called the police." He paused and shook his head, rolling his eyes. "We're grateful for your concern, Dr. Tripp—oh, are you a doctor in your field? No? Well—fine. Yes. You are. But that doesn't include interrupting my family's evening. Have a good one." He hung up, slamming the phone a little too hard.

"Thanks," I said. "I have to call Wendy again."

"And you should go, too, before it gets dark. The less you're out at night, the better," Reese said, and for a moment, I saw all of my dad in his face. It made me smile a little. And I reached up to squeeze one of Nick's hands.

I ran upstairs to use the phone in the hall to call Wendy again. "Silla?"

"Oh, Wendy, thank God." I slid down the wall to sit on the carpet in the dark, my knees pressed against my chest. "Are you okay?"

"Yes." She hissed the word. "Sorry, I don't want my parents to hear. They don't know anything's wrong."

"Ms. Tripp is probably going to call them."

"Ugh. Gross." A door shut, and Wendy spoke quietly but in her regular voice. "Are you okay?"

"Yeah."

"Good."

I needed to tell her. I wanted to explain everything. But

how could I tell her? Not over the phone, that was for sure. I'd have to lie, for now, at least. Maybe later . . . maybe later I could show her the magic. She deserved to know, since it had used her now. "I'm so sorry, Wen."

"It's okay, it was probably just low blood sugar. . . . I have to go, Silla."

My heart clenched. "Okay. I'll talk to you later, or in the morning."

"Sure thing. I—I'm sure I just need some sleep."

"Night, Wendy."

"Night, Silla."

As I hung up, a sickening feeling bubbled up from my stomach. I curled into a ball, forehead on my knees, and held it in. But I hadn't imagined it. Wendy, my only remaining friend, had been afraid to talk to me.

TWENTY-NINE

December 1942

Philip has left me.

I could not keep him here.

He left to serve as a medic in this war that has nothing to do with us — we who have lived beyond the scope of human things. I am fifty-three years old and look not a day over seventeen, and Philip, who was born a century before me, who has raised himself above them — We are better than they! They do not need or deserve our help!

It has been a year since he sailed. I came to stay with the Deacon again, who is the only thing that can cheer me. Everywhere is depression and hardship, but Arthur reminds me that all things end. He who has lived for centuries, whose blood is so strong and pure he barely need think on something for magic to happen. He says, "Philip will come home to us. He always does." When I rage and tear at my skin, he smears the blood away and turns it into nectarines. He has made a bower for me, like Titania's flower bed, under Kansas willow trees. I am shaded from sun and sheltered from rain, falling into the earth where it is warm and peaceful. I feel the heavy distance between me and Philip, and I feel the world tremble with death. It lulls me to sleep.

Philip's few letters have been filled with melancholy and veiled anger. I do not know how he can have lived for so long and continue to believe that men are good. "I can never make up for all of this death and pain, Josie," he writes. "Not with a million charms."

I write back, "Stop trying, Philip. Let go of it. Do what you can, but you are not God."

"If there is a God, Josie, he has failed us all."

I want to say to him, Philip, you can do more than turn water into wine. Why should you worry about God?

 # THIRTY

NICHOLAS

"Tell me your life story," I said over a basket of chicken fingers and fries. Fluorescent lights glared off every surface in the food court, making me wince.

We'd driven out in relative silence, both of us slowly shaking off the strangeness of the afternoon as best we could. I, for one, was looking forward to the inane normalcy of a shopping mall. The food court wouldn't have been my choice for our first date, but after the day we'd had I couldn't complain.

Silla smiled. "I was born in Yaleylah, grew up there, and will graduate from high school there. That's about it."

"Uh-uh. What's made you who you are?"

"I have no idea. Who am I?" Her smile turned teasing, but we both knew it was a valid question.

"Gorgeous, delicate, determined. A little bloody."

"Those are things I am, not *who* I am."

"Okay. A girl who risks everything for her family. A girl who trusts stalker boys because they have pretty smiles?" I tossed her my pretty smile.

"An open face," she said.

"Huh?"

"I thought you had an open face."

"You've changed your mind?"

She popped a French fry into her mouth. "What's your life story?"

"Born in Chicago, grew up there, will graduate from high school in Yaleylah."

Silla laughed and rolled her eyes.

"Let's try a different question. Tell me your favorite memory." I regretted the question almost immediately, when she glanced away from me and lowered the chicken strip onto her napkin.

But she answered. "Opening night of *Oklahoma!* I was Ado Annie, even though I was just a freshman, so it was amazing, but also kind of horrible sometimes because of jealousies and petty stuff. After the show, after the curtain call and bowing and applause, I went into the hallway still in costume, and I remember sweat running down my temples and ruining my makeup. The hall echoed with laughter and cheering and just this huge, hot energy of success. Mom was there, crying because she was smiling too hard. Dad gave me a hug and said 'Do I need to get myself a rifle?'" Silla's dreamy half smile dropped away. "Ado Annie's dad threatens several suitors with a rifle during the show. It made me laugh. And then I turned around and Reese shoved this huge bouquet of roses in my face. They smelled so, so good. Red, pink, yellow, white, and even this rich, dark purple color that was my favorite. He was standing there with his nose kind of wrinkled like he was trying to say something mean and big-brother-like. But instead he just shook his head and said, 'That was awesome, bumblebee.' And then Eric was there. He was one of the cowboys. And Wendy, who hadn't tried out, but did for everything after that—I don't think I've ever felt more alive than I did at that moment, in the big, boring hallway at school." Her eyes drifted closed. "My wig itched and the little boots I wore pinched my pinkie toes, and I just didn't care. Everybody loved me and I knew exactly why. It was like perfect communion."

Her hands were folded together, and the rings on her fingers managed to shine dully even in the crappy mall light. "I guess that's kind of an arrogant memory to be my favorite."

I pushed the basket of grease out of my way and covered her hands with mine. "I get it." It was normal. Her parents were alive. She was happy. And now her eyes shone just a little bit, with what was probably just the barest reflection of what it had been like then. "I wish I'd been there."

"Me too."

"We should get going, even though I don't really want to go back to all that. Ever."

"Yeah. But the sooner we find charms, the sooner we'll be safe for more—more of this."

SILLA

I held his hand while we walked through the plastic mall. I pretended we were just two people on a date. A normal date. I didn't want to think about blood or murder or magic. I couldn't think about Wendy, about her not wanting to talk to me, about what she must have been thinking.

As we searched the shops, Nick got me talking about video

games and designer jeans, favorite movies, colors, and toys. He'd been a Pokémon collector, and I confessed my preteen obsession with Power Rangers. And that Reese and I used to put on sunglasses and pretend they were visors so that we could battle demons from outer space. I'd been the Yellow Ranger, and he'd been the Green. Mr. Meroon's cornfield had been an ideal battleground.

At one of the jewelry kiosks, Nick bought a handful of questionably silver chains. I promised to pay him back, and he said, "Seriously, Sil. Any money I spend is less Lilith can steal from my inheritance when she screws Dad into an early grave."

I stared at him, lips parted. He'd said it with such casual disregard. "Do you really think that?"

Nick shrugged. "Usually."

"Why do you call her Lilith?"

"Oh." He grinned, mouth curved like devil horns. "Lilith was the name of the mother of all demons. In the Bible."

I couldn't help laughing. "She doesn't know, I take it."

"Nooo. Come on, let's go to a real jewelry store and get some nicer silver for the amulets."

"Nick, nicer equals more expensive."

"Well, think of it as me buying you jewelry, just instead of wearing it, you're putting it to more, erm, practical use." He tugged my hand.

We drove home into the sunset. It was hot pink and gold and this wicked, sharp teal melting into darkness. The wind burned my cheeks and nose, and I leaned back into the seat so that its icy fingers could tug at my hair.

Nick was driving very fast. Too fast to have to worry about aerial attacks. Both his hands gripped the steering wheel, at ten and two, and his arms were firm, not loose or relaxed. When he turned the wheel to take us around a curve, his shoulders angled, too, his whole body tilting with the motion of the car. I bit the inside of my lip and watched with my temple resting against the cool leather.

Impulsively, I put my hand on his thigh. He didn't move for a moment, then he skimmed his fingers over the back of my hand before grabbing the steering wheel again. His thigh flexed under my hand as he pressed the pedal down farther. A fresh rush of icy wind cut into my eyes and I closed them, concentrating on the rough denim of his jeans under my palm. It was my wounded hand resting there, and my pulse beat quickly along the length of the cut, focusing my attention, making the hair rise on my arm. The gentle, rapid rhythm connected us, and I just knew his heart was working hard, too.

My face flushed as the temperature in the car seemed to rise, until not even the wind made a dent.

I wanted his lips on mine, his arms around me. I wanted him laughing and telling me something mean about his stepmom. Or rolling his eyes at one of the peculiarities of Yaleylah. I just wanted him. The inside of my lip ached where I'd been chewing on it.

Every time I opened my mouth to demand that he pull over and let me kiss him, we passed another car or I caught a glimpse of a dark, shadowy bird flying into the swiftly moving trees, and I knew we had to get home. I knew if we stopped, we might stop forever.

NICHOLAS

We almost didn't make it back to Yaleylah.

I pushed the car faster and faster until I felt, or imagined, the shudder of strain when we curved, and only let up so that we didn't scream off the road and flip a bazillion times. I couldn't even glance at her. Her hand on my thigh was like a miniature nuclear explosion.

It took a clenched jaw, eyes on the road, and singing the theme of *Teenage Mutant Ninja Turtles* in my head over and over again to keep us on the road and me in my pants.

When the tires finally crunched over the gravel into Silla's driveway, I let myself look. Her eyes were tightly closed. "You okay?" I winced. "Sorry. I know better than to ask that."

She shook her head. "No, it's fine. I just—stop the car."

I did and twisted to look at her.

She put her hands on my face and kissed me.

For a second, neither of us moved. Then her mouth opened and she sucked my lip between hers and pulled herself forward by my neck. I fumbled to help her closer, lifting at her hips to get them over the gearshift. It wasn't easy, but we managed to keep kissing while we struggled and rearranged ourselves until she was sideways over my lap, back against the door and shoulder pressing the steering wheel. I had an arm around her back and the other hand tight to her thigh.

Everything fell away in a roar, as though the planet had cracked underneath us and it all collapsed into the blackness except for my car—except for us.

My hands found the hem of her shirt and slid under. Silla gasped when my cold fingers touched her skin, but she pressed into me and kissed harder. "Nick," she whispered, kissing again and again. Her hands ran up into my hair and she squeezed, pulling. The pain only made everything better, and I skimmed my hands up her sides. I could feel her breath shuddering through the quick motion of her diaphragm, and circled my thumbs up her ribs. Our kisses slowed, became more lingering as Silla held my face where she wanted it. My thumbs brushed the cups of her bra and I slid them around to the back, wanting—

Silla broke off, putting her cheek against mine. "Nick," she said again, and then, "Nicholas."

I stopped moving, just panted.

"We're—we're at my house. In the driveway."

My hands fell slowly to her hips. "I forgot."

"Me too. It's probably, um, good."

I just grunted. I should have agreed, pretended that I didn't want to take off all her clothes. But I wasn't lying anymore, and all that.

"Nick." The light made long shadows across her face. One eye was pale and bright, the other cast in darkness. It was hard to read only half her expression.

"The idea of you not being who you said you were . . ."

I waited. Watched her as she looked at her lap, at the radio, up at the darkening sky, and then directly into my face. "It scared me. I like you. A lot. You make me feel alive. Like the magic does, except it's just you. I mean, I want it to be just you. Not the magic. Not a lie or pretense or anything. I want to feel this way because you do, too."

The poem I'd thought of that afternoon, just before all the

shit went down, popped back into my head. "I do," I said, resisting the stupid urge to quote poetry at her.

"We should go inside." Silla climbed off my lap, ending up rather awkwardly on her knees in the passenger seat. Laughing lightly at herself, she opened the door and got out. I handed her the shopping bag.

"Silla?"

"Yeah?" She turned to me, and light from the front porch illuminated her completely.

"I should, uh, go. If Tripp called my dad . . . I turned my phone off, but I don't really want him to bury me for being too late."

After a moment where she just looked at me, Silla nodded. "Okay," she whispered. "I'll see you tomorrow. Be careful."

"You too. Night, babe."

SILLA

Inside, Reese was finishing a bowl of cornflakes. The entire kitchen table, except where he was eating, was covered in the contents of the magic box.

"Here." I dropped the plastic sack of silver next to his bowl.

"Judy's in the bath. But before we try to sleep, we should put salt at all the doors and windows, along with pinches of this heather flower."

"Sure. We didn't find any focus stones."

"We could try to use Dad's paperweights as focus stones. You know, maybe that's why he had that amethyst."

"Good thinking."

"Sometimes my brain works." Reese caught my hand and

tugged lightly so that I sat down next to him. "I've been thinking about something else."

I picked up his coffee mug and sipped at the dregs. "Yeah?"

"Nick."

"Oh, Reese, not now." I rolled my eyes, expecting some big-brother thing.

"This isn't about you having a boyfriend. It's . . . just think about it. He knows the magic, his grandpa died and left him that house at the right time. His mom and our dad have a past. And we don't know him that well. He lied to you about knowing the magic."

And Nick suspected his stepmother for some of the same reasons. "I can't believe that, Reese."

"Won't even entertain the possibility?"

"I did, and let go of it. It's not the truth, and you don't think so either."

"I don't?"

"No, or you wouldn't have let me go off with him just now."

"Silla."

"*Reese.* I know what it's like for somebody you know to be possessed. When Wendy was possessed, it was horrible—it felt wrong and disgusting. Nick doesn't feel that way. Besides, he was here with us, and the birds attacked him. And he's the one who saved Wendy. We can't just start suspecting everybody. You want to think it's Gram Judy, too, since she just got here when they died and we barely know her?"

Reese pushed his lips together and looked down at some papers on the table, flattening them with his hands.

"We can't live like that." I stood up.

After a moment, he said, "You're good for me, Silla."

"I know." I leaned down and put my cheek against his hair for a moment.

"He still lied to you. Which is the opposite of cool. I might have to punch him for that."

I laughed quietly. "You won't."

"I might."

"We worked it out. I promise."

Reese sighed, but it was more like a resigned growl.

Patting his shoulder, I said, "I'll be right back. Gotta pee."

Upstairs, as I washed my hands, I stared down into the porcelain sink, at the water spots on the faucet. I hadn't scrubbed the bathroom in days. Maybe this was helping both of us. Or just giving us something new to obsess over. I brought wet hands up to press against my face. The water was cold on my skin, cold and relieving. I blotted my face on the hanging towel, and in the mirror I saw Reese's bracelet. The one Dad gave him that he never wore anymore.

It sat on the shelves nailed behind the bathroom door. The tiger's-eye stone stared at me, tawny stripes glowing like it was alive. I turned and picked it up. The ring on my left middle finger matched it perfectly.

The inside of the silver cuff was etched with three runes.

I carried the bracelet downstairs and into the kitchen. "Reese."

He rumbled something and didn't look up from the papers he was working on. They looked like lists. I waited, sitting at the table next to him. After a moment, he glanced up. "Yeah? What are you doing with that?"

Flipping the bracelet over, I showed him the runes.

Taking it, Reese brought it close to his face and studied the inner circle. He frowned rather fiercely. "So?"

"Stop being defensive and think about it."

He set the bracelet down onto the table and took my right hand. "Are there runes on your rings?" Slowly he drew the emerald ring off my middle finger. It was the thickest and largest, and when he tilted it, we both saw the inner circle of tiny runes.

One by one, I removed the rest. Emerald, tiger's-eye, iolite, onyx, garnet, plus stoneless silver bands. One for every finger but my right ring. And each one inscribed with runes.

"That"—he pointed to the runes in my tiger's-eye ring, which matched the ones in his bracelet—"is the same as for the protection amulet. The one that might have been etched in the dirt outside, remember?"

"Do you think we can use these as the focus stones?"

Slowly, Reese nodded.

"Wear it," I said, scooting the bracelet closer to Reese. The tiger's-eye was as round and wide as a quarter, and winking at me.

"Sil."

"He wanted you to."

"Then he should have told us about all this. Maybe none of this would have happened if he'd trusted us."

"Maybe." I began replacing my rings, thinking of Nick's mom teaching him the magic and its not helping either one of them. The metal rings had cooled in the brief time away from my skin. It was like tugging on armored gloves.

"Why aren't you mad at him, bumblebee?"

Glancing up, I saw Reese wasn't looking at me but at the bracelet. He was holding it in his hands. "I . . . I never thought it was his fault."

"But he made choices that led to it."

"You don't know that."

"Yeah. I do. We do. And he didn't bother to prepare us, or Mom, to help him. To defend against this. He chose to be alone. Unfortunately, he didn't *die* alone."

"He loved us."

"Yeah."

"Maybe the rings and the bracelet were all he thought he could do. To keep us safe."

"Maybe."

Unwelcome thickness crawled up my throat. I worked my jaw, and swallowed sudden, shocking tears. I shook my head, blinked them away. I'd cried enough today. Reese was staring at the bracelet still, the skin around his eyes tight. He squeezed them shut, clenched his hands around the bracelet.

Standing, I put a hand on his head and petted his hair, like he'd always done for me. My fingers shook. Reese leaned his head against my chest, and I hugged him. I thought of that night I'd been telling Nick about, after my opening performance. When I'd been so alive because everyone knew me. Knew who I was.

Reese's arms came around my waist, and we held each other, alone together at the kitchen table.

THIRTY-ONE

July 4, 1946

Philip remains in France.

Some days I hate him for it. Other days I want to tear across the waters and find him, shake him until he promises to return with me.

I returned to Boston, to our old house, where I was born into this blood four decades ago. Here, I am a lonely rich girl whose husband abandoned her for war. Some weeks I entertain madly, laughing with suitors and the cream of Bostonian society. Some weeks I shut my doors and build stores of magic, grinding powders and pushing my magic into focus stones. I turn rocks into silver and gold to sell for money, and I barter curses and binding boxes because Philip would despise me for it.

But he left me and refuses to say when he will come home.

The Deacon came last month, and I entertained him as best I could. We traveled down the coast, and he showed me the cemetery where he found Philip stealing bodies so long ago. I like the Deacon for many things — his amorality is refreshing after Philip, and his imagination quite matches mine. But here in Boston, he seems superstitious and old-minded. For all that I am powerful and skilled, he frowns at my pants and makes clear that he is displeased by the general mood of the modern world.

I kissed him, and told him there might be things about the modern world he could admire, but he knows I only do it because I am furious with Philip.

He is correct, of course. My heart is fixed upon my Prospero, my lost wizard.

And so instead of having a passionate affair, the Deacon and I hunted for the bones of another witch like us so that we might surprise Philip when he returns with enough carmot to last thirty years.

THIRTY-TWO

NICHOLAS

It was late, so I tried not to slam any doors. The TV flickered from the den, and I could see both Lilith's and my dad's heads. I paused in the kitchen. I wasn't hungry, and my head throbbed slightly. Maybe left over from being possessed. Maybe from being tired.

My eyes narrowed. So much for Dad being worried about me. I strode to the den and perched on the edge of the single step leading down into the room. It was tricked out in black leather and those splattery kind of modern paintings that, now that I was thinking about it, looked a lot like arterial spray. "I'm home," I declared.

Dad twisted. "Nicholas Pardee, where the hell have you been?"

"Out."

He stood, and Lilith followed, just sort of gliding up behind him. Dad put his hands on his waist, a sure sign that he was about to emote. "Damn it, Nick, your school counselor called, and—"

"Everything was fine!"

"No need to yell." Dad's measured voice grated, and if I could have growled without it sounding ridiculous, I would have. Why couldn't he just yell back? Lilith slid her long hand across Dad's shoulders, as though he was the one needing comfort. "I'm glad you and your friend Silla are all right, Nicky," she purred.

"We are."

"Nick," Dad said, "you need to call me when this kind of thing happens. You're involved in a possible assault, and there are preparations to be made."

"You mean lawyer stuff? I don't need a lawyer. I didn't do anything—did she really say it was an assault?"

His eyebrows lowered. "She said there are conflicting reports about you hitting a young woman."

"You believe I would do that?" I felt sick.

"I just don't know, Nick. With all this sneaking around you've been doing. Spending time in a cemetery, and with a clearly disturbed girl—"

"She is *not* disturbed. I'm the one who should be worried about you, and *your* taste in women."

"Do not go down that path." Dad stepped forward again. "You have done nothing but disrespect me and my wife for months. Disregarding all the good Mary's tried to do, being hostile and openly disdainful, Nick. It will stop."

"Or what?" I crossed my arms over my chest. What was he going to do? Try to ground me? He wasn't here enough to enforce anything. Take away my car? I could walk to Silla.

Dad opened his mouth, but Lilith put a hand on his chest.

"Let's take a break, boys. Get some sleep. Talk in the morning when everybody's calmed down." She glanced at me. "Your father has had a long day, and couldn't retire until he knew you were home."

"Whatever. I'm here. Good night." I spun around and left as Lilith murmured something soothing to my dad.

I hated her.

Lilith was Josephine. She had to be. I didn't know why she hadn't grabbed me or attacked me or whatever. Preserving her identity or something, I guessed. And now she was getting Dad to back down, like she knew the truth about what had happened at school. Dad had met her right around the time Silla's parents were killed, then she'd convinced him, a city man to the bone, to move out here to the middle of nowhere? Right after my grandpa died? She could easily have killed him, too.

It all made sense.

I needed proof, some way of convincing Dad before she hurt him, too. It wasn't like I could tell him his mega-hot trophy wife was a nasty blood witch. Especially not now.

Instead of tromping upstairs, I paused in the kitchen at the cellar door. Mostly, Dad was using the cellar for wine, but several boxes had gone down there when we'd moved in. As quietly as possible, I popped the door open (it stuck, thanks to old construction), and winced while I waited and listened for movement from the den.

When nothing happened, I stepped down the first of the creaky stairs, feeling along the wall for the light switch. I'd been down here once, when we moved in, and even in the bright, hot afternoon had been grateful for the modern wiring. When the bulb flashed to life, it managed to flood out most of the shadows with weak white light. The stairway was narrow, and I tiptoed down to the concrete floor. There was another switch here, and I flicked it. The whole cellar was as large as the first floor, but it was divided up into as many rooms as the upstairs. This first room was lined with wine racks. They were maybe a fifth full with wine and a few random bottles of scotch and port. Sherry for Lilith. I briefly considered grabbing some whiskey to help me through the next hour, but decided I'd rather be sharp and on my toes.

The dank cellar curved around into a second room, which was really the only other one not just sitting empty. Boxes were piled high, mostly cardboard, but with several clear plastic bins holding all our winter clothes. That was a new concept for me and Dad—changing out winter and summer clothes. What was wrong with having them all out all year? But as with everything, Dad gave in to Lilith's suggestions without thinking.

Too bad I hadn't brought a flashlight: the words identifying the contents of every box were tough to make out. Mostly they said things like CHRISTMAS DECORATIONS and ROSE CHINA. A few had Dad's old comic books, which Lilith had banished from the library (and that was the only thing that ever made me want to read them myself). I grabbed a box that wasn't labeled, thinking if I was a body-snatching blood witch I wouldn't store my secrets in a box reading SPELLS AND CHARMS.

The cardboard was limp from the constant damp, and I easily pried open the flaps. Inside was a bunch of books. High school yearbooks, from some school in Delaware. Under the four volumes was a layer of letters addressed to Lilith. I pulled one out of its envelope and skimmed it. Love notes from a guy named Craig. Fortunately, they were more sappy than sexy. I dug a little deeper and found several sketching pads and a huge pile of little journals. I opened one to find the first pages or first paragraphs of about three dozen stories. Fiction things, one of which mentioned the main detective in one of Lilith's series.

Frustrated, I sat back on my heels. It was her stuff, all right, but regular old keepsakes, not the dark secrets I was hoping for. I guessed she probably kept that stuff closer to her. Maybe under her lingerie or something horrible like that, where I'd never look. Was I wasting my time?

I decided on one last scan of the boxes, and when I stood, I saw the box behind the keepsakes I'd just gone through.

The label was in different handwriting: DONNA, 12–18.

For a moment, I didn't breathe.

I dragged it out, but my fingers wouldn't obey when I told them to open it. I crouched there, staring at it for I don't know how long. It was like I knew something inside was going to tear me up, or piss me off.

It was filled with pictures. Mom must've had her own camera, and she photographed everything. I recognized the house from the outside and the cabinets in the kitchen, and there were two folks Dad's age who must've been my grandparents. Grandpa Harleigh looked vaguely familiar. I remembered him scowling, not smiling.

I didn't spend much time with those; I'd never spent time with my grandparents and didn't want to start feeling guilty about it. A lot of the pictures were taken in the graveyard and the fields around it, at all times of the year. The clothes everybody wore made me laugh a little as I flipped through a stack from the high school. Which was exactly the same. I even recognized old Mrs. Trenchess. Course, she hadn't been old at the time.

And then there was Robbie Kennicot, in stonewashed jeans and what I very generously decided not to think of as a mullet. His eyes were just like Silla's in the painting in their study. But he smiled way too much.

Mom's self-portraits almost made me throw the box away. She'd done that thing where you hold the camera as far from you as possible and push the button, and it captures a bunch of weird angles and perspectives.

Her hair didn't change much over the years, starting when she must have been in seventh or eighth grade. It was just thick and long, occasionally swooping back from her ears, other times just hanging straight and plain. Most of my own memories of Mom gave her shorter, pageboy cuts and a thinner face. It was weird seeing her like this. With bangles on her wrists and a really happy smile. There was one of her and Robbie, holding hands on the school bleachers. He must have taken it. Mom was kissing his cheek, her face all scrunched up from giggling. I wondered if she'd ever looked that cute when I'd been around. Or Dad. Surely she had. That's why Dad had loved her in the first place.

Staring at the photo of their obvious freaking bliss, the horrible thought occurred to me that it might not have been a very lot that kept me from being Silla's brother instead of Reese. Ugh. *Ugh.*

Rolling my shoulders as if that could banish the unfortunate thought, I let myself remember very clearly how I knew she wasn't even close to being my sister: the way she'd climbed into my lap and savaged my mouth.

The picture of Mom and Mr. Kennicot fit easily in my jeans pocket, folded in half. Had they snuck into the cemetery at night and regenerated bones? Made magic charms between kisses?

I had this urge to choose a few of the photos and send them to her in New Mexico or wherever with a note: *Found happier part of your life, the one I wasn't in.* Or just keep them in my pocket all the time so that when I did eventually see her again, I could show them to her and say . . . something. *Why don't I remember you this happy? What was wrong with me and Dad?*

I promised myself I'd be stronger than she'd been. I wouldn't hate the power. I wouldn't abuse it. My hands tingled as I thought of the magic, and I held them out before me. Tiny scratches from the bird attack itched with my pulse. But it was hard to focus on them, and I realized my hands were shaking.

I dumped all the boxes back where they belonged and hurried upstairs.

THIRTY-THREE

February 4, 1948

I hardly know him. Philip is thin and quiet. Not the quiet of churning thoughts or deep contemplation. It is a stillness that has settled around him like a wide black lake. It is a shield, a castle, that I cannot push through. Even the carmot has not made his blood boil.

I have tried to stir his blood, to drag him out into the world. I have kissed him and showered him with news. I have asked him what he's seen. What he's witnessed. He only shakes his head or closes his eyes. I bought a trio of canaries and possessed them all—I learned to sing with their throats and to carry them in an amusing sort of harmony. They almost sounded like the Andrews Sisters singing "Don't Sit Under the Apple Tree." Philip smiled, but only to please me.

The Deacon has convinced him to travel west, into mountains far from the pollution of men in order to find his peace again. I will not go. I will not.

I wish to tear this book into a hundred pieces.

THIRTY-FOUR

NICHOLAS

Dad came up to the attic to wake me for school. "We need to talk," he began ominously.

I scrubbed at my eyes, aching all over. "Jesus, Dad, can't I at least piss before we do this?" My neck was stiff and I just wanted to fall back into my pillows.

"I don't want you fleeing the scene before I get a word in." He frowned. As usual, he looked like he'd walked out of a catalog. Perfect hair already styled, perfect shave, tie knotted perfectly evenly at God knows what time in the morning. I swear he didn't even eat breakfast before brushing his teeth. Three times.

"Fine, fine. What do you want to talk about?" I plastered on a smile. Dad would recognize it as quickly as I recognized his patronizing one.

But he shook his head. "Your girlfriend. I think you should seriously consider not seeing her."

"What the hell?"

His lips pinched downward at my language.

"Seriously, Dad, what do you think you know?" My eyes

narrowed. "It was Lilith, wasn't it? What did that bitch say now?"

"Nicholas Pardee, you will not, I repeat, not refer to Mary by that awful name."

"Which one?"

He didn't respond. Dad tried not to give credence to things he found lacking with something even so small as a blink. The picture tucked into my jeans pocket flashed in my memory. Mom, giggling and carefree. There was no way she'd ever been that way with Dad. No wonder she hadn't turned to him when she'd needed him.

After a moment of us glaring at each other, I threw my covers back. "I'm going to get ready for school."

"Nick."

Dad's voice was quieter now, but just as firm.

The cool morning air chilled all my exposed skin. I kept my eyes glued to my knees.

"I spoke at length yesterday with the guidance counselor at your school. She told me some things about Drusilla Kennicot. Some very concerning things."

"Oh, yeah?"

"Her parents died in an appalling manner," he said, like they'd spilled red wine on Lilith's white carpet and hadn't apologized. "And young Drusilla is having a difficult time."

"So?"

"So, she might be needing better help than you can give, son. Think of her as being on the rebound."

"Dad, I'm not trying to help her. I just like her, okay?"

"I understand being drawn to that sort of broken individual, but it—"

"You mean Mom, don't you?" I looked at him, feeling ridiculously breathless.

Dad leaned forward in my computer chair, which he'd drawn close to the bed. "Yes. I don't regret anything, Nick, of course, but I don't want you to have to go through anything like what I did. What you did. Your mother was unstable, and I couldn't tell when we were young."

"You loved her too much?" I sounded derisive on purpose.

He hesitated, then said, "Yes."

Shock made me confess. "I, uh, I found a box in the cellar that's filled with pictures she took when she was in high school. I didn't even know she liked to take pictures."

"She used to hang a camera around her neck when she was"—Dad paused—"sober."

"I can get them for you. From the cellar."

He hesitated, his lips forming a thin line. "Maybe. We'll see."

"Sure."

"About Drusilla."

"Just Silla, Dad."

"All right. I just want you to think about her, about things. She's involving you in things you have no need to be involved with."

I almost laughed. "She isn't. Look, here's what happened. Her friend just had a bad afternoon—I don't know if Wendy was drunk or just, I don't know, upset. But Silla was trying to help her. All I did was grab her to calm her down. I don't know who's spreading lies, but that's the truth." I could feel the blood rushing into my cheeks and ears. I needed to call Silla so that we could get our stories straight. How could we not have talked about it last night?

After a moment watching my face, Dad nodded. "Very well, Nick. I believe you. I only want you to be careful. I am not blind—I see those cuts on your neck and the backs of your hands that you came home with last night. I don't know if you're fighting, or what is going on. But if you trust this girl, I'll trust your instincts."

I started to ask why he didn't trust my instincts about his own damn wife. But I swallowed it. Dad was deliberately choosing to believe me about a girl he didn't like. It was his clearest way of saying *Maybe you should trust my instincts, too.* I sat there in my boxers, feeling about ten years old. Dad got out of my chair and clapped a hand on my shoulder. "You call me if you need me at school. If they try to punish you for something that you didn't do. I'll be around today, working here. I can get there in ten minutes."

Guilt made it hard to talk. "Thanks, Dad," I managed.

He nodded, then turned to go. "See you downstairs, son."

"Dad."

He glanced back.

"You, uh, you love Mary like you loved Mom?"

He didn't even hesitate this time. "No. It's very different, but not any less."

I couldn't quite promise not to hate her, or not to think she was a soul-sucking psycho blood-witch wannabe. But I suddenly didn't want her to be.

THIRTY-FIVE

May 1959

    Can I allow an entire decade to pass without note? If I had been born to this time, or did not know what life in other eras and places could be like, I might have drowned myself.

    I moved to New Orleans for a time, losing myself in new magic. But every dance with Li Grand Zombi, every blessing doll, made me wish I could turn to Philip and ask if he'd ever thought to try honey to make a healing stick or dancing and singing to call blood to blood.

    Here was this magic, akin to ours but holier. Philip would have loved Louisiana Voodoo. I had to leave it behind, because his absence pressed too hard against my discoveries. But the rest of the country was empty. A black-and-white television pretending to offer life.

    There is nothing more to remember. This old book is useless to me now.

THIRTY-SIX

SILLA

Tuesday morning was cool enough that I needed a jacket. Reese dropped me off at school about fifteen minutes early so that I could get my things from Stokes's classroom, and the lot was mostly empty. Feeling naked without backpack or purse, I walked quickly toward the main building, hugging my corduroy jacket closed. The cold pricked at the little cuts on my hands from the bird attack. When all this was over, Reese and I would have to make one of the spell ointments for healing.

I ducked through a side door and skirted the auditorium to grab my backpack. Fortunately, Stokes didn't have a homeroom class, so his room was empty.

Standing alone in the room reminded me of the moment I'd realized Wendy wasn't herself. Of the clinging panic. I slipped my hands into my jacket pockets. My left hand found the crystals of salt we'd crushed with more heather flower. In the right-side pocket was my pocketknife. I'd be expelled for sure if they found it, but there was no way any of us were going to leave the house this morning unprotected. Reese and I had used permanent markers to draw protection runes over our hearts and smear them with blood. If we could have gotten away with putting them on our foreheads and hands, too, we would have. I'd told Nick to do the same thing when he called before school to go over our story.

Just in case Josephine was here, I'd be ready. *I banish thee from this body* is what Nick had said. Blood and salt would do the rest.

Blowing out a deep breath, I prayed Wendy would be safe.

I dug out my cell phone. The moment I turned it on, it vibrated.

There were three texts from Wendy. One from Melissa. One from Eric. Wendy's messages were from right before and after I'd tried to call her from Nick's cell. They just said, "Call me." Melissa's read: "WTF, S?" And Eric chewed me out for freaking on Wendy. That one actually made me smile a little. I was glad he cared.

I waited in Stokes's classroom for a few minutes, until I'd have just enough time to get to my locker and then my first class. When it was 7:56, I took a deep breath, put on my sea-green mask, and stepped out.

The hallways crawled, as usual, with scurrying kids, yelling and laughing and slamming lockers. I was the object of countless corner-of-the-eye glances and raised brows, of twisted frowns and tiny sneers. I was totally unprepared for that. I'd known there would be questions and maybe a little tension with people involved: Wendy, obviously, and maybe the *Macbeth* cast. But everyone in the school? What were they saying? I ducked my head and made a beeline for my locker. I had to act like everything was cool. Like I wasn't waiting for the bogeyman to leap out from every corner. In any shape. Act. *Act*. I could do that. I was an actress. I needed a brighter mask.

A smiling, glittery pink one, with pearls and flowers trailing down the side.

Mask firmly in place, it took me a second to remember what classes I had first, and then Wendy was there, grabbing my hand and pulling me around.

"Silla." Her mouth was pursed in a worried shape.

My body clenched in terror. I had to keep my other hand against my thigh or I'd have reached for the salt.

"Come on." She dragged me through the crowd and into the janitor's closet.

Pressed up against a stack of brooms, I waited. I couldn't make the opening gambit. All I could think of was Josephine staring out at me, of being trapped inside here while that monster rode my friend's body. How to tell without giving myself away?

Wendy peered at me through the dim yellow light. Then she opened her purse and pulled out a tube of shiny purple gloss and slathered it over her lips. I laughed, so incredibly relieved, and Wendy lifted her eyebrows and offered me some. I shook my head.

As she tucked the lip gloss away, she said, "Look, we don't have much time before the bell. I couldn't talk last night, and I shouldn't really text you or anything like that. At first they thought it was drugs—Mom and Dad, I mean—after Ms. Tripp talked to them. That had to be why I was acting erratically, or whatever. But I'm leaving at lunch to go to the doctor to make sure I don't have epilepsy or something. And my dad decided that it's your fault anyway. That's why no talkies or texting."

She grimaced. "Paul said he saw me run out of the building, you following, and that I punched Nick. Is he okay?"

I nodded.

"Oh, good. I thought about calling him, but I wasn't sure if I should or if he'd want me calling or if his parents knew or should know or what and now I'm babbling and you have to tell me what happened. Spill."

My mouth opened and nothing came out. Nick and I had decided on a general lie, but I didn't want to offer it to her. She deserved better. But did I have a choice? Quickly, I said, "You just suddenly freaked out—I think all the pressure of the audition and SATs coming up and everything, you know? You were babbling and then suddenly just ran off. I ran after you, and you got outside and—and went for Nick. He told me he said something obnoxious to you, and I guess you were so upset you didn't think and just swung. He grabbed you, held you off, and . . . that's it. You were bleeding and I—I had to go." I lifted a hand toward the wound under her jaw. A shudder clenched up my backbone as I remembered Josephine pressing the letter opener to Wendy's neck.

Wendy grasped my hand. "I'm scared, Silla. I hate not remembering."

"Wendy," I whispered, throwing my arms around her. I squeezed her hard, and she put her arms around my ribs and squeezed back. "I'm so sorry," I told her, overwhelmed by the cherry-vanilla reek of her hair. I didn't deserve her.

By lunchtime, the glitter was flaking off my mask. Three pearls dropped off and rolled down the tiled hallway.

Despite what I'd told Reese, I suspected everyone. All the teachers, all my classmates—everyone who looked at me could have been hiding Josephine inside them. Wendy and I passed notes like we always did, about superficial, totally unimportant things, and I tried to pay attention instead of thinking about the ritual that night or my looming meeting with Ms. Tripp.

Between History and Physics, I found a folded piece of paper slipped into my locker. In huge red block letters it read: LIKE FATHER LIKE DAUGHTER.

I tore it into tiny pieces and flushed it down the toilet.

Melissa, who I normally talked to in Physics, didn't look at me once. If it hadn't been for Wendy and our being cast as a trio, she probably would have ditched me weeks ago.

I hadn't done anything, but I was being blamed for everything.

As I detoured from my usual path to the cafeteria to go to Ms. Tripp's office instead, it was all I could do not to run to a bathroom stall and cry.

Tripp offered a sour-cherries smile as she held open her door. I entered silently, and she closed the door, gesturing for me to sit down. I did, clutching my backpack on my lap like a shield.

Today, her soft-and-simple attitude had vanished. The violet cardigan was more like a flak jacket than professional attire. She sat behind her desk for the first time, and folded her hands in front of her. I lifted my left hand and pressed it against my chest. I could feel the dried blood over the permanent marker rune, could feel the energy scorching between my palm and my heart even through layers of jacket and sweater. I was ready, just in case.

The tense silence ended when Ms. Tripp said, "I'm afraid we've come to a very serious situation, Silla."

"I didn't do anything wrong."

"Tell me what happened yesterday afternoon."

Closing my eyes because I was a crap liar when I didn't have a script, I said, "Wendy had some kind of panic attack. I couldn't calm her down, but Nick managed. The blood upset me, so I left. I had to go, even though she fainted or whatever."

Ms. Tripp was quiet long enough that I finally risked a look. She hadn't moved at all. "You and Wendy had argued?"

"Yes."

"About what?"

Part of me wanted to spill my guts. To let it all out in a dramatic monologue. What could I tell her that would make her leave me alone? That she wouldn't need to clarify with Wendy, or call Nick in for? Ms. Tripp gazed at me steadily until I said, "My dad."

Her smile tipped into sympathy, and she scooted back her chair to come sit with me. I let my backpack slide down to the floor.

"Can you tell me about it?"

I fiddled with my rings, turning the emerald around and around my middle finger. "Wendy agrees with you, that I should, uh, should stop defending him like I'm defending myself. That he might have made bad choices."

"And that angered you."

"Yeah."

Taking my hands loosely in hers, Ms. Tripp said gently, "Silla, dear, it's time you took these off."

Whatever I'd been expecting, it wasn't that. I flicked my eyes up to her face. Was she Ms. Tripp, really? Or was this another trick of Josephine's? "Why?"

Her eyes reflected the light falling in through the office windows. Normal. Safe. "You've got to let go of your trauma. Normally, I wouldn't propose pushing through it so quickly, but, Silla, with all this acting out, I'm afraid you are becoming a danger to yourself and even to others."

"Acting . . . out?" I'd never understood the meaning of the word *aghast*. But now, I was *it*.

Tripp made her pretty pout and turned my hands over. The parallel slashes on my palm, one pink and healed, the other scabbed and red, stood out against the little nicks from the possessed blue jays. "Deliberately hurting yourself is never a real way to feel again."

My palm tingled. "This isn't about making myself feel, okay? It was a—a fluke."

"A fluke twice?" She shook her head, and her massive curls bobbed. "I want to help you, Silla. I think if you let go of your dad, this huge burden will vanish. Admit your pain, and you can move on."

Did she get her grief training on the Internet? I jerked my hands away.

"Cutting yourself is unacceptable. It's dangerous and can lead to worse things. And now arguing with your friends, violence, the suggestion drugs were involved—Silla, I am very,

very worried about you. It's why I called last night and tried to talk. I don't want to recommend you be suspended, but it might be better for you to spend some time away from all this pressure."

My mouth dropped open. "Suspended!"

"If I have to, Silla."

"I have to go. Please."

"Come back tomorrow at lunch. I am going to insist on these meetings every day until I see some improvement. And if you fall out of line again, Silla, I'll recommend your suspension immediately."

I grabbed my backpack, trying to imagine a mask growing out of my skin.

"Think about what I've said, Silla," Ms. Tripp continued. "Think about letting it go. Let it out and cry or scream, or whatever you need to do. Just don't hurt yourself anymore. A lot can be said for little personal rituals." She glanced at my rings again. "I think taking those off would be a great place to start."

"I'll think about it," I promised, knowing I wouldn't.

I fled outside and flipped open my cell phone. Dialed Reese. It went straight to voice mail. Panic beat at my throat. "Reese, oh my God, where are you? I can't believe you aren't answering your phone. How do I know you're okay? I have to talk to you. I can't go home right after school—I can't skip rehearsal. Tripp is threatening to suspend me if I do anything wrong, and if that happens I won't have anything left. I won't be able to even be a stupid witch in the stupid play, and I've always been in the plays, Reese, I don't know what to do without it." I took a long, shuddering breath. "I haven't seen Nick all day, either. Everyone looks at me, and I don't know who they are. I think I might really be going crazy, Reese. God. Why hasn't she done anything? Where is she—"

My phone beeped that I had an incoming call. Reese.

"Oh, God," I answered. I closed my eyes and leaned against the hard yellow bricks of the building.

"Bumblebee, what happened?"

I babbled it all again. "And I'm scared, Reese. I have to stay, but I want to ditch, too, and get the magic over with. Be safe."

His calm voice washed into my ear. "Refresh the blood on your heart. It will keep you safe for now."

He didn't know. He was making it up.

"I love you," I said.

"I love you, too, Silla. Be careful. You'll be fine."

THIRTY-SEVEN

January 1961

The first month of a new decade. I heard on the radio a reminder to make resolutions to improve one's life. Such as: Always have dinner prepared on time. Keep your shoes shined and your hair tidy. Iron daily. Rest for fifteen minutes before your husband arrives home so that you will be fresh and gay to greet him.

I thought, I am going to find my errant wizard, and drag him home to me. There will not be another decade lost to his petulance and longings. I have had fifteen years to rest. Fresh is what he's getting.

THIRTY-EIGHT

SILLA

It was a relief to focus on rehearsal. It was a relief to have *made*
it to rehearsal with no Josephine encounters. And without
being suspended. I did it by huddling at my desk, ignoring
everything but the text in front of me. By keeping my eyes
down between classes.

Macbeth opened in two weeks—less than—and only had
four more rehearsals before we began tech runs. Assuming I
survived that long.

Between scenes, Stokes sent me into the hallway with
Wendy and Melissa to be fitted for our costumes. I had to leave
my jacket in the auditorium, and barely had time to transfer
the salt to my jeans. The knife was still in my jacket pocket.

Stokes had given the show a contemporary theme, and
we witches would be sporting a goth look. With black makeup
and everything. The sewing club was making us corsets
with lots of silver buckles. Madison, who was lacing me into a
mock-up, cussed me out for losing another half inch off my
waist.

"You do look awful, Sil," said Wendy, her arms raised so

that one of the freshman girls could pin down the top hem of the corset.

"Gee, thanks."

Melissa added, from her post against the wall, "It kinda looks like you ran through barbed wire." How nice of her to stop ignoring me in order to be mean.

"Have you been eating?" Madison asked. "Because really, this isn't going to hold your tits up if it isn't tighter."

I looked down. There was a quarter-inch gap between the lining of the corset and my breasts. Even though they were in a bra and under a sweater. "Yes, I've been eating, and sorry I'm not looking like I walked out of *Vogue*." I didn't bother keeping the bite out of my voice.

"It's a pain, and we have to keep redoing your stupid corset."

"I'll just stuff it or something."

"You aren't puking, are you?" Melissa asked.

"Melissa!" Wendy glared.

"Well, anorexia, psycho freak-outs, whatever."

Madison jabbed a needle at Melissa. "Bulimia. That's what puking is."

"God, whatever."

"And no," Wendy said, "she isn't."

I just stood there, mouth slowly falling open. Was Melissa possessed? No, I thought, she'd always been such a bitch.

"How do you know? You said she's too busy putting out for the new guy to stay with you when you pass out—"

"Don't." Wendy's cheeks exploded into fireworks of color, though, so I knew Melissa wasn't totally making stuff up.

I began untying the corset mock-up, tearing at the laces.

"Running away again?" Melissa smiled nastily. And Wendy actually paused for a moment, looking between us like she wasn't sure who to be angry at. All the freshmen were slowly backing off.

"The thing isn't going to fit anyway, so I'm leaving." I slapped it onto the tiled floor.

"Poor Silla!"

Wendy rounded on Melissa, but I caught her arm. "Don't. It isn't worth it."

"Yeah," Melissa sneered. "Besides, stay too close and you might get shot."

I hadn't been particularly angry before. But the meaning of Melissa's accusation seeped down over me like I'd been drenched with cold pudding. I stilled. Even my heart seemed to stop. I stared at her. "What?" I whispered.

She didn't answer except to lift her chin, jutting it out slightly.

"You don't know what you're talking about," Wendy hissed at Melissa.

"I know crazy is genetic. I know spending time with Silla is bad for your health."

"You don't know *anything*." I whirled around, wrapped in my own drama, and stalked into the auditorium for my backpack. I ignored the confused glance from Stokes and strode right back out again. I didn't care that I was ditching the last half of rehearsal.

The sun glared at me and I threw up my hands for shade. Most of the parking lot was still full. Everybody had practice or rehearsal or a club meeting or something. I was supposed to hitch a ride with Nick, but he hadn't been at rehearsal. Not even backstage. I'd texted him a few times during the day, but he'd only sent back one after lunch. A haiku about Mr. Sutter's toupee. Nothing since.

I marched through the lot. Home wasn't far. I'd walked it most of my life.

But as I wove through two lines of cars, I saw Nick's convertible. It was unmistakably shiny amid the old assortment of dusty compacts and station wagons and pickups. And the top was down. I climbed in and slouched into the passenger seat, arms crossed over my stomach.

NICHOLAS

She was asleep. In my car.

I stood next to the passenger side for a minute, looking down at her. The sun made her skin seem translucent and bloodless. For a moment, it didn't matter why I was falling in love with her. Just that I was.

As quietly as possible, I got behind the wheel and lifted my bag into the back. When the engine growled to life, she groaned softly and stretched. I didn't bother shifting out of park, watching her instead. Her eyelids fluttered and she sat up, rubbed her cheeks, and peered into the light. "Nick?" she murmured.

"Hey, babe. You need a ride home?"

"What time is it?"

"Almost five."

"Were you at rehearsal? I didn't see you there." She leaned

forward and turned in the bucket seat to face me. Her hair stuck out oddly in the back where it had been pressed against the leather.

"I had detention." I grimaced for her.

"What for?" She was biting the inside of her lip again.

"Nah, nothing much." Between fifth and sixth period, Scott Jobson had asked if she'd gotten those bruises for sucking my dick wrong. I shoved his face into the lockers and spent the rest of the day in detention. "Just had an incredibly bad day."

"Me too."

"Hey." I leaned forward so that I could dig the picture out of my jeans pocket. "Look."

She unfolded it slowly, and I watched her face. When she recognized her dad, her lips parted. She gripped the photo in both hands. "Oh, Nick."

"I found it last night. I found a bunch of my mom's stuff."

"They look so happy."

I picked at her hair, brushing it into some semblance of order. And I avoided her eyes as I asked, "Do you think we met for a reason?"

"Other than coincidence?"

"Yeah."

Tilting her head into my hand, she closed her eyes and said, "I don't think I care."

"Why not?"

"I'm glad we met. So if it was for a specific reason, fine. If it wasn't, fine. It happened. And I wouldn't change it."

What if I only moved here because Lilith killed your parents? The words didn't make it out of my mouth. "Are you ready for tonight?" I asked instead.

"Yes. God, yes. We set the potion out last night." She reached up and caught my hand, pulling it down into her lap. The photo quivered on her knee as she stroked my palm, then held out her hand for my left one. She examined them. "I like your hands."

"I like yours, too. Even though you cut yourself right through your life line."

"My what?"

"Life line. It's palmistry."

"You know the funniest things, Nick."

"I wrote a poem for you. Yesterday afternoon, out on the football field."

"Really?"

"Yeah."

"Can I hear it?"

"If I ever remember the first line."

"Nick!" Her laughter turned into a grin. "That's mean."

I laughed, too. "I wanted to see you smile."

A crow cawed from nearby, and Silla jumped. The smile fell off her face. "Let's go," she said, glancing at the sky.

THIRTY-NINE

October 10, 1967

    How the world can change in a few short years! Because men are short-lived and passionate, their children rebel and turn a country from a depressed shadow into a wilderness of neon love!

    I spent all of 1963 in a van, driving and driving across the country. It is amazing how everything transforms around us. So many new worlds, so many humans ready to give me attention and money. I hardly have to transmute metal into gold anymore. I've saved so much, and always, always have more to funnel in. Why? Because no one is afraid of witches anymore. They seek us out. They want me to show them the lands of death, to say, "You do not need pills, and you do not need a hospital. You need this amulet that I shall make with blood, spit, and yarrow. We will bless it under the full moon while we dance and make love brighter than the stars!" They want my magic to be real. They want me to be their goddess. And I am.

    Philip is reproachful, but I am irresistible to him now. I found him in California, working with his hands in the dirt on a farm. He saw me, and I woke in him that same sleeping need he woke in me when I was dying in St. James almost sixty-five years ago.

    He hungers for me more the stronger I am, the more he sees others want me. He needs me as I needed him. When I kiss him, I taste eternity on his tongue!

I said to him when we returned to Boston, "Philip, do you remember you thought of yourself as my Devil? Tempting me to throw off my innocence and embrace all this dark magic?" He replied, "I did my job too well." And he is morose enough to believe it. I love him all the more for his seriousness. He is my husband and father, my only real partner. I laugh at him, and tease him into happiness.

Oh, my diary. I have missed you these long years as I've traveled. I rather enjoy leaving you here, and opening your cover only when I think of it. Flipping through the first entries fills me with both sadness and joy, for I was such a child then, but I knew what I wanted, and I have it all. I am true to my path.

 # FORTY

SILLA

For once, the crunch of gravel remained in the background. Clouds had rolled in while I slept, so even though there was plenty of time before sunset, the air had a dim, foreboding feel to it. Or maybe I was projecting. But if I'd had to set a stage for this kind of blood ritual, I'd have used yellow-gray backdrops with industrial platforms and metallic trees. We witches would emerge down center, through stark flashes of red spots, and light candles until the entire stage was alive with fire.

Reese appeared on the porch as Nick and I climbed out of the convertible. He was wearing jeans and a plain black T-shirt. Very solemn. "Hey," he said. "I hope the rest of your afternoon was better than lunch."

"She was totally shit on," Nick said, "after what happened yesterday."

I almost smacked him.

"You feeling up to this, Sil?" Reese clomped down the porch stairs.

"Do I have a choice?"

Both Reese and Nick just looked at me. "Oh my God"—I

threw up my hands—"I could suffocate. Yes. Yes! I'm fine. Why don't you two cowboys stay out here and preach at each other about how you need to take care of your little women and everything. I'll go change into something more . . ." I faltered, glancing down at my yellow sweater. "More, um . . ."

"Bloody?" Nick offered.

"Yes." I swung around and made a valiant attempt not to stomp up into the house.

Dumping my backpack next to my bed, I switched out the sweater for a dark red button-up shirt. It wouldn't show stains as much and wasn't one of my favorites anyway. In the mirror, my face looked awful: white, thin, and delicate, with large purple-gray holes where my eyes should be. I needed a death mask like King Tut's, golden and brimming with life to hide the corpse beneath.

Scrubbing my hands through my hair made it stick up like an insane person's. I needed a cut. I'd had it all chopped off in July but hadn't touched it since. There were old highlights grown out a couple of inches so that you couldn't really tell the roots were roots anymore. If I was generous. I grabbed a handkerchief from my bureau and tied it over my hair like Cinderella. It hardly improved anything.

"Silla?"

Gram Judy stood in the doorway. Her own hair hung in two long braids on either side of her face. The smear of blood across her forehead looked both ridiculous and somehow natural. It had dried a little into the wrinkles between her eyes. "Hi, Gram."

"Judy," she said with a genuine smile.

I walked over to her and slid my arms around her waist. I pressed my cheek to hers and I hugged. Her arms came around my shoulders and she said, "Oh, Silla."

"It was a rough day."

She rubbed my back. "There, pet. We'll get this protection up, and find out who Josephine is pretending to be, and exorcise her permanently. Then you'll be able to relax and have a good time with your charming boy."

"Which has been your plan all along." I felt warmer, thinking about how Gram had been matchmaking for me from the very beginning. At least something was consistent. Gram hadn't changed a jot, even if I'd only known her for a few months.

"That's right." Squeezing my shoulders, she pushed back a little to catch my eyes with hers. "You know what this all means? All this blood stuff?"

I shook my head.

"It means you're strong. Strength is in your blood."

"I hope so."

She grinned. "I know so. Your dad was strong, and your granddad. I ever tell you how we met?"

"No."

"It was in 1978. He was in D.C. for a meeting, and I was marching for the Equal Rights Amendment. I sat down on the curb for a minute because I had a pebble in my shoe. It was a big man's boot I was wearing, being there for gender equality and all, and all of a sudden there was this shadow over me and a voice said, 'Isn't that ironic.' I glanced up, and had to shade myself from the sun with my hand. Your granddad thought I was asking for help to stand and he grabbed my hand and just hoisted me up easy as pie." Judy's face melted into a soft, girlish smile. "He was so pretty, Silla. But I told him off right there, that how dare he assume I needed help to stand, la-dee-da, and you know what? He apologized. Then took me out for coffee. I shouldn't have gone. Ditched my whole march!" She chuckled.

"That's the wrong kind of strong," I teased.

"Ha! Well, you know what I mean."

"You've done so many things. Traveled around the world by yourself. That year you were a hippie."

Judy laughed a single, uproarious laugh. "That was a tough one. Way worse than body snatchers."

With her braids, she looked like a not-quite-retired Viking princess. "I wish I was as brave as you, Judy."

"Baby, you sure are. You've withstood so much, you and that brother of yours. More than you should've had to."

Putting my hands on hers, I said, "I don't know if we ever said it, Judy, but Reese and I are glad you came."

"It's what anyone would have done."

It wasn't true, of course, that anybody would've. But you don't point out the lies everyone knows.

FORTY-ONE

April 1972

 Philip took my hand last Friday and said, "Josephine, grow old with me."

 I laughed, but saw he was serious. The Deacon gave him the carmot we mixed together from the bones of a blood witch like us. But those thirty years are nearly up. I have some time yet to make more, and to convince Philip to drink it with me.

FORTY-TWO

NICHOLAS

I stuck a long stick into the tripod of fire Reese had gotten lit before jogging off into the cemetery. Flames crackled up as one of the logs shifted, shooting sparks up. Standing over it, I let the smoke blow across my face. The bitter smell choked me, but it felt sort of like penance for something. It was different out here, not all contained in a marble fireplace with an iron grate keeping the heat and danger back. Here, if it wasn't watched, the fire could pick a direction and just tear through the grass. Reach the house or the giant bushes. Send everything up.

Pulling the old photo of Mom and Robbie Kennicot out of my jeans, I held it just close enough to the heat for the paper to bend. Mom's smile twisted. Part of me wanted to toss it into the fire, watch it turn brown and curl up. Instead I tucked it back into my jeans.

The grass crunched under my boots as I paced to the bushes and then back to the fire. I wished Silla'd hurry up, and the others. I wanted this over with. From the front of the house, I heard birds singing. The noise made my skin crawl.

And even though the sun wouldn't set for a while, the low clouds made everything darker. Between the house and the fence of thorny bushes, I was trapped.

Just as I started for the magic box, to pull out the blood-letter and at least arm myself with a bit of blood, the back door swung open, slapping against the side of the house.

Silla hopped down the concrete stairs to the patio. "Hey."

Relieved, I moved straight for her. All her hair was hidden under a bright red bandanna. I kissed her. She must have been expecting something else, because she squeaked and caught herself with her hands on my hips. "You okay?" she asked, her mouth an inch from mine.

"Just ready to do this." I kissed her again.

She pressed her lips firmly against mine, and then stepped back. With a sharp nod, she said, "Let's do it, then. Where's Reese?"

I nodded my head toward the bushes. "Cemetery. He said he'd be right back."

"Let's go get him." Silla took my hand and led me to the solid wall of bushes. Just like the night after the party, she knew exactly where to step to avoid the sharpest branches. I closed my eyes and let her hand guide me through. On the other side, I stepped up beside her and helped her up onto the wall. Stopping at the top, Silla took a long breath and gazed out over the slope of the cemetery. I climbed beside her. I'd never really looked at the whole thing laid out like this. Between us and the far side where the wall pushed up against the woods, the mis-matched headstones seemed like toys some giant kid had thrown across a field. A few loner trees bent over clusters of big stone crosses and more regular headstones. Their branches all leaned toward the south, molded that way by the wind, probably.

From this perspective, it all just looked pretty sad.

"I see him," Silla said, hopping down from the wall. I didn't move. I could just make him out, too, standing near the middle, where their parents were buried. After a few steps, Silla turned back to me. "Nick?"

I frowned at her. "Maybe I should wait here. I don't want to—uh—interrupt." Especially if he was talking to his parents.

Her face fell, and for a moment, she looked as sad as the graveyard. Beside a tuft of really tall yellow grass, with a marble headstone on the other side, her bandanna was a glaring red spot. "You're right," she murmured. "I'll be right back."

As she left, I called, "Silla?"

With a little laugh, she turned back around again. "Nick?"

"Be careful." I lifted my head to scan the sky. She got the message, and picked up her pace.

SILLA

The graveyard was awash in cool pink and gray from the reflection of the setting sun on the overcast clouds. My favorite time there, just like it had been when I'd first opened the spell book, first brought that leaf back to life.

This shadowy in-between time seemed the best time for magic.

I approached Reese slowly, not wanting to disturb him. But

I was curious. He hadn't come out here on his own before, that I knew of. So I sank my feet carefully, picking through leaves and dead grass.

He crouched at the foot of their graves, head down. His elbows were propped on his knees, and his hands just dangled down between them. The tight line of his shoulders and his closed eyes made my stomach clench up, too. I'd never seen him look so vulnerable. Stooped and still, like the statue of a sorrowful angel. I just stood, staring at my brother, heart aching.

Wind tickled my face and shook the trees. Evening frogs and cicadas picked up their songs, wailing their high-pitched competition. Wet anticipation clung in the air, promising overnight rain. Reese still didn't move. Not even when the breeze ruffled his dark hair.

"Reese?" I called softly, resting my hand on the huge stone cross beside me.

He rose up to stand in a single, smooth motion. "Hey. Time?"

I nodded and walked forward to take his hand. I squeezed it between both of mine. "You need a shave."

His mouth twitched up on one side. "Thanks, Sil."

"Mom wouldn't have tolerated that scruffy look." I lowered my gaze to his chest, not strong enough to keep looking at his sad eyes.

"She'd have hated your haircut, too." Reese pulled me into his arms rather roughly. "When this is all over, maybe we should leave."

"Leave Yaleylah?" I linked my hands around his back.

"Yeah. I should go to college, and you can come with me."

"I don't want to live in Manhattan, Kansas. The Little Apple," I teased, closing my eyes and pretending we were talking in the kitchen, with Mom and Dad listening. Mom would tug my hair gently for teasing my brother, and Dad would smile as he marked up Latin homework.

But Reese didn't respond like it was a joke. He sighed. The expansion of his ribs stretched my arms. "I don't have to go to K-State. I can go anywhere. Somewhere you'd be happy, too. Somewhere you can have a good senior year, far away from all this. Start new."

I thought about Nick. I didn't want to go somewhere I couldn't kiss him. But he'd be graduating in May and leaving to find his mom. I had no idea where our relationship was going. Where I wanted it to go. I pushed my face into Reese's shoulder. "Maybe Chicago," I muttered. "Judy has an apartment there still."

"Sure. Someplace. Anyplace that isn't here, really."

The gruff tone in his voice made me push back enough to see his face. He scowled at the ground, and my heart popped to see the shine of tears in his eyes. He looked at me, then away. "Everything here is dead, Silla."

"Not us." I found his hands and squeezed them, feeling tears prick my own eyes.

FORTY-THREE

August 1972

He has not given it up. He said, "I'm done. I want to know what it is like to stare in the mirror and see in my hair and on my face all the years I feel in my soul." Philip is melodramatic. He kissed me. "Josephine, we have been together, living wild, for seventy years. An entire human lifetime. And what do we have to show for it? Nothing. No one knows what we do, who we are. Who will remember us?"

"I am happy. I don't care about who will remember us in the future — because I'll be there."

"Stop taking the resurrection potion with me. Let our bodies revert to their own natural rhythms. I will marry you. We could have children, Josie. Can't you imagine how wonderful that could be? It is its own kind of magic. Better magic."

"I don't want to die, Phil. I don't want gray hair or aches in my joints."

"But children, I think" — he paused, and I don't know if what he said next was true — "I think we would make good kids."

I sighed. He will change his mind when he moves out of this funk. It is always ups and downs with Philip.

The Deacon and I will make fresh carmot together again, if Philip will not. And when we do, I will hide it in stir-fry. The soy complements the ginger nicely.

We will both live forever, together. I don't care about anything else.

FORTY-FOUR

NICHOLAS

I sat on the wall, with my elbows on my knees. The rough stone cut into my ass. It was freezing. I shifted, trying to get comfortable.

Everything was so gray. In the distance, the forest around my house was a dark gray blob against a lighter gray sky. Kind of like a forest of thorns surrounding the castle in some goddamn fairy tale. Only this castle didn't have a fairy princess inside, or whatever. It was the home of an evil stepmother. Literally.

Confronting Lilith was gonna be a bitch. How was I going to do it, after we got these protection amulets made? All I knew was that it would murder my dad when he found out he'd slept with more than one crazy witch. For once, I wasn't at all thrilled at the idea.

I was so caught up in staring at the dark trees, thinking about Lilith's sharp fingernails and whether or not I could get her to just back off and leave, I didn't hear her come up behind me.

The shuffle of grass warned me, and I started to turn, expecting Gram Judy. But a cold knife pushed against my neck, and her hand clutched my throat. "Hi, there, Nicky," she said, her breath warm on my ear. "Isn't this convenient?" It wasn't Lilith's voice.

"Josephine," I said, freezing up. The blade cut into my skin, and I tightened my jaw. My hands flexed into fists. I wanted so badly to jump away.

"Very good!"

Golden curls spilled into my sight as she tilted her head around, pushing the dagger into my neck and using my shoulder to climb over the cemetery wall.

It was Ms. Tripp. Looking younger than before in a leather jacket and tight jeans. She grinned. "Surprise!"

I swallowed, and the motion dug the knife in deeper. Pain shot down into my chest, and I felt the first long drip of blood hit the collar of my shirt. "What do you want?"

"Not you, alas." She rolled her eyes. "But it will be much easier to get what I *do* want if you're not being bothersome." Her free hand slid into her jacket pocket.

It was now or never. I knocked aside her arm.

The knife left a searing hot pain in its wake. Josephine stepped back in surprise, but just as I moved to tackle her, she withdrew her pocketed hand and blew something into my face.

Bits of powder pelted my cheeks and eyes. The dust went up my nose and I sneezed. Once and then twice, violently.

It stung my eyes, and I was blinking away tears. My vision narrowed and blipped out like the TV of my life had snapped off.

Small hands pushed at my chest and I stumbled back, flailing my arms to stop my fall. I landed on my ass, my head cracking back. The ground spun under me.

SILLA

The moment the sun sank past the horizon, I knew it. The silver edge to the gray light deepened into purple. Magic time.

Reese had walked forward and put one hand on their gravestone. "Wish you were here," he said quietly but offhandedly, like he was signing a postcard. "Okay, Silla, let's go." He turned to me and froze, staring over my shoulder toward the house. I whirled around.

Ms. Tripp.

She walked confidently, her leisurely steps bringing her through the maze of headstones. Instead of her usual sweater and neat bun, she wore a leather jacket and her curls bounced all around her face like a lion's mane. Her smile made the hair stand up on my arms. "You kids are making this too easy for me, really." She shook her head.

"Who the hell are you?" I felt the anger vibrating from Reese through my back.

"It's Ms. Tripp," I said, trying to keep my voice calm and even as I slipped my hand into my jeans pocket and curled my fingers around my pocketknife.

She shrugged. Casually, like we were meeting in a brightly lit restaurant and not a darkening cemetery. "Call me Josephine, if you prefer. It's what your dad preferred."

"Is that your real body?" I asked, refusing to rise to her bait.

Josephine actually spun for us. A little pirouette on one foot with her arms out.

It's what made me notice the blade in her hand. A big silver wedge of a butcher's knife.

We couldn't give her the chance to use it. As she planted

herself back onto the ground, I walked forward. "Leave us alone, Josephine. Get out of here. I won't help you get the bones, and we don't need you. We'll fight you."

Her face fell into a pout, and she raised her knife, tapping it gently against the side of her face. It left a smear of blood. "That was Nick's attitude, too, and look what happened to him."

My stomach dropped like I was on the upside-down loop of a roller coaster. "You're lying." I said it like a command, as if that would make it true. I flicked out my pocketknife.

"Oh, Silla!" Josephine grinned and pressed her hands to her chest. The knife was pale and hard against the black leather jacket. "You're delightful!"

Reese grabbed my shoulders, hard. "Ow!" I jerked, but he said, "Stop struggling, darling."

He said it, and so did Josephine, at the exact same time.

No. I twisted my neck, and he shook me, forcing my knees out so that I hit the earth hard enough to jar my teeth. I brandished the pocketknife, but they said, "Over here." Their voices pounded at me in stereo, one high, one low and oh so familiar.

How could I fight him?

Reese dragged me to the grave, where Josephine leaned her hip against Mom and Dad's grave marker.

I struggled against him, digging my heels in and pulling away—I tried to flip open the pocketknife, but he shook me again, jostling my brain, and then he threw me to the ground. The knife hit beside me with a thud. I got up onto my hands and knees, fingers sinking into the graveyard dirt. His hand reached around me, and he dug the pocketknife out of the grass.

Josephine grabbed my hair, pulling my head up. The pain brought tears to my eyes.

I didn't know what to do. Panic whirled in my stomach, making me go hot and cold in flashes.

Reese knelt behind me, his strong arms trapping mine, and I could smell him, my brother's outside, dry hay smell, with the undercurrent of oil that never quite went away because it had sunk into his skin and under his nails.

"If you'd only cooperated," Josephine grumbled as she bent in front of me, flashing the knife past my face. Reese finished the sentence, whispering harshly in my ear, "This wouldn't—be—necessary."

Pinned between my brother and Josephine, I closed my eyes and thought frantically for a way out. I just needed blood. Just a little, to banish her from Reese, and to—to get away from her.

"Please," I whimpered, grateful for the tears that plopped out of my eyes. "Please stop, I'll do what you want." The mask I fit over my face was a sickly yellow, like vomit and fear. "Please, just don't hurt me." I clutched at Josephine's jacket.

Our eyes met, very close together. Hers were a raging blue, dark and flecked with gray at the edges. Beautiful like a tidal wave about to destroy you. They narrowed, studying me with a predator's keen gaze. I held tight to my mask of terror, letting her see all the pain and fear I had for Reese, the doubt about what she'd done to Nick, the knowledge that she'd killed my parents and they couldn't stop her, either.

Josephine smiled. It softened her expression into one of almost friendliness, and she said very gently, "There, now, Silla. It will be better if you help willingly."

With a quick motion, she slashed my chest with her knife.

Pain exploded as blood poured down from my collarbone like a necklace. I faltered back, but Reese caught me.

"Just let your blood spill, Silla, and undo the curse you laid on this grave."

The reek of the blood burned in my nose, and I forced myself to open my eyes. Josephine stood and moved back just enough.

Turning in Reese's arms, I tugged down the neck of his T-shirt and slapped my bloody hand onto the permanent-marker rune I'd drawn over his heart that morning. "Be free, Reese!" I cried, pushing my burning magic from the raw cut over my heart all the way down my arm and into my brother.

The shock of magic blew us both back, and Reese and I landed several feet apart. Reese's eyes popped open wide and met mine, and I knew it was him in that instant. He leapt to his feet, a snarl on his face as he whirled to Josephine.

I scrambled out of the way, smearing my hand across my chest to ready more blood. Together, Reese and I would finish her.

With the roar of a warrior, Reese charged Josephine. She whipped her knife at him, and he caught her wrist in one hand. He had my pocketknife in the other. "You can't have me anymore, Josephine," he said. "My heart is shielded from you."

Josephine dug into her jacket and drew out a handful of something as dark as mud. She lifted it and threw it at Reese.

He dodged the flying dust, releasing her wrist at the same time. Baring her teeth, she stabbed the knife into his chest.

Through the heart rune.

The world dropped out from under me.

My scream caught in my throat.

Josephine held on to the hilt where it stuck out from Reese's ribs. She laughed.

Reese's head tilted down, and for a moment, he stared at the knife. So did I. So did Josephine.

I could not move. Couldn't breathe. My body was encased in stone. It wasn't real. It couldn't be real.

Reese took a deep, impossible breath, and then swung his arm around, burying my pocketknife high in Josephine's side.

Her mouth popped open, and her eyes widened.

The two of them leaned together, caught in a bloody embrace.

Josephine yanked herself away, hands clasping the knife in her side. She staggered back, fell against a headstone.

The cemetery spun like a merry-go-round as Reese dropped to his knees. I felt the contact vibration as if the ground was made of tin.

His hands gripped the hilt.

"No!" I shrieked, finally able to move. I jumped toward him, landing next to him and covering his hands with mine. "Don't, don't take it out."

"Sil." His whisper was like dry leaves rubbing on my skin. He pulled the knife out in one smooth motion.

Blood darkened his black T-shirt in a flood, and he swayed backward. I barely got behind him as he fell, landing on me. He coughed, his face contorting with pain. I wrapped my arms around him and grappled with the hole in his shirt, tearing. "I can heal it, Reese, I'll regenerate this, I can do it."

The smell choked me, and red flashed over my eyes: red-soaked carpet, red splashed over gravel, red in a thick, chunky mess around what was left of my dad's face. I squeezed my eyes shut and pushed my hands over the slick wound, feeling waves of blood pour over my fingers with the rhythm of Reese's heart.

His breath bubbled. I shifted out from under him, laying Reese down on the dirt. On my knees, I smeared my filthy hand across the cut on my collarbone, sending shocks of fiery pain straight to my stomach. Then I pressed my blood to his.

"Sil," my brother whispered. He reached up and touched my face. "Be well," he said.

It sounded like a goodbye, but it wasn't.

It was magic.

New pain scorched across my chest. The power surged up from the ground, from the air, from Reese. And into me. The leaves all around us flew up and spun around us in a tornado.

Reese flared like a firecracker.

Then his hand fell, slapping into the dry leaves of the forest floor.

NICHOLAS

Being temporarily blind was quite the eye-opener.

My blood rushed in my ears, pounding against my skull like I was trapped underwater. Over and over, my heartbeat drowned me in the noise.

Under me, the cemetery ground was cold and rough. I dug

my fingers into thick grass, gripping as if my life depended on it.

And it did.

It was just me and the cemetery.

I could hear everything. Grass against stone, the shuffle of my hands over dry leaves. Faraway wind blowing through trees. A billion bugs screaming like sirens.

For the briefest instant, I thought I could hear the clouds blowing past overhead.

Then a cry—Silla's cry. Fear shot through me. I had to help her.

Rolling over, I crawled to the cemetery wall. The rough edges were perfect. I shoved up and sat with my legs crossed, and before I could think harder, I reached up to the corner and dragged my hand over the edge as hard as I could.

The pain was immediate, and I shouted. Cradling my hand against my chest, I was suddenly glad that I couldn't see how badly I'd messed it up. Waves of pain pumped up my arm, and I felt blood and heat filling my palm.

I could do this. It was in my hands—in my blood. "Blood to heal," I whispered, thinking of my mom, who could do anything with just a little blood and a bad rhyme. Like the paper stars and hearts floating over my bed.

I cupped my hand, squeezing it, letting the blood pool grow. My eyes were shut because it was easier than remembering I couldn't see.

Bending close to my hands, I sucked in a deep breath, full of coppery blood. *I can do this,* I thought again. "Blood of mine, magic ignite. Cleanse my eyes, and restore my sight." I said it again as the itch drove up my spine and I felt the heat of magic burn in my scraped hand. In the total darkness, it was hard to believe anything had happened. I could feel myself blinking as I painted my own blood over my eyelids.

I repeated my crappy rhyme a third time. Then I pressed my hands flat to my face, fingers over my closed eyes. For a second, I didn't move.

Rubbing my hands down, I slowly opened my eyes, blinking away drops of blood.

Dim gray shapes blurred into view.

I grinned, and a burst of shocked laughter shoved out of me. I'd done it! I'd beaten that bitch, and could see again. I'd won. With only my blood.

I climbed to my feet, cradling my throbbing hand against my stomach, and looked out over the cemetery.

The first real thing I saw was Silla, stumbling toward me. Her hands left scarlet prints on every headstone she touched.

FORTY-FIVE

It is the worst thing I have ever done.

My real name is Philip Osborn, and I killed a seventeen-year-old boy because I was afraid to die.

# FORTY-SIX

SILLA

Seven hours after they declared my brother dead, I heard flapping wings against my bedroom window.

I'd been staring at the ceiling after hours of interrogation by Sheriff Todd, vomiting in the bathroom while Gram rubbed my back, and crying and crying as if my internal spigot had been turned to ON. I was tired enough that my blood felt like lead in my veins, but was unable to sleep. Unable to do anything but lie there while tears crept down my temples and into my hair. Nausea swam in my stomach like a goldfish.

I wanted him back, more than I'd ever wanted anything. I imagined regenerating his body, pushing life back into it. Seeing his eyes open and his lips pull back into a smile . . . but he was dead. Just like Mom and Dad, he'd died and left me for someplace else. Someplace better, I hoped. If anybody deserved heaven, it was my brother.

And his blood, like theirs, had soaked into my hands. Into the cloth of my jeans as I'd knelt in it. I'd smeared it everywhere: on headstones, on Nick. It had gotten on his face as I'd dragged him back to Reese's body. I squeezed my eyes shut. My head pounded, and my sinuses burned.

The wing beats shocked my heart into action. I jumped out of bed and ran to the window. Nothing.

It was six in the morning, and the far eastern horizon—past Nick's house, beyond the cemetery—glinted with gentle silver light. The maple tree in our front yard was still. My breath fogged the glass and I wiped it away, peering into the gloomy morning. Had I imagined the sound of feathers? Had it only been a gust of wind?

A crow cawed, and I almost swallowed my tongue.

Where was she? That horrible bitch! Tears scalded my eyes again as I thought of her, of her knife stabbing into my brother.

One of the branches of the maple jerked as a crow took flight. It flapped toward me, screaming. I slapped my hand flat against the window, and the crow wheeled back, settling down again on the maple. Then I could see them. A dozen black crows hiding behind the leaves. Watching me.

I whirled, ran downstairs, and slammed out the front door. The hard gravel poked into my bare feet, but I darted at the tree, waving my arms and yelling, "Go away! Leave me alone!" I hit the tree with my shoulder. "Go away!"

The smooth bark bit back as I punched and slapped at it with my hands. I grabbed the whole trunk in my arms and shook. Tears flooded my eyes, and the branches overhead shuddered. Leaves fell; the crows squawked and cackled. I screamed at them, then backed up and spread my arms. Their black wings flapped and beat, pushing leaves into my face. "Here I am," I said. "Take me if you want me." I could die, too.

But the noise faded. Leaves fluttered around my bare feet, reminding me of Reese, tossing a dead leaf into the air and laughing as it blossomed into a fresh green thing before settling on the cemetery ground.

I was alone.

The world around me blurred, and through my tears I couldn't see where the birds had gone.

I made my way back to the porch and pulled on my sneakers. The tears coating my eyes were like shellac, like a hard, crystallized film over my eyeballs that I couldn't get to go away. I hated it, and I rubbed at them. But something inside me was broken.

The chilly air pecked at my cheeks and bare arms. I bounced back and forth on my toes. The gravel crunched.

Reese had been a runner, and that's all I wanted to do. Run. Escape. I took off down the road, jogging at first to warm up my muscles, and then stretching my legs farther and farther until I sprinted full out. The gravel slid beneath me, and I panted. When my chest ached, I pushed on and didn't let myself stop. The pain cut more sharply than any knife, and my breath puffed out in front of me. In and out, in and out, harsh and smooth and then harsh again. My feet pounded, jarring my knees and my hips until the muscles loosened.

My vision swam in the darkness, and the nausea cooled down. The wind dried out my eyes.

I lost time and space for a brief moment: I was free.

Then I stumbled.

I slowed, caught myself, and then collapsed onto the gravel road, panting and heaving with effort. I rolled onto my back.

The tiny rocks poked into my shoulder blades, my hips, my calves. I spread out my arms and stared up at the sky. All I could hear was my raging breath. High overhead, the stars glittered at me.

Had it only been four days since I sat on the porch with his shoulder against mine, looking up at the constellations? Oh, God, it hurt. It was impossible that he was gone. Not him, too.

I began to hear the wind through the trees and singing crickets.

Sweat cooled on my forehead.

But my breath did not calm, or my blood stop racing. It built harder and faster, until I wanted to explode the way Reese had in July, after Mom and Dad died, when he'd punched a hole through the bedroom wall. My fists ached to do the same.

"Reese," I whispered. Then again, louder: "Reese."

Why had he left me?

"Reese!" I screamed.

Silence.

FORTY-SEVEN

To my children: Silla, Reese

    I pray with all the strength in me that you never have to read this. That I will defeat her today, and by tonight will have joined you and your mother for a late dinner in Kansas City. Together we will go apartment hunting for Reese, and everything will be as it should be. As it was supposed to be.

    Though that, I realize, is something I destroyed long ago: should be, supposed to be. When I made the decision I did, to take this body from the soul who rightfully possessed it.

    Here is my confession:

    I am not your father.

    I was born in 1803 outside Boston, Massachusetts, named Philip by my mother and Osborn by my friend the Deacon. I am a doctor and healer and magician, and because of her, a murderer.

    I had to escape her, my loves. I had to be free of Josephine.

    This confession is muddled, is it not? Reese should

be asking for details, and Silla for meaning. Oh, my children.

I stole this diary when I pretended to die, when I burned our house in Boston, and it is fitting that here, now, in what may be my final hours in this world, I should use it to confess to my children.

FORTY-EIGHT

NICHOLAS

At ten the morning after, my cell rang. I was wound so tight I almost fell off my bed.

Her name blinked on the screen. And I hesitated. I didn't know what to say.

I thought of the sheriff and Judy finding us in the middle of the cemetery, my arms around Silla, but not to comfort her, to pin her there, to keep her back from Reese. Her staring, comatose eyes. I thought of Reese's body, his blood everywhere and making me gag. His eyes half-open, his mouth slack.

I didn't know what to say to Silla, but I had to say something. So I flipped open the phone and walked to the window. "Hey."

"Hi." Her voice was soft, barely there.

Silence fell between us, and I pressed my bandaged hand to the cold glass. Under the bandage, stitches held together the gash I'd made on the cemetery wall. It throbbed, and the cold helped. I stared out past my fingers.

The woods looked so normal in the morning light. Not like the place the sheriff had tracked Josephine's blood trail to, not like the place they'd lost her. They'd searched Ms. Tripp's house and found several fake IDs—and not the kind you use to sneak into a club when you're sixteen. They were birth certificates and driver's licenses with her picture but different names. So they put out a statewide APB or whatever. Sheriff Todd didn't want to think she was coming back but had promised my dad there'd be regular deputies driving by our place and Silla's. Bullshit. They wanted her to be gone.

I looked past the forest to the cemetery.

It hadn't been hard for me and Gram Judy to convince everybody Ms. Tripp had been obsessed with the old stories, that it had made her crazy. If they suspected we'd done magic, too, they weren't saying anything to me about it. Maybe because everybody knew the rumors but nobody wanted to open a real investigation, real death, up to that kind of speculation. They were happier thinking Tripp had been behind it all. I noticed everybody around here liked to keep things working the way they wanted them to work. They didn't ask questions that might have knocked our delicately constructed story to the ground.

Except Dad and Lilith. I could feel them wondering. Right now they were downstairs, working together. They'd been remarkably quiet, both of them, all morning, mostly leaving me alone. Dad hadn't left for his usual four-day business trip, but hadn't pushed any kind of father-son bonding on me, either. Or said he told me so. It was like he was saying instead, *Son, I'm here if you need me.* I hadn't managed to find a way to let him know I knew what he was doing, and appreciated it, even if I didn't really want to talk to him at all.

And Lilith was acting like a human being. Breakfast had sucked, but not for the usual reasons. Dad and Lilith had kept up senseless chatter and passed me French toast and hash browns without forcing me to talk. I'd only sat there, chewing on a couple of forkfuls of potatoes that made me slightly nauseated, and feeling guilty for not talking. Then Lilith's elbow bumped into Dad as he was reaching for another helping of scrambled eggs, and her grape juice splashed onto the table-cloth. It wasn't even close to the right color, but I threw myself backward, my chair crashing to the floor. I covered my face with my hands and breathed and breathed and breathed.

All I saw was blood.

It had been Lilith who said, "Jer, take him into the kitchen for some cool water. I'll clean this up."

I didn't want her kindness. But I took it.

Cold leached into my head from the window, and finally I said the stupidest thing to Silla: "How are you?"

"Okay."

From the stereo behind me, Weezer was complaining about the girl you can't resist because she's only in your dreams.

She pulled a long, slow breath, then said, "I need to see you."

"Sure," I answered immediately. I wanted to kiss her, to remember she was still alive. To remind her that she was, too.

"Come to Dairy Queen."

"The . . . Dairy Queen?"

"Please."

We hung up. I grabbed a sweatshirt and slipped outside.

SILLA

Gram Judy sent me to get napkins.

It was the most inane thing, but she said I needed something to do. Since the funeral was tomorrow and we'd have a wake at our house afterward, we needed napkins.

I drove Reese's truck. The whole cab smelled like oil and hay and sweat. When I turned the ignition, Bruce Springsteen exploded out of the CD player. I hated the upbeat rock and extended guitar solos, but couldn't bring myself to turn it off.

My hands curled around the wheel, and I thought of Reese's hands. Of his sixteenth birthday, when he'd finally bought the truck. He'd wanted to go out with friends, but Mom made him stay in. It was a weeknight, and she said he could go out Friday. I helped her make fried chicken. Reese was being such an asshole, saying if he had to stay home he'd stay in his room—only he was cussing, and Mom was trying so hard not to cry. Dad came home, and when he found out Reese was pouting in his room, he told Mom and me to go ahead and set the table. I don't know what Dad said, but they both came down about fifteen minutes later, and Reese apologized to Mom. We ate dinner, and Reese opened his presents. I gave him some game for his PlayStation that he'd been really wanting, and Mom gave him a sweater and a credit for three hundred dollars off the price of his truck. He'd been saving up to buy it for a year, and that put him over the top. Dad told him that the truck was waiting at Mr. Johnston's, getting new tires, which were from Dad. Dad also gave him the bracelet with the tiger's-eye stone in it. We had ice cream and butterscotch cupcakes, which were Reese's favorite.

Maybe at the grocery store I'd buy a box of cupcakes to go with my napkins.

After I pulled into the parking lot at Mercer's Grocer, I had to rub at my sticky cheeks. I had that drowning feeling, like the memories and thoughts were a rushing river, surrounding me and pulling me under, and all I could do was fight for air. It left me shaking.

I climbed out of the truck and into the sun. Five other cars filled the lot, and I recognized them all. God, I hoped everyone would just let me go about my business. Maybe looking like a wreck would actually help with that. Gripping my purse, I tried to walk like I was fine, eyes on the asphalt before me.

Mr. Emory held the door open for me. "Hey, Silla girl, you're doing okay?" Wrinkles hid the corners of his mouth. I nodded, glancing briefly at his eyes.

A trick of the sun made their regular brown suddenly black and cold.

I jerked away, slamming my back into the edge of the door.

"Silla?" He cocked his head and light flooded into his eyes, reflecting normally.

"Um." I shook my head. "Sorry, Mr. Emory. I'm fine. Thanks," I whispered.

Lips pursed irritably, he nodded and backed away. Slowly, I confronted the inside of the grocery store.

Josephine could be anywhere.

Pressing into the glass storefront, I scanned the aisles of food. Two cashiers waited: Beth and Erica Ellis in blue aprons, sisters who'd worked as baggers forever until being promoted last year. Mrs. Anthony and her son Pete were in the canned fruit row. Pete was kicking his chubby legs from the kid seat in the cart. There was Mrs. Morris deciding between Cheerios and Frosted Flakes. Mr. Mercer, the owner, was back by the tiny butcher station talking to Jim, the butcher.

Any of them. All of them. I hadn't seen where Josephine's crows had flown off to. Maybe she was waiting for me to let my guard down. My heartbeat filled my ears as I walked steadily toward the paper goods. Everyone glanced at me. Watching. Just like the crows had. It was just like that awful day at school after Wendy'd been possessed. I saw enemies everywhere. And today, I knew kindergarten tactics like drawing runes over my heart were useless.

Even little Pete stopped kicking his legs as I passed.

I grabbed a bag of cheap paper napkins and barely re-strained myself from running to the checkout line.

Erica Ellis smiled sympathetically. "Did you find what you needed?" she asked, like she always did.

I laughed, and it sounded hysterical even to me.

She paused, glancing over at her sister with raised eye-brows. But what I needed was *not* in a freaking grocery store.

When she took my five-dollar bill, there was a new wari-ness there, like I might be contagious. She frowned at the cuts on my hands. I wanted to pull down my sweatshirt to display the long, jagged pink scar across my collarbone.

But behind her, I caught the hostile look on Beth's face. They could all so easily be enemies. Be Josephine.

So I said nothing, just grabbed my change and napkins and left.

NICHOLAS

The Yaleylah Dairy Queen was a small concrete building next to the grocery store where I'd gotten coffee with Eric, with giant, dirty windows for a front and a huge white and red sign. I could see the peeling plastic of the booths and the tired-looking kid slouched behind the counter before I was twenty feet away.

Fortunately, I was saved from going inside by a honk. Silla opened the door to Reese's truck as I turned. She slid out and went around to the tail to grab something out of the back.

I put my elbow up on the edge of the truck bed. She had Mom's lacquered box.

Silla offered it to me. "I don't want this in my house."

My chest tightened. "Oh. Okay." And here I'd been looking forward to telling her what I'd done to my eyes. Thinking maybe it would distract her a little, make her excited about the magic again.

Releasing the box into my hands, she stepped back, arms wrapped around her stomach. Before she turned away, I saw tears on her cheeks. Her hair hung lank around her face. All the quick pain of rejection broke up, and I just wanted to make her stop hurting instead.

"Silla, aw, Silla." I set the box hurriedly on the asphalt and reached for her. She didn't turn around, but she let me hold her shoulders, and even leaned back against me. I pressed my cheek against her hair. Her hands slowly slid up and crossed over her chest, and she gripped my fingers tightly. We still had each other. We did. I had to believe that. She wasn't rejecting me, even though the magic was part of me—was something I wanted. This was just a violent reaction to grief. It had to be.

"I see her everywhere, Nicholas."

"Josephine?" I didn't really want to say her name, and whispering it made it a little better.

"Yeah. I can't believe she just left."

"Neither do I."

"Everyone I look at—that's her. I couldn't go into Dairy Queen because Mr. Denley was there, staring at me. I froze, just waiting for him to pick up a knife and come after me. And in the grocery store, I was even afraid of a toddler."

I squeezed her, guilt sort of poking at my ribs since none of this had even occurred to me. While I'd been thinking about me, about my magic and the town believing us, about the first dead body I'd really seen, here was my girlfriend falling to pieces. I sucked. I'd make it up to her. "We'll figure something out." The protection amulets. We'd make them. We'd make them, just the two of us.

"I can't stop crying, either."

I hugged her as tightly as I could, trying to make her feel like I wasn't going anywhere.

After a long moment while cars drove slowly past and wind blew the warm sunlight off my face, she said, "Why does she get to be alive and Reese is dead?"

I was helpless. "I'm so sorry," I whispered.

"You broke my masks, Nick."

"What?"

"My masks. You ruined them."

She didn't sound angry, but I started to pull away.

"If you hadn't been able to see through them, I'd never have even thought for a moment that I didn't—didn't need them. But you just waltzed in and looked past and saw me and everything I was and could do—you knew the magic, you knew all the secrets." Her chest heaved and her voice hardened.

I let go of her, hurt. She kept her back to me.

"No one ever told us. The stupid, horrible secrets. Magic! Blood magic. And Dad knew it, and never told us. It's his fault that he died, and that Mom died. Reese was right. It doesn't matter who pulled the trigger." Silla whirled on me. "I know how he felt now, how Reese felt." Her hands balled into fists and she raised them between us. "Look! I want to hit something, destroy something. Anything. I'm so *angry*, Nick. Reese was right, and now he's gone and I'm alone."

I winced. I thought she had me, but how could I say that? Her whole family was dead.

"I'm sorry, Nick." Her eyes closed. "I just need . . . I don't know what I need. Take that box away from me. Please."

Maybe I shouldn't have listened. Maybe I should have pushed back. Because I was getting angry that I'd finally picked up the magic on my own, used it well and without being haunted by my mom's stupid choices, and now Silla didn't want it. Didn't seem to count me at all as somebody to need. Who needed her. I didn't know what that meant for us.

So I took my mom's box, and I left.

As I walked away, I heard her open the truck's creaking door. I heard her tears. But I only tightened my grip on the box until my messed-up hand began throbbing again. Reminding me, over and over, that the magic was part of me.

FORTY-NINE

She was poisoning me—Josephine, the witch who I created.

I called to the Deacon for aid, and he sent me here to Missouri, where long ago he'd settled, and so his blood is in the veins of this family. He surely didn't know what I would do to his great-grandson, Robert Kennicot.

I brought her diary, ripping out a few pages to leave for her as proof it was destroyed in the fire, and left all other memories of my life before I stole this one. Poor Robert. His mother called him Robbie, and so, too, did his girlfriend, Donna. After she fled, no one called him—me!—Robbie again.

She knew I was not her Robbie. I saw it in her face so long ago. When she ran up to me one morning and grabbed my hand. A smear of blood was pressed between our fingers, connecting us so suddenly that Donna could see the truth in me. I should have stopped her, but couldn't. Donna had such an open face, even in her fear, and I wished in that moment that I had been who she wanted me to be. But I was not. And I was not seventeen, despite this body. I haven't been a teenaged boy in too long.

The blood did not tell Donna what she was hoping for. Her power was not as sophisticated and nuanced as mine. She shook her head and her eyes filled with tears. "He's dead, isn't he?" she whispered. I nodded. And I stared as she fled, running straight through the cemetery toward her house.

I don't know if I lied to her. I killed him, no doubt. But when? Not the moment I took the body. No—for weeks I felt his will pressing gently against mine when I slipped into sleep. I don't remember when it faded. What day or time Robert Kennicot's spirit finally fell to pieces.

This sprawls widely off track, doesn't it, Reese? It would not make a decent monologue, would it, Silla?

But if I do not put down my secrets, how will I spend this remaining time waiting for her to come for me?

FIFTY

SILLA

Gram Judy drove us to the church in her little Rabbit. I just tried not to puke and watched the bright morning zip past. It wasn't very funereal. There was so much color everywhere: autumn leaves, blue sky, brilliant sun. All bold and sure of themselves. The opposite of how I was feeling. Reese would have said something obnoxious, but nothing appropriate occurred to me.

My stomach turned over, and I wished I'd brought the quickly vanishing bottle of Pepto-Bismol I'd been gorging myself with for the past twenty-four hours. It was worse when I managed to be hungry and nauseated at the same time. A stomach that growled and burbled simultaneously was certainly a recipe for some special kind of torturous hell.

"Silla, honey, how you doing?" Gram Judy asked as she paused at a stoplight. "We'll get through it," she continued when I didn't respond. *Like we did before* rang in the subtext.

I glanced at her. She'd dressed as nicely as I'd seen her since July, in a raw silk suit and giant pearl earrings. Her hair was up in a chignon and clipped in place with jeweled pins. It had been her idea to add a pearl necklace to my pink sundress, and a gray cardigan because it was too cold. She'd even gotten out a pair of scissors and trimmed a couple of the more outrageous chunks of my hair, and clipped barrettes in a pretty pattern. I looked like a little kid out for Easter, not her brother's funeral.

We arrived at the church, and I took the cowardly route of letting Gram Judy play nice instead of doing so myself.

I was only here for one reason.

I left Gram at the front pew, greeting people and shaking hands, and climbed up to the communion table, where I could stand before the coffin. The wood was shiny yellow. I touched its smooth finish. My hand was pale against it. I averted my eyes from the open half. I didn't want to see him, even though I'd agreed to the open casket.

Yaleylah shuffled and murmured as it gathered behind me. There was sniffling and the slick clacking of heels on the floor. To my right, Mrs. Artley played a quiet tune on the piano.

Now was the moment.

Closing my eyes, I dug into my purse for the spell book. Such a small, old-looking thing to have caused so much pain. I pressed it to my stomach. Memories of it flashed through my head. Unwrapping it at the kitchen table, shoving it at Reese, holding it open on my lap, listening to his deep voice as he listed ingredients.

My stomach lurched. I'd never laugh with him again over grilled-cheese-and-tomato sandwiches, or yell at him when he left his sweaty running shorts on the bathroom floor, or accuse him of drinking too much, or make fun of his questionable girl-friend choices, or push him into getting an engineering degree instead of *farming*, for God's sake. Reese, who was smart and took care of me and—

I couldn't breathe. My chest pinched, and I leaned into the coffin. I wanted to slam my fists into it, to break it into a thousand pieces and fling them everywhere.

Finally I looked at him. It wasn't him, not really. As unrecognizable as my own face had been in the mirror this morning. A waxy death mask. His hair was combed back, the stubble I'd teased him about gone. Face peaceful—but falsely so. It wasn't like when he slept. It was empty.

I tucked the book against his chest. "I'm so sorry, Reese," I whispered. I never should have made him try the magic. Never should have let myself feel the burn of its power, or believed it could bring any beauty into our lives.

All it had brought was death. And now I would bury the magic with my brother.

NICHOLAS

After the funeral (which sucked), I dropped Dad and Lilith off at home and walked back down the road to Silla's house. I wanted to avoid the forest path and cemetery.

Cars flooded the street, and I had to pick my way around them. As I approached the house, an empty sort of dread settled in the pit of my chest. On the roof, about a dozen crows roosted. Watching everything. Not really doing anything. Not playing or squawking like crows usually did but sitting there. Chilling. Occasionally one flapped its wings.

I walked faster. Silla was probably going nuts. And tonight, after everyone was gone, we'd make those damn protection amulets, finally. So that bitch couldn't hurt anyone else.

Silla was in the kitchen, dutifully accepting casseroles and Jell-O salads in her pink dress. A clunky silver bracelet pressed against the bones of her wrist. I'd never seen it before—but it made me realize that she wasn't wearing any of her rings.

I stood at the door as she let church ladies hug her and shook men's hands. Her lips barely moved as she spoke.

Wendy burst in, and hugged Silla. Her shoulders shook, and Silla just clutched at her back, eyes dry. The kitchen was invaded by drama club kids, pushing around and trying to get to Silla to tell her how damn sorry they were.

The whole thing was sorry.

I was about to force my way in, too, to rescue her from the swarm, when Silla rescued herself. She smiled tightly and said something. Wendy hugged her again, and Silla just pulled away, shoving through the crowd.

"Silla." I reached out.

She blew right past me. For a second, I went cold, thinking she still wanted me to go away. But I'd seen that look on her face, the torn-up expression and her eyes not seeing anything or anyone.

I dashed up the stairs after her.

On the second floor, she pushed into a purple bedroom. I followed, and stopped suddenly. Masks covered the walls, staring at us with a hundred empty eyes. I don't know how she slept under so many eerie faces. I barely managed not to frown at them.

Silla flung herself onto the bed, grinding her face into the pillow.

The empty eye sockets of a white and green checkered mask glared at me from over her head. It wore a jester's hat.

"This is creepy, Sil."

She flipped around and sat up, eyes wide. "Nick!"

I held up my hands. "I thought you could use a punching bag." *See, this is me, the new and improved Nick Pardee, available to girl-friends and crazy people in their time of need.* I never would have been here for any of the girls I saw in Chicago. But I couldn't imagine not being here for Silla.

Her lips pressed together, and she looked into her lap. "Nick. I can't do this."

I knelt at her knees but didn't touch her. I wanted to, but wasn't sure she wanted me to.

"Just look at me!" She spread her hands. "I'm a mess! I can't stop crying, and it all just hurts so much. I can't eat—I'm nauseated all the time, and my head aches, and it's just awful."

"Your brother died, babe." I said it as lightly as I could, and gently touched her knee. "And you lost your parents just a little bit ago. There's still a crazy bitch stalking you and crows covering your roof. You aren't supposed to be okay."

Her jaw dropped. She stared at me. For once, I had no idea what was whirling behind her eyes. I hoped she wasn't going to ream me, or tell me to leave. I swallowed hard, forcing my hand to stay in place on her knee.

Then suddenly she slid forward and fell down into my arms. She wrapped hers around my neck and pressed her cheek against mine. I closed my eyes. The whole length of her fit against me as I knelt on the carpet. My arms encircled her easily, and her breasts pushed against me through her thin dress. I heard the blood roaring in my ears and held her tighter, smelling her shampoo, her delicate perfume. Tears made her cheek sticky, but I didn't care. This was why I'd come. We needed each other.

A breeze ruffled the purple curtains at the window, letting in the muffled sound of conversations and the crunch of gravel outside. The masks on the walls ranged from happy, grinning faces to horrible demonic glares.

"What is all this stuff, anyway?" I murmured. "The masks?"

Without moving, she said, "They're theater masks and Venetian masks. Most are from catalogs and stuff."

"They're watching me."

"Yeah," she said softly. She curled a hand up in the ends of my hair, tickling my neck. "Like guardians."

Rubbing her back, I said, "They're kind of creepy."

I could feel her smile against my ear. "Yeah. I like that, too."

I laughed a little. Of course she did. "You eaten anything today?"

"No."

"You should."

"I'm not ready to go downstairs again."

"Okay, babe. I'll go get something."

"Will you tell Judy where I am?"

"Sure thing."

I started to pull back, but she caught my shoulders and said, "I'm sorry for yesterday. What I said."

I couldn't keep the smile off my face. "Don't worry about it."

"I'm so glad you're here."

"Me too."

She leaned onto her heels, looking tiny and desperate against the bed, with her feet tucked up under the pink dress and her hands limp in her lap.

"I'll be right back," I promised as I stood, feeling pretty damn good for a guy at a funeral.

FIFTY-ONE

For years, I convinced myself I had never been Philip but was only Robert Kennicot. I went away to the university, I met Emily, and I loved her effortlessly. Your mother was majoring in biology, always teasing me about my Latin, as if I were archaic and boring.

I will die now, for her. For all of you.

When you were born, Reese, I had never been so full of magic as I was the first time you lay between Emily and me. When all our hands touched, when I saw my nose in your nose. You stared at everything, just watching, not reaching to touch or put it in your mouth. Just watching. It has always amazed me, the depth behind your eyes, even when you were barely a few months old. Emily always said you were as stubborn as I, and as thoughtful. Reese, son. I beg you not to pursue this. If you find these confessions because I have died, put them away and continue on your path. Become a great scientist, a farmer. Work the land, as your hands have always told you. Think no more on the mistakes of your father.

FIFTY-TWO

SILLA

When the only ones left were Gram Judy's bunko buddies, Nick and I went outside. It was nearing sunset, and with the crows at our back, we followed my regular path through the forsythia. The prickly branches scratched at my hair, and I showed Nick the best way to duck and twist around the grasping thorns. On the other side, the cemetery was quiet, overgrown, as usual. Except for the backhoe hunkered down between rows of graves.

Reese's grave was blanketed in loose sod just to the north of Mom's and Dad's. There was no headstone yet. That took a while—and I hadn't picked an epitaph. Judy had put several before me, but I hadn't been able to focus on the words.

"Why'd they leave it out here?" Nick asked, jerking his chin at the backhoe. "Eager to make another trip tomorrow?"

I just shook my head. "They probably borrowed it from Mr. Meroon. I bet the parish's is over at the other cemetery."

"So Meroon uses the same tractor for tilling land and burying the dead. It has a nice sort of circularity." Nick picked up his flask and held it out over the fresh grave. "I have tainted the inside of my flask with beer. For Reese?"

"Yes."

He tipped the contents out, and the yellow-brown liquid cascaded briefly onto the grass. The stream caught the dying sunlight and turned into a band of gold.

Crows hid all over the cemetery. They tucked themselves into shadows, some hunkered down like feathery fluff balls, and some stood with their necks stretched and tall. A handful, a dozen, I wasn't sure. They didn't move toward us or cry out to one another; they just watched. Silently, unnaturally.

I leaned against Mom and Dad's headstone, drawing runes in the dirt and then scratching them out. A crow landed about fifty feet away. Nick picked up a rock and threw it, hitting the ground near the crow's feet. The crow flapped backward, cawing angrily.

"Thanks," I said. I dropped the stick and put my hands in my lap. "Do you ever wonder if it says anything about our relationship that we're always meeting up in a cemetery?"

"That we're eternal and peaceful?"

I smiled. "That isn't what I was thinking."

"You're right. You don't make me feel peaceful." The little smile fell off his mouth, and some intense look replaced it. We watched each other for a moment, until I had to glance away. I fiddled with Reese's bracelet, heavy on my wrist. My rings were tucked under my pillow, strung together on a silver chain. Reese's blood was crusted in the setting of the emerald and the iolite. I couldn't wear them.

Nick didn't say anything, just stared down at my wrist, too, as the tiger's-eye caught the light of the sunset. Until a crow cried out. Nick glanced at my eyes, tossing another rock.

I nodded, gathering up sticks and crumbled headstone marble into my skirt. Together we stood, and launched a volley. We were silent, arms swinging, rocks and twigs peppering the ground with tiny thuds and crunching into headstones.

The crows yelled at us and, in unison, broke away, flying off toward the forest.

Mauve-edged clouds swept past overhead, leaving behind a darkening night sky. I walked to the nearest headstone that wasn't my parents'—a squat, rectangular tower—and picked at the green lichen hugging one corner. I wished it was so easy to chase away the memories of Reese's heart's blood spilling over my hands.

Coming up behind me, Nick said, "I think the cemetery is at the center of everything."

"Huh?" I frowned at him and shivered. With the sun set, the cardigan over my summer dress wasn't enough.

He put his arm around me. "The cemetery. It's connected to the magic. All the dead bodies, they've got to have some power. Right? That's why Josephine wanted your dad's bones. For the magic. Why else? She wants his bones, and it must be because whatever makes our blood special makes our dead bodies special, too. Otherwise, why not dig up any old grave?"

"Yeah."

"And you must know they say things about this place having been cursed for generations? Your family and mine have been here, have been buried here, for that long."

The silence stretched out, but it wasn't tense or brittle. More like dough. Thick and sticky, settling over us like a blanket. Then a crow called, and it was echoed by another on the far side of the cemetery.

My sigh was violent enough to expel every molecule of air.

Nick pressed his forehead into mine. We just stood there, heads together, hands on each other. Breathing his air was almost as nice as kissing him.

"We'll figure it out, babe," Nick said.

I tilted my chin and kissed him. My fingers curled into his jacket, and I tugged him against me easily.

Nick opened his mouth, and I grabbed his head. He tasted so good. The same—exactly the same, and I knew how to kiss him: where his teeth were and how he moved his lips.

I pulled, lifting myself up, and Nick grabbed my hips to boost me onto the monument. His fingers twisted at my thin skirt as I parted my legs so that he could get closer. Wrapped around him, pressed against him, I was warm.

For whole breathless minutes, we kissed. I unbuttoned Nick's shirt, and he jerked as my cold hands touched his skin. But he sighed back into the kiss, holding me closer with his hands fisted in my skirt. The rough scrape of his jeans on my thighs made me dig my fingers into his back, wanting him more, needing harder than I ever had in my life.

His mouth tore away from mine, and he scoured down my neck with kisses. My head lolled back and I gasped, clutching at him.

He raised his hands up from my hips, his palms hot on my

ribs even through the thin dress. I wanted out of it, I wanted everything between us gone. I tugged at the collar of my cardigan, twisting to get it off.

But Nick stopped. He caught my hands. "Silla," he whispered.

I stared at him, but his eyes rested lower than mine, at my throat. Releasing my hands, he slowly, and very gently, unbuttoned the top button of the cardigan and unfolded it off my chest, like unwrapping a gift. His face was so open I thought that if I tried I could see into his thoughts. Wonder, fear, panic, tenderness shared space in his expression, and Nick drew one finger along the scar lining my throat, just over my collarbone. "God, Silla," he said, his voice hoarse.

"It's okay," I whispered, touching his lips. "It's okay."

He ducked his head and pulled me close, hugging me.

I wound my arms around his neck and relaxed against him. Our breath evened out together, synchronized perfectly.

Nick said, "We should, uh, go get the spell book and all the rest of the stuff."

"What?" I pushed away.

He scrubbed a hand down his face, then back up through his hair, leaving it mussed. "The amulets, babe. We have to finish the amulets. It's been two whole days, and we're just lucky she hasn't attacked and apparently needed time to recover. There's no way she's really gone."

"We can't."

"Why?"

"The spell book is gone."

"What?" He grasped my hands. "What happened?"

"I buried it with Reese."

His eyebrows lowered, and he frowned. It was fierce and angry, not confused. "Silla, we need it. How else can we stop Josephine?"

"We can't, Nick! She's stronger than us, and she's killed so many people! We can't fight her. So I buried the thing she wants so badly. Where she can't get it."

"You're giving up? Just like that? What if she comes after you again? She will, for the exact same reasons as before."

I shivered and pulled my hands from his. I reached down for a jagged rock, and made a long, shallow cut through my palm.

"Silla!"

Nick snatched the rock away from me.

I held out my bleeding hand. "I don't want this power. Look at it. Look how it bleeds out of me. What if all it does is bring death like this?"

"It isn't the magic—it's the person using it."

"You don't know that."

"Yeah, I do. The blood is what we make it."

"Your grandpa knew; he said it was evil. That what your mom was doing was."

"But we don't know what she was doing!"

"Maybe it was just the magic itself. Maybe Mr. Harleigh knew it couldn't be used for good."

"But your dad, all his spells are good. For good!"

I shook my head. "But the price, Nick. The sacrifice is too much. My brother, my mom, they both died for it—and even a rabbit is too much."

"It's part of who you are, Silla."

"I don't want it."

"That's what my mom thought, and she tried to kill herself and then drug it out of her."

"Maybe she had the right idea."

Nick was in my face in an instant. "Don't say that. Don't *say that.*"

The air was warm between us. Cold on my back. I got off the monument, pushing around him. "I'll say what I think is true," I said quietly.

Lips pressed into a frown, Nick tore the bandage off his left hand. He put the rock against the stitches knitting his palm together, and sliced. Blood gushed. Hissing through his teeth, Nick dropped the rock, reached out with his unwounded hand, and grabbed my bleeding one. He jerked me forward and slapped our bleeding hands together.

Power cracked somewhere deep inside me, like lightning. And then a long summer roll of thunder rumbled from my center out toward our joined hands. All my blood was alive. I met Nick's eyes and they were wide. I could almost see sparks of reddish lightning reflecting in his pupils.

"This is what we are, Silla," he said. Then he paused, shook his head. "This is *who I am.* I know it now." Snatching his hand from mine, he clenched it until blood dripped onto Reese's grave. "Tell me when you decide who you want to be."

With that, Nick strode away from me, into the shadowy cemetery.

My palm burned, and I turned it over to watch the blood pool. All around me, the crows screamed.

NICHOLAS

The October air cut against my hot cheeks as I plowed through the field on my way home. I kept not breathing and then having to suck in a huge, choking breath to catch up with myself.

Everything was so, so clear. My hand freaking hurt, but the fingers moved, thank God. I cradled it against my stomach as I hurried home to stanch the bleeding. But it almost didn't matter. I'd get up to the attic, pull out the box, and use the holy water and willow leaf to heal it up. Mom had done it when I skinned my knees.

The woods enveloped me, and I dove in. The path wasn't here, but I could just barely make out the glow of my house, so I'd be fine. Trees scratched at me, and I batted them away. I thought of when Silla had said she didn't want the magic, and of how it had made me want to shake her. And I thought of kissing her, of how I'd wanted so much more than only kisses. Of the burn of magic between us.

A root snaked out and grabbed my ankle. I landed with a grunt on my palms, wrists jarred and knees popping with instant bruises. Furious pain coursed up from my cut hand. I just lay there, aching, my cheek against the cold ground. Damp leaves plastered themselves to my skin, and I breathed in cool, moldy air. Wind shivered through the trees, dropping more leaves down around me, soft and quiet as snow. I smelled mud and wet wood and—blood. Old, rotten blood.

My eyes snapped open and I pushed up, hissing at the pain. As I clutched at my hand, I peered into the darkness, at the bulbous shadows near the base of the tree trunk beside me. Something huddled there. The carcass of a raccoon, guts spilled out everywhere. My eyes picked out the details, and I realized, swallowing back a sour taste, that there wasn't any blood. I smelled it but didn't see it. The raccoon was totally eviscerated, but the intestines glowed pink and white and pale blue in the bare moonlight. Every drop of blood was gone. I faltered back onto my ass, shoving away.

Branches creaked overhead, and I jumped to my feet, then spun around.

The whole woods groaned.

Skidding and sliding, I ran for the lights of my house.

FIFTY-THREE

Drusilla. Your mother almost didn't agree to the name. We've told you this story before, that I said it was the name of a Roman empress and Emily found out she was the sister of the crazy, possibly incestuous Caligula. I could not tell her, nor you until now, that Drusilla was the name of my mother, who died a hundred and fifty years ago, alone and unknown, and is buried in a simple grave with only her given name upon it.

When you were born, I wept. And I remember thinking, for the first time in fifteen years, how glad I was of what I had done. I would not have changed anything that had led to the moment I held you in my arms. I was not—am not—sorry.

Emily insisted we call you Silla. My sweet, gentle Silla, all these things I write down will capture your imagination, and you would follow them into the face of God if you could. Or the Devil. As I begged your brother, so I beg you: only be yourself. Forget these bloody things when Josephine is gone, and if you can, forgive me.

FIFTY-FOUR

SILLA

The crows followed me into my dreams, and I woke up over and over again, batting away black wings that turned out to be my sheets. I sweated and panted and pulled Reese's crumpled T-shirt against my face, breathing in that hay-and-oil smell.

It was sick and weird, I knew, but in the middle of the night I didn't care. I pretended the smell would never fade, that he was right in the other room. That I wasn't totally crazy.

I got my cell phone. It glowed an eerie blue against the dark of my bedroom. The light reflected along the ceramic and glass planes of all my masks, their empty black eyes reminding me of Nick, of how he'd disliked them—of how he'd yelled at me, pushed me back. *Tell me when you decide who you want to be.*

Scrolling through my address book, I passed his name and came to Wendy's. I'd never apologized for the things I'd said at rehearsal the day Reese died. I typed: SRY SO CRZY. MISS U. THX 4 BNG HR. SEND MESSAGE? My phone blinked. I tapped the green button. Message sent. At two-thirty in the morning.

Then I lay back and stared at the ceiling. *You know what this all means, Silla?* Gram Judy had said. *It means you're strong.*

I didn't feel strong. I felt alone and terrified. Helpless. Dad had kept this secret, and he'd left me. Taken Mom with him. Reese hadn't been able to stop it, hadn't been able to fight it. And if he couldn't, how could I possibly? I didn't want this, not any of it. I wanted my life back, the one where the worst thing I had to worry about was that my best friend was dating my ex-boyfriend and I hadn't been cast as the lead in the play. But of course, if I had my old life, I would've been Lady Macbeth.

Art thou afeard / To be the same in thine own act and valor / As thou art in desire?

Was I afraid of making a new life? Afraid of what it might entail? How did one choose such bloody deeds as ours?

Nick had. My father had. He'd studied it for his entire life, and lived in peace until he died, so far as I knew. And the Deacon. The Deacon who had sent me the spell book—he had chosen this life, too.

Who was he? Where was he? Could he help with Josephine? He'd said in his letter that he communicated with Dad—that Dad told him he was proud of me. Of my strength.

I owed it to my parents and to Reese to stay alive. To fight. I owed Nick and Judy. And Josephine had a lot coming to her.

But what did I owe myself?

Tell me when you decide who you want to be.

I had a choice to make.

With the first light of dawn, I was up and moving. I scoured the bathroom until my shoulders ached and I was light-headed from bleach smell. Despite a bandage and heavy-duty cleaning gloves, the cut on my palm ached. When the bathroom sparkled, I put together a casserole with all the vegetables left over from the memorial service. I scrubbed the microwave and emptied out the fridge, things that Gram Judy had thought too minor to matter in our day of cleaning. But in my mood, nothing was too slight.

Judy left around ten to meet Mrs. Margaret for yoga, and donuts afterward. She tried for a few minutes to get me to go, but not terribly hard. I did stop her, though, with a hug when she was pinning her salmon and turquoise Sunday hat over her braids. She patted my back, rather delicately. "Don't crush my hat, love."

Releasing her, I said, "Sorry."

Judy patted my cheek. "I won't be late. Be careful. We'll be okay."

As she climbed into her beat-up little Rabbit and zipped away, I wished I took as much of life on faith.

A few minutes later, I'd pulled on one of Reese's sweatshirts for strength, slid the chain with my rings around my neck, and was gripping the study door frame, trying to decide where to begin my search for the Deacon.

I only stared at the hardwood floor, unable to take the first step.

My breathing sped up. I needed music to distract me.

In ten minutes, Reese's old CD player was plugged in. It squatted on the floor beside the door, music whirring softly. Gentle guitar chords strummed, reminding me of the steady revolution of car tires.

We'd had a professional cleaner come down from Cape Girardeau to get rid of the stains in July. Gram Judy had arranged it when Reese had refused to let her help with the funeral costs. For a couple of weeks, the house had smelled like chemicals. I hadn't minded, but Reese had bitched about his food tasting like peroxide. He'd threatened to buy sticks of incense or pour whiskey all over everything. I remember imagining the whole house going up like a bonfire. Judy had bought a bunch of flowers and lined the hallway with them. Roses and peonies and carnations: things with vibrant or cloying scents to counter the chemical stench.

Now it smelled like kicked-up dust and old books.

It was a dead room, guts torn out by the same thing that had killed my whole family.

Standing in the center of it, I felt all the empty weight crush down onto my shoulders. The music crooned, but beyond that, the house was silent.

I was alone.

"Stop," I told myself. My voice rang against the music. I held out my wounded hand and gently touched the gash across my palm. It was red and throbbing. *Who am I?* Silla Kennicot, lost and washed-out cutter? Afraid of her own blood, always crying, always alone? Or Silla Kennicot, magician? Strong friend, in control of her own power? It was an easy choice to want to make, but taking the first step felt like leaping over a chasm of fire.

FIFTY-FIVE

Do you remember the day you did magic, Silla? Reese scraped his knee bloody, and you were so upset that you were the one crying. You were five years old. You put your hands on his knee and cried and cried. Reese pushed you away after a minute, saying "Stop, Silly, stop." The wound was healed. You so naturally tapped into the power, your immense need to make your brother's pain go away was enough to call the magic and heal. I was never so proud of you.

And I know that now you will be able to do what is necessary if I fail today.

FIFTY-SIX

NICHOLAS

My cell rang at eleven-thirty. I'd only been awake for an hour.
"Yeah?" I hadn't checked the incoming number and was pretty
freaking surprised when Silla said, "Nick."

I didn't think she'd want to talk to me for a while, after last
night. I wasn't sure I wanted to talk to *her* for a while, either.
But her voice had me sitting up straight at my computer and
glancing out the window toward the cemetery and her house. I
had to tell her about the raccoon.

"Are you there?"

"Yeah, I'm here." I cleared my throat.

"I'm in my dad's study, looking for a way to contact the
Deacon."

"The . . . oh, the guy who sent the book."

"Yes. I figure since the book is buried, and Josephine isn't,
he might be the only person who can help us. He knew Dad. He
probably knew Josephine." She sounded certain, and calm. Like
she was talking about her plan for studying for final exams.

"Good idea." I leaned back into my chair. The joint
creaked. I should've told her about the raccoon right then. But

if she wasn't over her whole suicidal-didn't-want-the-magic thing, I'd just have to deal with it myself.

After a pause, she said, "I was hoping you might come help me."

"Yeah?"

"A second pair of eyes. I might not see something that stands out because I've been looking at my dad's office for my whole life."

"Yeah."

"And"—she took a deep breath—"I'd like to apologize to your face."

I huffed out air like a popped air mattress. "Okay."

"Good." Her smile was audible.

"I'll see you in a bit."

"Nick, be careful. There are crows all over my front yard."

We hung up.

Dad and Lilith had left for a matinee performance of some "cutting-edge" play that they were driving the two-plus hours to St. Louis for, so I didn't have to make any excuses. I headed straight over.

Reese's truck was in the drive, and I parked next to it. Three crows were chilling on the hood, arguing over a bit of purple ribbon. They squawked at each other but ignored me. I headed straight through the unlocked front door, calling "Silla? You here?" Music filtered out from the rear of the house. I followed the singing.

The door to her dad's study hung open, and I walked right in. "Silla?"

A portable CD player blared some girly country-pop-rock,

and I leaned down to unplug it. There was no sign of her, other than the chaotic jumble on the desktop. "Silla?" I called again as I moved around the huge desk. A brass lamp glowed faintly yellow, casting light onto the top of her head. She was crouched behind the desk with her legs crossed and a random collection of objects in her lap.

"Oh, Nick." She gently moved the knickknacks to the floor and stood up. She was wearing a sweatshirt about five sizes too big for her. "I didn't hear you come in."

"I can't believe you left your door unlocked."

Silla shrugged. "Did the crows bother you?"

"Nope."

Her eyes slowly rose to my face. Her expression was guarded, but not *masked*. "I didn't mean it last night. About your mom."

"Good. Because it was stupid."

One corner of her mouth twitched up. "I didn't sleep much, worrying about it. And you."

"Me?"

She shrugged. "And myself. And every possible thing I could worry about. I don't want to spend the rest of my life afraid like that. Grieving. I want to act. Even if it means murdering a king."

"*What?*"

"Oh, um"—Silla offered me a cheesy smile—"I was using Lady Macbeth for pep talks."

"Sounds like the opposite of healthy." I reached out and brushed my thumb against her cheek.

She caught my hand. Pulling it down, she studied it, rubbed

her own thumbs over my palm. The deep gouge from last night was only a raw pink line. Like the scar on her collarbone.

"Magic," I said lightly, noticing that she had her own hand wrapped in medical tape. "You should let me fix yours."

"I think . . ." She raised her face. "I think I need the wound right now. As a reminder of last night. Of what you said." She pressed her lips together and nodded once, fiercely. "Of who I want to be."

I lifted her hand and kissed the tips of her fingers. The air between us was warm again. "So. We're looking for the Deacon."

With a heavy sigh, Silla dropped back to the floor and skimmed her hand over the assorted items: a pair of old glasses, a glass paperweight, some quill pens with ratty plumage.

Hunkering beside her, I pointed at the pens. "Your dad used those?"

"He had ink pots and everything. They're in the top drawer there." She glanced up at the desk; then her eyes flickered at me. She lifted the glasses. "I don't know what he used these for. See? The lenses are pink."

"Rose-colored glasses? I could use a bit of that." The rims were silver and twisted in an odd S curve, and the earpieces were shaped like candy canes. "Oh, I remember him wearing these."

"You . . . remember?"

Robert Kennicot glares down at me, through the weird glasses. "Robbie would not have approved, Donna Harleigh. You have gone too far." I closed my eyes, pressed my fingers against them.

"Nick?"

"Mom used to look for your dad through a mirror, the far-sight spell. And . . . I think I remember him looking at me through them, but talking to me like I was Mom . . . and Sil"— I met her worried eyes—"he said 'Robbie would not' like he wasn't Robbie. But it was definitely your dad."

"You mean someone possessed Dad's body," she whispered.

"Something like that . . . maybe." I shook my head. "I'm not sure." Picking the glasses back up, I asked, "You mind?"

"Go ahead. Tell me what you see."

I settled the strange glasses onto my nose, and pushed the wire over my ears. Then I looked at Silla.

And fell backward onto my ass. "Shit!"

Her hand glowed with this reedy red aura. It bled out from her, stretching in tendrils. Toward me.

"Nick?" She leaned up onto her knees. The red wavered around her, less like liquid—more like a heat mirage. I glanced down at myself. The tendrils grasped at me, weaving around my hand.

"Uh, Silla. Um." My eyes must've been huge. I couldn't stop staring. "The glasses are magic."

She frowned. "What?"

Reluctantly, I pulled them off. It took a second for my eyes to refocus. I handed the glasses to Silla.

With a massive frown, she put them on. "Everything's a little pink."

"Look at yourself."

Her mouth fell open when she raised her hand. "Oh, God." She climbed to her feet, still staring down at herself. "This is amazing. And weird."

I smiled. She looked funny with the delicate round glasses perched on her nose.

"We're connected, Nicholas." Her eyes followed the long tendrils. "Probably because of whatever you did last night."

"Or just how I feel about you."

She froze, lips parting slightly. "Oh, Nick."

I just looked at her. Thinking about the poem I'd written for her on Monday. Before all this had gone down.

Swallowing, she distracted herself from what I'd said by turning slowly in a circle, scanning the room. "I wonder if we can see any kind of blood magic?"

"I don't know."

"Oh!" She froze, staring at one of the squares of bookshelf. "Sil?"

She walked toward the shelf, hands out, and removed the stack of hardbacks leaning there. They dropped to the floor with a sharp thud. "This is glowing—sort of a red-gold, not exactly like what's connecting us." She shuddered and pressed a hand to the back of the shelf. "It's a false back, I think." Knocking on it, she peered in closer. The knock echoed hollowly.

I joined her at the shelf. "Maybe there's a trigger or opening mechanism or something."

Chewing on the inside of her lip, Silla ran her fingers along the edges. "Here!" She pushed on the bottom corner, and the panel popped out. She handed it off to me and reached inside.

She pulled out a portfolio, bound shut with a strip of leather, and a small Moleskine-like journal. Silla set them on the desk, on top of a scatter of sticky notes and old bills. She unwound the leather quickly, and pulled out sheets of paper thick with writing. "Spells."

The first one I picked up contained a diagram of a triangle inside a circle, and a bunch of notes and arrows and scratched-out words. From the top of the page, I read, "Triangle first, then the circle, or the energies won't be bound."

"It's my dad's writing," Silla whispered. She flipped through. "God, some written in Latin. Like a code. It'll take a bit to translate everything. But they look like they're all for a huge, complicated charm—more stuff like what's in the spell book, but less finished." Silla glanced at the little journal. Slowly, she set down the spell notes and caressed the journal's cover. It was plain black, with a thin red ribbon marker sticking out the bottom like a tongue. With a large sigh, she lifted it and opened it. "Nineteen-oh-four," she read.

I leaned in as she continued. "I am Josephine Darly, and I intend to live forever." Silla dropped the journal.

Touching the journal, I said, "Let's take all this to my house. Dad and Lilith are gone for the day, and we can spread out and have the place to ourselves."

"Yeah." Silla nodded.

FIFTY-SEVEN

SILLA

I left a note for Gram Judy, stuffed my backpack with my marked-up Latin dictionary and everything from Dad's secret cubby. Nick took salt out of the pantry, and as we walked to his car, we filled a plastic sack with gravel for throwing at crows.

On the way, they winged silently overhead. Pacing us. I wanted to scream at Josephine that we had her diary—that we'd find whatever weaknesses were inside it and destroy her.

We got into the house unscathed, though. They didn't even dive close or caw. They only landed gently on the lawn as we ran in through the garage.

It was amazing that I had enough energy to be thrilled by Nick's bedroom. Playbills and posters made it look like he'd leached all the color and emotion out of the stark house and splashed it onto his walls.

We spread out across the floor, which was piled with horrible rugs. Oriental rugs and modern geometric rugs; even a shag rug. The chaos suited him.

Nick propped himself on his elbows, his legs stretching

back toward the stereo, and began to read the diary out loud. His finger tapped with the low beat of some weird music he called Swedish electronica. His eyes and lips had relaxed into an expression of slight amazement, and I stared. And listened. I imagined brushing my lips across his eyelashes, skimming them along his wide cheekbone. He hadn't bothered, apparently, to slick back his hair this morning, and it flopped around his ears and down his neck. It looked soft.

I closed my eyes, stretched out beside him, and listened as he read to me about Josephine, about how she'd learned the magic from a mysterious doctor named Philip, about their lessons and theories, the decades they spent together. Josephine was insane, clearly, but I think if I hadn't known she would eventually start killing people, it would have been easy to relate to her. She was just so excited about the magic, and determined to use it to live a good life. And she was in love. I understood why she enjoyed possessing people, and Philip's difficulty with it made me feel better about failing so abysmally at it myself.

She even wrote about sacrifice. Philip taught her that the magic required balance, that our blood is strong but can be used for good or evil. It must have been wonderful to have a real teacher. Josephine mentioned the Deacon, too, who seemed to be an ancient wizard. Though it was hard to believe they'd all really been alive for so long.

The entries were extremely spotty and scattered over time, and occasionally there were pages missing. Some torn out, some scrawled through so fiercely we couldn't read them.

And then there was the resurrection powder—carmot— she talked about that. It was made of the bones of the dead, and was how they were able to live for so long.

As Nick finished that particular entry, he fell silent, just staring at the page.

"You're thinking about it, aren't you?" I asked quietly.

"It's impossible not to."

I took his hand, wove our fingers together. "Living forever."

"There's just so much you could do. See anything. Travel, learn, do . . . anything."

"Have twenty different jobs."

"Write a novel. Or ten."

"Be a rock star."

"President," he laughed. "Though I guess that scrutiny would be a problem."

Too bad it came at a price. I sighed, pushing the temptation away. It was a thing to worry about another day. "I'm surprised my dad isn't mentioned. I mean, something had to have made her hate him so much."

Nick leaned over and kissed me. "We'll figure it out."

We took a break to eat a frozen pizza, then kept reading.

Josephine became less and less stable after World War II, alone as she traveled across America, occasionally with the Deacon and then back with Philip. But she was clearly becoming unglued. After Nick read the entry about Josephine hiding the resurrection powder in Philip's food, he flipped the page and stopped. "Oh, Jesus."

"What?" I took the diary out of his loose hands.

There on the next page was my dad's writing.

It is the worst thing I have ever done.
My real name is Philip Osborn, and I killed a seventeen-year-old boy because I was afraid to die.

My breath stuck in my throat in a huge, spiky ball. I didn't want to read on, but I had to. "Oh, God," I whispered. "My dad was Philip. He . . . oh my God."

Nick's voice was strangled. "My mom could tell. She knew he wasn't himself. Knew that . . . what Philip did."

Everything from Josephine's journal suddenly spun like a roulette wheel, and when it stopped, all the colors and numbers fell into place more surely. My dad . . . Philip. The experimenting doctor, the teacher, the one who thought we were witches and devils but who tried to save lives. He'd tried so hard, and believed the magic could be good.

But he'd created Josephine. And loved her, even?

Nausea, light and dancing, whirled in my stomach. Nick pushed over the pages in the diary, skimming down with his finger. He stopped when he saw his mom's name again.

Nick put his head down. I picked the book out of his limp hands and read. The whole thing was a letter to me and Reese. Written in the final hours of my dad's life. A letter to us, explaining what he never could before. My eyes watered and I wiped furiously at them.

At least I had answers now. I touched Nick's arm. "Read this with me. It's—it's about you, too."

You deserve to know, my children, why I did not teach you these things.

Silla was seven and Reese nine, and it was time to begin, if ever I was going to.

I stepped out of the car, arriving home from school, and a boy, maybe eight years old, was sitting in our front yard. He staggered up and then sat back down as though he were injured. I went to him and crouched, held out my hand. "My name is Robert," I said. "Who are you?" But even then I knew he was familiar. His face, his eyes, I knew them. He held out a scraped and bloody hand. "I fell," he whispered. Just as I took his hand to investigate, he clamped onto my wrist and stood fully, strongly up. "I banish thee!" he yelled, and pressed his other hand, also bloody, to my forehead.

My head bubbled out and I ached, but I did not lose my grip on my body. For it is mine, after so many, many years. No child's spell could undo it. Nor the spell of a woman who loved its former owner. I stared into the boy's flat eyes, at the matte-black pupils with no reflection. "You are not who you claim to be." The boy scowled and said, "Give Robbie back to me!"

After so many years, it was Donna Harleigh. I whispered a sleeping charm, and the little boy collapsed. I carried him into my car and drove down to the Harleigh farm. Inside, Mr. Harleigh met me in a fury, but when I asked where Donna was, he went with me to find her unconscious in her bed. And Mr. Harleigh understood even as I did. He said, "Her *own son!" and vowed to me that he would see things righted.*

And so I knew what became of Donna, that she has a son and was so filled with hate for me that she used his body, his very strong blood, to try to save the real, long-departed Robert Kennicot.

Looking down at her, and at her used son, I knew I could not teach that magic to my children. I had to save you from it, protect you from it. I taught it to J, and look where that brought me. For darkness clings long in the blood, and history never forgets what we do to our children.

Nick put his hand over the words, pressing the diary to the carpet. "I woke up with a fever, and heard Grandpa yelling at Mom about being evil. About having done a terrible thing. Now I know."

Our shoulders pressed together, and I leaned my head against his. "We'll be better than them."

"Yeah." Nick rolled his shoulders and set his jaw. "We have to keep reading. Find out what happened. My mom is old news."

We bent our heads back over the journal.

And I did not regret my decision until today. Because Josephine is here in Yaleylah.

She came to the school, and I saw her in a flash, just from the corner of my eye. I told myself it was not her. It couldn't be. The heat was getting to me, the loneliness of the school building in summer. After nearly thirty years, she could not have found me.

But she waited for me outside in the parking lot. Exactly as she always looked. Beautiful face, lioness eyes. Her lips were painted scarlet. "Philip," she whispered. "I cannot see my reflection in your eyes."

Her voice. Oh, God, it cut to me. I could not move. If she knew where I worked, she knew, too, where I lived. She knew my wife's name, my children's names. The sun was so hot. "Josephine," I said.

Her fingers curled up into fists. "I thought you were dead."

I didn't answer.

"I loved you!" she screamed. "For a hundred years, I've loved you!"

"Leave me alone, Josephine."

"As you left me, Philip? Or Robert? Should I call you Robbie, darling?" She stepped closer, in that stalking, slow walk of hers.

I was quiet again, my eyes darting around, hoping for someone to come near, hoping as much for no witnesses.

"How could you stand it, Philip? My stalwart, righteous doctor? Even I always return to my body." She touched her lips, her chest.

I was afraid, am still afraid. Her eyes were wild and dark—as if it were not a human soul behind them but a crow or wolf or eagle.

We stared at one another in silence as the sun beat down. The asphalt shimmered with heat, and her skin shone with sweat. She spun away from me, and drove off in a little silver car.

I came straight home. I told Emily to go get you, Reese and Silla, and to take you away to Kansas to find an apartment for Reese. An easy excuse.

Magic is sunk deep into the earth around the house—I will wait here for Josephine, with my binding box, and one or another of us will walk away.

I pray I will hold you again, that you will never find this. Never need to know your father's past, his sins. For my sins are great ones.

That was all. I was breathless, and I read the last entry straight through again. "God, Nick," I whispered. "God, this was the last thing he did. Oh, God." I took a deep breath and let it out shakily.

"It's a lot to take in." He put his hands around mine and rubbed. The friction warmed me up immediately.

"I need—I want some air."

We clung to each other as we headed downstairs, fingers entwined. My bones ached. It was hard to think about what we'd read. Hard to imagine Dad not being my dad. Or Nick's mom possessing him, her own son. Josephine, showing up at the school . . . maybe even interviewing that very day for her counselor's position. Insinuating herself into our lives. But after reading her journal, I knew how conniving she was, how certain of herself and selfish.

Nick led me out through the kitchen and stark living room, through glass doors and onto a patio. I rolled my shoulders. We stood there, hand in hand. The sun was behind the house, and I wished I could feel it warm my skin. Instead, as wind ruffled the short back lawn, I realized there were strange black lumps on the ground at the edge of the woods. "Nick." I let go of his hand.

"Yeah?"

"Do you see that?"

"See what?"

The lumps looked like old black trash bags left out to rot. "At the woods." I walked straight onto the grass.

"Hey." Nick grabbed my arm. "Careful."

"They're animals," I whispered. "Birds and squirrels and . . ." I shrugged him off and lengthened my pace until I was jogging toward the trees.

"Silla!" He came after, footsteps soft. "It could be dangerous—they might be diseased. Or worse." But I couldn't look away from the dead animals.

A crow called from behind us. A flock of them was flapping its way down from the roof. Several landed on the patio, then hopped closer. Like they were driving us at the forest.

I stopped and squatted near one of the bodies. "It's dead. A fox." I shook my head, then raised it to look up into the trees. Wind brushed through the red-tinged leaves. Beyond, the sky was a drab and unterrifying gray.

"I forgot—last night, I found a dead raccoon, totally drained of blood," Nick said, warily keeping his eyes on the crows behind us. They kept hopping closer. Their beady black eyes were angry and hostile. "The glasses."

We ran back up to the attic, and I dug the glasses out of the backpack. Nick swung open his window, and I pulled them over my ears.

Instantly my vision flooded red. I stumbled back.

"What? What?" Nick caught me, his neck craning to see what I was seeing.

"It's all red, Nick. All of it." My voice shook, higher than usual.

"Seriously?"

"It's like the forest sucked the magic out of the ground and just runs with it—like the trees are all alive with blood instead of water and sunlight."

"And—and the animals?"

"Patchy red."

"And those crows?"

Slowly, I turned, nausea gripping my middle, and looked out at the sky. Thin lines of dark red connected the crows like a bloody spiderweb. "They're all connected to each other— the whole flock. With red. Like the trees. The entire forest is possessed."

FIFTY-EIGHT

NICHOLAS

The doorbell rang. Silla, positioned at the window, jumped.

"I'll get rid of them," I said, skimming my hand down Silla's back. I cursed the fact that since my windows all faced the rear of the house, I couldn't see the car that had pulled up. She nodded and said, "I'll start going through Dad's portfolio." After kissing her neck, I jogged down the stairs.

The art deco clock hanging on the second floor landing told me it was just past four. Way too early for Dad and Lilith. I considered pretending we weren't home, but my convertible was parked right out front.

The doorbell rang again, rewarding my headache with the dulcet tones of "Frère Jacques."

When I swung the door open, I frowned. "What are you doing here?"

It was Eric, standing there in his favored rehearsal garb of sweats and a long-sleeved shirt. His hair stuck up in twelve different directions, and he lowered a cigarette from his mouth to scowl and say, "Nice, Nick. I'm here to find out if you're coming to school tomorrow. Especially rehearsal. I was thinking you'd make a great stand-in for some of the fight choreography. Patrick blows when it comes to taking a hit."

"I'm considering school tomorrow," I said slowly as Eric offered me a drag and leaned his butt back against the doorjamb.

"Naw, I have my own vices."

He raised his eyebrows. "Ashtray?"

"Just toss it outside when you go."

"God, you're an asshole."

"Well, I'm busy, okay?"

"Silla upstairs?"

I pressed my lips together. "Don't go there."

Eric held up his hands. "Hey, far be it from me to interfere with a little post-funeral *grieving*."

If only that's what was going on. If. Only. "Look, hopefully I'll be at school tomorrow, okay? To help you play with your pointy sticks."

He paused, staring at me with his eyes narrowed as if he couldn't decide whether or not to make a joke out of that last line. I was mildly impressed he even considered taking the higher road.

Finally he saluted me with his cigarette. "Enjoy, man."

I closed the door, not letting my smile fall away until there was no way he could see me. I stood there, head leaned back against the front door, eyes closed, and wished that getting into Silla's pants was the biggest of my concerns.

Nick tromped out of the attic, and I focused on Dad's notes, dragging out the huge Latin-English dictionary. The first spell was called *loricatus*. Armor.

That sounded promising.

I skimmed a little, frustrated that it was taking so long, and wishing Wendy was here. She'd always been better at Latin than me, much to Dad's chagrin.

I kept flipping through the pages, wishing like I had when I was taking the class that I could just take a nap with the pages under my pillow and while I slept the translations would trickle in through my ear.

"To bind."

This one was all in English.

Silla, I created this spell to use against her. I do not believe in using the magic offensively, but there may be no choice. If I fail, I pray you never have to use this.

Hands shaking, I read through the spell. The ingredients were wax, red ribbon, a physical piece of the subject to be bound, and a box. You pressed the hair or fingernails, or anything like that, into the wax, shut it into the box, and tied the ribbon around it. A drop of blood to lock the knot, and then the whole thing was buried. With a rune over the top of it. To bind a spirit into a place or person, you had to make a circle around it with the rune at all the corners.

A wordless cry of dismay fell from my lips.

The rune Reese had found behind the house. It was so similar to the protection rune, we'd assumed it was the same symbol. But this was it. I felt it in the tingle of my palm. There'd been a binding around my house, not a warding. It had been a spell to trap something inside.

Dad had tried to bind Josephine. That's why he'd let her come to him at the house instead of luring her elsewhere. But Mom must've come home, and flipped it all around so that Josephine captured Dad instead.

Yes, there at the bottom of the page it read: "Spirit-binding, not physical." It kept Dad from jumping when she killed him.

It also meant that if we found Josephine's body, we could do the same thing to her. And she had to be in the forest. Her body, I mean. That's where her blood trail had gone cold, and with all the dead animals, she must have used them to possess the whole freaking forest. But her body was dying, or at least broken enough that she couldn't get out.

I turned back to the armoring spell.

NICHOLAS

The moment I pushed open the attic door, Silla raised her head and grinned. "This spell, Nick, the armoring spell, it's my rings!" She held out her hands and I grabbed them, hauling her up. "I've had protection from her all along, and . . ."

"It's why she never possessed you, or even tried," I finished for her.

Silla nodded, knocking her forehead against my lips. "And why she was always trying to get me to take them off."

Tilting up her chin, I kissed her.

"Nick," she said. "Put this on." Silla pulled back and stripped the bracelet off. "It was Reese's. He never—he never wore it, though, or he'd have been . . . safe." Her eyelids fluttered. "You should wear it. I'll put my rings back on."

I frowned. She pushed the bracelet into my hands. The metal was warm from being against her skin, and I suddenly wanted to wear it because she had. But as I slid it over my wrist, I couldn't help thinking of Reese. Of all that blood. The bracelet tingled, and I didn't have the first clue if it was magic or my own nerves.

Systematically, Silla pulled rings off her necklace and jammed them onto her fingers. "I always thought they were just comforting, but this . . . my whole life Dad was building up armor for me." She smiled up at me, and it was the most beautiful smile I'd ever seen.

The window glass rattled as something slammed into it.

We jumped away, whirling around.

A crow beat its body against the glass. Silla ran for it, yelling "Get away!"

Another cry rang out, then another, and then it was a cacophony of crows screaming at us.

I was at the window instantly, pressing close behind Silla. A massive flock of them swept around the backyard. Like a hundred shadows come to life. Their feathers glinted in the bright afternoon. One dove at the window, and Silla leapt back into me.

Then I saw it. Peering through the scattered birds, I saw Eric.

At the edge of the forest, he hung ten feet in the air, snarled in the branches of a tree. Blood stained the whole front of his shirt.

 FIFTY-NINE

NICHOLAS

I didn't move, even though my heart danced jaggedly in my chest. Silla spun around and went to dig in my desk, finding a pair of scissors that she held out like they were a miniature sword.

The crows had settled down, and all I heard was a soft mechanical buzz. My stereo. The album had ended. I hit the power button and realized my hand was shaking. I had to keep it together. But all that blood, just like Reese . . . I should have made sure he got to his car. This was my fault.

I fisted my hands and pressed them into my eyes as though I could force away the memory of Silla's face and neck splattered with blood, of her bloody handprints on the headstones.

"Nick?"

My hands fell away at her quiet voice. "Sorry, just . . . we still don't have a plan."

"We have to bind her. The spell she used to bind my dad so that he couldn't jump free when she killed him."

"Bind her into her body, you mean?"

"Yeah." She went to the magic box and pulled out the spool

of red thread and piece of beeswax. Tucking them into the front pocket of her huge sweatshirt, she came back. "We need a little box. A matchbox, a—a card box, anything we can seal this up in. And we have to get to her body."

"Okay."

She touched my cheek. "This might be it, you know."

"I know." I turned my face and kissed the tips of her fingers. Then I leaned over and kissed her lips.

And Silla didn't move, didn't even breathe.

When I leaned back, she opened her eyes. I focused on them, on the curve of the lid, on the tight, curling lashes.

I kissed her again, and the air around us warmed. My blood burned, ached from fingertips to toes and where our lips touched. "Silla."

"Yeah?" She met my eyes with determination, with this edge of wildness.

I kissed her again, but harder.

"It's okay, Nick. We can do this."

I couldn't say anything.

SILLA

Downstairs, I waited with the binding spell ingredients tucked into the kangaroo pocket of Reese's sweatshirt while Nick searched for a proper box.

Outside, the crows blanketed the grass, standing between the back door and the forest where Eric was suspended. I took long, deep breaths. Tonight was it. I was going to find Josephine's body, bind it, and trap her there forever. I squeezed my hands around the scissors in my pocket.

Nick came back and offered me a thin metal box with a painting of a lily on its cover. "Will this work?"

"I hope so." I popped it open. One of Lilith's business cards was stuck to the roof. I dug it out, and Nick tossed it to the floor.

"Oops. Left one." He quirked up his eyebrow. Even though he couldn't quite bring himself to smile, I saw the satisfaction he got out of destroying something of hers.

Through the thick sliding glass, we could see crows hopping around on the grass, barking and cawing at the forest. And at the row of rats crawling along the two branches holding Eric up. I swallowed a deep breath.

Nick unlocked the sliding glass door, and shoved it open. We walked out together.

Although the sky continued to hold light, the afternoon sun was low enough that here in the center of the woods everything was dim and shadowed, like looking through a dark lens. I winced, realizing I should have grabbed the blood-sight spectacles. But then I'd have to look at the horrible red stain painted across the whole forest.

As we approached, the blanket of crows parted for us. They flapped back over the lawn and watched us with their tiny black eyes. Feathers ruffled and beaks clacked quietly. I pressed closer to Nick and finally looked at Eric, suspended between the trees.

His eyes were closed, head hanging. His whole body was limp. It swayed gently, almost peacefully. Blood matted his hair to his skull, had turned his shirt scarlet. And a steady stream of bright red drops trickled off the toe of his sneaker.

"Josephine!" I yelled. "Show yourself. We know you're out there."

Eric's blood pattered on the leaf-strewn forest floor. Silla said, "Let him go."

It was easy to ignore the crows behind us, thanks to the row of nasty rats in front of us. They clung to the branches with their tiny claws. Some were missing eyes, and most had blood matting down their fur. Not just rats. Zombie rats. It would be totally awesome if it wasn't so real. "Come on," I said with as much scorn as I could dredge up. "You aren't scaring us, you're just being as annoying as ever. No wonder Philip ditched you."

The trees shook, and a rain of red-stained leaves fell. A crow cawed behind us, then a second and third. "They're coming closer," Silla said quietly. I glanced back. They were lined up, wings out like the eagle on the U.S. seal.

Silla gasped. When I looked, I saw that Eric's head had lifted. His eyes were closed, and his whole face was coated in blood. Like someone had dumped him in a bathtub full of it, and hung him up to dry. His lips parted, and he said, "My beasts will tear you to shreds if you approach, Silla Kennicot."

It was Eric's voice, but flat and low.

"Did you hurt him?" I demanded.

"No, Nick, I did not. And I suggest you not take that tone with me." Eric's lips pulled back into a grimacing smile that bared all his teeth.

Silla stepped in front of me. "What do you want?"

To kill us all, I guessed. I pressed my shoulder against Silla's so that we were an obviously united front.

"We're gonna do a little magic." Eric's mouth twisted into a sneer.

A crow jumped into the air and flapped up toward Eric's shoulder. The rats chattered and screamed, clambering closer to Eric. The crow backed off. Silla grabbed my hand and squeezed.

I crossed my arms over my chest. "Why should we help you?"

One of the rats scuttled up onto Eric's shoulder and slid its nose through Eric's hair, then hopped up to his head. Its claws pricked into Eric's forehead. Fresh blood welled up and ran down over his closed eyes. "Because," he said, ignoring the stream of blood skimming the corner of his mouth, "if you don't, I'll kill him."

"What do you want us to do?" Silla asked.

"You're going to heal me, with that shining bright blood of yours."

Silla tucked her hands into the front pocket of her sweatshirt. "Josephine, why don't you just use Eric to heal yourself?"

I hoped Silla didn't mean it; she just wanted to get Josephine to tell us where her body was.

Another rat walked awkwardly down a tree branch to pick at Eric's face with its nose. "His body," Eric said, "lacks the power of the Kennicot flesh."

"Seems like you're doing fine without it." Silla flung her arms out. "You've got control of a whole forest and a ton of rats—plus his body."

Eric's eyes snapped open. His expression twisted into a leer. "I want my own body back, girl."

"It's hurt, isn't it?" Silla stepped forward, and I didn't like the aggressive way her shoulders tensed. "Is it hidden in the woods? Broken? Dying? Are you dying, Josephine? What happens if your body dies?"

"You cretin," Eric spat. A handful of the crows snapped their wings. Eric's whole body shuddered, and the rat perched upon him chuckled angrily, claws digging in. "You're going to heal me, and you're going to give me Philip's precious spell book, too."

"We don't have it," I said.

The trees shook again, stirring more leaves. "Where is it?" Eric shrieked. I clenched my hands into fists. His voice was strained beyond recognition. Did he know what was happening to him? What I'd let happen?

Silla lifted her chin. "It's safely buried six feet underground with my brother. What you want, what I want, unreachable."

Josephine cackled: a rough, squishy sound through Eric's throat. "Perfection, my darlings! We'll dig him up, take the book, and take his strong, unprotected bones for my carmot."

"You'll try." Silla gripped my hand.

"I always do." Eric's head tilted. "Nick, you go inside and get some salt, and we'll get started."

I glanced at Silla. Were we still playing along? She nodded, and said, "Go."

SILLA

The distant *slick* of the glass door signaled that Nick had made it inside. Crow wings flapped slowly, patting the dry autumn grass. The rats chattered from the branches of the trees.

Eric's body swayed.

His eyes were closed, his face slack. I wondered how hard it would be to bind Josephine while convincing her that I was trying to heal her. If she figured it out, or panicked, what would she do? Could she get out, take Eric's body, or an animal's or something, flee somewhere safer? I couldn't let that happen. She couldn't hurt any more people. The only thing to do was to bind her and destroy her.

Coldness dripped through me as I realized I was planning murder.

It was too dark to see much of anything in the forest. The trees were black and the space between them full of shadows. Moving shadows. It wasn't only rats—on the ground, now that I focused, I could see other animals, too, huddled between roots and ducked under small bushes. Their eyes gleamed. Rabbits, raccoons, possums, and several foxes. And they were dead—many of the corpses Nick and I had seen that afternoon were now blinking at me. Staring at me. Even smaller birds hopped among the menagerie. They shouldn't have been all together. Rabbits don't just hang out with foxes, or little mice, like the ones gathered in a herd just below Eric's dangling shoes.

Josephine was in them all.

Her power had to be enormous. How could the binding spell contain her? What if it wasn't enough to bind her body— what if we had to bind all the trees and every single little animal she possessed? Was I strong enough?

The silence dripped down my skin like rain. Goose bumps rose on my arms and neck. My palm, the one with the cut I'd made last night, to show Nick my poisonous blood, ached and itched. I opened my hand, staring down at it.

I'd kept it broken to remind myself what Nick had said. *This is who I am.*

All it had taken that night in the field, the first time I'd kissed Nick, when the flowers had exploded around me, was blood. Reese had healed the deep cut on my chest with just will, blood, and need. And banishing possession, and possession itself . . . so many of the spells only required blood. Blood and . . . imagination. Oh, boy, did I have that in spades.

I just had to want it more than Josephine.

I looked back to Eric. I hated that his eyes were closed. Like Josephine wasn't really paying attention to me. But she had so many other eyes. Rat eyes. Fox eyes. Crow eyes. "Josephine. Tell me why you want the spell book. Why does any of that matter if all we ever need is blood?"

"You want to talk philosophy, Silla? Right now?" Eric's eyes snapped open and his fingers twitched.

"I'd rather find your body and tear it into a dozen pieces." But what I wanted was for someone—anyone—to explain this stupid, impossible magic to me.

She laughed, and even through Eric's weary voice I could hear her delight. "Wouldn't you just. But very well. A quick lesson: It's hard to pull your will out of the reality you've always known, isn't it? Even when you see with your own eyes? Taste with your own tongue? The spells help us form our will. Fire symbolizes certain things to us—cleansing, destruction, transformation—things that have been the same or nearly so for millennia. Ritual bridges the gap between what we sense with our hands and eyes and ears and what we believe is possible in our hearts and minds. And words are the sharpest tools we have to trick our minds into having faith that the magic will work. Belief, will, faith—whatever you want to call it. I have only met one person who had such a complete understanding of the magic, had such faith in it that he could make mountains move without a word."

"The Deacon," I said, before I could stop.

"Yes. The Deacon. A humble name for one near godhood."

I shivered at the worshipful tone in Eric's voice. And was suddenly glad I hadn't tried contacting the Deacon. Inside the kangaroo pocket, I held tight to the cold metal of the scissors.

The back door slid open, and I glanced over my shoulder, reluctant to turn my back on Josephine's forest. Nick had a blue paper bag of salt under his arm.

He came to stand beside me. "Okay, we have what you want."

Eric's head lifted, eyes open and staring.

"Now what?" I called.

Eric's face parted in a gruesome smile. "Now Nick and I go desecrate some graves."

"I will *not* help you do that!" Nick shouted.

"You won't have a choice. Your body is mine."

I laughed. I actually laughed. "You're so wrong, Josephine. You can't have us. We have armor." And I held out my rings. "You should know that."

"Oh, silly, silly girl." Eric's mouth pulled into a mocking frown. "Didn't you *know?* Armor like that only works for the person it's made for."

Nick whispered in my ear, "Be bound, to the ground."

The grass at my feet exploded up, spitting chunks of earth at me, and thick, snakelike roots grabbed hold of my ankles. I kicked and jerked away, but fell back and slammed into the ground. Pain jolted up through my bones, and I tasted blood on my tongue a moment before sharp pain caught up to where I'd bitten the tip.

Roots kept bursting up through the ground, winding around my legs. I yelled, wordlessly, reaching down and tearing at them. Crows took to the sky, screeching and beating their wings. The roots stilled, but I was stuck. They tightened when I pulled, like a Chinese finger trap. I twisted onto my stomach and searched, but Nick was gone.

 # SIXTY

NICHOLAS

It was like being in the dog dream, where I'm bombarded by images and sensations and can't control them or make any sense of them—but it doesn't matter anyway, because my brain hasn't really kicked in. It was so much worse than before, in Silla's front yard. I'd been able to fight then, push and feel the capillaries in my fingers and toes burn. Now I was nothing but a viewer.

But I'm glad I wasn't fully engaged.

The ground trembled, and I saw flashes of a great mechanical arm in front of me, thudding into the earth again and again.

A thing, a slimy, awful thing, clung inside my head, made my feet move, my hands move, directed my eyes and lips. I heard slick thoughts that weren't my own, longings and anger and old, old sorrow, crowding me as I watched the backhoe excavate Reese's grave.

SILLA

The sky was perfectly clear above me. In the circle of forest where I lay tied down with roots, it was dark and shadowed, but up there, where the crows wheeled in frenetic circles, it was light. The sun shone.

Below me, I felt the earth. I imagined it sinking down for miles, through dirt and bedrock, through tectonic plates, and all the way to the burning core of the world. How far down did Josephine's reach extend? She had trees, birds, animals. Why not the earth itself?

She had Nick. And Eric. She'd had Reese, and I could not let everything now spiral out of control like it had so quickly the night he'd died.

I pressed my eyes closed. I had to free myself, to find Josephine's body and bind it before she hurt anybody else. The scissors.

Digging in, I withdrew them and sat up. Most of the crows had flown off, but a few hopped around me. They watched, flapping their wings. I'd have to be fast, because Josephine would know what I was doing. The other possessed woodland creatures were hiding. Waiting for something. Eric's limp body swayed slightly in the wind. My stomach twisted; I put the scissors against one of the roots, and sawed at it. The blade cut in, smoothly, and I kept slicing. It took forever to hack through, and several of the possums had crept out from under the trees.

They looked like alien rat-monsters. These had blood on their snouts.

I slashed at the next root, and heard a crow caw. There was grunting. It sounded like pigs. Did Nick have wild pigs in his woods? I didn't look. Instead I cut at my wounded palm, and smeared the blood over both hands. I grabbed roots and ordered, "Release. Now. Let me go!" I imagined them snaking back, quickly. I was good at imagining—I did it all the time and it made me a great actress, being able to slip into another reality for a few hours, to believe I was someone else. I could do it.

I closed my eyes and imagined being free. "Release me. Release. Release." The memory of Nick using poetry to focus surfaced. My brain scrambled for rhyme. "Roots release me, let me free. Earth release me, let me free. Blood release me, let me free." I built up the picture in my mind: the roots cracking and breaking apart.

The roots crumbled into ashes.

Gasping, I stumbled to my feet and turned to face the forest. The possums chattered at me, hissing through their horrible teeth. Shadows fluttered overhead. Crows. They circled like vultures. Josephine was everywhere.

I would have to bind the whole forest.

A mask. I needed a mask for this. But not an imaginary one, slipped on only in my mind's eye. I needed a real one.

Holding out my bleeding hand, I smeared my fingers through the blood, and pressed them to my cheek. My skin burned as the power inside me came crashing out. I painted, streaking blood across my forehead, down my nose, over my chin.

Red, dark, and dangerous.

It was the most genuine mask I'd ever put on. My power, my self. Me.

This is who I am.

NICHOLAS

I was inside the grave. Surrounded by walls of wet dirt. Under my feet: Reese's casket. The pale shine of it was encrusted with mud. All I saw, as my body crouched down, was how white it was, how it gleamed like the moon, or marble.

A click and slow creak as I unlatched and opened the top half of the casket. There he was. His face was slack and gray, mouth hanging open, eyelids half parted. The shadows under his cheekbones were greenish, and his hair fell limp onto the satiny pillow. My heart pounded, blood roaring in my ears like a tornado.

And the smell slid up into my nose. I felt my tongue work as I gagged, but couldn't lean back or climb out or run. I couldn't even close my eyes.

My hand rose to my mouth, but instead of covering my nose, I bit my own finger harder than I'd bite into an apple. Pain sharpened my awareness, and for a moment, I was free. I stumbled, landing on the casket hard enough to crack it.

Then the brief freedom was over, and I crawled forward, reached down into the casket, and with my bleeding finger painted a rune onto Reese's corpse's forehead.

The skin broke. And a piece of it slid away, down his temple, trailing ooze like a tearstain.

A fat red drop of blood splashed down from above, smacking into Reese's cheek. Then another.

I looked up—I didn't want to, but I had to.

A fox crouched at the edge of the open grave, a broken crow in its long jaws. It dropped the crow, and my hands caught it. They held it out so that the blood spattered onto Reese's heart, staining the suit he'd been buried in.

I closed my eyes. *I can close my eyes.* I threw the crow aside. Nausea swept through me, and my bitten finger throbbed. I felt it down to my toes. But I didn't care that it hurt. I controlled my body again. She'd let me go.

Just as I pushed up to my knees on the coffin, Reese's eyes opened.

Yelping, I fell back again. His eyes were glassy. Dead. But his hands came up and gripped the sides of the casket. He pulled himself to sit. And looked at me. His ruined, grayish hands reached into his lap, and he grasped the spell book.

His lips shook, and a harsh whisper slid out, puckering my skin with horror.

"Nick."

His breath smelled like rank perfume. He reached for me, but I jolted away, fast. A rough sound like choking burst out of him. He was laughing. Of course—it was Josephine.

Reese's body stood up, and she turned him to face the grave wall. It was a struggle, but he heaved up over the side.

I pressed into the earth and tried to keep breathing.

SILLA

It would take too long to run all the way around the forest, so I had to go through it, and through all of Josephine's possessed animals. I walked closer, holding the scissors out like a sword, my injured hand tucked against my side to keep the blood flow down.

A row of squirrels prattled at me, their little snickers cold and awful. Maybe they wouldn't do anything. Maybe they were only watching.

I reached the edge, where the first trees rose up and spread out their branches. Beyond them was nothing but shadows. The trees twined so close together, and there was so much undergrowth, the sun barely penetrated.

Swallowing, I thought of Nick. I had to get to him. Had to bind Josephine so that she couldn't hurt him. Or kill him.

Screw the animals. It wasn't like there were tigers in the woods. So long as I didn't run into any wild pigs, I should be fine.

I gripped the scissors and strode in.

"Silla."

It came from above. "Oh, God." Eric's eyes were open. Against the mask of blood, they were extremely pale. "Eric?" Was it him? Had Josephine let him go?

"Silla, I feel . . . Help me down." His head lolled.

The branches he was tangled in wrapped around his arms, curling under his shoulders and around his chest. Even if I could get up to him, what would happen if I freed him? It was at least a twenty-foot drop. He'd break bones.

"Silla," he whispered again.

A crow landed on a branch, shaking Eric's body as it bobbed closer, wings out. It cawed. Eric winced. His throat worked like he was going to puke.

"Hang on," I called. If it was Josephine, I still had the scissors.

I put my bloody palm against the nearest tree with its

branches holding him aloft. Leaning into it, I said, "Put him down. Bend your branches, and set him onto the ground." I was descended from the Deacon's blood. I was strong enough. All I needed was blood. "Obey me," I whispered, lips brushing the bark. I couldn't think of any stupid rhymes. "I bled for you, obey me." I visualized the trees bending, untwining, letting him go.

A rustle and crack alerted me, and I spun. The trees bowed, lowering Eric down. They shifted in the darkness, looking more like liquid than rough wood, like sinuous black ribbons and rope slowly placing Eric onto the leaf-strewn forest floor.

I ran to him. He lay prone. "Eric?" I bit my lip, hesitant to touch him.

"Thanks," he whispered without opening his eyes.

"Are you hurt?" It was amazing that he was alive. Much less whole.

"Yeah, but . . . not bad. I think. I just need to lie here."

"Do you know what's happening?" I eyed the raccoon shuffling closer to us. It sat back on its haunches and clasped its tiny hands together.

"Little bit." His face spasmed, and he coughed.

"I have to go—to get Nick. We should move you out of the forest. The animals are, um, possessed."

Swallowing, he opened his eyes and turned his head. A string of mice had joined the raccoon. "Jesus, your face," he muttered.

I gritted my teeth together. I had to go, but I couldn't just leave him.

"I'll be okay." Eric's voice sounded raw. "I can get out. I'll get to my car."

"I'll be back when I can."

"Wait." He dug into his jeans pocket and pulled out a lighter. "Fire."

I scuttled around for an appropriate torch.

NICHOLAS

Chunks of dirt pelted me, but I clawed through them. I dragged myself up out of the grave, finally, and lay down across a line of blood. The smell was thick in the air. Rot, sulfur, burning hair, fresh earth, tangy blood. With the arm of the backhoe, I heaved myself up. I had to get back, before anything happened to Silla. Before Josephine possessed me again.

Without the armor, it probably didn't matter, but I used the last bit of blood on my finger to paint the protection rune over my heart.

It couldn't have been more than five minutes since they left, but there was no sign of the corpse. I thought of last week, of being alone and blind, not with Silla when she needed me. I had to find her now.

I ran.

SIXTY-ONE

SILLA

I ran.

The trees were too tight together, cutting off the last of the fading sunlight. And a handful of crows darted ahead of me, pressing me in a direction that would lead me out of the forest at the wrong angle to get to the cemetery quickly. But they screamed again and again until I wanted to flatten my hands over my ears to block it out. Instead I swung my torch at them, yelling. They banked away, but kept coming around in front of me to drive me left.

A dark form darted into my way, and I skidded to a halt as the deer's head swung around to knock me over. I landed in a bush, barely keeping hold of my torch. The deer bared its teeth and whined like a child. I stood up, fire in hand. "Back off!" I screamed, flailing my arms. Crows dive-bombed it, but it swung its antlers around, and they were forced away, bawling their displeasure.

The deer hopped back, whined again, a long, squeaking bleat. I slashed at it with the torch and tried to dodge around it. It kicked out with a hoof, catching my thigh. I yelled, swung the torch again, and it darted back.

The rest of the crows herded me on, no matter which direction I tried to go. How was I supposed to search for Josephine's body when they kept pushing me and pushing me?

One darted down and screamed in my face. I fell back, my hand landing in soft mud. Warm mud. The torch sputtered and I grabbed it up again. The mud was tinged red.

Crows cawed and I saw it. A golden curl poking from between two roots. Her body had literally been swallowed by the forest. I stuck the end of the torch into the ground and dug the spell components out of my sweatshirt pocket. With the scissors, I cut the curl away from the mud, and I pressed it into the wax, which I held close to the fire so that it softened enough for me to mold it into a tight ball, with the hair worked deeply in.

As I worked, the crows kept talking. I couldn't think about them, as long as they didn't attack. I opened the card case and stuck the wax inside, pushing it into the corners and flattening it out so that I could snap the case shut. Finally I wound the red thread around the box again and again, whispering "Be bound" with every beat of my heart.

I sealed it with a drop of blood. Then I stuffed the torch into the base of the tree. Dry grass lit with a whoosh of air.

I stood up and pushed on. The crows flew with me now, not against me.

The edge of the forest came into sight—a flat, dark expanse of fallow field before the crumbling wall of the cemetery. Squinting and tightening my fists, I pumped harder.

And I erupted out of the trees.

Directly in front of my brother.

I lurched back. His eyes were pale, whited-out like with cataracts, and the skin sort of hung off his bones. Blood smeared across his face and dripped down onto his chest, splattering the tie he'd been buried in. His clavicle punched up at his skin as though waiting to sprout through at any moment.

"Sister," Josephine said through his dead lips, and I recognized his voice. It was harsh and rattled, but it was his.

"Get away from me!"

"Come, Silla, it's your brother." His lips smiled, the skin cracking like they were seriously chapped. Clear fluid oozed out.

"Help me, Silla, and we'll live forever together. All we need is the powder from his bones."

"No, never." I stared at his face, at the hanging skin. I was empty; I was hollow. *Reese.*

He held up the spell book. "Back up, and we'll go heal my body. It's almost all over, darling."

I slapped my hand against his chest. "I banish thee from this body!"

The corpse twisted and shuddered, and bile choked me, coating my tongue with acid.

NICHOLAS

The crumbling cemetery wall gouged my hands as I vaulted over, then raced for Silla where she struggled with the Reese corpse on the track of gravel road.

He lifted the spell book and slammed it into Silla's face.

She collapsed backward, and I flung myself at him. I hit

with a wet *thunk,* and we crashed to the ground. The rotten smell gagged me, and then the corpse was back on its feet, dragging me up off the ground. I punched back with my elbows, kicked with my legs. But it didn't feel pain, hardly seemed to notice my efforts. Like kicking and punching Play-Doh. I couldn't get away.

Crows circled overhead, faster and faster.

I forced my eyes open as Reese's arm came around my neck. "I'll enjoy spilling your blood," Josephine spat through Reese's dead lips. "All I want is to live again—how difficult is that?"

The arm tightened, and I couldn't breathe. Orange light flashed in my peripheral vision.

"You—just—don't—understand!"

I flung my head around, only then hearing the crackle of flames. The forest was on fire. "Fire," I whispered harshly.

The arm around my neck loosened as Josephine flung us both around to face the forest.

"No," she yelled, "my body!" Crows dive-bombed us, their wings brushing my face. She released me, raising Reese's arms to smack them away. But they drove her at the trees.

Two crows snagged their claws in his hair. Reese's body folded abruptly, and he crumpled to the ground.

I panted for a moment, staring at the leaping flames. She was in there. Her body was. It had to be anchored in there somewhere, and if it burned, so did Josephine.

I crawled to Silla. Her head lolled to one side, and her entire face was painted with blood. From a gash in her temple, fresh blood trickled quickly into her hair. She wasn't moving. Barely breathing.

The crows that had hounded Josephine darted around me now. Hopping frantically.

Closing my eyes, I whispered, "Blood and earth, hear my appeal: through skin and flesh, readily heal." Again I said it, but louder, and then again. The heat built up, and I begged her to stay, begged the blood and magic to work.

My heart churned over and over, aching, and I leaned down to kiss Silla's lips. They were hot—as hot as mine. "Silla," I whispered.

She gasped for breath.

SILLA

Everything was black.

My whole body ached, tingling painfully like when your foot falls asleep and then all the blood rushes back in. I couldn't move, but felt tears film over my eyes and spill down my nose. I heard a scream, and smelled smoke. And blood. So much blood. My throat was raw, my tongue heavy. I tried to move my arms, and I think my finger twitched. My heart resonated hollowly inside me.

I sucked in a long breath, and cold air rushed in along with a mouthful of smoke and sticky blood. I could taste it running down the back of my throat.

Wind cut into me, and I coughed.

"Silla?"

Nick. I turned to him, burying my bloody face against his filthy shirt. I fisted my hands behind his back.

"Babe. Silla." He sounded like he was going to laugh. "Oh my God!"

"Reese." I remembered Reese's body with the flesh dripping off. Pink muscle. Yellow bones.

"Come on, babe." Nick struggled to get us both standing up. "We have to get away from here. The forest is burning."

"But." I stumbled to put weight on my feet. "But Josephine."

"She's dying in the forest."

I pushed away from him, tilted my face. His half smile was the best thing I'd ever seen. But I shook my head. It rolled with nausea—brain nausea, like my whole body wanted to vomit. "We have to bind her in there so that she'll burn—or she'll only escape again." Digging the card case out of my pocket, I held it up. "It's ready to go. Remember the rune." I leaned over and drew it in the sticky mud with my finger.

A cacophony of crying animals and cracking wood blared from the woods, and wind rose up, blowing toward the trees. My eyes ached like I'd been staring into the sun. "Help me, Nick." I stood up. The fire glared between the black trees. A dozen crows leapt into the sky and flew around the forest like a crown, wheeling and cawing and chasing any little jays or robins that tried to flee. A crow dove at the ground, shrieking at a fox, chasing it back. More and more crows arrived, winging over us, encircling the woods as a living barrier.

I dragged Nick to one of the trees. "Make the rune. We do it with blood, at the four corners of the woods, starting here, running clockwise."

"It's too far."

"We can do it. We have to." It was almost over.

Nick tightened his jaw but nodded.

NICHOLAS

The only thing that kept me going was Silla's hand in mine.

SILLA

Every step meant being closer to destroying the thing that had killed my mother, my father, my brother. Maybe Eric. Every step meant closing the circle, completing the trap.

NICHOLAS

The forest screamed as it burned. Cries from animal throats ripped together, winding around to create this one, awesome shriek. Heat tightened the skin on the left side of my face as we rushed around the perimeter. Step after step, through tall grass, over the road, stopping three times to paint a blood rune on a tree.

SILLA

A cluster of crows fell from the sky, trailing flames. The rest cried and flew, like black glinting sparks rising off the huge bonfire the forest had become. Their wails were lost in the snarling fire, in the column of eye-searing smoke.

NICHOLAS

We fell to our knees when we returned to the beginning. As I painted the rune onto a tree, Silla dug at the earth and buried the card case. We clutched our hands together, dripping our mingled blood onto the final rune, and Silla screamed, "Be bound, Josephine. Be forever bound!"

A snap of heat exploded. My ears popped. Silla and I were knocked backward. I didn't try to stand but just stared up as the stars vanished behind billowing smoke, and wrapped my fingers around Silla's.

The forest howled.

SIXTY-TWO

SILLA

I lay with my head tilted to one side. I could see orange glow against black grass; I could see my brother's profile. His body was surrounded by crows. They hopped around, heads cocked and wings ruffled. Touching their beaks to his hair, his hand, his pants.

The crows. They'd stalked me but never attacked me. Warned us when Eric was possessed. Led me to Josephine's body. Held all the animals in the woods so that she couldn't escape the binding.

And Reese had been so good at flying with them.

I sat up.

"Silla?" Nick's voice trembled. I knew he was tired—I could barely move myself. So much blood lost, so much running and desperation. But Reese—Reese was here. He was alive. The knowledge cracked through me with a surge of adrenaline.

"The crows, Nick. They're . . . it's Reese." I crawled on my hands and knees into the center of them. "Oh, God, Reese!"

The crows exploded into the air, flapping around me. I

stared at Reese's dead face, imagining it sunny with life again. Imagining his laugh. The creases at the corners of his eyes when he smiled.

"We could bring him back," I whispered.

"Sil."

"With the regeneration spell. Just like with the leaf."

Nick dragged himself next to me and took my hand. "Silla," he whispered. "Think."

Excitement raged through me like white light, buzzing in my ears. "I am! Bring back his body, and his spirit is right here. All around us in the crows." I flung my hands out at them, outrageous laughter spilling upward from my guts, shaking my backbone and ringing in my ears. "We can heal his body, regenerate it, and then he'll be able to jump back in. Reese!" I called to them, to all the flapping, agitated crows. "Reese, I can fix your body, you can have it back!"

The crows—*Reese*—cawed at me. My head swam and I gripped my knees, pushing my nails into them until it hurt. The idea—the promise of having my brother back—was almost too much. I turned to Nick. He would help me.

Nick was watching me, not the crows. His expression was drawn and tired, hard to read. "Nick," I said.

"I'll help you, babe, if this is what you really want."

I grinned wildly, even as the world spun around me. I knelt so that I didn't fall over, beside the corpse. I could do it. I had enough left in me. Soon it would be my brother.

NICHOLAS

I couldn't look at her eyes. I couldn't.

She held her shaking hands over Reese's chest. There was no need for more blood—we were both covered in it already. Neither of us moved. I wanted to knock her aside, push her down, yell at her that this was wrong. He was dead—the body was dead—and bringing it back wasn't any better than Josephine had been, or my mom had been. We couldn't give life. We weren't God.

The bloody mask was smeared almost completely off her face, in streaks that made her terrifying. She stared down at her brother. My chest constricted. Blood flowed so slowly through my veins, dragging me down. Turning me to stone while I watched my girlfriend prepare to resurrect the dead.

But she didn't move. Her breath wheezed in and out. The hazy air stung my eyes.

A crow cawed. It landed on Reese's forehead, claws breaking into his loose flesh. I drew back. Silla didn't move. The crow cawed again, and I stared at its eyes. It—he—tilted his head and glared at Silla. He raised his wings and stood there, posed.

Silla's face crumpled. "Reese," she whispered.

Oh, Silla, babe. I couldn't say anything. I couldn't make this decision for her, no matter how much I wanted to. No matter how wrong it was, she had to decide. I couldn't take this away from her.

A choking cry exploded out of her mouth.

I reached out and our hands gripped together, squeezing. She wrapped her bleeding hand around her stomach. "Reese," she said.

The crows took flight, spinning and singing, against the orange and smoky sky.

She collapsed to the side, against me. I circled my arms around her, stroked her hair, pushed my lips against her head. Her shaking vibrated through my whole body.

The heat of the fire dried the sweat off my face. Its crackles and roaring ripped through the air. I could barely breathe.

Silla whispered something, and I lifted her chin so I could hear. "Reese, Nick. We have to—have to hide the body."

My hands tightened on her. She was right. With this fire, we'd be swarmed with cops and locals anytime. Silla got to her feet, swayed in place. I joined her, and my own weariness almost swallowed me up. Too much blood loss, too much adrenaline and energy wasted. But we had work to do.

We dragged Reese's body into the forest, hacking on smoke. I grabbed a blazing branch and set it at his feet so that we knew he'd burn. Tears tracked down Silla's cheeks the whole time, but when it was finished, she rubbed her hands on the grass and lay down, rather serene. I worried she'd lost it for a moment, but then she reached out for my hand and said, "It's not a bad way to go. A funeral pyre like this."

I squeezed her fingers and said, "Like old Viking kings."

"You really do know weird stuff." There was a smile in her voice.

We lay down together, near the cemetery wall. Silla put her head on my shoulder, and I closed my eyes. The world spun slowly under me, like I was being flushed down a toilet.

SIXTY-THREE

NICHOLAS

My memory was fuzzy still, even at the hospital. Apparently, blood loss will do that to you. I barely know how we got there. I just remember standing in the checkered hallway as they wheeled a barely conscious Silla away. Dad sort of caught me when I started to pass out again, and then I was blinking up at a dingy popcorn ceiling. Through the thin mattress, I could feel the bar under the small of my back, where the top half of the bed would angle up if I pushed the right button. There was no noise except a ringing in my left ear. When I used my hands to lean up, I realized there was a needle in my arm attached to one of those long plastic tubes, which was in turn attached to a bag of clear liquid. Saline or something.

It was a small but private room, with an old TV on an arm attached to the wall and a window with heavy blue curtains drawn across it. I was light-headed, but otherwise okay. Nothing ached or burned or pinched besides a general malaise that clung to my skin like I'd been awake for way too long. Only I'd just woken up.

From outside the closed door, I began to hear the muffled sounds of a hospital at work.

I studied the needle in my arm, wondering if it was okay to just pull it out. Surely I wouldn't bleed all over everything. Or die. Briefly, I imagined all my insides squeezing out through the tiny needle hole, in party shades of green and violet and pink.

The door opened.

It was Lilith, wearing an orange dress trimmed with rows of black fur. *Fur.* Like she'd come from the freaking opera. Which, I guess, she kind of had. Her hair was falling out of its perfect coif. Which I'd never seen, not even at six in the morning before her coffee. But she pressed her lips together, which were perfectly painted this awful, shiny red, and said, "Nick, don't you even think about getting out of that bed."

I gripped the edges of the thin mattress. "Where's Dad?"

"Talking with the doctors. And the sheriff."

"And Silla?"

"Unconscious but . . . fine." Lilith's eyes shone with something not quite evil. "Your friend said the fire was an accident."

I rubbed my eyes to stall. "Um. Friend?"

"Yes. The boy who called us. Eric. He has a few injuries. Broken ankle, quite a bit of blood loss. He says you and Silla saved his life."

There was a strange undercurrent to the information. As though what Lilith was saying was urgent. What was I missing? Some weird code?

She continued, "He said you were going to build a fire in

the backyard, to burn a few of Reese's things. Your own little memorial, as it were."

I stared. Lilith was feeding me my story. So that when the sheriff came and asked me, I'd say the same thing Eric had. She was freaking helping me.

"The only damage was to our property, Nick. Your property, which your father holds in your name, of course, until you're of age."

God, I was slow. I licked my lips and said, "So—Dad could hold us responsible. Press charges. For the fire."

Lilith nodded, crossing her arms under her breasts. She tapped the orange fingernails of her right hand against her left elbow. One at a time. "I believe I can talk him out of it."

"Why?" The word burst out before I could stop it. I should have asked what she wanted in return, or just accepted her help and promised my forever gratitude.

She spread her hands wide and plastered an innocent expression over her face. "Why not? It was a tragic accident, but you survived, and certainly your father has plenty of money and properties, Nicholas."

"God, don't call me that," I whispered.

"I'll go speak with your father about putting this all behind us." She turned and put a hand on the door handle.

"Wait."

Lilith paused with her back toward me, knowing what I was going to ask.

"What do you want in return?" *My firstborn child? Ten years indentured servitude?*

Spinning on her heel, Lilith offered me her brilliant shark's smile, the one that caught Dad every time. She looked about ten years younger. "Ah, Nick. All I want is the truth. I want the real story. The one with all the magic, the one with murder and jealousy and history. The one with that cemetery at its center."

I gaped at her.

"Ta, Nick. Think quickly." Lilith flashed her smile again, and was out the door.

Turned out, they believed the ridiculous story. Believed we'd been stupid enough to set fire to the forest accidentally.

And I told Lilith the truth the next morning. I think she believed me. The crows that hung around the hospital, and that followed our car several miles out of town, certainly helped. Maybe it was about time to purge her nickname from my brain and stick to Mary.

SIXTY-FOUR

SILLA

My eyelashes stuck together, and it was almost impossible to force them apart when I woke up.

"Silla!"

Wendy leaned over my bed. My own bed. I'd woken up in the hospital that morning, terrified that everyone was dead. But Judy had been there, and given me a story for the sheriff. Said she'd talked to Nick, and had gone out to the cemetery to fill in Reese's grave with the backhoe.

The doctors said I was only exhausted from the adrenaline and trauma, and to get rest. Which had been easy. I'd barely made it up to my room, I was so tired.

Behind Wendy, all my theater masks watched like a private audience. I moved my tongue, which was dry, and started to sit up. There was no nausea. No dizziness. Just the sleepy need for caffeine to wake up my bones.

"Silla!" She sat back on my desk chair. "We've been so worried. You've been asleep for twenty hours!"

"Water?" I said hoarsely. My throat burned. I couldn't believe I'd been asleep for a whole day and still felt like crap.

"Oh, yes!" Wendy twirled around and grabbed a bottle of water off the nightstand. She looked good. A breeze from the open window teased at her hair. My eyes strained to see out the window, searching for crows.

Wendy touched my arm, then helped me sit up to drink. After downing half the bottle, I only felt a little better. "How is—is everyone?" *Have there been crows? Where's Reese? Did I imagine they were him?*

"Eric's fine. His ankle is broken, from running out of the fire, he said. He also said you saved his life." She pursed her glittery pink lips, and I remembered that Josephine was gone.

"Yeah, something like that," I murmured, wanting her to leave so that I could lie back down. Or run outside to look for Reese.

She quieted. "I can hardly believe what everybody is saying about you and the cemetery and the fire. Mrs. Margaret and Mrs. Pensimonry have been plaguing Judy with questions about you and the fire, about your whole family, and whether you're . . . well, crazy." Wendy winced apologetically.

"It's okay, I think I am."

Grabbing my hands, she squeezed them until I yelped. The doctors had stitched up my palm. "Sorry," she said, letting my hands go like they were poison. But she stared at the bandages. "You really are . . . hurting yourself, aren't you?"

I opened my mouth. It was the time to tell her the truth if I ever was going to. But even though the magic was a part of me, it was too dangerous to involve other people. I was too dangerous. Tears filled my eyes and I let them, giving Wendy the only mask she could understand. I nodded, and the tears plopped down onto my hands.

"Oh, Sil." She climbed onto the bed and put her arm around my shoulders. "You—it's just been too much. But I'll help you. So you don't have to do that anymore."

"I think," I whispered, inventing the lie on the spot, "I think Judy is going to take me away. To Chicago, where I won't be trying to live all the time where they lived." More tears fell as I remembered talking to Reese about moving away together. And I knew Judy wouldn't mind. That only left Nick.

I hugged Wendy. A huge part of me couldn't imagine leaving her behind. But what other option did I really have? Especially if the whole town was talking again. My family had been the center of their attention for months now. I was done. I sighed. "Where's Nick? Is he okay?"

"Yeah, but"—she frowned—"his dad moved them into a hotel in Cape Girardeau last night. I should go call him, actually, to tell him you're awake."

"Sure."

She hugged me tight again, and then slipped out of the room. Climbing out of bed, I dragged myself along the wall to the window.

I turned my face toward the east, toward Nick's house and the forest. It was black and decimated, like the crumbling ashes of an ancient city. Towers and bridges ruined and fallen into decay. Smoke still rose in tiny ribbons from several places. But nothing outside our circle had burned. Not a single thing.

And I didn't see any crows, though I searched the sky for them.

Soup was the only thing my stomach could handle. I was all-over fragile, muffled, and shaky.

It hadn't sunk in, what had happened. While I ate, my eyes caught the shifting ruffles of the blue curtains over the sink, and I forgot whole swaths of that night. Then the spoon clacked against my teeth, and it rushed back. I had to stop eating and close my eyes.

Gram Judy moved around the kitchen, present but not speaking, like she could tell I wasn't ready to talk but wanted me to know I wasn't alone. Wendy had left with a kiss on my cheek, and promised to come back and check on me. I watched Judy, wondering how I was going to tell her about Reese and the crows. Would she believe me? Or think I'd been totally out of it?

When the gravel outside crunched, I put down my spoon. Judy scooted out the door, and I heard her in the front hall, greeting somebody.

Nick came around the corner, in a pinstripe vest and black pants, and I was across the room and in his arms before I knew I'd moved.

His arms were around me, lifting me onto my toes, and I could smell his hair goo and the hotel soap clinging to his neck. He kissed my hair and said my name.

I couldn't let go, even when he whispered in my ear, "Hey, babe." I just held on, fingers in his hair, struggling not to wrap my legs around him, too. "Come on," he laughed lightly. "Let's sit."

We did. Me in his lap. He spoke, and I brushed my fingers along his cheekbone and kissed him randomly, in the middle of words. He was telling me what had happened, how Eric had managed to get to his car and Judy had seen the fire from the house and come running. How we'd been taken to the hospital, and the story Eric had told to cover for us. About his deal with Lilith.

When he said, "Dad's dragging me back to Chicago," I put my fingers over his lips.

"I'm going, too."

Nick's eyes widened, and then he smiled. "Yeah?"

"Yeah. I can finish high school anywhere. Especially somewhere nobody knows me. Might be good to not be around so many . . . reminders. Judy has an apartment there, and I've already been thinking about leaving. Reese had even talked about it with me. Before."

He wrapped his arms around me again. After a long moment he said, "How are you feeling?"

"Delicate. Strong. A lot of things. I think you saved my life."

"I think you saved mine, too."

I thought of the crows again, falling out of the sky and trailing fire. Helping us bind her. Flying overhead. We hadn't saved Reese.

"What is it, babe?"

"Nothing. Nothing. I was just thinking about the crows."

"About Reese."

Relief closed my eyes. He believed it, too. Thank God. "Yeah. I haven't seen him. Or them."

"They were at the hospital. Flew halfway to Cape Girardeau with us."

"Oh." Where were they now?

"He'll be around. Probably as tired as us."

I opened my hand, the one with the long, healing slashes from the binding spell. Then I took his hand, and laid our wounds side by side. "Tell me it was the right thing to do."

Nick covered my hand with his, pressing our hot, healing cuts against each other. "It was."

NICHOLAS

I stayed the rest of the day, and we cooked soup with Gram Judy, talking about Chicago. The plan to move back made her wrinkled old cheeks pink with excitement.

After dark, Silla and I left Judy in the house, though I could tell she'd have rather we stayed. Once in the backyard, we pushed through the forsythia, and the house lights fell away. The cemetery spread out before us. I took Silla's hand, and we stood there for a moment. Her breathing was calm, and I watched it puff out through her lips and hang in the cold night.

She turned her face toward my house, where I could still see smoke floating up in thin wisps from the decimated forest. "I haven't heard them all day," Silla said, staring at the smoke.

"Come on, babe." I squeezed her hand. The cemetery was ghostly white, and I was struck by the way it opposed the black starkness of the burnt forest.

At random, we picked a headstone surrounded by long, dry grass. Far away from her parents' graves, from Reese. It was unspoken, but neither of us wanted to go back there.

I leaned back against the cold marble, and she sat between my legs. I held her, cheek against her soft hair. Everything was so silent. There was no wind or traffic noises. No birds, no bugs, even. Closing my eyes, I focused on Silla, on her warmth in front of me, and the gravestone cold behind me. And me in the middle, alive.

"Nick, do you think it's ever worth it to live forever?"

"Be a rock star?"

"President?" She smiled.

I kissed her hair. "No. It isn't possible."

Silla was quiet. "Not without turning into a monster."

A crow's call tore a ragged hole through the silence. Silla sat up straight, face lifting to the sky. She was like a statue, a cemetery angel raising her eyes to heaven.

A handful of crows flew toward us, wings synchronized. They settled down onto the surrounding gravestones. Except one. It landed directly in front of Silla, hopped closer, then cawed at her.

She said, "Reese. God, Reese." Her words hung in the air the way her breath had. "In the name of truth," she whispered, paraphrasing *Macbeth,* "are you fantastical?"

The crow cocked its head, and I tightened my hands on her arms. The other crows flapped off their perches and joined the first on the ground.

All five crows paused. Then the first cawed again and bobbed its head.

They surrounded us, five points in a circle. Silla stared at the black eyes of the first one and reached out her hand.

ACKNOWLEDGMENTS

I want to thank the following people, without whom *Blood Magic* simply would not exist:

Natalie—who sacrificed everything I sacrificed, shared my insanity, watched endless hours of *Criminal Minds* at two in the morning because I was too stressed to sleep, lived in a dirty house, and kept me standing when my knees were weak, all because she believes in me.

Maggie Stiefvater—for daring me to do it. All of it. And for calling me on the carpet when I didn't.

Brenna Yovanoff—for teaching me how atmosphere can be a character, too. And for being a little bit demon, a little bit flower girl.

Laura Rennert—who makes me feel like a rock star even when things aren't going too well, and cheers with me when they are. For charging ahead like a white knight and for calling me to say she can't call me.

Suzy Capozzi—for "all the blood, none of the vampires" and convincing me that I'd written something pretty good after all. Her insight and enthusiasm know no bounds!

Jocelyn Lange and her team in subsidiary rights—nobody

has been better at making my dreams of world domination come true!

Everyone at Random House—their support continues to astound! I feel like every time I turn a corner there are amazing new people pushing me forward.

The Gothic Girls—Carrie, Dawn, Heidi, Jackie, Jackson, Linda—for making me feel like one of them, even before I had a deal.

Early readers online—Star, Amber, Nikki, Laura, and Kate, who always begged for more.

My mom, dad, and brothers—for the gift of reading, nights at Ponaks, and making me strong. The carriage house awaits!

Especially my little brother Travis—for assuming I'd be able to put him in a book someday.

Robin Murphy—she suffered through the first novel I wrote, and even said she liked it.

My godfather, Randy—for always asking how the writing is going, and always doing my taxes.

ABOUT THE AUTHOR

TESSA GRATTON has wanted to be a paleontologist or a wizard since she was seven. Alas, she turned out to be too impatient to hunt dinosaurs, but is still searching for someone to teach her magic. After traveling the world with her military family, she acquired a BA (and the important parts of an MA) in gender studies, then settled down in Kansas with her partner, her cats, and her mutant dog. She spends her days staring at the sky and telling stories about magic. Visit her online at tessagratton.com.